CW00554319

Inspector Morse:
A Literary Companion

Paul Taylor

LUX IN EXTREMO CUNICULO

All correspondence for
Inspector Morse: A Literary Companion
should be addressed to:

Irregular Special Press
Endeavour House
170 Woodland Road
Sawston
Cambridge
CB22 3DX

❋❋❋❋❋ ⭘ ❋❋❋❋❋

Overall copyright © 2016 Baker Street Studios Limited
Text copyright remains with the author
All rights reserved
Typesetting is in Times font

ISBN: 1-901091-66-X (10 digit)
ISBN: 978-1-901091-66-3 (13 digit)

Cover Concept: Antony J. Richards
Map: Reproduced by permission, www.dailyinfo.co.uk © Daily Information Ltd.

❋❋❋❋❋ ⭘ ❋❋❋❋❋

All rights reserved. No part of this publication may be reproduced, stored in a
retrieval system, or transmitted, in any form or by any means, electronic,
mechanical, photocopying, recording or otherwise, without the prior permission of
the Irregular Special Press.

❋❋❋❋❋ ⭘ ❋❋❋❋❋

Every effort has been made to ensure accuracy, but the publishers do not hold
themselves responsible for any consequences that may arise from errors or
omissions. Whilst the contents are believed to be correct at the time of going to
press, changes may have occurred since that time or will occur during the currency
of this publication.

INSPECTOR MORSE:
A LITERARY COMPANION

Introduction

The late Chief Inspector Morse was rather fortunate in obtaining the skilful writing endeavours of Colin Dexter (or, to put in another way, Dexter was rather skilful in writing about the fortunate Endeavour Morse). Dexter both recorded the course of investigation of a number of the Inspector's cases and also arranged for publication of those records. Dexter has relayed thirteen major cases in substantial detail, and a further eight (nine if Chief Inspector Bell may be tangentially included) in abbreviated form. How these are referenced, and how entries are laid out, is explained later.

This Companion is intended to be exhaustive and contain almost all relevant names, places, institutions, subjects of interest, and esoterica. It is arranged as an encyclopaedia in that entries appear alphabetically (with extended articles on a number of themes). Any errors in the text can be attributed to one of three sources – Morse's imperfect recollection, my own faulty interpretation through guesswork (often uninspired) on crucial minutiae, and Dexter's mistakes in transcription (if any); Dexter is happy to admit to such mistakes (and one gets the feeling that their presence is not a cause of great concern to him). There are also, no doubt, a (good) few unintentional omissions, careless mistakes, and faulty cross-references.

A number of entries have been included specifically for any readers who neither live in Oxford nor England (nor indeed Great Britain). These entries are intended for further elucidation of what may appear to be basic knowledge to, for example, a good many Oxonians. While the BBC may enjoy a worldwide reputation, *The Archers* (as a radio serial) is probably less well known; an 'English breakfast' is not universally understood (nor eaten); dons, proctors, and porters have their own particular significance in an old university city (or town); certain products, shops, or forms of transport may not be readily available in Australia or the Americas; and so on.

This Companion has struggled somewhat with recent history. Smoking used to be allowed on the upstairs floor of double-decker buses but has not been for some years; platform tickets were once common at railway stations; the internet and the World Wide Web were in their relative infancy during the period of Morse's most prolific activity; mobile or cellular phones were once (hard as it may be to believe) non-existent.[1] References, therefore, may occasionally appear to be somewhat of their time though also linked (where possible) to the current day; as a general rule, ages of individuals are given as of the date of their appearance in a case. Further, where photographs appear they tend to be from 'now' rather than 'then'. If Morse had ever

---

[1] The first reference to a mobile phone appears in 1994 (CAIN: p305). Abbreviations for cases appear on page 6.

taken a picture of his own Lancia car, it is yet to surface (and one guesses that he had rather more important or interesting things to do).[2]

It is worth noting, perhaps, that the life of another famous detective (Sherlock Holmes) has attracted rather a lot of interest – particularly where there appear to be contradictions or apparently inexplicable lacunae. Fry (1997: pp91-94), while making a good case that annotations of Chesterton rely on the fallacy that his *Father Brown* stories constitute a 'canon', cogently argues that it "... is the details that fascinate us with Holmes ..." (p93). Whether Holmes attended either Cambridge or Oxford University (or, indeed, both) as an undergraduate has not been satisfactorily resolved to this day; exactly where he travelled between May 1891 and April 1894 remains a mystery although many plausible suggestions have been put forward. Quite omnisciently, Doyle (1981: p983) predicts in the Preface to *The Case Book of Sherlock Holmes* that: "Perhaps in some humble corner of ... a Valhalla, Sherlock and his Watson may for a time find a place, while some more astute sleuth with some even less astute comrade may fill the stage which they have vacated." One would not necessarily argue Morse to be more astute than Holmes (though he is vastly more human); whether or not Lewis could be described as less astute than Watson is, indeed, a moot point.

Similarly, the life of Morse (purely as recorded by Dexter) creates a number of problems. For example, while it is known as a fact that Morse attended St John's College (Oxford) there is simply no record in that College's membership lists of such a student. The employment records of the Thames Valley Police Force are also silent. If there were a reason for such gaps, the present author would be both surprised and delighted to hear of it. It is also worth recording that, by printed volume, the casebook of Morse exceeds that of Holmes by a considerable margin (though the number of known cases investigated by Holmes is, of course, far greater than those of Morse).

The Works

There is, regrettably, a finite number of cases investigated by Morse of which we are aware through publication (and these effectively total twenty-one). It is on the written word that The Works are based and any references to Morse in media other than the written word (and that as told to, and transcribed by, Colin Dexter) will remain beyond this Companion. It would be unthinkable for the real Morse (as a serving police officer) to appear as 'himself' in, for example, any television programmes that purport to give accurate details of the cases. Any such programmes would need such a range of gifted and talented actors, sensitive direction, and enhanced production values that it simply beggars belief that they could be successfully made and attract an audience of several millions not only in the United Kingdom but around the world.

---

[2] It has been claimed that Morse had a Brownie camera as a child (WOOD: p83) but "... Morse knew little (well, nothing) about photography ..." (WOOD: p175). Further, according to NEIG (p53), Morse apparently *never* owned a camera in his life.

Further, just as one might argue that a line should be drawn between the Holmesian canon (as transcribed by Arthur Conan Doyle) and "Sherlock Holmes and the Voice of Terror" (a 1942 Universal Studios film starring Basil Rathbone wherein Holmes battles the Nazis), a principle needs to be established. Television interpretations of Morse may be wonderful, creative, and superbly acted - one can even imagine certain actors in the lead roles - but they are not the words of Morse as told to Dexter, nor Dexter's recording of the cases.

Obviously, since the death of Morse in 1998, there can be no further cases and, as Dexter seems adamant that he has no notes of any others that remain to be transcribed, the caseload must be closed.[3] Rather a shame for all of those who enjoyed Morse's ingenuity, irascibility, imagination, lusts and addictions, and good fellowship but there remains the treasury of the published works. It is, probably, an exaggeration to paraphrase the words of Drabble (1974; p7) who writes, of Jane Austen, "... there would be more genuine rejoicing at a complete new novel by (her) than any other literary discovery short of a new major play by Shakespeare". Substitute 'case' for 'novel' and change 'her' to 'Morse' and you may appreciate both the depth of my admiration and the extent of the exaggeration. And how odd that Drabble demands a 'major' play by Shakespeare? I think one may settle for a minor one…

Symons (1985) usefully comments about the works of G. K. Chesterton whose "... short (Father Brown) stories are a diet too rich for everyday consumption. Two or three, not six or seven should be read at a sitting. And they have their faults …" (p77).[4] A case could surely be made that no such stricture applies to the records that Dexter has supplied. They provide addictive reading, repetitive reading, and a glorious mixture of entertainment and enlightenment. This Companion has mined fairly extensively but many discoverable nuggets still remain: for example, was it Diocletian or Poirot who grew tomatoes and cucumbers (WEAR: p2), what was Coleridge's interest in candles (SERV: p110), what was the literary allusion picked by Barbara Moule (JWEL: p298), or (apart from a literal translation) what is a *camera hypothetica* (LBUS: p123)? By all means read Dexter to find the solution to one of Morse's cases but, I strongly suggest, just read the books anyway for sheer pleasure. It is an exercise, I maintain, that is well worth pursuing not once, but many times.

The Cases and References

All references in the Companion are to the 1997-2000 paperback editions published in the United Kingdom by Pan Books (except where noted). Dates of original publication by Macmillan are given below as 'first published' where appropriate. Page references are used extensively – to both allow the astute reader to challenge anything potentially controversial or surprising and, more pedantically, to provide a basis for verification. At the end of the brief

---

[3] Dexter has recorded further work that involved Lewis alone but, with the absence of Morse, these are not further referenced in this Companion. He has also written a *very* short story where the two detectives discuss ambiguities in clues such as "Yellow additive to food" (7) when confirming letters could equally give 'mustard' or 'custard' (*The TIMES* 15th October 2009).

[4] Fry (1997), in an essay on (or rather a review of) 'The Annotated Father Brown' argues that there is no justification in giving Brown anywhere near as much attention as properly deserved by Holmes.

description for each case (which appears alphabetically i.e. *Last Seen Wearing* appears under L rather than W for WEAR) there is a list of main personnel who have a separate entry in this volume (without mentioning, of course, Morse and Lewis). Not all names are listed after a case but only those who play a prominent part.

Title	First Published	Case Date	Abbreviation
Last Bus to Woodstock	1975	1971	LBUS
Last Seen Wearing	1976	1975	WEAR
The Silent World of Nicholas Quinn	1977	1975	NICQ
Service of All the Dead	1979	1978	SERV
The Dead of Jericho	1981	1979	JERI
The Riddle of the Third Mile	1983	1980	MILE
The Secret of Annexe 3	1986	1985/86	ANNX
The Wench is Dead	1989	1989/90	WNCH
The Jewel That Was Ours	1991	1990	JWEL
The Way Through the Woods	1992	1992	WOOD
The Daughters of Cain	1994	1994	CAIN
Death is Now My Neighbour	1996	1996	NEIG
The Remorseful Day	1998	1998	REMO
As Good as Gold	1994	Various	See below

This compendium contains 11 accounts (most of which originally appeared in an earlier compendium (*Morse's Greatest Mystery* in 1993). Richards and Attwell (2003: pp37-38) give a comprehensive history of publication dates and where these first appeared. Of these cases, the following are of interest here:

	Case Date	Abbreviation
Dead as a Dodo	1990	DODO
Neighbourhood Watch	1990	WATC
The Carpet-Bagger	1992	BAGG
Morse's Greatest Mystery	1992	MYST
The Inside Story	1993	STOR
As Good as Gold[5]	1994	GOLD
Last Call	1994	CALL

Page references herein to these seven cases are from Dexter (1994).

Evans Tries an O-level also appears in this compendium; it has a very brief reference to Chief Inspector BELL (and some details about Oxford Prison) but, while well worth reading, has no further part to play here. And the same goes for the similarly included *A Case of Mis-Identity* (a Sherlock HOLMES pastiche).

---

[5] Published by Pan but in association with Kodak.

The Burglar	1995	BURG

According to Richards and Attwell (2003) this first appeared in book form in 1995 at a Convention in Nottingham. Haining (1996) has it appearing in *You* magazine (issued with *The Mail on Sunday*), but gives the year as 1994. Page references are to the case as appearing in Haining.

Entries in the Companion

These are arranged in the style of *alphabetical order* and such an order ignores gaps and hyphens. So, for example, the NEWS OF THE WORLD follows NEW ROAD but precedes NEWSPAPERS. Each entry is headed in **bold type**. Most entries are identified by reference to the case (or cases) in an abbreviated form (e.g. REMO for The Remorseful Day). A large number of entries contain cross-references to elsewhere in the Companion and these are shown in CAPITALS (with the exceptions of Morse, Lewis, Strange, Max, and Oxford). Footnotes are used sparingly and are numbered sequentially within each letter.

All and any material facts that may identify a criminal or compromise the solution to any case have been brutally suppressed. The names of all people appearing in the cases have an entry (although most of these are rather brief);[6] many of these are simply listed under APPENDIX D (with, one hopes, no slight to the persons involved) when they have limited or no impact on the detection of a crime; this category also includes a number of named entries out of sheer bloody-mindedness. References to well-known poets, composers, artists (of all other types), and writers appear only if relevant or from other interest; how 'interest' is determined is vague, idiosyncratic, and occasionally deliberately perverse. Names mentioned in, and the authors of, the hundreds of quotations that head most Chapters are only rarely recorded.

All place names in The Works are recorded, including those beyond Oxfordshire (unless they simply appear with no further relevance to the text: examples of these include Australia ('Ostrighlia') from MILE (also appearing as 'Ostrylia' in WOOD: p190), Belsen from LBUS, and Tenerife from WOOD; even so, some of these non-relevant places seem to have crept in). Many place names are recorded only under APPENDIX E. Map references – which are, of necessity, occasionally rather vague –appear for many street and place names within Oxford and its environs; that map of Oxford City and of the surrounding area can be found on page 10. Brand names appear throughout the Works. These only appear as entries in this Companion if they are somehow relevant to any case, further one's understanding of the character of Morse or Lewis, or may require some slight explanation. It is, therefore, assumed that 'Barclaycard', 'luncheon vouchers', or 'Green Shield stamps' do not need entries but 'Prestige' and 'Letts' might.

---

[6] Descriptions are taken from the Works; it is no mere coincidence that female characters are often described (by and large and simply) by their physical attributes.

Apology

Many of the following entries may appear totally otiose and there is no defence beyond claiming a desire to be inclusive (though it may not necessarily be a bad thing to be a snapper-up of unconsidered trifles – or, as Holmes states, in *The Boscombe Valley Mystery*, "You know my method. It is founded upon the observance of trifles."). Compiling such a work has a smack of obsession about it and is coupled with a compulsion not to allow disorder (or deficiencies) in the alphabetical progression. The hooked atoms demand, for me, some sort of interconnection.

Inevitably, there is also a large dose of pedantry (putting it politely). Dexter would be one of the first to admit to a slight lack of precision in recording details – the colour of Morse's eyes, for example – and there is something rather soul-destroying about recording such scarce minutiae.[7] I would maintain that these add to, rather than detract from, the joys of Morse. There is, perhaps regrettably, a tradition in these matters: Keating notes (1989: p29) how one correspondent pointed out that a reference in an Inspector Ghote story mentioned a train passing the Sandhurst Road High Level Station (when it should, of course, have been the Sandhurst Road Low Level ...) and Shepherd (1978) devotes parts of his seven chapters on the Holmesian Canon to explaining how Watson could have been wounded (by that Jezail musket) in both shoulder and leg (with an illustration, no less). Shepherd also suggests that the villain's reference to a bittern on Dartmoor (in the Baskerville case) was a somehow confused mistake when he foolishly lost his head on meeting Dr Watson.

In delving into Morse (and Lewis *et al*) I take some comfort from the words of Armstrong (writing of those who try to analyse 'laughter'):

> "The learned and philosophic have given laughter their most serious consideration, and as they pore over the spritely and elusive thing, tearing it with the dry and colourless terms of science and philosophy, the tables are frequently turned on them and the Ariel which they are anatomising so absorbedly shakes himself free, straps them upon the operating table and sets about anatomising them in turn, and the earnest analysts of laughter become themselves laughable." (1928: p28)

No amount of nitpicking, analysis, probing, or pseudo-scholasticism will ever pin Morse to the table (for which much thanks).

Paul Taylor

---

[7] The matters of the age difference between Morse and Lewis, the colour of the former's eyes, the choice between a Lancia and a Jaguar, and Lewis's origins are all explored in the main text. That being said, Dexter employs a *most* remarkable consistency and inner cohesion in his records.

Contents

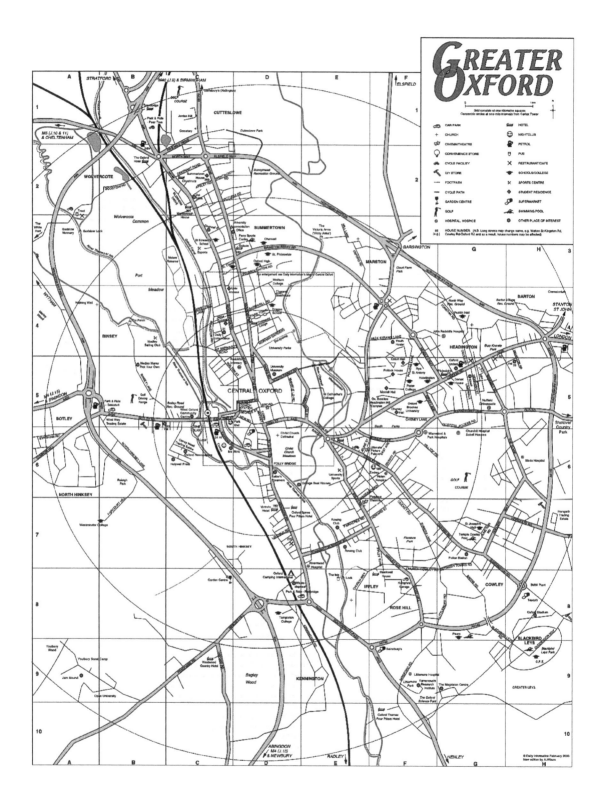

A

AA (Alcoholics Anonymous) An organisation that Morse has never joined, though he has obviously considered the amount he drinks as the following exchange witnesses:

Morse: "What's the matter with you this morning? I hope you're not becoming an alcoholic … you want to be like me, Lewis. I'm a dipsomaniac."
Lewis: "What's the difference?"
Morse: "I think an alcoholic is always trying to *give up* drink."
Lewis: "Whereas such a thought has never crossed your mind, sir?"
Morse: "Well put!" (ANNX: p232)

AA (The Automobile Association) This organisation (founded in 1905 in London to assist the growing number of motorists – specifically to avoid police speed traps) awards 'stars' to denote varying standards that may be expected at hotels, restaurants, and other establishments (including the HAWORTH HOTEL and the BAY HOTEL). Their signs, of black stars on a yellow background – or yellow on black – are readily visible, it would appear, in WOODSTOCK in particular (LBUS). The AA also publish, among many other works, *Hotels of Britain* and it is from this book that Morse picks, at random, the SWISS LODORE HOTEL for a holiday (SERV: p69). He decides not to take up a later chance pick in Inverness.

ABC Cinema The name of a once proud chain of cinemas (with an outlet in GEORGE STREET). BROWNE-SMITH, inter alia, has paid to see mild PORNOGRAPHY here during vacations (MILE: p35). In 1998 *The Full Monty* is being shown (REMO).[1]

Abingdon Home to the RICHARDS and the WHITE SWAN pub, Abingdon is some half a dozen miles south of Oxford; Abingdon also houses the Central TV studios (NEIG: p14) and the studio of Manual McSevich (MINOR). It is a pleasant (enough) market town on the River Thames.

Abingdon Road A major street in Oxford, leading south from ST ALDATES. It is home to the Elite Booking Service Agency (MINOR) and also the REDBRIDGE Waste Recycling Centre (WOOD: p300), otherwise known as the Waste Reception Area (REMO: p104). **Map D6 - E8**

ACC See ASSISTANT CHIEF CONSTABLE.

Ackermann, Rudolf (1764-1834) He arrived in London (from Austria) in 1795 and has been credited with creating a school of fine art lithography. He published his *History of Oxford: Its Colleges, Halls and Public Buildings* in 1814 (which contains works by a number of artists). He is erroneously referred to as Ackerman (WEAR: p24). **Plate 1**

---

[1] Some commentators have suggested that the phrase 'the full Monty' was originally a description of the ENGLISH BREAKFAST but on such matters one should remain silent here.

Acum, David A French teacher, since 1973, at the City of Caernarfon School (but formerly a French teacher at the ROGER BACON school – where he taught Valerie TAYLOR, among others). He sports a beard and apparently met his wife at EXETER UNIVERSITY (where he studied Modern Languages). They live at 16 St Beuno's Road, Bont-Newydd (some 2 miles south of CAERNARFON).

Acum, Mrs Morse calls to see ACUM at his home on chance and, instead, meets an attractive woman, naked but for two towels. Morse feels as lecherous as a billy-goat (WEAR: p225).

Ainley, Eileen Married to Richard AINLEY. They live, without children, at 2 Wytham Close WOLVERCOTE. **Map B2**

Ainley, Richard (Detective Chief Inspector) An officer with the THAMES VALLEY POLICE. He had, unsuccessfully it seems, investigated the disappearance of Valerie TAYLOR. The driver of a JAGUAR killed him in a road accident on the 1st of September 1975 (WEAR).

Alcohol See entries under BASS, BEER, BITTER, GIN AND TONIC, REAL ALE, WHISKY, and WINE (and the appropriate section under 'Morse'). A number of brand names are recorded – for example, Monica HEIGHT drinks a gin and Campari (NICQ: p112), Angela STORRS fancies a Dry Martini (NEIG: p94), and a flagon of Woodpecker cider appears (SERV: p137); the HAWORTH HOTEL has at least four bottles of Veuve Cliquot Ponsardin 1972 (ANNX: p104) while Sheila WILLIAMS drinks Möet & Chandon Imperial Brut (JWEL: p3; WOOD: p96); Joanna FRANKS is offered Running Horse beer (WNCH: p163); a Louisa HARDINGE drinks Cointreau (WOOD: p23), and Julian STORRS drinks McEwan's Export Ale (NEIG: p30). Of somewhat bizarre interest are the 'cocktails' on offer in the FLAMENCO TOPLESS BAR (MILE: p20) including, for example, the 'Soho Wallbanger – a dramatic confrontation of voluptuous Vodka with a tantalizing taste of Tia Maria'. Sarah JONSTONE drinks a rather more recognisable cocktail – a Tequila Sunrise (ANNX: p44) – and Morse fantasises about Karin ERIKSSON drinking Cognac (WOOD: p268). St Julien 93 (a powerful red wine from the Haut-Médoc) has been served at LONSDALE College (NEIG: p286); the 89 or the 90 are preferred vintages. The Ailish cocktail (REMO: p259) served at The RANDOLPH (Cognac, Kümmel, Fraise Liqueur, topped with chilled champagne) appears to have been named in honour of Ailish Hurley, Morse's favourite barmaid (p314).

Aldrich, Phil A mild-mannered American (born 1922) on the HISTORIC CITIES tour (JWEL). He has poor hearing but a good motive for being in Oxford.

A-level The name of the 'advanced' level of national examination in England, usually taken in at least three subjects, at the age of eighteen (or so). Success at the top grades does not guarantee a place at OXBRIDGE; failure to achieve top grades militates against such an achievement. The exam system of O-levels ('ordinary') and A-levels underwent a number of changes during the course of Morse's investigations (and not necessarily to his liking). Students from abroad may sit A (and O) levels courtesy of the SYNDICATE; those from nearer home may sit the exams courtesy of the LOCALS.

Alfred Street This narrow and cobbled lane joins BLUE BOAR STREET and BEAR LANE to the HIGH and is used by Morse to get from a haircut to the BEAR pub – a trifle early (NEIG: p90). Perhaps he should have chatted to the barber for a little longer. The origin of the name, adopted in the nineteenth century, may relate to the supposed founder of UNIVERSITY College – Alfred the Great. The street was formerly known as Vine Hall Street (or Bear Lane). **Map D5**

Alibi Chambers (2003) gives 'the plea in a criminal charge of having been elsewhere at the relevant time; the fact of being elsewhere …' and this definition appears as the heading to Chapter 40 of ANNX. The WORKS also have (in JERI: p147 for example), 'the plea in a criminal charge of having been elsewhere at the material time' from the Oxford English Dictionary. See also Diogenes SMALL. A number of the problems that beset Morse (and Lewis) arise from seemingly unbreakable alibis; a number of those problems are solved. The nature, purpose, and operation of alibis are explored in REMO (pp278-279 in particular).

Al-Jamara A sheikdom in the Middle East governed by Sheik Ahmed Dubal. It is rich in high quality oil and has been dealing with the SYNDICATE since 1970 (largely through the Al-Jamara Education Department).

All Souls This college (founded 1438) occupies a somewhat marvellous location in Oxford with facades on the HIGH and RADCLIFFE SQUARE. It is primarily an academic research institution and has no undergraduates. **Map D5**

Anagrams see LITERARY CURIOSITIES.

Anchor, The A pub close to POLSTEAD ROAD. Honey (1998) has it in Heyfield Road but Hayfield Road is also recognised. Morse enjoys 2 pints of John Smith's Tadcaster BITTER here (NEIG: p356). **Map C4**

Andrews Ancient History Tutor at LONSDALE College, where he has been for some 15 years (MILE: p121) and Master since 1980. He lives out of college with his family in KIDLINGTON and is slim and bespectacled (MILE: pp112-113; 116).

Andrews, Eddie A SOCO. He has probably worked with Morse before the NEIG case – he certainly understands why two cans of beer at a crime scene (coupled with the presence of Morse) are empty (p270). Andrews is also involved, as the second in charge SOCO officer, in the REMO case (p153). It is believed DEXTER once taught him.

Angel, The A pub in BREWER STREET, London; it sells BASS and is almost opposite the PENTHOUSE club.

Angel Inn A former pub in the HIGH and destination for nineteenth century coaches from BANBURY (WNCH: p139) and, one guesses, elsewhere. Honey (1998: p16) calls it '…

Oxford's most important coaching inn … with upwards of ten coaches leaving every morning at 8.00am'.

Archers, The A radio soap opera (originally billed as an 'everyday story of country folk') that can be heard on the BBC's Radio Four. Morse often listens to the omnibus edition, broadcast on a Sunday morning but has also been known to tell Lewis not to visit in the evening until the programme is finished (WNCH: p183); he rarely misses an episode but occasionally work intervenes (WOOD: p235).[2] Morse also listens in his car (CAIN: p221).

The series began in 1950 on the BBC Midland Home Service and coverage was extended to the whole of the United Kingdom in 1951. It is set in the fictional village of Ambridge; Ambridge can be found in the equally fictional county of Borsetshire in the absolutely factual West Midlands (and south of Birmingham). Until 1972, the producers and writers worked in collaboration with what was then the Ministry of Agriculture and the programmes helped, inter alia, to inform farmers and others about best practice. The first leading characters were Phil and Grace Archer, the latter dying conveniently in a fire in September 1955 in what was commonly seen as a spoiler for the opening night of the launch of Britain's first independent television company (ITV). The 15,000th episode was broadcast in November 2006. The theme tune (*Barwick Green* by Arthur Wood) has now been heard, with omnibus editions and at a very rough calculation, close to 20,000 times; it is, indeed, widely recognised and very easily hummed.

Aristotle There are many mentions, indeed, of Aristotle and Aristotelian theory in the WORKS – beginning with LBUS (pp91/122). Morse is clearly knowledgeable about Aristotle and his writings – he understands, for example, the concept of *immediate cause* (WEAR: p299), that the truth is somewhere in the middle (NICQ: p89), and he has been known to stand in the pose of Rodin's statue of the Greek (WEAR: p208).

There are further references – to the *Nichomachean Ethics* (JERI: p126; WOOD: p346), by implication to the Golden Mean (JERI: p251), and to Aristotelian intellect (MILE: p82). ANDREWS describes BROWNE-SMITH as an Aristotelian: "… it was always the half-way house between the too much and the too little …" (MILE: p117). He wonders if Morse understands. There is no doubt that Morse understands.

An example of Aristotelian syllogism is given (WNCH: p155) about the ownership of Joanna FRANKS' shoes and Sturdy (MINOR) mentions inductive reasoning and Aristotle (WOOD: p238); Ellie SMITH has lips '… marginally on the thin side of the Aristotelian mean …' (CAIN: pxx). James Hughes (MINOR) exhibits Aristotelian curiosity – and as a four-and-a-half year old brings therefore much delight to his parents (CAIN: p304).

---

[2] The timing of the omnibus edition on a Sunday is relevant in challenging a witness statement (CAIN: pp34/39/168).

Aristotle Bridge A bridge over the OXFORD CANAL (number 240) leading to ARISTOTLE LANE. **Plate 2**

Aristotle Lane The location of the only recreational open space in NORTH OXFORD. One can also find allotments here. Aristotle Lane is Morse's favourite Oxford street-name (NEIG: p94). **Plate 3**, **Map C4**

Arkwright, Doris She lives, perhaps, in Worcester Road, Kidderminster. While her actual address is a matter of some confusion, she does (at least) turn out to be an '... extraordinarily attractive brunette ...' (ANNX: p282).

'A' Roads A designation used throughout the United Kingdom to identify major routes that have not been accorded the status of motorways. Oxford is well (or poorly, it rather depends on one's point of view) served by such roads – notably the A34, A40 (parts of which are known as the Northern Ring Road), and A44. Morse believes the A49, north of Leominster, '... is one of the prettiest roads in England.' (SERV: p218). At the junction of the A34 and the A44 there is a roundabout with a service area (Pear Tree); from here, Christine GREENAWAY catches a Park-and-Ride bus into Oxford (WNCH: p121) and Margaret DALEY circumnavigates the roundabout while 'agonizingly preoccupied' (WOOD: p242).

As Good as Gold A brief case for Morse and one involving much bending of the rules and discussions of the ethics of fabricating evidence, all within the context of new guidelines from the Home Office on dealing with terrorism. Lewis almost falls prey to temptation (and Beamish Cask Pour stout takes on a significance). (GOLD) *Main personnel* DI CRAWFORD, Kieran MULDOON.

Ashenden, John A guide on the HISTORIC CITIES tour. He was born in 1956 and educated at a Leicester comprehensive school. His failure to gain a place at CHRIST'S COLLEGE in 1974 was a severe disappointment and contributed, in part, to his later fascination with PORNOGRAPHY.

Ashmolean A world-famous and very grand museum in Oxford. Its collections include much Art and rather more Archaeology. Morse intends to see 'again' the Tiepolo and the Giorgione (SERV: p48) and the Museum is the intended recipient of WOLVERCOTE TONGUE. There is a reference (JWEL: p9) to its pictures by Holman Hunt and Millais. In 1990, the museum was displaying an Oxford-blue banner reading *Musaeum Ashmoleanum apud Oxonienses* ('... among Oxonians').[3] Three of the Trustees of the Museum are invited to a dinner arranged by the HISTORIC CITIES tour (JWEL: p88) and KEMP plans to hold a slide-show in the Elias Ashmole Memorial Room (p105). The museum is attached to Oxford University. **Plate 4**, **Map D5**

---

[3] Oxonians usually refers to University members and Oxfordians to the town though this distinction has often been blurred.

Assistant Chief Constable A senior rank in the police. An unnamed ACC interviews Morse and, rather skilfully, denies him an undesired promotion while putting him in charge of a case (JERI: pp160-162). One guesses that the same ACC also hears the solution to the case (JERI: pp 285-291). Also see RANK.

Aunt Sally A pub game, fairly common in Oxfordshire and neighbouring counties. The game involves throwing sticks at a ball on a spike; the object is to dislodge the ball without hitting the spike (REMO: p148).

Azed The pseudonym of Jonathan Crowther, a CROSSWORD compiler (particularly for *The Observer*) and compared by Morse to Gary Kasparov (NEIG: p180), thought by some to be the XIMENES of chess.[4]

---

[4] Chess references are rare in the WORKS. Another may be found in REMO (p181) where a problem is surveyed like "… Capablanca contemplating his next move …"

B

Bacon, Roger See ROGER BACON COMPREHENSIVE SCHOOL.

Baines, Reginald He is the 'second master' at the ROGER BACON COMPREHENSIVE SCHOOL with responsibilities for, inter alia, both the timetable and teaching mathematics. He has a fair amount of savings – with the Oxford Building Society, Lloyd's, and the Manchester Corporation – though the relevance or not of this is a little unclear at first. At the time of Morse's investigation, Baines is aged 55, balding and grubby, speaks with a slight North Country accent, and is unmarried; he will remain unmarried (WEAR).

Bainton Road This thoroughfare provides a useful link (taken by, at least, Morse JERI: p21) between the WOODSTOCK ROAD and WALTON STREET. **Map C3**

Baker, George A lorry driver who tries to help the police in identifying what sort of vehicle may have been involved with one or two hitch-hikers (LBUS).

Baker, Yvonne She lives alone in Bethune Road, Stoke Newington (London) and is interviewed by a Morse entertaining (but controlling) certain lustful thoughts – by any reckoning, she is a honey (WEAR: p272). She appears to have shared a little history with Valerie TAYLOR and also offers to share a little time and fun with Morse (WEAR: p335/6). Morse appears to decline her offer but is in her flat rather a long time – from 10.30pm until well after the last Oxford train from PADDINGTON has departed.   .

Ballard, Mr and Mrs At one point this couple claim to live at 84 West Street, CHIPPING NORTON (ANNX: pp37-38) though they plan to move to Cheltenham. Their stay in Annexe 3 at the HAWORTH HOTEL is rudely interrupted.

Balliol College Benjamin Jowett was an influential Master (1870-93); the high academic standards set by him gradually spread to other colleges (NICQ: p24). Little is revealed about the college in the WORKS; it seems to feature more for being walked past by Christine GREENAWAY (WNCH: p74) and ASHENDEN (JWEL: p50) or being stood outside (at the Master's Lodge) by members of the HISTORIC CITIES tour (JWEL: p89). The foundation date of the college is traditionally given (by the College) as 1263. It is one of the larger colleges. Indeed, the college website refers to it in what it intends to be flattering terms as '…. being big and old …' **Plate 5, Map D5**

Banbury A town of some 40,000 people in North Oxfordshire. Some might say, churlishly, that its main claim to fame is the nursery rhyme beginning 'Ride a cock horse to Banbury Cross' but it is pleasant enough. The OXFORD CANAL passes through the centre of town.

Morse nearly falls asleep at the wheel in the outskirts (WEAR: p233-34), and BARTLETT claims to have attended a meeting there at Banbury Polytechnic (NICQ: p165). According to

Brewer's (1996), Banbury was the location where a puritan hanged his cat on a Monday for killing a mouse on Sunday; it is still the location for TOOLEY'S YARD.

Banbury Road One of the main roads leading into (or out of) Oxford to the north of the city. There are many fine Victorian villas (in the style that has been known as Venetian Gothic) on both sides of this thoroughfare '… as though Ruskin had been looking over the shoulders of the architects …' (ANNX: p17). The further north one goes, the less Venetian the scene. Lewis notes Linton Road and Belbroughton Road on his right-hand side as he drives up the Banbury Road from ST ALDATES to KIDLINGTON (SERV: p200). The numbering of houses – crucial to the solution of the ANNX case – is explored by reference to the Banbury Road (p172). Exactly where Morse lives is explored in the entry under his name. **Map C2-C3-D4-D5**

Bannister Close This may be found on the BLACKBIRD LEYS Estate. The police are particularly interested in the flats at numbers 13 and 14 (GOLD). There is also a like-named Close just off the IFFLEY ROAD. **Map H9**

Barclays Bank Their branch in The HIGH manages accounts for, inter alia one imagines, ST FRIDESWIDE'S, George WESTERBY, and Oliver BROWNE-SMITH. They helpfully forward a letter to Morse (MILE: p155).

Barker's Garage An establishment in the BANBURY ROAD, they provide services to both Morse and, in the past, Jennifer COLEBY (LBUS).

Barron, John A builder (and decorator) and local to LOWER SWINSTEAD. He is aged 41 years at the time of the REMO case, married with two young children (aged six and four), and has been carrying out some work for Debbie RICHARDSON. He was formerly in the Special Air Service Regiment (p296) and the hymn *He Who Would Valiant Be* has some special significance for him (p323).

Barron, Linda Wife of John and a slightly overweight brunette. She tells Lewis (REMO: p286) that her husband's favourite meal is egg and chips (at which point, John understandably goes up in Lewis's estimation).

Bartlett, Richard The son of Dr BARTLETT and his wife. He has been diagnosed as a schizophrenic and is a voluntary patient at Littlemore Hospital under Dr Addison (NICQ).

Bartlett, Thomas G. PhD, MA. He is Secretary (i.e. head) of the Foreign Examinations Syndicate, a body organising the setting and marking of exams for foreign students. In this capacity, he also acts as Secretary to the SYNDICS, the board that oversees that work. He is in his mid- to late-fifties, a stickler for procedure, a little deaf, described as 'Pickwickian' (NICQ: p69) and married (living with his wife in BOTLEY). He has travelled to the Middle East.

Bass A brewery, established in 1777 at Burton upon Trent (also known as Burton-on-Trent; REMO: p423). Its distinctive red triangular logo was the first to be registered as a trademark (in

1876). The history of the brewery since 1777 is far too complicated to detail here; suffice it to say that it was once famous for providing REAL ALE. The beer is also available in cans (REMO: p299).

Bath The HISTORIC CITIES tour visits this (historic) Somerset city (known to the Romans as *Aquae Sulis*). ASHENDEN manages to list a number of names associated with the city when speaking to members of the tour – Beau Nash, Henry Fielding, Fanny Burney, Jane Austen, William Wordsworth, Walter Scott, and Charles DICKENS. He also refers to *The Wife of Bath's Tale* by Geoffrey Chaucer, which the diligent ROSCOE is reading as the *Tale of the Wyf of Bathe* (JWEL: p275). As an aside, Morse knows that Chaucer was born in 1343 (REMO: p96).

The city has (among *many* others) locations such as the Circus and Brock Street (NEIG: p407), the Roman Baths, and enjoys the presence of the Bath Festival Choir; in 1996 they may be heard at the Abbey, singing Fauré's *Requiem* (NEIG: pp264-265, 390). It is a little under 70 miles from Oxford (NEIG: p268). Morse very much enjoys a stay here at the ROYAL CRESCENT HOTEL when sharing the Sarah Siddons suite (NEIG).

Bay Hotel The name of a fairly superior (well, two AA stars anyway) hotel on Marine Parade (Lyme Regis, Dorset; phone 0297 442059). It has views encompassing Portland Bill and the historic Cobb Harbour. Morse takes a break here in 1992 (room 27; WOOD: p11) and decides it is time to re-read *The Odyssey* and brush up on his knowledge of both architecture and snooker. And he also meets Louisa HARDINGE.

Bayley, Paul A neighbour of Sheila POSTER and a History graduate from MAGDALEN. Despite being lank-haired and large-buttocked, he has a certain charm – though Morse does take an instant dislike to his earring (STOR: p169).

Bay Tree Hotel An establishment in BURFORD (REMO: p235). No doubt much could be written about it but the WORKS are largely silent.

BBC The British Broadcasting Corporation; a major provider of public service television broadcasting (on channels BBC1 – and BBC2 in the 1970's and 1980's). Morse has appeared on BBC1 television making an appeal for information in the case of the murdered Sylvia KAYE and the PHILLIPSONs watch the 9 o'clock news (WEAR: p237) on the same channel; Morse watches, at the Lewis's, the *Six O'Clock News* (CAIN: p347). He does not, however, watch *Newsroom South-East* (REMO: p13), preferring to get his news from 'the wireless'.

The BBC also provides a radio service ('the wireless') and on one of these channels (Radio Four) can be heard *The ARCHERS* and *DESERT ISLAND DISCS*; Morse is a keen listener to both as well as Radio Three, which broadcasts classical music and live concerts. On Radio Four one may also listen to the *Morning Service* (NEIG: p249) and the *Today* programme (NEIG: p110) – the latter containing early morning news, discussion, and analysis; the programme is a favourite of Angela STORRS (NEIG: p215).

Bear, The A famous and popular pub on the corner of ALFRED STREET and BLUE BOAR STREET; the cover of Honey (1998) is adorned with a picture of it. Apparently, there has been a pub on the same site since 1242. The pub does not officially open until noon (much to Morse's initial disappointment) and has been run by Steven and Sonya Lowbridge for the last 5 years (NEIG: p90). Morse drinks Burton ale here. He not only admires their extensive collection of ties – 'purchased' by a succession of landlords for a free drink or two - but also is surprised to find that a particular type he is seeking may be purchased from MARKS AND SPENCER'S.

The pub is comparatively small and often filled with members of nearby colleges (including CHRIST CHURCH, ORIEL, LINCOLN, and UNIVERSITY colleges). It is while washing his hands in the gents here that Morse briefly contemplates where all the plugs in the world have gone (NEIG: p92); no answer is forthcoming. **Plate 6, Map D5**

Bear Hotel A rather plush and large hotel in WOODSTOCK. There was an inn (of sorts) on the site in the thirteenth century; the present building boasts an ivy-clad façade, oak beams, open fireplaces, and stone (rather than brick) walls. Morse would like to invite Laura HOBSON here for a quiet or a noisy drink – and does so – but there are more urgent pressures in the case (WOOD: p328).

Bear Lane A street in Oxford not far from LONSDALE COLLEGE (LBUS: p229). **Map D5**

Beaumont Street Here one may appreciate the '…curving sweep of the Regency houses' (JERI: p20). It is also here that Morse mentally '… debated between the ASHMOLEAN, just opposite on his right, and the RANDOLPH, immediately on his left. It wasn't a fair contest'. (SERV: p60). **Map D5**

Beer Although Morse has been known to drink beer from cans (LBUS: p118), it is usually in company (or alone) and in pubs (or hotels) that '… the glorious amber fluid …' (WEAR: p192) is drunk. Morse's favourite is 'best bitter', always by the pint (or pints), and always savoured. Morse has no time for artificial beer, preferring 'real ale', conditioned in the cask, and drawn to the glass by a pump (preferably by a barmaid). Morse does not appear to be a member of CAMRA (the Campaign for Real Ale) but certainly sympathises with its aims. The smell and, dare one say, romance of beer wafts throughout the WORKS (and is often detected by others on Morse's breath). Apparently, in 1998, a pint cost about a pound (REMO: p207). A number of brand names may be found under the names of the individual PUBLIC HOUSES in which they are served or in individual entries. Morse has often been counselled that beer makes a lumpy mattress and spirits, a hard pillow (REMO: pp360-361). See also BITTER and REAL ALE.

Beerbohm, Max The author of the comic tale *Zuleika Dobson* (subtitled *An Oxford Love Story*) published in 1911. It was, perhaps, this novel that promoted the idea of the SHELDONIAN heads as being those of Roman Emperors. Morse has not read the book (JWEL: p70); a shame, as he may well have enjoyed Judas College and a number of Oxonian suicides. See also the RANDOLPH.

Begbroke A village some 2 miles south of WOODSTOCK. It is the home of the GOLDEN ROSE pub (LBUS: p85) and the DALEY family (WOOD).

Belisha crossing Now more commonly known as a 'zebra crossing', the Belisha Beacon is a flashing orange globe on top of a black and white striped pole, both indicating where pedestrians may cross a road and to alert motorists to that fact. It is named after the then Minister of Transport, Sir Leslie Hore-Belisha, who introduced them to Britain in 1934 and such a crossing is sometimes patrolled by a LOLLIPOP man (or woman). Crossings without the aid of those dedicated public servants may be a 'Pelican crossing' (NICQ: p196; SERV: p37) where traffic lights control the flow of both pedestrians and vehicles. The more sophisticated of these crossings have a flashing 'Green Man' showing when it is safe to cross (CAIN: p110).

Bell, Inspector A Chief Inspector (later promoted to Superintendent) with the Oxford City Police in ST ALDATES (LBUS: p231), he and Morse have met several times before their involvement in the KAYE case. Lewis also recalls 'the old days' when Bell was based at KIDLINGTON (WNCH: p126). He does rather tend to be involved at the start of a death or murder, make a little progress, and then get overtaken by Morse (for example, in NICQ and SERV though the latter is officially because of his 'flu'); in both these cases, his immediate superior is Strange (SERV: p129). He is able to impress junior officers (such as WALTERS in JERI: p53) but, perhaps, others notice his limitations and his promotion is as much a way of getting him off the front line, as it is a 'reward' (JERI).

Bell is married with children ("ungrateful little buggers" SERV: p94), drops his aspirates, and is tall with black hair (JERI: p37). His sense of humour is rather feeble – as witness his 'joke' in JERI (p59): "(She) probably put her bank balance on some horse at ten-to-one and it came past the post at twenty-to-six!" A number of equally feeble varieties of the joke exist. He believes Morse to be the "cleverest bugger I've ever met" (JERI: p38) and is not averse to asking him for help (p156) despite being officially (by time in the job and length of service, one guesses) his senior (p161). His promotion does, of course, make him officially Morse's superior.

Bell makes an appearance at a murder scene in NICQ (p182) and also (obviously talented, this man) organises the security for a visit by some Chinese dignitary (JERI: p82). He is still a Superintendent in the ANNX case – asking Morse if he wants more officers (p90). By the time of the JWEL case he has become a Chief Superintendent, remarking that Morse causes as many problems as a pregnant rabbit (JWEL: p244).

Bell Inn A noted, and picturesque, inn in West Street, CHIPPING NORTON (ANNX). The building dates from the mid-eighteenth century. **Plate 7**

Bell's A brand of whisky drunk by Morse (and Margaret and Tom BOWMAN; ANNX: pp208/221). It is named after Arthur Bell who joined a trading partnership in 1845 as a salesman, becoming a partner six years later. In 1895 the firm changed its name to Arthur Bell & Sons and registered its 'signature' brand a year later. Arthur died in 1900.

Bertnaghboy Bay This can be found by KILKEARNAN, Connemara on the west coast of Southern Ireland (WNCH: p201). A large cemetery overlooks it.

Bicester A town in Oxfordshire of some 30,000 people. Its position – in terms of transport links – has led to what some may call an over-developed expansion. It has a number of streets (including BURE PLACE and Sheep Street) and a public toilet (REMO: p89). The town name is pronounced to rhyme with 'blister'.

Biffen, Tom Landlord of the MAIDENS ARMS. He is known as Biff (understandably), is short and square, and wears a beard and an earring (REMO: p122). He also has tattooed arms, suffers from vertigo, and enjoys fishing every Tuesday. He is still legally married but separated and has little contact with his wife or their young children (Joanna and Daniel). His favoured tipple, especially when nervous, is Captain Morgan rum (reflecting, perhaps, his time in both the Royal and Merchant Navies).

Binyon, Catherine Wife of John. Morse finds her journey to Leeds to be *very* interesting (ANNX: p283).

Binyon, John An erstwhile factory-hand from Leeds who had a large win on the football pools from Littlewoods in about 1975. This jackpot enabled him to buy and manage, with Catherine, the HAWORTH HOTEL and to obtain an AA star (ANNX).

Bird and Baby A common soubriquet for the EAGLE AND CHILD. Sheila WILLIAMS refers to the pub by that name (JWEL: p138) as did the literary group, the Inklings.[1]

Bitter The most common variety of English beer (one need not count lager here) is often 'best', occasionally 'cooking', and has a great variety of tastes, strengths, and manufacturers. Morse has been known to drink bitter on a few occasions. See BEER.

Blackbird Leys An estate (one of the largest areas of council housing in England) in the south-east of Oxford and the scene of various anti-social behaviours including a smashed shop in Verbena Avenue and the crash of a getaway car near the Horspath roundabout (CAIN: p268). Most of the housing is low-rise but there are also tower blocks. Joy-riding, high rates of unemployment, and the full panoply of social deprivation have bedevilled the estate. **Plate 8, Map H8 - H9**

Black Dog A pub in ST ALDATES opposite to the great portal of CHRIST CHURCH. Morse happily waits here, rather obviously with a pint of beer, for ROOPE (NICQ: p144).

Black Horse A pub (of unknown location but, one guesses, not too far from CHIPPING NORTON) that Margaret BOWMAN wishes she had gone to after a funeral (ANNX: p12).

---

[1] A larger group than often supposed but three members (C.S. Lewis, J.R.R. Tolkien, and Charles Williams) formed the core. Lewis (not C.S.) has some thoughts about them – see the EAGLE AND CHILD.

There is no indication whether Morse had ever drunk there; there is no indication that he had not (especially as it is within striking distance of Oxford).

Black Prince (The) A pub in WOODSTOCK. One of its main attractions is a reasonably sized car park. A boon in a town bedevilled by parking restrictions, the car park also affords an appropriate location for the last hours of Sylvia KAYE. The pub opens at 11.00 a.m. on weekdays and contains a reasonably select cocktail lounge (staffed by a reasonably select Gaye MCFEE); shields of Oxford colleges may be found adorning its walls. The pub is passed (at speed) by Lewis and Morse on their way to CHIPPING NORTON (ANNX: p199).

Black Prince, The A racehorse running at Chepstow on 30th September 1971; it is backed by Lewis to win (on Morse's advice), and Morse 'each way' (so that if the horse comes into the first 3 or 4 – depending on the number of horses running - a proportionate amount of the odds will be returned as cash). The betting and the race result provide an early indication of how the relationship between the detectives may develop (LBUS).

Blackwell's A prestigious bookshop, founded in 1879 by Benjamin Henry Blackwell in the BROAD where it can still be found (though with somewhat expanded and extended premises – the basement Norrington Room is now huge). The firm, proud of its family tradition, has expanded into publishing and has a large number of bookshop branches, particularly in university towns or cities. It has long enjoyed a close relationship with the University of Oxford and schools (for example, Donald PHILLIPSON has an account) and DOWNES spends almost an hour browsing their second-hand books (JWEL: pp95-96). Morse buys the first volume of Sir Steven Runciman's *History of the Crusades* here in 1996 – though he is not sure why (NEIG: p337). The bookshop erroneously appears as 'Blackwells' rather than 'Blackwell's' in LBUS (p61) and NICQ (p283) but correctly in WATC (p123) when Morse saunters around the shop for half an hour. Blackwell's Book Services – concerned with the wholesale side of the business – may be found in Hythe Bridge Street (ANNX: p133). **Plate 9**

Bladon A village in Oxfordshire; it is famous as the burial place of Sir Winston (and Lady Clementine) CHURCHILL (LBUS: p10).

Bland, George MA, A former member of the SYNDICATE (replaced by Nicholas QUINN) who has moved, with subsequent regrets, to AL-JAMARA to work. (NICQ).

Bleak House The 'greatest novel in the English language' for Morse (WNCH: p87); DEXTER has: '... (it) is the greatest and most poignant story in the whole of English literature.' (Folio Society prospectus: 2006). Morse re-reads it (for probably the umpteenth time) in the JWEL case (p314). It is the ninth novel by Charles DICKENS and first published, in parts between 1852 and 1853.

A useful (but undated and unaccredited though extensive) leaflet used to be provided by, one guesses, the Curator(s) of the now like-named building: 'Charles Dickens and his Bleak House'. This appears, for what it's worth, in the Bibliography as 'Bleak House'. In it, one learns that at the time of Dickens's death (1870) the house he had bought in Broadstairs (Kent) was still officially known as Fort House. However, Dickens apparently thought of it as a 'bleak house' and the leaflet suggests (with some referenced evidence) that *Bleak House* is based on the building of 'Bleak House' although it locates that building elsewhere (in St Albans). Fort House was officially renamed Bleak House in about 1899 or 1900. Finally, the leaflet asserts (p5) that Dickens was inspired, while living in Fort House, to call his novel written there *Bleak House*; that during his lifetime it was accepted by the public that the novel's title was thus inspired; and that Fort House was usually referred to as Bleak House since about 1850. Much useful information can be found in Sutherland (2005).

Blenheim (1704) First of the four major battles won by John CHURCHILL in the War of the Spanish Succession. See also RAMILLIES, OUDENARDE, and MALPLAQUET. *Blenheim* was also the name of a coach running from the ANGEL INN to London in the nineteenth century (WNCH: p139).

Blenheim Close The home-cum-office of Rex DE LINCTO may be found at number 45; the Close is in KIDLINGTON (STOR).

Blenheim Palace One of the grandest of stately homes set within an estate of some 12,350 acres in WOODSTOCK. The very size of the estate may raise certain problems in any police search of the grounds.[2] Named after the battle, construction of the Palace began in 1705 with Sir John Vanbrugh as the architect. The Palace and estate were the gift of a generous Queen Anne (and a supposedly grateful nation) to John CHURCHILL. The estate features a little in LBUS and rather more so in WOOD (and the record of that case provides a helpful map). Particular areas of the Estate (much of which was laid out by Capability Brown) are described in some detail in the latter case (pp311-315): these include the route of the River Glyme (through Queen Pool, then under Vanbrugh's Grand Bridge) into the lake and over the Grand Cascade at the southern end, the Triumphal Gate, and Eagle and Combe Lodges. The Blenheim Tapestry (LBUS) may be found in the Green Writing Room. George DALEY works at the Blenheim Garden Centre (WOOD); Winston CHURCHILL was born here (at the Palace rather than the Garden Centre).

Bloxham Drive Occasionally referred to as Bloxham Close by Morse, this road of terraced houses features prominently in the NEIG case (just as the traffic-calming sleeping-policemen feature prominently in the Drive). The odd-numbered houses run from 1 to 21. Occupants include JAMES, OWENS, Queenie Norris at number 11, and the Jacobs family (including Emily: NEIG: p114). A stone-deaf lady (Arabella Adams) lives at number 19.

It may be found in KIDLINGTON (and is, presumably, named from the village of Bloxham, which is near BANBURY). At the start of the NEIG case, various parties (including Conservative and Labour) are contesting a local election in the Gosforth ward – as witnessed by various posters displayed in the Drive.

---

[2] Especially as much of the estate is wooded; it even has its own saw-mill (WOOD: p314).

Blue The colours associated with CAMBRIDGE and Oxford are light-blue and dark-blue respectively. A light-blue tie (bearing the legends 'Burton', 'St Michael', and 'Munro spun') is of some relevance in identifying a body (SERV: p116) though the fact that the door of 14B MANNING TERRACE is of the same colour is not (SERV: p282). Charles RICHARDS drives a light-blue Rolls Royce (JERI) but is possibly making a fashion statement (as he appears to have no known connections with CAMBRIDGE) and, on a certain day in July 1992, the sky was such a hue of blue (WOOD: p138). There is a regimental nickname of the 'Oxford Blues' – originally the Royal Horse Guards in 1690 (from their commander, the Earl of Oxford) – that, through the years, became part of the Blues and Royals (Brewer's 1996). Joanna FRANKS wears '… an Oxford-blue dress …' (WNCH: p48). Of more relevance to Morse is the jazz band - Oxford Blues (ANNX: p276) – to which Edward WILKINS and Charlie Freeman belong.

Julia STEVENS has an Oxford-blue front door (CAIN: p211), Donnington Bridge is (bizarrely for Oxford) Cambridge-blue (p304), Rachel JAMES has Oxford blue pillowcases and a matching duvet (NEIG: p112); no doubt this list could be expanded – by, for example, the mention of Shelly CORNFORD's Oxford blue pyjamas (NEIG: p192), a press release including 'The socks were of navy-blue cotton, with two light blue rings round the tops'. (MILE: p128), or (even) Peter SHERWOOD's pants (CALL: p259).

Blue Boar Street On one of its corners stands the BEAR public house. It was also the location of the Blue Boar Inn (which is now the site of the Museum of Oxford); of fleeting interest is the fact that Boswell stayed at the Inn in April 1763 (Boswell 1950: p240). **Map D6**

Boar's Hill A small promontory (and village) to the south west of Oxford. It once afforded an excellent view of the city centre (and that view was the inspiration for Arnold's 'DREAMING SPIRES') but this has been somewhat restricted by buildings. Anthony Hughes (MINOR) lives in the village (CAIN: p303).

Boat Inn A delightful pub at THRUPP; the landlord is known to both Morse and Max (MILE: p69). As they (and Lewis) are there after OPENING HOURS are over, he kindly offers (at a cost) to provide a bottle of GLENFIDDICH (MILE: p72). Morse and Lewis drink here at the denouement of the case (pp271-273).

There is a bizarre reference connected to the Boat in the NEIG case (pp65-66) – although in KIDLINGTON, Morse asks Lewis if he knows of a real-ale pub nearby. If Morse does not know pubs in the area, then who does? Lewis suggests going to the Boat; Morse responds with: "Excellent." And later enjoys three pints of Best Bitter (at the expense of Lewis). It is a good bet that the Boat is the 'muzak-free' pub noted in REMO (p72).

Bodleian Library The library is spread between a number of buildings (including the RADCLIFFE CAMERA). It is the main research library of the University of Oxford and is also a copyright deposit library. Morse consults the curator of the Medical Science Library about brain tumours (thankfully, not his own) in MILE (p121) and Christine GREENAWAY works here as the senior of three librarians in the Lower Reading Room, having progressed from such menial tasks as answering a query on the authorship of *Wind in the Willows* (WNCH: p73). The New Bodleian houses an Archive Room and here Sheila WILLIAMS tried to be enthusiastic about a set of Henry Taunt photographs (JWEL: p106).

Bonnington Hotel This may be found in Southampton Row, London. Near to here, Philip DALEY tries to beg (WOOD: p336).

Bonn Square A small public area at one end of QUEEN STREET and a daily home to various drop-outs (SERV: p33). Nearby is a branch of Selfridges (a chain of department stores) with 'light-beige brickwork' (SERV: p138). In the square can be found the 'Uganda' monument (SERV: p141). The monument is properly known as the Tirah Monument (from the 1897 campaign on the Northwest frontier in the province of that name). **Plate 10**, **Map D5**

Bookbinder's Arms A pub in the BOTLEY ROAD where at least a light lunch and a pint of Guinness may be purchased (LBUS: p106).

Botley A large (and mainly residential) development to the west of Oxford.

Botley Road A westbound route from Oxford leading, eventually, to Swindon. The premises of CHALKEY AND SONS can be found here. **Map B5 - C5**

Bovril A trademark and the name of a thick yeast extract (sold in a distinctive jar); a spoonful dissolved in hot water provides a 'beefy' drink. Lewis enjoys his while dunking chunks of bread therein (WEAR: p246). Ted BROOKS (CAIN: pp158-159) calls for a cup of the beverage while recovering from a mild heart attack (low on the Richter scale).

Bowden, Jimmy (Alfred) A neo-Marxist from Trowbridge who gained a First in both parts of the Classical Tripos (in, one guesses, 1977) at CHRIST'S COLLEGE. He moved to a Junior Research Fellowship at Oxford only to die 3 years later (JWEL). He is buried in HOLYWELL CEMETERY (p52).

Bowman, Margaret Wife to Tom; she is aged 36 in 1985 and works for the University Examining Board, her plans to become a stewardess on Boeing 737s having failed to reach fruition though she appears to have a tendency to otherwise spread her wings (ANNX). Is it she or Tom who owns a book called *The Complete Crochet Manual* – or, more importantly, the postcard from 'Edwina' that can be found within it?

Bowman, Thomas (Tom) Husband to Margaret; they live at 6 CHARLBURY DRIVE (about a mile from where he works in CHIPPING NORTON). He has passions – for PORNOGRAPHY and ALCOHOL (ANNX: p7) – but, unlike Morse, hides both rather than one of them.

Bradley, Jasper J. A classicist and a member of LONSDALE (NEIG). His book, *Greek Moods and Tenses* (Classical Press), has been favourably reviewed in Classical Quarterly; it deals (presumably in some depth) with the aorist subjunctive but there is not enough space here to delve further into this fascinating subject.

Brakspear An award-winning brewery, originally in Henley but now in Witney, Oxfordshire. The BITTER is certainly known to Morse. The brewing family was distantly related to Nicholas Breakspear, the only Englishman to become Pope (as Adrian IV) – a fact of which both Max and Morse are well aware (JWEL: p221).[3]

Brasenose College An aerial photograph can be found in the upstairs lounge of the CHERWELL MOTEL. The college bears a remarkable architectural and historical similarity to LONSDALE and has sometimes been confused with it. Brasenose claims a foundation date of 1509. DOWNES is a Fellow (JWEL: p81) and Edgeley (MINOR) an undergraduate. Elias Ashmole left without taking a degree; Walter Pater was a Fellow, and the cobbles outside were snow-covered in January 1986 (ANNX: p217). **Plate 11, Map D5**

Brasenose Lane A small lane leading between TURL STREET and RADCLIFFE SQUARE and an occasional home to various drop-outs (SERV: p33) and undergraduates. **Map D5**

Bream, Sir Clixby[4] A distinguished mathematician and Master of LONSDALE (in 1996 at least). He is about to retire (as the Founders' Statutes demand) but maintains a very active interest in his potential successors. His wife, Lady Muriel, died some three years ago and there was no issue from the marriage. He has come to love Oxford (although educated at CAMBRIDGE) and has been able to prolong his tenure a little. Oxford is not his only love. He had a trial at hockey for England (in his youth) and has been known to drive a Daimler car and enjoy a pint of Old Speckled Hen (NEIG: p98) in West Ilsley; while the pub is not named, there is a good chance it is The Harrow.

Brewer Street A thoroughfare in SOHO and the location of the club wherein John MAGUIRE works (WEAR). The street (or, rather, a narrow lane off it) is also visited by BROWNE-SMITH (MILE: p18). The Sauna Select, a massage parlour, is also just off Brewer Street (MILE: p40) as is 'Le Club Sexy' (albeit renamed 'Girls Girls Girls') – with some fairly splendid architecture above the ground floor (NEIG: 206).

Broadmoor Lea This sounds rather like a pleasant council estate in Oxford. It is, in fact, the location of near riots with car-thefts, joy-riding, stone-throwing, and so on; the problems are of national interest as Morse reads about them in *The TIMES* while on holiday (WOOD: pp100-101). The riots continue for some time and even provoke copy-cat disturbances in neighbouring Berkshire and Buckinghamshire. It adjoins the BLACKBIRD LEYS estate (WOOD: p40). **Map H8**

---

[3] Morris (1978: p166) has that Nicholas was the first recorded Vicar of Binsey (a very small settlement on the Thames) and thus the Oxford connection is maintained.

[4] The forename of Clixby is probably associated (somehow) with the Lincolnshire village of the same name. Clixby lies between Scunthorpe and Grimsby (and should not, one ardently hopes, be confused with Claxby which lies further south).

Broad, The One of the major thoroughfares in the centre of Oxford (and well-described in any number of guidebooks rather than here). Morse asks Lewis to park the Jaguar just outside the Old Clarendon: "All the traffic wardens know my car. They'll think I'm on duty." (CAIN: p79). **Plate 12**, **Map D5**

Broad Street An apparent incline in Lyme Regis; Morse struggles up it in search of a newspaper (WOOD: p25) and gets rather out of breath.

Brontë, Charlotte Author of *Villette* (LBUS: p60) and *Jane Eyre* (WEAR: p329); Morse is certainly aware of the first book (but has not read it) while the presence of a school copy of *Jane Eyre* in Yvonne BAKER's flat causes him some concerns. The last book that student nurse Fiona Welch has read is *Jane Eyre* – the fact that she found it pretty boring is a moment of some slight sadness for Morse. Part of Morse's bedtime reading is *The Brontës* by Juliet Barker (NEIG: p189).

Brooks and Gilbert A firm of estate agents in West London (and active in Cambridge Way, WC1) with a sideline in the removals business (MILE). They are involved – however tangentially – in the removal of lives as well as goods. The GILBERT appears to be Alfred (MILE: p238).

Brooks, Brenda The 52-year old wife of Ted and a cleaner for Julia STEVENS (CAIN). She was previously married (to Sid, who died) and her adult daughter is no doubt a child of that union. She enjoys cake-decorating but an injury to her hand (her husband is to blame) causes her some difficulties in this skilful hobby despite the support of a Tubigrip bandage and then a glove.

Brooks, Edward (Ted) He was formerly a SCOUT at WOLSEY COLLEGE (Staircase G, Drinkwater Quad) but has since moved to the PITT RIVERS as an attendant (which gives him access to all keys for the exhibits). He is, by all accounts, a thoroughly nasty piece of work and appears to deserve little sympathy for his heart problems (CAIN). He has been married to Brenda for some 13 years (and one wonders which of them chose the *Pie Jesu* from the Fauré *Requiem* for their wedding service);[5] they live in Addison Road, EAST OXFORD (CAIN: p211) and have savings of some £19,500 with the Halifax Building Society (p293). He is, crucially, of medium height and build (p289).

Broughton Castle An historic building on the itinerary of the HISTORIC CITIES tour (JWEL: p39) though not, in fact, visited. It is not far from BANBURY and still retains architectural elements of its origins in the 13th century.

Brown, Howard Born in 1918 and married to Shirley since 1947; he has clearly been in Oxford before he visits there on the HISTORIC CITIES tour. Like Mole (*The Wind in the*

---

[5] According to Morse, this *Requiem* was chosen by three out of four of the last Popes for their funerals (speaking in 1996; NEIG: p5).

Willows) he senses and smells his old territory when looking at the Keeper's Lodge to the PARKS (JWEL: p18).

Brown, Shirley Wife of Howard, they probably live in a house called Wardley (JWEL: p332). This may seem rather irrelevant but it is not to Morse.

Browne-Smith, Oliver (Maximilian Alexander) MC, MA, D.Phil. At prep-school he was nicknamed 'Omar'; at the more grown-up Oxford, 'Malaria'. During the Second World War he was a lieutenant with the Royal Wiltshire Yeomanry and was present (and wounded) at the second battle of EL ALAMEIN. He served in North Africa and Italy, acted as Major, and was awarded the Military Cross in 1945 (MILE: p169). He is 66 years old (and fairly tall) at the time of the MILE investigation but, according to his doctor, is unlikely to live for much longer. It is unclear at first whether or not the missing first joint of his right index finger (MILE: p16) will aid the investigation into a body found in the canal. He has been at LONSDALE College for some 30 years and is now a Senior FELLOW, residing at Room 4, Staircase T, Second Quad. He is known for his accuracy in using the English language (see HOUSMAN) and appears to be a stickler for the OXFORD COMMA (MILE: p52). He has been a literary pedant for many years – Morse recalls him (he was one of Morse's MODS tutors) barking away at any trivial spelling mistake (MILE: p53). He also examined him in GREATS (p63). For reasons too revealing to explain, he writes a long and painstakingly grammatically correct letter to Morse; his reference therein to '*istam epistolam*' confirms, inter alia, that he knows Morse reads Latin (p162; the phrase translates as 'that letter'). His surname, taken with his initials, appears to be a ripe ground for anagrams (though 'I'm Morse, own bath' does not really seem to get one very far).

Brown's A restaurant at the very bottom end of the WOODSTOCK ROAD where Eddie STRATTON has a bottle of red wine. JWEL has it in ST GILES' (p163) but the actual address is 5-11 Woodstock Road – an easy enough mistake for Stratton, the American, to make.

Bull and Stirrup A 'mean-looking, ill-lighted, spit-and-sawdust type of pub' (LBUS: p277) in WALTON STREET. Morse met PALMER there one evening and a shabby tale, appropriate to the environs, was revealed.

Bull and Swan A local pub for CECIL and OWENS in KIDLINGTON. It is known (of course) to Morse and he lovingly recalls some of its beers – BRAKSPEAR, BASS, and Bishop's Finger (NEIG: p120).

Bulldog, The A pub found opposite CHRIST CHURCH. Morse has at least two pints while contemplating a body found on top of the tower of ST FRIDESWIDE'S (SERV: pp115-17). A day or so later, he is joined there by Lewis (Morse has, of course, left the pub and done other things in the meantime) when Lewis, rather surprisingly, drinks three pints of beer (SERV: p171-3; 199). Ted BROOKS may have also drunk here (CAIN: p84) and Morse pops in – to see how the landlord is – in CALL (p269).

Bullingdon A prison in BICESTER and once the temporary home of Harry REPP (REMO). Details of a typical discharge from a prison (including the Discharge Certificate and the Central Reception Area) may be found on pp85-86. The Governor is an old friend of Morse (p106). Not necessarily to be confused with the Oxford Dining Club of the same name.

Bure Place The location of the BICESTER bus station (REMO: p89).

Burford A most pleasant Oxfordshire town, particularly described in REMO (pp232-233). Streets include Witney and SHEEP and the High, which leads to the bridge over the River Windrush '...with all the birds and the bright meadows and the cornfields ...' (p233). It has a Secondary School, a Police Station, and a Social Services office. Burford is home to Harry REPP and Debbie RICHARDSON (and a number of others). It is unclear whether Repp and Richardson worship at St John the Baptist (p236) but thought unlikely.

Burford and Cheltenham Building Society A building society with, one sincerely hopes, branches in (at least) Burford and Cheltenham. Debbie RICHARDSON has an account with them (REMO: p219).

Burglar, The Morse and Lewis investigate a suspected burglary – only, it seems because Morse once used to live near to the victim and knew him. Page references elsewhere are from Haining (1996). (BURG). *Main personnel* ROBERTSON.

Bursar Traditionally, the treasurer in a college though the role often encompasses a range of administrative duties. There are many references in the WORKS (such as those at MILE: p37 and JWEL: p102).

Bus This form of transport features large in the life of Oxford; route numbers have changed over the years (the number 4, for example, to the number 20). Buses, since the early 1970s at least, are operated by a single employee (the roles of driver and conductor being merged) and enjoy the benefit of 'bus lanes' (LBUS: p104). The main bus station in Oxford is in GLOUCESTER GREEN (and here, also, Oxford City Link coaches arrive from Heathrow; CAIN: p341).

Park-and-Ride buses may be caught in many places and certainly at the Pear Tree roundabout (WNCH: p121); for some strange reason they are known as unhyphenated Park and Ride buses in SERV (p63). Other references to buses include the Circular Bus Tour (JWEL: p146), a Nipper Bus (JWEL: p339), and a Freedom Ticket and a red Oxford City double-decker (CAIN: xiv). Smoking was once allowed on the top of double-decker buses.

C

Cabriolet Taxis Services Based at OXFORD RAILWAY STATION. Their services are used by ROOPE (NICQ: p231) and, no doubt, other citizens.

Caernarfon An historic town, replete with castle (Edward the First), statue of Lloyd George, Caernarfon Tech, and the City of Caernarfon School (where David ACUM teaches). It is in the County of Gwynedd, in North West Wales. Morse, somewhat heroically, drives himself there on a 5-hour journey from Oxford (WEAR).

Cambridge A town in the east of England, famed for its University. It claims to be a City but such claims have yet to be fully recognised except by the 'City' council and Cambridge City Football Club (based in Milton Road). The University has enjoyed a long (and occasionally friendly) rivalry with that at Oxford, the latter claiming (with some justification) to be the older of the two institutions. Cambridge University is collegiate and a number of graduates have appeared in the WORKS.

A sister (Betty) of Celia RICHARDS lives in Girton village, a short way from the town (JERI). The HISTORIC CITIES tour stops here (at the UNIVERSITY ARMS) but inclement weather means their planned visits to Grantchester and the American War Cemetery at Madingley are cancelled though those to King's College and the Fitzwilliam Museum take place (JWEL: p9). Also see the entries for CHRIST'S and MAGDALENE and, for example, the entries for DEXTER, QUINN, ROOPE, OGLEBY, Lionel LAWSON, BOWDEN, and HOUSMAN.

Camelford Absolutely nothing to do with CAMFORD (or OXBRIDGE for that matter). It is a small town in Cornwall, on a busy road, and between Bodmin Moor and the Atlantic Ocean.

Camford A term used by HOLMES (in, for example, *The Adventure of the Creeping Man*) to not only conflate the universities of Oxford and Cambridge but also to confuse them as an aid to hiding the true identity of any particular college. The phrase has never achieved the general currency of the more familiar OXBRIDGE. According to Brewer's (1996), the term was used (if not coined) by Thackeray in *Pendennis*.

Canal Reach A cul-de-sac in JERICHO and home to Anne SCOTT and George JACKSON (among others). The ten houses here were all built in the nineteenth century (JERI). Canal Reach is 'ridiculously narrow' (JERI: p90). At 2 lives a heavily pregnant woman, at 6 a middle-aged, tattooed giant of a man, at 8 a slim and bespectacled young man (possibly a Mr Green) who knows a great deal about the local area (and who works on the production line at COWLEY), and at 10 George JACKSON. At 1 lives a very old man (who identifies the occupant of 8 as 'Mr Green'), at 7 Mrs Elsie Purvis, and Anne SCOTT at number 9. No photographs can be provided – Canal Reach is 'now straddled by a new block of flats' (JERI: p301). **Plate 13**, **Map C5**

Canal Street To be found in JERICHO. It is very easy for pedestrians to visit but motorists are advised to avoid the parking restrictions and leave their car elsewhere. And this comment applies to all of central Oxford. **Map C5**

Cape of Good Hope, The A pub visited by Morse after seeing Joseph GODBERRY in COWLEY. It is on The PLAIN (effectively a roundabout) and was once known as The Hobgoblin. It had, according to the Oxford University Company of Archers (such an organisation does, of course, really exist), successfully shed its image of drug dealing and violence in the recent past.

Carfax The major crossroads in the centre of Oxford where four main roads meet – HIGH Street, ST ALDATES, QUEEN STREET, and CORNMARKET (**Map D5**). The name is derived from the Latin 'quadrifurcus' meaning 'four forked' (but one guesses that the French *carrefour* or *quarrefour* has somehow intervened). The University sees Carfax as the centre of Oxford and it has been used to qualify residence e.g. a professor at one of the COLLEGES may be required to reside within '25 miles of Carfax' for a certain number of months of the academic year. There are a number of shops and businesses, including a branch of Lloyds (where the BROOKS hold an account; CAIN: pp292-3).

Carfax, Lady Frances HOLMES investigated her disappearance in the nineteenth century. The manager of the Hôtel National at Lausanne was a certain M. Moser (immediately arousing suspicions of an early anagram). It is not recorded how the surname of Lady Frances was derived.

Carfax Tower '… a great, solid pile of pale-yellowish stone that stands on the corner of Queen Street and Cornmarket …' (ANNX: p207). The tower is all that remains of a thirteenth century church and is some 74 feet tall; it may be climbed by internal steps (when, of course, open) for a good view of Oxford. **Plate 14**

Carlton Road A street in NORTH OXFORD which forms a convenient route between Morse's flat and the FRIAR BACON pub in Elsfield Way (ANNX: p278). **Map C2**

Carpet-Bagger, The Morse has no direct involvement with this case and Lewis simply does not appear. Morse does, however, offer a suggestion as to someone's nickname in the police canteen and may or may not have been seen earlier in a Jaguar with a young lady (p241). Police officers mentioned (but not further referenced herein) are Sergeants Hodges and Russell and Chief Inspector Page. (BAGG). *Main personnel* Barry WATSON.

Carroll, Lewis See CHRIST CHURCH; Carroll is 'exhibited' in the OXFORD STORY.

Cars Morse originally owned but rarely drove a LANCIA (preferring for much of the time to travel as a passenger and let Lewis take the wheel). By the time of the JWEL case, the car was changed to a JAGUAR. It does seem that both Morse's predilection for alcohol (and comfort) and Lewis's for fast driving may have influenced this choice. See the entries under JAGUAR and LANCIA.

Other models or makes of car included in the WORKS are Mini, Volvo, Rover, Sunbeam, Fiat, and Zodiac (all LBUS), Morris Oxford (WEAR), Morris 1300 (NICQ), Peugeot (REMO), Metro (WNCH: p142, NEIG: p287, and WATC: p121) – and Metro 1300 (ANNX: p197) – and MG Metro (JWEL: p235), Porsche (ANNX), Vanden Plas (NICQ), Cadillac (NICQ), Allegro (SERV), a 'panda-car' (i.e. a marked police car; SERV: p159), Ford (SERV), Rolls Royce and Roller (JERI: p9 and CAIN: p155 respectively), BMW (WNCH), Ford BMW (JERI: p195), Daimler (MILE and NEIG), Maestro (ANNX), Austin (ANNX), Maserati (ANNX: p223), Ford Anglia (ANNX), Dormobile (ANNX), Vauxhall Cavalier (JWEL), Fiesta (JWEL), Mercedes (WOOD: p15), Land-rover (WOOD: p131), Land-Rover (sic) (CAIN: p306),[1] Honda (WOOD), Sierra (WOOD), Ford Escort (CAIN), Citroën (NEIG), Toyota Carina (REMO), and a (Ford) Cortina (GOLD).

The references to cases bracketed above are not unique. For example, Mini is found in JERI (as a Mini Clubman on p103) as well as LBUS but such a list would be even more tedious than the one appearing here. Not quite so tedious (or it is, perhaps) is the fact that Lewis has an old Mini (MILE: p176).

Casa Villa A guesthouse in the BANBURY ROAD. McBryde (MINOR) is lucky to find a room here (WOOD: p335).

Cassock 'A long robe or outer coat worn by clergy and choirboys' (Chambers 2003). Once removed, the person who once wore one is 'discassocked' (SERV: p3) though Chambers (2003) has yet to recognise the word.

Catte Street This links RADCLIFFE SQUARE to the crossroads at the eastern end of the BROAD. Alan HARDINGE parked his car here '… and went straight up to his rooms in LONSDALE.' (WOOD: pp353-354). **Map D5**

Cecil, Della (Adèle Beatrice) She lives at 1 BLOXHAM DRIVE and is an attractive ash-blonde. She is the local agent for the Conservative Party (though for some reason the postcode and telephone number on her card appear to be inaccurate). Her late father served in the Army in India (NEIG: p329).

Chalkley and Sons A firm supplying household fittings (such as tiles and wallpapers) from their premises on BOTLEY ROAD. The firm employs, one guesses among others, John SANDERS (LBUS).

---

[1]The correct title for the vehicle is a "Land Rover"; hyphens may have been used in the past but they have been, for some time, totally redundant.

Champollion, Jean-François (1790-1832) A French Orientalist and Egyptologist, famed for deciphering the Rosetta Stone (LBUS: p57). Morse does, of course, have a specific interest in cracking a number of codes throughout the WORKS.

Charities A number of charities appear in the WORKS. Lewis tries to identify a charity sticker (ANNX: pp165-166) and contacts, inter alia, Christian Aid, OXFAM, War on Want, the Save the Children Fund, the RSPCA, but not NACRO (the National Association for the Care and Resettlement of (Criminal) Offenders). NACRO, since its foundation in 1966, has not had 'criminal' in its title: a minor *faux pas* by Lewis. The children's charity, Barnardo's, is also mentioned (JERI).

Charlbury Drive The home address of Tom and Margaret BOWMAN in CHIPPING NORTON (ANNX).

Charles, Dawn A receptionist (for over three years) at the private HARVEY CLINIC on the BANBURY ROAD. She is vivacious, dark-eyed, long-legged, left-handed, and well figured (NEIG: p12) but not quite as well behaved as a receptionist should be. She lives in Woodpecker Way on the Charles Church Estate in BICESTER. For some reason, Morse dislikes the name Dawn (p12).

Charlton Road An address in NORTH OXFORD, home to Jennifer COLEBY, Sue WIDDOWSON, and 'Mary'. (LBUS). **Map C2** or **C3**, or **D2** or **D3**.

Chaucer Crescent It is unclear exactly where this may be found (but one guesses it comes off CHAUCER ROAD). At number 14 lives Bill ROBERTSON (BURG). **Map D4**

Chaucer Lane A street in BURFORD and home to the semi-detached house of Harry REPP and Debbie RICHARDSON (REMO). Its exact location is difficult to find; perhaps REPP gave the police a false address.

Chaucer Road A street (somewhere) in NORTH OXFORD and home of the SYNDICATE. **Map D4**

Cherwell Arms A pub, some 50 yards from the WATER EATON ROAD (JWEL: p224). Here Morse has two pints of BRAKSPEAR, Lewis a half of the same (all bought by Lewis). It is, apparently, '… a quietly civilized public house where the quietly civilized landlord kept an ever-watchful eye on the Brakspear and the Bass.' (NEIG: p142). It is here that Morse (drinking two pints of BASS) explains to Lewis that he needs the sugar in beer so that his artificially produced insulin has something to counteract – otherwise, he would "… be in one helluva mess". (NEIG: p251).

Cherwell Motel Situated on the A40 road; in the upstairs lounge at least, the food is (apparently) 'carefully cooked and appetizingly garnished'. (NICQ: p17)

Chesterton Hotel A venue in Bath used by the HISTORIC CITIES tour. Morse addresses the party in the Beau Nash room (JWEL).

Chipping Norton A small and attractive market town, some 20 miles to the north west of Oxford. Some may find it regrettable that some of its residents refer to it as 'Chippy'. The town's archivist is able to check as far back towards Domesday, as local records allow, stating categorically that there is no number 84 in West Street (ANNX: p90). The BALLARDs and the BOWMANs reside in Chipping Norton; it also has some fine pubs including the BELL and the BLACK HORSE.

Cholsey A village in Oxfordshire. It has a station on the Reading to Oxford railway line. The grave of Agatha Christie (in St Mary's churchyard) had not – by 1996 – been visited by Lewis or his wife (NEIG: p85).

Christ Church Known, in Oxford at least, as 'The House', Christ Church is (for some) the grandest of the colleges. It was founded by Cardinal Wolsey in 1524 (on the site of St Frideswide's monastery) and re-founded in 1546; the connection between the Cardinal and WOLSEY COLLEGE is a little unclear though the colleges share many features. The chapel of the college is also Oxford Cathedral (more properly known as the Cathedral Church of Christ). Full details of the Cathedral may be found in Pevsner and Metcalf (2005: pp238-255); Batsford and Fry (1934) usefully describe it as '… the smallest, shyest, and squarest of our 'greater' cathedrals. Yet it well proves that modest size need be no bar to great architectural beauty and interest.' (p133). Tom Tower houses the bell Great Tom (WNCH: p124), the loudest bell in Oxford and weighing about seven tons.

Sheila WILLIAMS plans to take a group of tourists on an 'Alice Tour' (JWEL: p40). Such a tour will include mementoes of Charles Lutwidge Dodgson ('Lewis Carroll') and visit the Deanery, the Dining Hall, and the Cathedral. Dodgson was a 'Student' at Christ Church (a Student being the equivalent of a FELLOW in other colleges).[2] **Plate 15, Map D6**

Christie, John A serial killer who was convicted in London during the 1950s. His story was investigated by Kennedy (1965) and his book was made into a popular film released in 1971. Morse is (presumably) very much aware of the case (LBUS: p97).

Christ's College Re-founded in 1505, this CAMBRIDGE college numbers BOWDEN, DEXTER and Lionel LAWSON among its alumni (though ASHENDEN failed to get in). Morse well knows the works of Milton (who was here between 1624 and 1632).

Churchill Hospital Lewis visits this hospital when checking blood donor records (MILE: p97) as does Julia STEVENS for a rather more personal and serious reason (CAIN: pp94-97). The hospital has a Blood Transfusion Centre (MILE: p240). It can be found in New Headington. **Map G6**

---

[2] WOLSEY COLLEGE also calls its Fellows 'Students'.

Churchill, John The first Duke of Marlborough; BLENHEIM PALACE was built for him from a design by Vanbrugh. The fourth Duke of Marlborough arranged for 'Duke's Cut' to be dug between the Thames and the OXFORD CANAL in 1796; this is where the body of Joanna FRANKS was found in 1859.

Churchill, Winston A rather influential British twentieth century statesman; he was born in BLENHEIM PALACE and is buried nearby in BLADON (LBUS).

Cigarettes Brands of cigarette mentioned in the WORKS are Benson and Hedges, Embassy, Woodbines, Marlboro, Silk Cut, and Dunhill (this last being the choice of brand for Morse[3] and Monica HEIGHT (NICQ: p155) and Louisa HARDING (WOOD: p14) as well). The relatively recent introduction of compulsory health warnings on cigarette packets helps Morse to confirm that someone has been in the crypt at ST FRIDESWIDE'S a lot more recently than at first suggested (SERV: p196). A large number of personnel in the WORKS smoke cigarettes – including, of course, Morse – but it would be a sign of a little too much addiction to record such details. See also the section under Morse headed *Smoking*.

Clarendon Building This fine Grade 1 listed building was designed by Nicholas Hawksmoor. It was the original home of the OXFORD UNIVERSITY PRESS. See the BROAD.

Clues It would not be helpful to list the 'clues' that assist Morse (and Lewis) in solving cases (particularly because Morse has a tendency to leap to the wrong conclusions early in any investigation). Examples of the other type of clues can be found under CROSSWORDS.

Cobb Road A road in Lyme Regis (WOOD: p25). It appears to lead, unsurprisingly, to the Cobb (the harbour break-water).

Codex Vaticanus 'Morse handled them with the loving care of a biblical scholar privileged to view the *Codex Vaticanus*.' (ANNX: p245). 'Them' is a four-page letter or rather the parts thereof. The Codex Vaticanus is considered to be the oldest extant version of the Bible and was written in the first half of the fourth century. According to the Catholic Encyclopaedia (1907), the written material is fragile and access to it is highly restricted.

Colebourne Road An address in West London; a woman known as Yvonne lives at 23A (MILE: pp44/207).

Coleby, Jennifer A worker for the TOWN AND GOWN ASSURANCE COMPANY. She lives in a rented house in CHARLTON ROAD and is interviewed by both Lewis and later Morse without, at first, revealing crucial information. (LBUS).

Colleges Not all of the Oxford colleges (and only the merest smattering from CAMBRIDGE) are mentioned in the WORKS. See the entries under ALL SOULS, BALLIOL, BRASENOSE,

---

[3] For example JWEL: p268, WOOD: p35, and NEIG: p258.

CHRIST CHURCH, CHRIST'S, EXETER, HERTFORD, JESUS (twice), KEBLE, LADY MARGARET HALL, LINCOLN, LONSDALE, both MAGDALEN and MAGDALENE, MANSFIELD, MERTON, NEW, ORIEL, PEMBROKE, QUEEN'S, RUSKIN, ST CATHERINE'S, ST HILDA'S, ST JOHN'S, ST PETER'S, TRINITY, UNIVERSITY, WADHAM, WOLSEY and WORCESTER. The word 'college' appears herein with or without a capital C almost entirely at random. Non-Oxbridge higher educational establishments appear under their own names e.g. EXETER UNIVERSITY. See also SCHOOLS.

Coombe Street The location of garage parking for residents at the BAY HOTEL in Lyme Regis (WOOD: p15).

Co-op The usual abbreviation for Co-operative Stores or Shops (which once issued tokens and dividends as a reward for regular shoppers). Tokens for milk were used by Mrs Thomas (see MINOR), by PHILLOTSON (CAIN: p76), and by Lewis (WOOD: p275). The Jacobs family (NEIG: p62) have two pints of Co-op milk delivered.

Corn Dolly A pub in Frewin Court off CORNMARKET (JERI: p126). Morse meets Edward MURDOCH here (JERI: p128); the latter drinks Worthington E (a brand of beer long out of favour with connoisseurs). According to Honey (1998), it is better known as The Dolly.

Cornford, Denis Jack A Fellow, and candidate for the Mastership, of LONSDALE (NEIG). He has rooms on the Old Staircase of that college. Born in 1942, is a graduate of MAGDALEN, and married to Shelly since 1994.[4] He is a Reader in Mediaeval History and has created something of a stir with a paper re-dating the Battle of Hastings ('the momentous conflict between Harold of England and William of Normandy' (p22) to the year 1065. He attracts rather less interest (from his wife) in his theory that the 1348 Black Death statistical evidence had been widely misinterpreted. He is slim and pleasantly featured and has rooms in HOLYWELL STREET (whence he and Shelly enjoy the proximity of the KING'S ARMS and The TURF TAVERN – as well journeying further afield to, for example the KING'S ARMS in the BANBURY ROAD).

Cornford, Shelly Ann She met Denis during his sabbatical at Harvard and married him in 1994 (to the surprise of his colleagues). She has been married before (as Benson), was born in about 1970, and has a Master's degree in American History. She has legs a little on the sturdy side, wavy brown hair, and a quiet New England accent (NEIG: p23).

Cornmarket A shopping street in central Oxford. The Covered Market (CAIN: p328) lies to the east. **Map D5**

Coroner A judicial officer, usually with legal or medical qualifications. His or her role is often to investigate the circumstances surrounding an unnatural death (occasionally having

---

[4] NEIG (p226) has Lewis stating that Cornford is "… a Lonsdale man himself …" He is clearly listed as a graduate of MAGDALEN on p21 – at least by reference to his MA and DPhil. There may, of course, be absolutely no significance to this apparent confusion.

determined beforehand whether or not a death is unnatural in the first place). The Coroner's Court in Oxford is mentioned in JERI (p82) and a Coroner's Sergeant (an aide) appears in SERV (p242).

Costyn, Kevin An unpleasant youth, 17 years of age. He is (just) a pupil at the PROCTOR MEMORIAL SCHOOL and shares a birthday (25th May) with his teacher, Julia STEVENS. He is slightly deaf, has an interest in the martial arts (where he once met Ellie SMITH), and stands for the right-wing British National Party in his school's mock elections. He lives with his mother ('… a blowsy, frowsy single parent …' CAIN: xviii) in a council property in, what is a possibly accurate description, a street known as 'Prostitutes Row'. One of his bedroom walls is adorned with pictures of Jimi Hendrix, Kurt Cobain, and Jim Morrison; his bedtime activity appears restricted to listening to his Walkman and reading pornography (such as the paperback *Eroticon IV*).

Cotswold Gateway Hotel An establishment in BURFORD and one where Morse has two pints of cask-conditioned ale and his first cigarette of the day (from a packet bought by Lewis; REMO: pp244-245).

Cotswold Hotel An establishment in BURFORD and the scene of (at least) one liaison (REMO: p98).

Cotswold House A double-fronted guesthouse in the BANBURY ROAD (managed by Anne and Jim O'Kane) and the scene of at least one illicit relationship (WOOD). Morse has been known to drink whiskey (rather than whisky) here (NEIG: p405). Opposite the hotel may be found Wentworth Road; from here, Karin ERIKSSON made an unfortunate telephone call (WOOD: p372).

Cotterell, Jane She is the Administrator (very much a capital A) of the PITT RIVERS (CAIN). Tall, slim, and prematurely white-haired it seems to be the diffident smile on her lips that encourages Morse to contemplate a minor flirtation. Had he but realised, he may have found himself pushing on an open door.

County Hall There appears to be only one reference to this Oxford castellated nineteenth century building (and that is in WNCH: p123). **Map D5**

Coverley, Christine A teacher at BURFORD Secondary School. She is aged 27 years in 1998 and is small, skinny, flat-chested and spotty-chinned (REMO: p269) - but she does have one admirer.

Cowley A suburb of Oxford known for its car and engineering works and to the extent that a headline in the *OXFORD MAIL* talking of 'Cowley Men' is sufficient to identify them as factory workers (SERV: p115). There is also a reference to the 'Rover plant' in GOLD (p27). Unlike Oxford, the derivation of the name does not appear to be bovine; Ekwall (1960) links it to either a personal name or 'a block of wood, a log' together with an open space or a meadow. **Map G8**

Cowley Road A number of 'dingy digs' (JERI: p56) may be found in this road (which runs to COWLEY from the PLAIN). Morse sees it as an area of contrasts: "… of the drab and the delightful; of boarded-up premises and thriving small businesses; of decay and regeneration …" (CAIN: p172). Perhaps one of the thriving small businesses is The Golden Scissors hair salon (CAIN: p213). It is also the site of a 'squalid domestic murder' investigated by Morse (WOOD: p67) though no notes of this 1991 case have been discovered. Part of the Oxford bypass is known as the Cowley Ring Road and here, in a lay-by, Kevin COSTYN was conceived (CAIN: xviii). **Plate 16, Map E6-F6**

Cowley Tyre and Battery Services As may be expected, a firm providing tyre and battery services to, among others, a leading person in LBUS.

Crawford, Detective Inspector He is based at HQ and is having a rather difficult time with providing suitable evidence against MULDOON. His attempts to enlist Morse and Lewis to his aid are similarly problematic. His stab (GOLD: p7) at naming the wife of Julius Caesar – Pomponia – appears to satisfy Morse (who is having trouble recalling the correct name of Poppeia). His most noteworthy contribution is, perhaps, an accurate comment on Morse: "… there's a big streak of integrity somewhere …" (p14). He is lucky enough to be offered a glass of GLENFIDDICH in Morse's flat (pp36-37).

Crosswords There are many references throughout the WORKS to crosswords - beginning (in LBUS: p17) with the clue (A) "Take in bachelor? It could do" (3).[5] The crossword of choice for Morse is that published daily in *The TIMES* (where the crossword could once be found on the back page). More complex puzzles are found in *The LISTENER* '… but since the death of the great Ximenes (**Plate 17**) he had found few composers to please his taste. On the whole he enjoyed the Listener puzzles as much as any …' (LBUS: p74). Indeed, the preamble to one *Listener* puzzle prompts a useful and deductive chain of thought (LBUS: p75). Other publications are noted below. There have been many, many books published on crosswords; Putnam, for one, has the grace to contain a succinct explanation of clue types (1974: pp12-17). Clues appear here largely (but not precisely) in the order that they appear in the WORKS.

> *The Times:* The first crossword in this paper appeared on the first of February 1930. Richard Browne, the crossword editor, has been quoted as saying: "The Times thought it was rather beneath its dignity to have it in a serious paper. It first appeared in the foreign weekly digest – but was so popular it was placed in the hallowed precincts of the main paper." (*The Times* October 19th 2006 – which also reproduces the first crossword). Gradually, the clues became totally cryptic and the instruction 'anag.' after a clue was dropped, such anagrams being indicated in any number of subtle fashions. Until (at least) the 1990s, the occasional quotation would appear with the missing word being the answer;

---

[5] All the clues in the WORKS are listed in this article; the answers are found at the end of it.

Morse recalls Wordsworth thus appearing (LBUS: p176) and impresses Louisa HARDINGE by knowing that, according to Coleridge, (B) 'Work without Hope draws nectar in a _ _ _ _ _' (5) (WOOD: p46). The need to have a decent grounding in the Classics reduced over the years. The crossword has become '... a national institution, rated as the benchmark of acumen and flexibility' (Dexter 2006c). The crossword had traditionally been easier on a Monday (it being felt that one shouldn't be too taxed at the start of the working week) and this is confirmed by Morse (WOOD: p112; REMO: p73). Morse's usual approach (presumably on any day of the week) is to tackle the bottom right-hand quarter first (JWEL: p225); another method, not recorded by Morse, is to trawl through the clues until an answer is assured, fill that in and then look at no other clues bar those that intersect with the one entered solution. At some point in time during the 1960s, the then editor Edmund Akenhead introduced a set of 25 standardised grids and the crossword changed to only having a grid wherein there were always either an equal or greater number of intersecting letters (Browne 2006). However, the CAIN case records Morse struggling over the final clue (C) 'Kick in the pants' (3-5) with the now near-completed grid showing only the letters "– I – – L – S –" (pxxvi). A similar example is found in STOR (p197) where the clue reads (D) 'Gerry-built semi is beginning to collapse in such an upheaval' (7). Morse has " – E – S – I – left to complete". One is at a loss to explain how these apparent contradictions have arisen. *The Times* runs its own annual National Crossword Championship. Dormant for a few years, it began again in 2006 and was won, in 2007, by Peter Biddlecombe.[6] A guide to the various clue types for the paper is given in Greer (2000). A crossword (*Morse – Whodunnit*) is reproduced in *The Times* (2005) from the 18th March 1993 edition.

Timing *The Times*: As what can only be seen as a challenge to himself, Morse regularly (if not always) marks the time he has taken to complete this crossword in the space beside it (usually by writing the start time and, if successful, the total time taken). Thus, in WOOD (p44), he writes 8.21 (pm) but still has clues to complete almost a quarter of an hour later. This somewhat breaches his avowed policy of only allowing himself 10 minutes (WEAR: p97) – in which time he almost always completes it. Noted times for completion or near completion are 9 and a half minutes (WEAR: p197), *about* 10 minutes (WNCH: p136), 12 and a half (NICQ: p188), 'between Oxford and Didcot' on the train (WNCH: p234) where he fills in the one remaining unsolved answer with bogus letters to impress any fellow passengers, 10 minutes (WOOD: p69), Oxford to Didcot again with one clue remaining (WOOD: p264), 10 and a half (REMO: p73), and 11 minutes (STOR: p197). No time is recorded for the crossword he completes in the police canteen (ANNX: p168) nor in a particular hotel (NEIG: p409). His best time, ungrammatically announced to Lewis, is 6 and a half minutes (REMO: p380); it may have been the last crossword he ever did. The year 1994 seems to have been particularly good for Morse. Twice he reaches six minutes bar one clue – first in the GOLD case (pp25-26) and then in that of CAIN (pxxvi); six minutes would have been his record. According to the subheading (viii) in GOLD, the fastest time

---

[6] DEXTER welcomed the return of the competition in *The Times* of the 6th October 2006. Bizarrely, the heading of the article was "Times should clue it adequately (8)" with the *nine-letter* 'crossword' as the answer.

for completion of *The Times* (under test conditions) is 3 minutes and 45 seconds and such is recorded in *The Guinness Book of Records*.

Other crosswords Lewis is fond of the Coffee-Break in *The DAILY MIRROR* (for example, LBUS: p17 and JERI: p272), and he and Mrs LEWIS often attempt the Quick Crossword in the same paper 'of an evening' (JWEL: p225). Morse has been known to complete the *Country Life* crossword (JERI: p270) and also dabble with The *DAILY TELEGRAPH* (WEAR: p120), solving the clue (E) 'Has been known to split under a grilling' (7). He also recalls a 'brilliant' puzzle in *The Observer* set by XIMENES (JWEL: pp283-284). It was a sort of *double-entendre* crossword – where all the clues were susceptible of two quite different solutions. Solvers who followed the wrong set would end up with an insoluble clash of one interlocking letter. Morse regularly attempts the crossword in the OXFORD TIMES (taking 12 minutes over one example; WNCH: p235) and helps Walter GREENAWAY solve the clue (F) 'Bradman's famous duck' (6) in that paper (WNCH: pp136-137). *The Guardian* also makes an appearance – with the clue (G) 'Girl in bed – censored' (6) in SERV: p150 as does *The Independent on Sunday* with (H) 'Some show dahlias in the Indian pavilion' (6) (NEIG: p259). NICQ (p167) has 'The case was throwing up enough clues to solve a jumbo crossword ...' without suggesting a place of publication but *Country Life* is identified as the source of an eleven-minute success (JERI: p270).

Other solvers Monica HEIGHT has a stab at *The Times* (NICQ: p194) and BROWNE-SMITH completes its crossword (on a train) between Oxford and Reading (MILE: pp15-16), including the clue (I) 'First thing in Soho tourist's after?' (8). Polly Rayner (WOOD: p99) tries to solve the SWEDISH MAIDEN verses by seeing the word BEGBROKE as a crossword clue – with beg as a synonym for 'ask' and broke referring to the Anglo-Saxon 'brok' i.e. brook or 'stream'. She is, perhaps, ingenious but, also perhaps, totally wrong. McCLURE is interested in crosswords and encourages Ellie SMITH to approach the same (CAIN: p56).

Crosswords and detection There are a number of references to how solving a crossword is allied to solving a crime. For example, part of the heading to Chapter 26 of WNCH (and therefore p153) is from Chesterton's *The Napoleon of Notting Hill*: '... if you look at a thing nine hundred and ninety-nine times, you are perfectly safe; if you look at it for the thousandth time, you are in frightful danger of seeing it for the first time'. Morse believes that this is just the same with crossword puzzles – one can look and look (and look again) at a clue but its solution may be hidden until you approach it afresh and from a distance (and look at it for the first or thousandth time). And in WEAR (p42) Morse, believing he has cracked a difficulty in the case, thinks it is "... just like doing a crossword puzzle. Get stuck. Leave it for ten minutes. Try again – and eureka!" Further, he tells Lewis that if he is stuck on a crossword, he stops thinking about it, considers something different, comes back – and gets the solution; and this is the approach he adopts in tackling a particular murder (JWEL: pp225-226).

Strange is no good with crosswords but he does know that you can stop, think of (for example) Brigitte Bardot, and then successfully come back to a clue (REMO: p20). Lewis has compared the odd chain of thought he often unexpectedly starts off in Morse with helping him do the crossword (JWEL: p141) and Morse likens a knot in an investigation with misunderstanding which part of a crossword clue is the definition and which the wordplay (NEIG: p315). Further, when trying to work out how he came to a particular conclusion, Morse realises that (while it may be possible to describe the mental gymnastics involved in solving a crossword clue) it was harder to unravel his detective psychological process (CAIN: p350).

Crossword compilers (and publishers) have been known to make the rare mistake and it is of these that Morse thinks when trying to get the correct angle on a particular case (WOOD: pp384-385); it was like finding the supposed answer to a clue unsatisfactory before receiving an erratum slip with the *correct* clue on (and then the *new* answer – "shining and fitting").

Compilers Those creating *The Times* crossword are uncredited by name. Mentioned in the Works are QUIXOTE, XIMENES, and Ichabod (a setter for the Oxford Times; JWEL: p281). Not mentioned but included here (for the succinctness of his definition of the nature of a cryptic clue) is Afrit (A.F. Ritchie) who is quoted in Brewer (1996: p270): "I need not mean what I say, but I must say what I mean". Biographical details of a number of compilers appear in Crowther (2006). According to the *Guinness Book of Records*, the most prolific compiler (who has done so for *The Times* and many other publications) is Roger Squires. **Plate 18**

Bogus clues At least two appear – an unnamed doctor invents (J) 'Girl takes gun to district attorney' (6) (SERV: p150) and Morse raises a question in clue form (K) 'It's striped: what about ze panties?' (5) (WOOD: p70). And, perhaps, a third: (L) 'The girls and pints are out of order' (10) from JERI: p129.[7]

Some further cryptic clue examples ... The heading to Chapter Two of WEAR has this, from Ximenes: (M) 'We'll get excited with Ring seat' (10); on p97 of the same case appears: (N) 'Eyes had I – and saw not?' (6) and p141 gives: (O) 'Code name for a walrus' (5). In NICQ (p188), one finds (P): 'In which are the Islets of Langerhans' (8) – perhaps not too cryptic – and MILE (p90) gives (Q): 'He lived perched up, mostly in sites around East, shivering' (6,8). (R) 'Elephant-man has a mouth that's deformed' (6) appears in NEIG: p180 and earlier in the case (p1) is found (S): 'Stand for soldiers?' (5-4). The last clue to appear (REMO: p73) is the appropriate (T): 'Stiff examination' (7).

... and some easier ones Well, perhaps not always easier to solve. Lewis struggles over (U) 'Carthorse (anagram)' (9) in *The MIRROR* (MILE: p193) and mistakenly enters CAM for

---

[7] A partial clue, which requires a definition part such as '... for youngsters'. But the clue as it stands cleverly echoes 'The lads for the girls and the lads for the liquor are there' from HOUSMAN's *A Shropshire Lad* (such line appearing as the heading to Chapter 16 of JERI).

(V) 'River' (3) because it fits in with COD for (W) 'Fish' (3) (NEIG: p264); indeed, he admits that sometimes "... I can't even do the *Mirror* coffee-break one" (WOOD: p83). DEXTER (2008) has suggested that one of the harder (if not impossible) clues is (X) 'Yellow food stuff' (7) where the last 6 letters are USTARD.

Some further references and general matters "In a Definition-and-Letter-Mixture puzzle, each clue consists of a sentence which contains a definition of the answer and a mixture of the letters." Don Manley, *Chambers Crossword Manual* and quoted as the heading to Chapter 22 of WOOD. A good example would be (Y): "Person with crimes to unravel." (9,5); this may be found in Dexter (2006a). Morse knows about bovine stomachs because of crosswords (REMO: p224); one guesses that this would include the abomasum, the omasum, and the (delightfully-named) manyplies. And Morse, '... a crossword fanatic from his teens ...' (CAIN: p22) is able to rattle off a list of Ks commonly used – King, thousand, kilometre, Kelvin, and Köchel – as abbreviations.

It does seem that Morse and crosswords are irretrievably linked (which is rather a good thing). A 2007 investigation by Drs Friedlander and Fine of the University of Buckingham into the cognitive skills and motivation of cryptic crossword solvers asks a large number of questions – one of which is 'How did you get interested in solving e.g. through Inspector Morse?' Further, *The Times* (during June 2007), were celebrating what would have been the 20th anniversary had Morse appeared on television by offering a linked prize for winning entries to the Saturday crossword. And, finally, a rather clever clue – not directly linked to Morse but apposite – appeared in *The Times* (23,572; 11th April 2007): 'Personal growth after much bitter experience? (4,5)' (with the answer as 'beer belly').

Answers to clues: (A) Bra, (B) Sieve, (C) Hip-flask, (D) Seismic, (E) Sausage, (F) Donald, (G) Banned, (H) Howdah, (I) Stripper, (J) Brenda, (K) Zebra, (L) Striplings (M) Wagnerites, (N) Watson, (O) Morse, (P) Pancreas, (Q) Simeon Stylites, (R) Mahout, (S) Toast-rack, (T) Autopsy, (U) Orchestra, (V) Exe , (W) Eel, (X) Custard or Mustard, (Y) Inspector Morse.

See also ANAGRAMS (under LITERARY CURIOSITIES), The *LISTENER*, QUIXOTE, *The TIMES*, XIMENES, and APPENDIX A.

Crown and Castle A pub (in 1859) at Aynho (WNCH). There is still a pub in the village but it is (in 2006 at least) called the Great Western Arms.

Crown Inn See AA (AUTOMOBILE ASSOCIATION).

Crowther, Bernard (Michael) An English DON and Senior FELLOW at LONSDALE COLLEGE; married to Margaret for some 15 years, they live in Southdown Road, North Oxford, and have two pre-teenage children (James and Caroline). He is aged 41 in 1971 and has been in the British Army. He is keen on the works of DOWSON, knows something of *Cymbeline*, and quotes casually from Milton ('abhorrèd shears': LBUS: p68). He has been known to disparage the efforts of OXFORD UNITED (LBUS: p39).

Crowther, Margaret Married to Bernard CROWTHER. She works part-time in the School of Oriental Studies.

Crozier Road A sunless thoroughfare just to the west of ST GILES'. Philip WISE lived at number 14 in the 1940s (DODO). **Map D5**

Cumnor Hill The scene of the death of Alan HARDINGE's daughter, Sarah (WOOD: p52) and that of Robert TURNBULL (NEIG: p16). Both these accidents are unrelated (beyond the obvious fact that it may be worth exercising a good deal of care when cycling or driving in the area). It is also home to Robert and Sylvia Grainger (STOR). **Map A6**

Cutteslowe A residential area off the BANBURY ROAD and to the north of the A40. Gladys Taylor, friend of Margaret BOWMAN, lives here in a council house (ANNX) as does Janis LAWRENCE (CAIN). The estate was built in the 1930s and, apparently, achieved some notoriety for the 'Cutteslowe Wall' (erected to segregate Council tenants from those living in NORTH OXFORD – perhaps a case of 'Town and Down'). The wall was demolished in 1959 (CAIN: p218). WATER EATON ROAD gives another access to the estate (JWEL: p80) and the Cutteslowe Roundabout is known to be a busy one (CAIN: p240). **Map C1-D1**

Plate 1 (Left) An Ackermann print: Augustus Pugin – *Oxford High Street, Looking West* (p11).
Plate 2 (Right) Aristotle Bridge from the canal (p15).

Plate 3 (Left) Aristotle Lane Allotments by Francis Hamel (Spring 2004) (p15).
Plate 4 (Right) The Ashmolean (p15).

Plate 5 (Left) The Door to the Master's Lodge (p17).
Plate 6 (Right) The Bear (p20).

Plate 7 (Left) The Bell Inn (p21).
Plate 8 (Right) Tower blocks on Blackbird Leys (p22).

Plate 9 (Left) Blackwell's in the Broad (p23).
Plate 10 (Right) The 'Uganda' monument (p26).

Plate 11 (Left) Brasenose College (p27).
Plate 12 (Right) The Old Clarendon Broad Street (circa 1910) (p28).

D

Daily Mirror, The A newspaper of large circulation but, perhaps, lesser news (or, a fair amount of news but with a different emphasis). It is the paper of choice for Lewis who happily tackles its basic CROSSWORD and reads the horoscopes; these horoscopes are also read by a hostess at the FLAMENCO TOPLESS BAR (MILE: p20). Morse has been known to read it on occasions (LBUS: p18). The '*Mirror*' was long known as a campaigning paper and for its support for the Labour Party in British politics.

Daily Telegraph, The The title of a daily newspaper with a crossword. Morse attempts it with the same methodology as *The TIMES*; he finds it easier and completes one example in seven and a half minutes (WEAR: p120). Mr Prior, a security guard, with an interest in matters royal, also reads the paper (ANNX: p197).

Daley, George He lives, with wife Margaret and son Philip, at 2 Blenheim Villas, BEGBROKE (and has lived there for some 18 years). At the bottom of a hawthorn hedge beside the slip-road on which the ROYAL SUN stands, he discovers (while walking his 8-year old King Charles spaniel) a camera and the rucksack (adorned with a Swedish flag) of Karin ERIKSSON (WOOD: p61).[1] Had he immediately passed these items to the police – rather than taking them home - much trouble may have been saved (though as JOHNSON was the detective in charge at the time this may not necessarily have been the case). He is in his mid-forties, fond of wearing a pork-pie hat, needs glasses for reading, and slim of build (pp152-153). He works on the BLENHEIM estate and drives a van provided by them. His purchase of a video recorder – ostensibly to watch sport such as England's 1966 football World Cup victory and Botham's cricket miracles – allows him to indulge in much pornographic recreation (WOOD: pp243-244).[2]

Daley, Margaret Wife of George, mother of Philip, and a pleasantly spoken and neatly dressed woman. But her husband and son cause her many concerns. She attended the Douay Martyrs' Secondary School in Solihull (WOOD: p244).

Daley, Philip Son of George and Margaret and a troubled teenager at the Cherwell School (and wherever he goes, it seems). His interest in photography is to have unforeseen consequences. He does not appear (at the behest of the Oxford Magistrates' Court) to answer a charge under the Aggravated Vehicle Theft Act (WOOD: p329), preferring to move to London.[3]

---

[1] The dog's name was Mycroft (WOOD: p71). He was put down by a vet in 1992 (p155) and, understandably, plays no further part in the case.

[2] Botham's success is likely to have been that during the 1981 Ashes test matches against the Australians. He effectively turned certain defeat in the third match at Headingley into victory and ended the series with batting and bowling figures of 399 and 34 wickets.

[3] More accurately, the Aggravated Vehicle-Taking Act 1992.

Dates The first recorded case occurred in 1971 (LBUS) with the discovery in late September of the body of a young woman. The last case (REMO) took place in 1998. Between these crucial dates a certain amount of (though not much) confusion exists. For example, Lewis first comes into Morse's orbit 6 years before 1979 (JERI: p165), i.e. in 1973, but seems to have first met Morse in 1971 (LBUS). One could always agree with Morse himself: "Never my strong point – dates." (SERV: p154).[1]

LBUS: This case can be dated to 1971 by the reference to the film *RYAN'S DAUGHTER* (released in the UK in December 1970). An alternative date *could* be 1973 to tie in with the statement that Lewis first knew Morse 'six years ago' (JERI: p165) as JERI is firmly dated to 1979. A matter of little consequence, perhaps, but *RYAN'S DAUGHTER* (while popular) would have been unlikely to be shown for two years in a cinema and 1971 is the preferred choice herein. The 29th of September is identified as St Michael and All Angels' Day and Chapters are headed by dates (e.g. Chapter 4 is 'Friday 1st October'), which agree with 1971.

WEAR: The date of this case is a little more problematic than others. For example, there are many references to the day, date, and month (such as Friday 12th September or Sunday 24th August), which give the year as 1975 (and this falls in with the rest of The WORKS). However, a reference (p44) refers to 'two years ago' and gives a key date as Tuesday 10th June – the day of the disappearance of Valerie TAYLOR from her school. The 10th of June in 1973 was a Sunday and only in 1969 and 1980 are there 'correct' Tuesdays. It must be assumed that the day Valerie disappears (which is certainly a school day) is, in fact, the 12th June 1973. There is, however, a further confusion created by a reference (p196) to the Vladivostok Summit being planned; as everyone knows (surely), this summit took place in November 1974 rather than 1975. And one more complexity – Strange and Morse meet (p11) some 'three and a half years later' than an incident described in the first ten pages. If that incident, involving the sexual activities of Valerie TAYLOR, took place in 1972 then, thankfully, she may have just reached the age of consent. The case is dated, for this Companion, as 1975.

NICQ: The case has many dates recorded e.g. Friday 31st October or Friday 21st November. The only appropriate year is 1975 and this suggests that Morse had little rest from WEAR before becoming embroiled in the next recorded case.

SERV: Friday 7th April (SERV: p71) and Monday 3rd of April are given as dates (p237) and these confirm the year of investigation by Morse as 1978 (although many of the events occur in 1977). There are a number of other confirming dates.

JERI: A key date is given as Wednesday 3rd October, which gives the year of the case as 1979 (JERI: pp21; 174). There are other confirming dates in the text. We also learn that

---

[1] Though Morse does take some interest in a 1993 *Oxford Almanack* (dated MDCCCCLXXXXIII) – at 14 letters, the lengthiest designation of any year (CAIN: p20). The date is more usually written as MCMXCIII.

Morse is 50 years old and that he is 'a bit paunchy, more than a bit balding' (p4). As a matter of idle interest, the winner of the Miss World Competition (p158) was Gina Swainson from Bermuda and the United Kingdom entry came second.

MILE: The heading to Chapter One is, usefully, 'Monday, 7th July'. The only appropriate year is 1980 and there are numerous dates confirming that year throughout.

ANNX: The case takes place between December 1985 and January 1986 (most Chapters are headed by day and date). This does raise the question of what Morse and Lewis were doing for the last 5 years or so (and provides a golden opportunity should DEXTER ever discover some of his notes from this period).

WNCH: The back cover of the Pan edition usefully has '... on a Saturday morning in 1989 ...' Morse goes to hospital. The text also gives Morse recalling that it was now 44 years since the end of the Second World War (p24), and that a Nurse's party is held on Friday 22nd December. The matter seems beyond doubt until one reaches p234 to be told that the 11th of January was a Friday. The 11th of January 1990 was a Thursday and the 11th a Friday in 1991; would Morse have thought about the case for more than a year before coming to a conclusion? However, 1989 is accepted here.

JWEL: The published (and dated) itinerary of a group of American tourists (pp38-39) confirms the year as 1990 (e.g. Thursday, November 1st).

WOOD: Morse is determined to take a holiday '... for this year, for the year of our Lord nineteen hundred and ninety-two ...' (WOOD: p5). There are subsequent confirmations – for example, Tuesday 14th July (p 116) to make the date of the full investigation of the case 1992 (although much of the nefarious activity takes place earlier).

CAIN: The opening words of Chapter One are: 'Just after noon on Wednesday, 31st August 1994, Chief Inspector Morse was seated at his desk ...' Further investigation seems a trifle redundant.

NEIG: The Prolegomenon is headed by 'January 1996' and the narrative of subsequent events follows directly with, for example, a reference to '15 January' on page 13. For the avoidance of doubt, a number of the early Chapters are dated (the 4th being 'Wednesday, 7 February').

REMO: Page 5 of the notes of the case has '... Wednesday, 15 July 1998 ...' and as 1998 the case is therefore dated. More intriguingly, the Prolegomenon records a conversation in hospital between an unnamed man and Yvonne HARRISON during which she reveals that she is soon to be 48 years old (p5). The case indicates the conversation took place in, probably, 1997. While the male has many attributes of Morse (for example, a typically suggestive and lewd conversational style), he also refers to his home life using the word 'we', to having a number of videos (p3)[2], and uses 'em' for 'them'; perhaps a stranger person than Morse?

Of the shorter cases:

DODO: The first sentence contains the date of 'early February in 1990' and as such the case is dated.

WATC: There is a reference (p120) to the Welsh National Opera performing *Così fan Tutte* at the Apollo Theatre (see NEW THEATRE) in Oxford. The opera came to Oxford on Wednesday the 11th of July 1990 on the final leg of a 15-date tour. Bryn Terfel (no less) featured as Guglielmo (though WATC fails to record this).

BAGG: There is scant information in the notes to the case. There is, though, a reference to Nigel Mansell (p236) in the context of an expert racing driver. Mansell was world Formula One champion in 1992 and this date has been (somewhat arbitrarily) decided upon. References to a Jaguar and Morse's grey hair are too vague to narrow the dates. While the notes of the case contain many references to PC WATSON the only semi-significant fact is that he is 'newly recruited'; no mention is made of his age (he was known to be 'young' in 1990 in the JWEL case).

MYST: A reference to the 'old Jaguar' being repaired probably puts the case between 1992 and 1994, and a mention of a working Tuesday, clearly just before Christmas (both p46), gives a likely date of Tuesday 22nd December 1992.

STOR: The '... morning of Monday, 15 February, 1993' appears on p168 and this seems quite clear enough.

GOLD: Apart from the suggestion that Morse will soon be retiring (p13) being a little premature, the case can easily be dated by the reference to the 31st of March as a Thursday (p30). And that date is taken here as being 1994.

CALL: Despite some effort, no trace has (yet) been found of the Greek Archbishop who died in a brothel in Athens (p268) and this has been of no help in dating the case.[3] However, the presence of Laura HOBSON puts the case after 1992 and the death of MAX. The changing price of rooms at the RANDOLPH (p262) has not been *fully* explored but a semi-educated guess gives the date of the case as 1994. £140 for the relevant length of stay would seem very attractive now.

BURG: There is nothing in the text to indicate a date. It is suggested that 1995 is likely only because that is when the case was first recorded.

---

[2] Morse does not have a video (WOOD: p331; NEIG: p273) until some time after 1996. He certainly has one by 1998 (REMO: p361, for example).

[3] Archbishop Seraphim of Athens died there – in Athens rather than a brothel - in 1998 at the age of 85.

Daughters of Cain, The A former don from WOLSEY COLLEGE meets a violent end and there appears to be a link to his time at that college and allegations of mischief on the staircases (particularly involving drugs). PHILLOTSON organises the scenes-of crime investigation but is soon removed from the case and Morse takes over (with Lewis, once he has finished his egg and chips), happy not to have been involved with the body. Much is learned of what SCOUTS do (and not do), something of the PITT RIVERS Museum, a few procedures relating to fingerprinting, and a little of Morse's opinions of facial jewellery. Knives play a large part and the common question of how to dispose of a body is given a (probably) unique answer. Morse's thoughts turn a number of times to retirement during this case; in short, he begins to feel his age and tells Strange that "I shall only be going on for a couple of years, whatever happens." (p5). Quotations may be found heading the Chapters. Apparently, a number of Biblical scholars interpret the phrase 'the daughters of men' (*Genesis 6,4*) as meaning 'the daughters of Cain'. Some even go so far as to suggest that those daughters are non-believers but further into these murky waters one need (and should) not tread here. The notes of the case are helpful in speaking of: "Women set apart from the rest of their kind by the sign of the murderer – by the mark of Cain" (p317). (CAIN). *Main personnel* Brenda and Ted BROOKS, Julia STEVENS, Eleanor SMITH, McCLURE, and Kevin COSTYN.

Daventry Avenue A street in SUMMERTOWN between the BANBURY and WOODSTOCK Roads. Here may be found Daventry Court, once home to Felix McCLURE (in one of 8 flats). The layout and occupants of Daventry Court are detailed in CAIN (p16). The rather odd numbering is a possible way of meeting the fact that number 5 is below number 6. **Plate 19, Map C3**

Davies, Ashley Once an undergraduate at WOLSEY COLLEGE, he failed to get his degree (having been rusticated and then failing to return). He lives with his parents at 248 Northampton Road, Bedford and is interviewed there (at some length) by Lewis (CAIN: pp145-152). During this process one learns that he met and befriended Matthew RODWAY at the University Conservative Association and the East Oxford Martial Arts Club – but they later argued over a girl. It is not the first time that the thickset Davies has fought.

Dead as a Dodo Morse is asked to help unravel a bit of a mystery dating from the Second World War (and does so without the assistance of Lewis). The case is certainly of interest as it contains the first mention of Morse's JAGUAR – assuming the information under DATES is correct (DODO). *Main personnel* Philip WISE and a couple of WHITAKERs.

Dead of Jericho, The A case in which one learns a great deal about the history and street layout of JERICHO (a map is usefully included in the published version), a little about Morse's date of birth, and something of a small publishing firm run by Charles and Conrad RICHARDS. Morse and Lewis investigate what appears to be a SUICIDE and then what could be an example of manslaughter. Most of the Chapter headings are quotes and some of these are explored under QUOTATIONS. The heading to Chapter 19 is a definition of the word 'ALIBI' and how Morse tackles this issue is crucial to the solution of the case. (JERI). *Main personnel*

Gorge JACKSON, Edward MURDOCH, any RICHARDS beginning with a C, and Anne SCOTT.

Dead Sea apples A fruit said to grow near the site of the biblical Sodom. When plucked, they turn to smoke and ashes. Margaret BOWMAN thinks her food tastes like them (ANNX: p13) because of the mess her life is in.

Deafness An affliction that is central to the NICQ case but there are other references in the WORKS. The Oxford Centre for the Deaf and Hard of Hearing is based in Littlegate Street, at the foot of ST EBBE'S Street; one of their correspondents is Nicholas QUINN (NICQ: p80) to whom they write about lip-reading classes.[4] There is a reasonable amount of information about the skills – and pitfalls – of lip-reading (pp249-250) and the solution to the case involves a particular pitfall. In REMO, one learns that 'traffic lights' and 'driving licence' produce very similar lip movements (p42). QUINN also uses Otosporin eardrops, which are designed to combat bacterial infection; this may be linked to his deafness. The RADCLIFFE INFIRMARY has an Ear Nose and Throat Department (NICQ: p127). Phil ALDRICH has incipient otosclerosis – a disease of the inner ear bones where the bones become fused (JWEL: p296) – and both Cedric DOWNES and Mrs Wynne-Wilson (MINOR) have poor hearing. Simon HARRISON is largely deaf (REMO) and both REPP and FLYNN have attended lip-reading classes at OXPENS. Dr ULLMAN wears a hearing aid (WATC).

Dean, Barbara She has worked for the THAMES VALLEY police since 1992 and as Strange's personal secretary since 1995. He may have flirted with her (or vice versa) but only one time is recorded (in REMO).

Death is Now My Neighbour The record of this case opens with details of a quiz; it is reproduced, along with some answers, in APPENDIX B. Before long, Morse and Lewis are investigating a murder (or two) and the stench of blackmail wafts through the potential motives they discover. Almost everyone involved in the case appears to have a secret (or two) and affairs abound. The Master of LONSDALE is about to retire and his succession is not a straightforward issue; something is learned of college politics and the determination of wives to further the careers of husbands; a little is also learned of triskaidekaphobia. The subject and nature of DIABETES is a regular theme and concerns about Morse's health grow more serious; Morse even shares some of these concerns himself. The record of the case has quotes (and a few dates) heading the Chapters. Morse utters the line: "Death is always the next-door neighbour". (p75). His Christian name is revealed on the last page. (NEIG). *Main personnel* Clixby BREAM, Dawn CHARLES, Denis and Shelly CORNFORD, Rachel JAMES, Geoffrey OWENS, Julian and Angela STORRS.

De Bono, Edward Modern thinker; his *A Five-Day Course in Lateral Thinking* has been read conscientiously (and enjoyed) by Morse. From it, he takes the question of 'how can one drive up a dark alley if the headlights are not working?' and the best of the answers is to use one's

---

[4] Morse is unable to lip-read (WNCH: p171).

blinkers or indicators (LBUS: pp73-74). The same principle applies to a motorist stuck in a snowdrift or a blizzard (MILE: pp129/257).

De Bryn, Maximilian Theodore Siegfried The full names of the police surgeon known to most as Max (and all information has been entered under that name).

Deddington Road This may be found close to BLOXHAM DRIVE and provides a convenient parking spot for Morse and Malcolm JOHNSON (NEIG).

De Lincto, Rex The fat, short, balding (and slightly deaf) Chairman of the OXFORD BOOK ASSOCIATION (STOR). His name seems ripe for an anagram (Dixon Lecter, perhaps).

Deniston, Wilfred M. Author of *Murder on the Oxford Canal* (privately printed in 1978 by The Oxford and County Local History Society; full details of acknowledgements and sources may be found in WNCH: p42). He is an ex-Indian Army Colonel (with the awards of OBE and MC) and, unbeknown to Morse, keen on the works of HOUSMAN (WNCH: p12). He and Morse share a little time in the John RADCLIFFE HOSPITAL where Mrs Deniston gives him a copy of her husband's book. He lives with his wife, Margery, at 46 Church Walk, WOODSTOCK (WNCH: p209).

Desert Island Discs A popular radio programme on BBC Radio Four. It was created by Roy Plomley (**Plate 20**) in 1942 (with the first guest being the bandleader Vic Oliver) and is still broadcast today (though not by Roy Plomley). Each week, a guest is invited to choose their eight favourite pieces of music which, should they be cast away on a desert island, may give them solace, memories, or simply pleasure. From these eight, a further sole favourite must be chosen. The complete works of Shakespeare and a copy of the Bible would be made available but each guest can also choose another book together with a luxury item, which must have no practical use (and also be inanimate). The programme takes the form of an interview about the guest's life and achievements interspersed with extracts from their chosen music, giving them the opportunity to explain exactly why such a piece has been chosen. Guests are often asked what they would most like to 'get away from'; Morse's answer would be 'Committees' (LBUS: p195). Some of the luxuries chosen include: for Sir Tim Rice (the lyricist), a telescope; for Jan Morris (whose book on Oxford appears in the bibliography), a hot water bottle; for P.D. James and Patricia Cornwell (respective amanuenses of the detective Adam Dalgleish and the medical examiner Kay Scarpetta), paper and pencils and notebooks and pens. Minette Walters, winner of both the American Edgar Allan Poe Award and the British Gold Dagger Award for crime fiction, chose Van Gogh's *Irises*. The theme tune to *Desert Island Discs* is the redolent *By the Sleepy Lagoon* composed by Eric Coates (with seagulls added for the programme). The 2000th guest on the programme was the actor John Thaw.

Morse considers whether or not to replace his 8th choice (the *In Paradisum* from the Fauré *Requiem*)[5] with the slow movement of Dvořák's American Quartet (JWEL: p113) though he

---

[5] The *In Paradisum* is also much admired by Julian and Angela STORRS (NEIG: p285).

appears to have these on cassette rather than disc. A few years later he is still uncertain of numbers 7 and 8 but does send a complete list to Claire OSBORNE together with details of the versions he has of MOZART's *Requiem* (WOOD: p126). DEXTER, according to Bird (1998: p123), appeared on the programme in February 1998. His choices were *In Paradisum* from Fauré's *Requiem*, *Abide with Me*, Chopin's *Étude No. 5*, MOZART's *Clarinet Concerto K.622*, *The Long and Winding Road* by the Beatles, Gerald Hoffnung relating *The Bricklayer*, *On Going to Sleep* by Richard Strauss, and the finale to *Götterdämmerung*. His chosen book was the poems and papers of HOUSMAN and his luxury, a pair of nail-scissors.

Detective (fictional) See the entries under DESERT ISLAND DISCS, DICKENS, POIROT and Wimsey (MINOR). Mention is also made of Perry Mason (SERV: p120) though he could, one guesses, be classed more as a lawyer.

Dew Drop Inn A pub in SUMMERTOWN. Morse has two pints of beer here (after already visiting the RANDOLPH); it seems it is a convenient location on the way to MANNING TERRACE (SERV: p322). Margaret BOWMAN also uses the pub on her lunch breaks (ANNX: p142). The pub has been commonly frequented by Malcolm JOHNSON (REMO: p180). Morse rings for him there (on a borrowed mobile phone) – and appears to know the number off by heart. He enjoys (no doubt) a pint of Best Bitter here while Lewis contents himself with a half of Beamish (WATC: p126). **Plate 21**

Dexter, (Norman) Colin Born in 1930 and raised in Stamford (Lincolnshire); he went up to CHRIST'S College to study Classics and later taught that subject. Increasing deafness meant a move from teaching and into the world of examination-setting and marking. He has lived in Oxford since 1966; JWEL is dedicated 'for my wife, Dorothy' and MILE 'For My Daughter, Sally'; he was awarded the OBE in 2000 (see *overtaken by events* under LITERARY CURIOSITIES). A clue set by Jeremy Morse – 'Contra-revolutionary hero who made the tumbril proceed (6)' - spurred him to a little action, including a great interest in solving and setting CROSSWORDS.[6] That Dexter should know two people called Morse seems like a touch coincidental. He may well have learned (and been expert at) Morse code as Haining claims (1996: p288) but, in light of other evidence in his relationship with the detective Morse, this seems a little irrelevant. Dexter is quoted in *The TIMES* (21st November 2006; p8) on how he recorded Morse's cases: "I didn't write. I just jotted down a few words in between *The ARCHERS* and going down the pub". He has contributed articles to the annual journal issued by the HOUSMAN Society. See also 'Dexter' in the bibliography. **Plate 22**

Diabetes Morse has been gently cautioned by a consultant at the John RADCLIFFE HOSPITAL that his drinking (Morse's rather than the consultant's) may lead to diabetes (WNCH: p37). In 1989, when Morse is in hospital, he is tested for diabetes and found to be clear. The Consultant, commenting on Morse's drinking, suggests, "Give him a couple of years!" (WNCH: p166). Prophetic words, indeed (though they are out by a good fraction of a decade). In February 1996, Morse refers himself to the SUMMERTOWN Health Centre,

---

[6] The answer is 'Carton' (as in Sydney).

concerned that he may have diabetes (NEIG: p233). His blood sugar level is extremely high – suggesting diabetes mellitus and hyperglycaemia – and he is rather rapidly taken into hospital (by ambulance).[7] Either abnormally high or low levels of sugar are dangerous. He is formally diagnosed as a sufferer and put on an insulin-drip. Matthews (MINOR), the Senior Consultant at the Diabetes Centre of the RADCLIFFE INFIRMARY, advises him that there are three basic causes – hereditary factors, stress, and drinking – and here one learns that Morse's father was diabetic latish in life. Despite telling Dr Matthews that his alcohol consumption is between a third and a half of the truth, Morse is scored ten out of ten on this cause. NEIG helpfully lists a number of the treatments available: 'single-use insulin syringes, Human Ultratard, Human Actrapid, Unilet Lancets, Exatech, Reagent Strips, Enalapril Tablets, Frusemide Tablets, Nifedipine Tablets …' (pp244-245).

Morse learns to inject himself with insulin and demonstrates the same, to a wincing Lewis, in the CHERWELL ARMS (NEIG: pp251-252); he has been known, however, to forget to do the same (p333). He is also advised to take four readings daily, with a pen, to check his blood sugar level. By the time of the REMO case, Morse is a regular at the Diabetes Centre and on four hefty injections a day (self-administered) and still manipulating his blood-sugar readings. At a fairly thorough review in May 1998, Morse's general condition gives no real cause for concern to Professor TURNER. In July, Morse is examined by Sarah HARRISON (and advised that he has nice feet). The origin of the word 'diabetes' is the Greek for siphon; Morse is not alone in suffering from this illness and some carry a Diabetic Card (Peter SHERWOOD, for example, in the CALL case).

Diamond Close A street presumed to be in Upper Wolvercote (ANNX: p256) though its exact location is a little hard to determine. At number 17 (formerly a council house but now in private ownership) lives Edward Wilkins (ANNX). **Map C2**

Dickens, Charles (1812-70) Creator of, among many other characters (of course), 'Bucket of the Detective' in *BLEAK HOUSE*. Morse playfully alludes to himself as "Morse of the Detective" (LBUS: p122) and BROWNE-SMITH refers to Morse as "… a man of the Detective …" (MILE: p166). There are references to *Little Dorrit* in both WEAR (p298) and REMO (p34). Of all the works by Dickens, Morse ranks *BLEAK HOUSE* first and *Little Dorrit* second (MYST: p46). And Lewis has heard, at least, of the character of Scrooge (MYST: p45).

Dickson A detective constable with the THAMES VALLEY POLICE. 'Dickson was almost always in the canteen' (SERV: p200) and, however impolite it may sound, eats rather a lot. He is described as having a 'bulky figure' (NICQ: p54), is unable (at first) to tell a 16-year girl from her mother (NICQ: p124), and fails (when acting as duty-sergeant) to recognise the relevance of a message from the Shrewsbury Constabulary (SERV: pp167, 196, 198). He also fails to record the address of Simon ROWBOTHAM who may, or may not, have some relevant information (MILE: p74). His weakness is for amply jammed doughnuts and Morse has been

---

[7] An abnormal *reduction* of sugar in the blood is hypoglycaemia. According to SMALL, the condition is easier to spot than to spell (NEIG: p384).

known to greet him with "Fingers a bit sticky this morning, Dickson?" (MILE: p91). Morse has also called him 'delinquent' (MILE: p145). See also DIXON.

Disprin A brand name (since 1948) for a soluble aspirin with a recommended dosage happily ignored by Morse (LBUS: p117). Winifred Stewart (MINOR) also takes this medicine (MILE: p217), as does Sarah JONSTONE (ANNX: p30) and Karin ERIKSSON (WOOD: P736).

Dixon, Sergeant According to JWEL: p180 he is 'newly promoted' and this does provoke the suspicion that DEXTER may have heard Morse speak of DICKSON and made a simple error in transcription. If there is a real Sergeant Dixon, one does, of course, offer apologies for any unintended slight. However, as his sergeant's stripes are 'newly stitched' (JWEL: 285) this suggests a transfer to the uniformed branch (not unknown). Certainly, he is on night duty in 1990 (WATC: p129) and plays a small part in the STOR case. There is, though, a further confusion – in 1998, some 8 years after the JWEL case, Dixon is still only 'recently elevated' to sergeant (REMO: p59). Certainly, a Sergeant Dixon takes an important phone call in a later case (WOOD: p383). And it is believed that Sergeant Dixon has ordered *Housewives on the Job* for himself – only to be disappointed in scenes of washing-up and potato-peeling (NEIG: p44); perhaps he was less disappointed with the film *Grub Screws* that was shown on his stag-night (p273). Not the brightest of officers – he has been described by Morse, no doubt accurately, as "… the lowest-watt bulb …" and his spelling leaves something to be desired (p218). Thankfully, perhaps, he is due to retire in 2003 (REMO: p59). The same Dixon relishes jam doughnuts (NEIG: p181 and REMO: p58) – could this be another coincidence of which Morse is so fond? Were Homer to have described him, he might well be 'Dixon-delighting-in-doughnuts' (REMO: p72). His last recorded doughnuts appear on pp438/441 of the REMO case; a fitting end to his place in the WORKS.

Don Usually a fellow or any member of the teaching staff of a university. There are, of course, many female dons at Oxford. Hobhouse (1939: p102) has: 'The women dons devote much of their thoughts to the dangers of masculine society'.

Donavan F.T. The first husband of Joanna FRANKS (WNCH: p46). His size gave him the nickname of 'Hefty' and he was a conjuror and magician by profession, appearing as 'Emperor of all the Illusionists' at the City of Nottingham Music Hall in 1856. He had also written, in 1853, *The Comprehensive Manual of the Conjuring Arts*. It appears he died in 1858 and is buried at BERTNAGHBOY BAY.

Donnington Bridge Road This runs between the IFFLEY ROAD and, via Weirs Lane, ABINGDON ROAD and is part of the route taken by Brenda BROOKS to the REDBRIDGE Waste Centre (CAIN: p292). **Map E7**

Downes, Cedric MA Oxon, He is a graduate of JESUS COLLEGE (Oxford), Fellow of BRASENOSE, a mediaeval historian, and also a speaker for the HISTORIC CITIES tour when it reaches Oxford. He was originally from the Midlands and is, regrettably (though, for the JWEL case, importantly) going a bit, more than a bit, deaf (p79); he wears a hearing aid and has a special attachment on his home telephone. He is married to Lucy and they live at the end of LONSDALE ROAD (with a garden conveniently backing onto the Cherwell; p81).

Downes, Lucy (Claire) Married to Cedric and some 11 years his junior. She is fair-skinned and blonde, fully-figured, and fully-sexed (JWEL: p81), and – not that it really matters - a Scorpio (p236). It does, at first, seem to matter that she spends some time on Harley Ward in St. Pancras Hospital.

Dowson, Ernest (1867-1900) Poet and decadent. His poems, including one guesses, *Non Sum Qualis Eram Bonae sub Regno Cynarae* (1896) – with the line 'I have been faithful to thee Cynara! In my fashion' – are favourites of Bernard CROWTHER. The title is taken from the odes of Horace (Book 4.1) and roughly translates as "I am no more the man as in the reign of the Good Cynara". An extract appears as the heading to Chapter 70 of REMO. It is clear that Morse is *au fait* with the works of Dowson. He adds the line: 'One day of the great lost days, one face of all the faces …' to a note that he sends to Claire OSBORNE (WOOD: p355). The line is from *Impenitentia Ultima*. During an interview with Julia STEVENS, Morse notices a copy of Dowson's Poems. He quotes, from memory, the lines: 'They are not long, the weeping and the laughter, Love and desire and hate …' (from *Vitae Summa Brevis Spem Nos Vetat Incohare Longam*)[8] and would be happy to continue (with, one hopes, 'I think they have no portion in us after We pass the Gate'). Dowson attended the QUEEN'S COLLEGE but failed to obtain a degree.

'Dreaming Spires' A common enough reference to Oxford (though not common in the WORKS). The phrase is from Matthew Arnold's poem *Thyrsis* and the relevant lines are: 'And that sweet city with her dreaming spires, She needs not June for beauty's heightening …'

Dudley Court A block of flats built on the site of the old SUMMERTOWN Parish Cemetery (WNCH: p198). **Map D3**

Duke of Cambridge A pub in London, WC1 that Morse walks past (MILE: p193). One guesses that there was something wrong with the pub though this is mere surmise.

Durrants A traditional hotel in George Street (*not* the one in Oxford but, rather, behind Oxford Street in London). It has good facilities, comfortable beds, and tasteful cuisine (NEIG: p325).

---

[8] The line is from Horace: "The brief sum of life forbids us from enduring long".

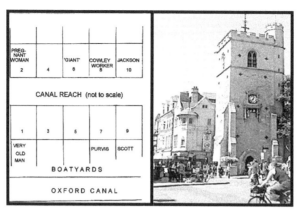

Plate 13 (Left) The residents of Canal Reach (p31).
Plate 14 (Right) Carfax Tower (p32).

Plate 15 (Left) Christ Church (Tom Tower centre) (p35).
Plate 16 (Right) Shops in Cowley Road (p39).

Plate 17 (Left) A young Ximenes (p39).
Plate 18 (Right) Roger Squires (left), prolific compiler (and an admirer) (p42).

E

Eagle and Child Often known as the 'Bird and Baby', this charming pub can be found in ST GILES'.[1] According to Dunkling and Wright (1987), the name is derived from the heraldic arms of the Stanley family, the Earls of Derby. Morse and Lewis drink beer here (ANNX: pp96-97). On this occasion, Lewis has rather more beer than usual and, on reading the plaque to the Inklings (reproduced in ANNX), imagines a series of fundamental emendations beginning: 'CHIEF INSPECTOR MORSE, with his friend and colleague Sergeant Lewis, sat in this back room one Thursday, in order to solve ...' **Plate 23**

Margaret BOWMAN manages to find an extremely rare and vacant parking space opposite the pub (ANNX: p202); if only she had been so lucky in love. A potential witness in the WOOD case recalls the time most particularly as he was just about to be off to the pub at noon (p59) and McBryde (MINOR) has two pints of splendidly conditioned Burton Ale here (WOOD: p335) though Karin ERIKSSON has only a half of lager and a ham sandwich (p372). Dawn CHARLES drinks here while doodling on a Burton beer-mat (NEIG: p12) and Morse pays a visit 'just after 11 a.m.' (REMO: p207). Philip WISE and Dodo WHITAKER used to meet in the 'ill-lit bar at the rear' (DODO: p82).

East Oxford Where Nicholas Greenaway (MINOR) is christened (NICQ: p294) and Ellie SMITH, an excellent swimmer, has kept her figure in trim by regular visits to the Temple Cowley pool (CAIN: p153).

East Oxford Conservative Club Ted BROOKS drinks here; it hardly sounds the sort of place that Morse would frequent (CAIN: p109) but one never knows.

Edwards, Jane A 'recent' (probably 1995 or 1996) addition to the typing pool at the KIDLINGTON HQ. In 1996, at least, she acts as Morse's secretary. She is young, blonde and a "... pretty little lass ..." according to Strange (NEIG: p157), though Morse feels he is losing his lust when thinking of her. She comes highly recommended from the Marlborough College in the HIGH and her secretarial skills include a Pitman Shorthand speed of 120 words per minute (NEIG: p196). Morse tears her off a strip, later apologises, and she is one of the few people to try and contact him when in hospital (NEIG: p246).

Egg and chips This is, of course, a favourite meal of Lewis and some details are provided under that entry. Here, though, it should be recorded that Morse also has (or at least had) a certain fascination with this basic meal: '... lingering over things – as he'd always done as a boy when he'd carved his way meticulously around the egg-white until he was left only with the golden circle of the yolk, into which, finally, to dip the calculated balance of his chips' (WNCH: pp153-154).

---

[1] A brief footnote to the BIRD AND BABY refers to the Inklings.

El Alamein The site of two battles (July and October/November 1942). Much detail – including the exploits of the tank-driving GILBERT brothers and BROWNE-SMITH – may be found on pp3-9 of MILE. Such detail is not repeated here and the curious reader (who wishes to know more about the tank battle for the ridge at Tel Aqqaqir and the participants thereof) is referred to the appropriate pages. The ridge is also known as Kidney Ridge (MILE: p170). The battles have been seen as a major turning point in the Second World War in favour of the Allies.

Elizabeth, The A fairly expensive (but some would say worth it) restaurant in ST ALDATES. Ruth RAWLINSON, at least, enjoyed a marvellous meal there (SERV: p275). Nicholson (1976) simply notes that it has been in the Good Food Guide since 1961; Nicholson (2006) comments more effusively on its French traditional cuisine and delicious sweets.

English Breakfast 'Few English families living in England have much direct contact with the full English Breakfast' (JWEL: p84). This early feast is also sometimes simply known as the 'Full English' (p160).[2] Although enjoyed on holidays, the daily routine for many tends to be cornflakes and a slice of toasted Mother's Pride bread. Vegetarian readers or dieters may wish to turn away now – what follows is a vivid and rather extreme description of the genuine article: '... a milkily-opaque fried egg; two rashers of non-brittle, rindless bacon; a tomato grilled to a point where the core is no longer a hard white nodule to be operated upon by the knife; a sturdy sausage, deeply and evenly browned; and a slice of fried bread, golden-brown, and only just crisp ...'

The recipe varies from place to place and expands from a core of bacon and eggs to include, inter alia, sausage, mushrooms, tomatoes, toast, fried bread, baked beans, black pudding, sauté potatoes, and (rarely on the same plate) smoked kippers. The egg part is usually fried but devil-may-care breakfasters have been known to indulge in poaching and scrambling. A kidney (usually grilled) is optional (at least at the ROYAL CRESCENT Hotel – NEIG: p368).

Morse has been restrained enough when in his flat to restrict his choice to a self-cooked bacon, tomatoes, and mushrooms (LBUS: p74). After an innocent night's sleep and a shower, '... a fried breakfast of high cholesterol risk', taken at home, launches a zestful Lewis on his way to the HAWORTH HOTEL (ANNX: p87); he enjoys a similar breakfast in a later case (REMO: p62) but one imagines there have been a few, at least, in the intervening years.

Alternative breakfasts might be such as that enjoyed by John Smith (MINOR) – Flora margarine and Cooper's Thick Cut Oxford Marmalade (ANNX: p151) – or that by Janet ROSCOE of grapefruit, unbuttered toast and diabetic marmalade, and decaffeinated coffee (JWEL: p85); or even that by Rachel JAMES of a hard-boiled egg, toast and Frank Cooper's Oxford (NEIG: p53). Della CECIL is more traditional and enjoys (one assumes) her eggs, bacon, mushrooms, and sausages (NEIG: p326).

---

[2] A horse, 'Full English', is thought to have run at Sandown Park in 1992 (WOOD: p253).

For Morse, an English breakfast (perhaps preceded by a bowl of Kellogg's Corn Flakes) is the biggest single joy of any holiday (WOOD: p27). For much of the time, though, Morse is not on holiday – and, as such, a breakfast then may consist (for example) of three cups of instant coffee with toast, butter, and Frank Cooper's (NEIG: p155). The RANDOLPH serves a full meal under the name of the Good Morning Breakfast (REMO: p347).

English National Opera A company, renamed as such in 1974 from the Sadler's Wells Opera, and based at the London Coliseum; there is a reference to a 'prima ballerina' from Sadler's Wells in SERV (p74). It claims to be Britain's only full-time repertory opera company and was acclaimed for its 1970s tour with the RING CYCLE. Morse attended their performance of Die Walküre at the NEW THEATRE in September 1975 (WEAR).

Eriksson, Irma She is the mother of Karin, Katarina, and Kristina and lives in Flat 6B, Bergsvägen in Bromma (a suburb of Stockholm). Her figure is plump, her eyes hazel, and her manner with Lewis is (at first) mildly flirtatious (WOOD: pp215-218) – which Lewis enjoys. She has, dare one say it, Swedish tastes in decoration and her flat contains a set of Dala horses and some Carl Larsson prints. Her husband, Staffan Eriksson, had left her a year or two ago; she and her daughters are Roman Catholics.

Eriksson, Karin She disappears near WOODSTOCK in 1991 – her rucksack is found – and becomes known as the SWEDISH MAIDEN. She is the middle of three daughters born to Irma ERIKSSON from Uppsála, Sweden. She seems to have developed a yen for travel – to the Arctic Circle in 1989, the Holy Land and a kibbutz in Tel Aviv in 1990 (after finishing secretarial school) and, in 1991, to London and thence towards Oxford as part of a planned longer journey to see a relative in mid-Wales. Among the possessions found in her rucksack was a slim copy of *A Birdwatcher's Guide* (WOOD: p64) with a number of birds marked as seen on a separate sheet of paper (with only one spelling mistake). **Plate 24**

Eriksson, Katarina The oldest of three sisters, she is married and works at the European Commission in Strasbourg as an interpreter (WOOD).

Eriksson, Kristina The youngest of three sisters, she is still at school at the time of the WOOD case.

Evans, Dorothy Allegedly a cousin (a few times removed) of the ERIKSSON sisters, she is (in fact) one of the old style of 'Aunties' – a friend of the family. She lives in an isolated guest-house ('Birdwatchers Welcome') in Llandovery (South Wales and on the A40) – the home of the RED KITE (WOOD: pp318/269). Morse and Lewis (the latter driving) go to visit her and it is on this memorable journey that Morse refuses Lewis's offer to stop for 'a quick pint'. It is unclear whether or not this refusal has any effect on Morse's interviewing technique (which lays and springs a rather clever trap on her; pp319-322). She is also known as Dot or Doss – and, sarcastically, Auntie Gladys to Morse.

Ewers, Mrs Susan A SCOUT at WOLSEY COLLEGE (CAIN) with responsibility for Staircase G in Drinkwater Quad. Her cleaning and stores cupboard is marked as 'Susan's Pantry' (wherein may be found a number of branded products such as a Hoover or two, Jif, Flash, Ajax, and Windolene). Morse is particularly interested in her knowledge of any drugs activity on her staircase and she answers at least one of his questions truthfully (p89).

Examination Schools The official place for the display of examination results - once verified in the presence of the Clerk (MILE: p97). The buildings are also used for various University occasions and lectures; they front the HIGH. Lewis makes his first visit here (MILE: p95) and is slightly overawed by the décor (and the busts of University Chancellors). Morse spends more than a most helpful hour with the Curator (MILE: p240).

Executive Hotel Situated just off Park Lane, London. Mrs PALMER has been known to make new friends here, in the Cocktail Lounge, on a regular – and usually temporary - basis (ANNX: pp111-112).

Exeter College Founded in 1314 as Stapledon Hall (by Walter de Stapledon) and refounded in 1566 by William Petre. Alumni include Philip WISE, Alan Bennett, and J.R.R. Tolkien. **Map D5**

Exeter University Formerly a University College, it was granted full University status by Charter in 1955 (presented by Queen Elizabeth the Second in 1956). The University has campuses in both Devon and Cornwall and has gained a good reputation for both academic and leisure activities. David ACUM met his wife here.

Exocet A missile much in use in the 1970s and the 1980s with a fearsome reputation (not always deserved). Morse launches his own verbal Exocet against Max (MILE: p111).

F

Fawlty Towers A hotel in Torquay once renowned for its incompetent owner (WNCH: p81). OWENS has a video of the TV programme made about it (NEIG: p272).

Featherlite A brand of condom made by Durex. An empty packet of the same is the only item Morse discovered during a police search in North Staffordshire (ANNX: p219); and Philip DALEY possesses a packet, two thirds empty (WOOD: p273).

Fellow A number of definitions exist (including that of a worthless or contemptible person) but the most common use in The WORKS is that referring to a senior member of a COLLEGE or of the governing body of a university. Fellows may be, of course, of either sex.

Field House Drive A turning off the WOODSTOCK ROAD and close to the location where a blackmail plot almost reaches its culmination (JERI). **Map C2**

First Turn A quaintly named road leading from the WOODSTOCK ROAD to WOLVERCOTE. It is traversed by Eddie STRATTON (JWEL: p339). **Map C2**

Fish and Chips A traditional meal of battered fish (often cod) and chips; it is best eaten out of a newspaper (according to Mrs Lewis; Morse agrees).

Five Mile Drive A road linking the BANBURY ROAD and the WOODSTOCK ROAD to the north of the A40 (SERV: p17). **Map B2-C1**

Flamenco Topless Bar, The An establishment in SOHO, serving various exotic drinks (see ALCOHOL). The Bar is visited by Morse (MILE: p177) – for business rather than pleasure.

Fletcher's Arms, The A public house in NORTH OXFORD; it is unexceptionable and attracts an ill-assorted yet amiable clientèle (LBUS: p37) but it is also close to Morse's flat. Here he enjoys a lunchtime of four pints of BITTER while ignoring the suspicious ham sandwiches (WEAR: p316). The pub name is recorded as The Fletchers' Arms in WEAR.

Flynn, Paddy (Patrick) A cabdriver for Radio Taxis (with offices in King Alfred Street),[1] and living in Morrell Avenue, Oxford. Slightly surprising finds in his flat are a CD of *Great Arias from Puccini* and the contents of a battered case. He is aged 39 years in 1998 and has seen neither his wife nor his two daughters for some time. He has had at least one job involving a trip to the home of the Harrison family, *The Windhovers* (REMO). The veracity of his ALIBI needs to be proved (or disproved).

---

[1] There is an ALFRED STREET and a King Edward Street in central Oxford and both are close to the location as described in REMO (p216). Radio Taxis also seem to have an office in WARWICK STREET (p289).

Folly Bridge Following ST ALDATES to the south, this bridge crosses the Thames and leads to the ABINGDON ROAD; the current structure was erected in 1825-1827. It is mentioned in SERV (p118), WNCH (p93), and CAIN (p302). **Plate 25, Map D6**

Football There are scant references in The WORKS to this fairly popular spectator sport. This is hardly surprising considering that Morse's '... life would not have been significantly impoverished had the game ... never been invented' (CAIN: p8). A game between Arsenal and Tottenham is mentioned (LBUS: p60) and a 0-0 draw between England and Holland (JWEL: p21). There is a brief reference to Birmingham City FC in REMO (p299) but only as a gentle dig at a whining accent. There are a few more references to football pools (see under Lewis and Morse). Also see the entry for OXFORD UNITED.

Foreign Examinations Syndicate See the entries for the SYNDICATE and SYNDICS (NICQ).

Franks, Joanna Her story is told in *Murder on the Oxford Canal* (DENISTON 1978). Wife of Charles Franks, her tomb-stone recalls that she was tragically drowned on the 22nd of June 1859 aged 38 years. Her father was one Daniel Carrick.

Freeman, Celia Switchboard-operator at the RANDOLPH and a pleasantly spoken and courteous woman (JWEL: p100). She has previously worked for Dr KEMP and her note-taking of callers is precise (p172).

Freeman, Margaret Once the secretary of BLAND at the SYNDICATE but now, in 1975, the secretary of QUINN. Slim and plain, she lives with her parents (because she is slim and plain, perhaps).

Friar Bacon, The A pub a little way back from the A40 Northern Ring Road. It is named after Roger Bacon (as is, of course, the ROGER BACON School) and has a sign depicting the said friar pouring a glass of liquid. Morse and Lewis spend a fruitful session there – the beer is pleasing to the critical palate of Morse (SERV: p295) – when many details of a particular case are explored and explained. The pub serves Morrell's beer and one guesses it is a Morrell's BITTER that encourages Morse to exclaim: "By Jove, the beer's good here!" (SERV: p300).

Morse also visits the pub prior to a meeting with Mrs Murdoch (JERI: p220) before walking the few hundred yards to his flat. It would seem that the pub is Morse's local: '... he stepped out with a purpose in his stride towards his nightly assignation at the Friar' (ANNX: p31). According to Honey (1998), there are only two pubs called The Friar (rather than the Friar Bacon). The first was demolished in the 1960s redevelopment of ST EBBE'S (making it an unlikely candidate) and the second is in Old Marston Road, some two miles from Morse's flat, (a more unlikely option still). Morse had planned to take part in the final of a pub quiz at the Friar Bacon but duty called him away (ANNX: p51); the pub has a lounge bar (ANNX: p275) wherein certain groups play music and thus driving Morse to the relative calm of the public bar (p277). It would, of course, be something of a tragedy should the pub be demolished to make way for a block of flats (but these things are known to happen).

Fuller An otherwise unidentified female police constable (LBUS: p79).

Newly wed and in bed	Mrs. Laura Wynne-Wilson (deaf old lady)
Flat 1	Flat 3
Empty	Away in Tunisia
Flat 5	Flat 7
Ground floor	
Empty	Out on a charity walk to 'Save the Whales'
Flat 2	Flat 4
McCLURE	Redecorating and listening to The ARCHERS
Flat 6	Flat 8
First floor	

Plate 19 (Left) Probable layout of Daventry Court (p51).
Plate 20 (Right) Roy Plomley (1960) (p53).

Plate 21 (Left) The Dew Drop Inn (p54).
Plate 22 (Right) Colin Dexter (p54).

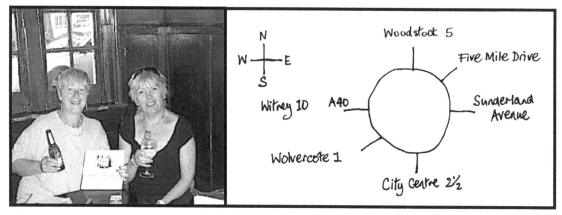

Plate 23 (Left) A pair of happy ladies in the Eagle and Child (p59).
Plate 24 (Right) A police sketch of options for Karin, the travelling Swedish Maiden (p61).

G

Gardener's Arms, The A pub found in Plantation Road. Morse and Max repair here after the examination of the corpse found at the nearby HAWORTH HOTEL. According to Honey (1998), the lessors (ST JOHN'S COLLEGE) threatened not to renew the lease in 1977 but were persuaded to do so after a petition from local residents. It is here that Morse reveals to Max that a word that he is always turned on by is 'UNBUTTONING' (ANNX: p80).[1]

Gardner, Dame Helen (1908-1986) A fellow of ST HILDA'S College, emeritus Merton Professor of English Literature, and editor of *The New Oxford Book of English Verse*. Morse hears her speak at a meeting of the OXFORD BOOK ASSOCIATION and she inspires him to revisit the *Four Quartets* of T.S. Eliot – which he had once committed to memory (JERI: pp28-29).

Gaudy BROWNE-SMITH recalls that the BURSAR always said at a Gaudy: "Let them have the good stuff first." (MILE: p37); it is also at a Gaudy in LONSDALE that Denis CORNFORD notices his wife (after Madeira, red wine, and gin) in a slightly compromising situation with Julian STORRS (NEIG: pp24-25). The Dean of LONSDALE is anxious to wrap up business matters in order to attend a gaudy (NICQ: p4).

George, The A pub 'past the railway station' in Oxford (WATC: p46). The landlady is Mrs MICHAELS. Its generous patrons raised £400 in aid of the Littlemore Charity for Mentally Handicapped Children.

George and Dragon An inn on the Edgware Road, London. Charles Franks lodged here in 1859 – wrongly recorded as 1869 in the record of the case (WNCH: p48).

George Street The location of the NEW THEATRE, the Department of Social Security (REMO: p217), the ABC CINEMA, and a printer of Parish Notes for ST FRIDESWIDE'S (SERV: p234). **Map D5**

Gideons International A Christian organisation, founded in 1899, which evangelises by placing bibles in the human traffic lanes and streams of life (particularly hotel rooms). Morse refreshes his memory of a biblical reference by recourse to a copy in one such room (MILE: pp219/220); a further copy of such a bible can be found in at least one room of the HAWORTH HOTEL (ANNX: p83); and yet another copy in a hotel just north of Russell Square, London (JWEL: p248). The Gideons appear to remain busy.

Gilbert, Albert Twin brother of Alfred. Both he and Alfred enlisted in the Royal Wiltshire Yeomanry in October 1939 and both were later promoted to corporal (MILE).

---

[1] Attributed by Morse to Philip Larkin, the poet, but as yet untraced. Larkin attended ST JOHN'S COLLEGE. See UNBUTTONING.

Gilbert, Alfred Twin brother of Albert (MILE). He was wounded (as was Albert) at the second battle of EL ALAMEIN. Of the twins, he is the more cultured and Emily Gilbert – his sister-in-law - suggests that had Albert and Alfred been together in Salzburg, the former would see *The Sound of Music* and the latter attend a MOZART concert (MILE: p219).

Gilbert, Emily Wife of Albert Gilbert and living in Berrywood Court in the Seven Sisters Road, London. Morse (even when giving her bad news) finds himself '... almost loving the woman who was weeping out her heart against him' (MILE: p208).

Gilbert, John Youngest of the Gilbert brothers. He was posted to North Africa in mid-1942 and died that year (MILE). How he died is not revealed until a good way into the case (but see SUICIDE).

Gilbert Removals It is a little unclear who owns this firm (one guesses a GILBERT or two) but it is clearly linked with BROOKS and GILBERT. The Removals firm are active in LONSDALE College (MILE: p140).

Gilels, Emil (1916-1985) A Russian pianist; his playing of Beethoven's Piano Sonata Opus 90 is fondly recalled by Paul MORRIS (SERV: p22).

Gin and tonic A popular drink combination found both in Oxford and beyond. Pedantically, the plural should be 'gins and tonics' (LBUS: p94; NICQ: p17; MILE: p57) or, when drunk by Americans, 'gins and tarnics' (SERV: p60). Brands of gin mentioned are Booth's and Gordon's (JWEL).

Glaister, John Author, with Edgar Rentoul, of *Medical Jurisprudence and Toxicology.* The bulky book can be found on the shelves in Morse's office (NICQ: p90) and, rather more surprisingly, on the shelves of OGLEBY (NICQ: p211).

Glenfiddich A brand of WHISKY. The merits of this drink are gently debated by Morse and Max in MILE (p73) while discussing the case in the BOAT INN. It was, apparently, once advertised as 'A Touch of the Malt' (JWEL: p8). Morse savours a large and satisfying swallow of the brand though discreetly placing the half-empty tumbler from the sight of Lewis (JWEL: p49) and is just about to take a nightcap of the brand at home when the phone rings (WOOD: p337). Both Eddie STRATTON and Sheila WILLIAMS consume 'considerable quantities' of this delightful drink (JWEL: p339) and Morse and Laura HOBSON do the same in his flat (WOOD: pp380-381). To encourage two hours of blissful sleep, Morse has been known to pour himself '... a goodly measure ...' (NEIG: p168). He has also been known to ask Lewis to stop outside Oddbins when he is running low on supplies (REMO: p144) – and purchases two bottles (not necessarily *just* because there is money off a double purchase) two pages later. Shortly before Morse's death, Lewis smuggles a couple of miniature Glenfiddichs into his hospital bed (p416) – and Morse is given the chance (which he takes) to have a final dram (p419).

Gloucester Green The location of the main Oxford bus depot. **Plate 26**, **Map D5**

Godberry, Joseph He was a soldier in the First World War and, many years later, became a LOLLIPOP man, living in the Oxford Road, KIDLINGTON. He is now (following being hit by a motorcycle in 1974) retired and in a home in COWLEY. When interviewed by Lewis, his recollection of the day on which Valerie TAYLOR disappeared may (or may not be) valuable in solving the case.

Golden Cross, The A pub off CORNMARKET. It is here that Morse memorably recalls that he had always 'believed that his mind functioned better after a few beers …' (SERV: p207).

Golden Rose, The A large and thatched public house in BEGBROKE; it offers a lounge bar and a garden (with the added attractions of a jovial-sounding landlord and an amply bosomed landlady).

Goose Green An area of land in WOLVERCOTE abutting the OXFORD CANAL. Eddie STRATTON passes through it on his way to the TROUT INN (JWEL: p339). There is no obvious link to the same-named area of conflict in the Falkland Islands. **Map B2**

Granada TV A firm providing rented television sets to, among others, John MAGUIRE. The company also used to make its own television programmes.

Granny Bonds The established nickname for index-linked savings certificates (CAIN: p225). Their introduction was originally restricted to those over retirement age.

Grapes, The A pub, since 1820, in GEORGE STREET. Ashley DAVIES had a fight here in his first year at University (CAIN: p149).

Great Clarendon Street A road leading from WALTON STREET through the heart of JERICHO. The buildings of the OXFORD UNIVERSITY PRESS run along much of its southern boundary. **Map C5**

Greats 'The Faculty of Literae Humaniores, the study of the Classics, Philosophy and Ancient History … the first examination is called Classical Honour Moderations or Mods, and final school is known as Greats'. (From Hibbert 1988 under Literae Humaniores). 'We are in the University of Oxford, at the marks-meeting of the seven examiners appointed for Greats' (MILE: p10). Dr BROWNE-SMITH is one of the seven members. Morse was examined in Greats '… on that bleak day some thirty years ago' (MILE: p62). As MILE is dated to 1980 this suggests a last year at the University of 1950 (but see the comments under the entry for Morse on *University* – where 1954 is preferred). Also see LITERAE HUMANIORES.

Great Western Hotel Found at PADDINGTON Station. Morse meets Mrs PALMER here (in the Brunel Bar). He enjoys the half-price drinks of Happy Hour and almost enjoys a very happy hour with Mrs Palmer (ANNX). His bladder seems to be in rude health – he drinks four pints before needing to visit the Gents (ANNX: p128). Phil ALDRICH arranges, unsuccessfully, to meet his daughter in the Brunel Bar at this hotel (JWEL: p194). Julian STORRS and Rachel JAMES also drink here; STORRS has half a pint of Smith's BITTER but it is not clear whether this is John's or Sam's (NEIG: p33).

Green, Mrs Charlady to Morse; she does Tuesday and Saturday mornings (WNCH: p3). It is she who discovers a sick Morse and calls an ambulance for him (spurred on, perhaps, by her recollection of how her husband died); she later visits Morse in hospital (p80). She has trouble with her feet and visits her chiropodist (though Morse would call that person a *kyropodist* (WNCH: p107).

Greenaway, Christine She is a 30-year old, slim, blonde divorcée and a librarian at the BODLEIAN (where she has been since for the last six years). She has a long history of desire to be a librarian (WNCH: p73) and, of course, one should be thankful that such people really do exist. She is a modestly active member of a number of organisations – CND, Greenpeace, the Royal Society for the Protection of Birds, and the Ramblers' Association among others, and lives in the village of Bletchington. She visits her father, Walter, in the John RADCLIFFE HOSPITAL and encounters Morse on the same ward (and eventually brings him the exciting *Insurance Guide and Hand-Book 1860*). Morse recalls her eyes as being '… almost as blue as his own …' (WNCH: p79).

Greenaway, Frank An upstairs neighbour, with Joyce, to Nicholas QUINN. He works nights in COWLEY, seems to support OXFORD UNITED, and brings Joyce a box of Black Magic chocolates, among other things, to celebrate her parturition (NICQ).

Greenaway, Joyce Married to Frank, she spends a fair amount of time (in Private Room 12 at the RADCLIFFE HOSPITAL) thinking about the name for their newly-born son.

Grosvenor Street A road in NORTH OXFORD and home to Simon HARRISON at number 5 (REMO: p356). The street is a little difficult to find (and bears no link to the Grosvenor Road that is south of North Hinksey).

Grove Street A road in SUMMERTOWN (and where a cobbler repairs Morse's shoes: WNCH: p81). **Map C3**

Guinness Brief mention is made of this drink in WEAR (p139) and JERI (p171). On a rare occasion, Morse and Lewis and Strange all drink (at least one pint) in the ROSIE O'GRADY (REMO: p188). Perhaps the Irish music has something to do with it.

H

Hamilton Road Running east from the BANBURY ROAD to the Cherwell (JWEL: p77). Sheila WILLIAMS lives here in a semi-detached house (JWEL: p83). **Map D2**

Hampton Poyle A village about a mile north east of KIDLINGTON. It seems to have been the scene of an unsolved murder (REMO: p18).

Hardinge, Dr Alan He is a small, neat man, a Fellow of LONSDALE College (with rooms in the front quad) and has recently lost his young daughter, Sarah, through a cycling accident on CUMNOR HILL (WOOD: p52) where he lives (p276). He is married to Lynne (once a librarian at the BODLEIAN) and their other daughter is at Durham University. He has had a sterling academic career – a double first in Natural Sciences and a PhD from CAMBRIDGE, and two years' research at Harvard (WOOD: p220).[1] But he does have a penchant for PORNOGRAPHY, or, as he prefers, "… a lifetime of sexual adventurism" (WOOD: p221).

Hardinge, Louisa She is not necessarily to be confused with Louisa Harding (MINOR) nor with Lynne Hardinge (see below). She is a guest at the BAY HOTEL (room 14) and meets (and entrances) Morse there; he rightly suspects that Louisa Hardinge is not her real name (and has his doubts about the address she gives - 16 Cathedral Mews, Salisbury – and her claim to run a model agency).[2] Her attractiveness, fondness for crosswords – she completes most of *The TIMES* in 20 minutes (WOOD: p14) – and susceptibility to drink make her an ideal target for Morse. Even on her brief acquaintance with Morse she is able to pronounce: "… judging from the amount of alcohol you get through you're probably never in your office much after opening time" (p47). See also Claire OSBORNE.

Hardinge, Lynne Wife of Alan, she is slim, grey-haired, and aged 50 years. After the death of her daughter, she throws herself into charity work for help the Aged, Meals on Wheels, Victim Support, and Cruse.[3] She is aware that her husband is not quite as faithful as, no doubt, he once promised he would be (WOOD: p286).

Hardy, Thomas (1840-1928) His novel, *Jude The Obscure*, is largely based in 'Christminster', otherwise known as Oxford. Morse appears to be well-versed in Hardy's novels and poetry (on one occasion quoting a chunk from *Tess of the d'Urbervilles* by heart (WNCH: 117); it is about the burial of the infant Sorrow, appears towards the end of Chapter 14, and is word-perfect. His recognition of Aldbrickham as Hardy's name for Reading and Spring Street as the address of

---

[1] His PhD thesis is entitled: 'The comparative body-weight of the great tit within the variable habitats of its north European distribution'. (WOOD: p223).

[2] Morse suggests this address is the Cathedral Close rather than Cathedral Mews (WOOD: p48) but offers no real evidence. See also REGIS.

[3] Cruse offers bereavement advice. While the name appears to be an acronym it does, in fact, originate in the widow's 'cruse' – a jar of oil which never ran out – and signifies that support will be given for as long as it is needed (*Kings 1,17*).

Jude and Sue Fawley (from *Jude the Obscure*) helps to establish the true identity of Mr and Mrs Smith (ANNX: p99). The Smiths own a book called *The Landscape of Thomas Hardy* (p160). Morse receives an anonymous letter (ANNX: p243) wherein the female sender expresses her love for him; she has been reading a biography of Hardy (and mentions that fact); Sarah JONSTONE has, by reception, a copy of Michael Millgate's *Thomas Hardy – A Biography* (OUP 1982) (ANNX: p281) though there is no guarantee that she is the only admirer of both Morse and Hardy. She may be embarrassed at her misspelling of 'embarassed'. An extract from his poem *The Convergence of the Twain* (about the sinking of the *SS Titanic*) appears as the heading to Chapter 56 of JWEL. A longer extract (from *The Photograph*) appears at NEIG: p89 as Gerrard, Morse's barber, recites the last verse. There is a time and a place to rehearse tired jokes about Wessex girls; but not here.

Harrison, Frank Husband of Yvonne and a Portfolio and Investment Manager at the Swiss Helvetia Bank in London. He has a company flat in Pavilion Road (REMO).

Harrison, Sarah[1] Daughter to Frank and Yvonne and a junior consultant in the Diabetes Centre at the RADCLIFFE INFIRMARY (where she is interviewed by Lewis in the Blood-Testing Room). She is slim, in her late twenties, a brunette, lives in JERICHO, and has a pleasant singing voice (REMO). For a while, Morse is under her care.

Harrison, Simon Son to Frank and Yvonne and a proof-reader (sic) at the Daedalus Press in Oxford. He contracted meningitis when a 6 year old (his parents then living in Church Lane, somewhere in Gloucestershire) and this led to irreversible and substantial deafness (with a little more hearing in his left ear than the right).

Harrison, Yvonne (c1949-1997)[2] A nurse (working on Ward 7C at the JR2) and once living in LOWER SWINSTEAD (in a prestigious house called *The Windhovers*). A phone call prompts the second investigation (in 1998) into her death (in 1997). Her extensive circle of acquaintances (she had once, for example, nursed Morse and called him 'a sensitive soul') provides much meat for the REMO case.

Harvey Clinic, The Opened in 1971 in the BANBURY ROAD, this private clinic employs Dawn CHARLES as a receptionist. It specialises in the diagnosis and treatment of cancer and its 25th anniversary was attended by the Lord Mayor of Oxford in, one hopes, 1996.

Haworth Hotel Originally called the Three Swans Guest House, this extended building may be found between the BANBURY ROAD and the WOODSTOCK ROAD (ANNX: p18) some 12 minutes walk down from MIDDLE WAY (p30). The newly built annexe appears to be in the Banbury Road itself (pp54/95) and the Hotel may also be there – Margaret BOWMAN drives

---

[1] Bishop (2006) has her as Sarah Harris.
[2] Her gravestone, reproduced in REMO (p67), gives her date of birth as 1947. It may be examined at St Mary's in the village of her residence. Harrison is recorded as saying, in 1997, that: "I'll be forty-eight this Thursday". Further, she is identified as a '48-year old' in a report of her death (p14). Perhaps she lied about her age.

past it on her way to ST GILES' from Ewert Place (ANNX: p205). It is now owned and managed by John and Catherine BINYON. Morse does not appreciate their taste in décor; he finds purple carpets and reproduction paintings (Renoir's *Les nues dans l'herbe*, for example) distasteful (ANNX: p60). It has not been possible to find a reproduction of that reproduction for reproduction here. The hotel has expanded its trade by themed breaks. The one held on New Year's Eve (1985) offers a variety of trademarked games (Monopoly, Scrabble[3], and Cluedo), a fancy dress dinner party, *Auld Lang Syne*, and a murder. The Hotel is compared (unfavourably, of course) to the Waldorf Astoria (ANNX: p194).

Hayfield Wharf See HYTHE BRIDGE STREET.

Headington Effectively, a suburb of Oxford (to the north east) and home to the Lewis family and the John RADCLIFFE HOSPITAL. It has a technical college (WEAR: p290) where lip-reading classes are run (NICQ: p80). One may also find one of the many WHITE HART pubs here. Headington Hill, a sub-suburb, is mentioned in WOOD (p346) and is the location of the WEA classes attended by Josephine PALMER (LBUS). **Map G4-G5**

Headley Way Part of the Oxford ring road and part of the journey by ambulance when Morse is taken into hospital (WNCH: p4). He also gives Ellie SMITH – in a motoring rather than an athletic sense – a lift involving a turn here (CAIN: p255). **Map F4-G5**

Height, Monica M. MA. A linguist and the only female graduate staff member of the SYNDICATE. She was married at the age of eighteen and lives in a bungalow in OLD MARSTON with her daughter Sally. It is not clear if she ever gets to the forthcoming performance of *The Messiah* for which she has a programme (NICQ: p155).

Hertford College Founded in 1282 but dissolved and recreated on a number of occasions. Alumni include Jonathan Swift and John Donne; Thomas (MINOR) is a college member. Also see NEW COLLEGE LANE. **Plate 27, Map D5**

High, The Probably the grandest street in Oxford, leading from the CARFAX tower to the PLAIN. The High also affords entrance to the Covered Market (where Strange has extolled the bargain of cheap drinking glasses; REMO: p24). **Map D5-E5**

Historic Cities of England Tour An organisation that provides a guide (John ASHENDEN), deals with the hiring of guest speakers, arranges accommodation, and plans itineraries for tourists from (at least) America. On the occasion of the JWEL case, the tour has moved to Oxford, the accommodation is the RANDOLPH HOTEL, and the guest speakers include DOWNES, KEMP, and WILLIAMS. The party of tourists – eighteen women, nine men (and of these, three registered husband-and-wife combinations) – are, indeed, all Americans (JWEL: p16). The group is rich, elderly, and from what has been called the *abcde* brigade – alcohol,

---

[3] The contest for the Mastership of LONSDALE is ironically described as crossing swords in '...a mighty game of Scrabble...' (NEIG: p216).

bridge, cigarettes, detective-fiction, and ecology (p9). Their itinerary is London-Cambridge-Oxford-Stratford-upon-Avon-Bath-Winchester. The Tour Company has its headquarters in Belgravia (JWEL: p214).

Hobson, Dr Laura She is a pathologist working for the police, has a temporary flat in JERICHO, and works as a protégée of, and an assistant to, Max; she has only known him some 6 weeks before she discovers his (still live) body.[4] It is she who telephones Morse with the news. She has a husky, north-country accent, appears to be attracted to older men (even having had a mildly erotic dream about Max), is in her early thirties, and objects to being called 'dear', or 'darling'. It is only revealed in the CALL case (p260) that she is blonde. She drives a bright-red Metro car (CAIN: p311). Her grammar ("I am she") impresses Morse (WOOD: p184) and he is immediately attracted to her (as she may be to Morse) but her use of the word 'exited' – to mean 'died' – causes Morse to wince (p281); she is certainly anxious to gain Brownie-points on her first real enquiry (p255).[5] Unlike Max, she is prepared to give a reasoned estimate for the time of a death (p326) and does so again in a report in the CAIN case (p102 – which also reveals her past interest in the martial arts). She reports (but not in person) on a murder in the NEIG case (p127); on this occasion, Morse refers to her as "our distinguished pathologist" (perhaps with a hint of sarcasm). She reports on a second death in the same case but Morse prefers the word 'instantaneous' to her choice of 'instant' (p259). At one time, Morse agrees with Lewis's description of her as a "smasher" (WOOD: p283). She makes a brief appearance in REMO (pp155-157; 189) and another in an earlier case (STOR: p169/173) when Morse has ambivalent amatory feelings for her. In the CALL case she raises the question of which came first, the chicken or the egg. Morse's suggestion by way of reply matches that given under LITERARY CURIOSITIES.

Holmes, Elizabeth Jane The mother of Roy and a wheelchair user. As Elizabeth Jane Thomas she was something of an athlete. It is, at first, a little unclear what her previous marital and maternal status has been though some detail is subsequently provided by DIXON's notes (REMO: p320).

Holmes, Mycroft The elder brother of Sherlock HOLMES and seen by some to be the greater in mental capacity (though by all to be the less active). Morse is compared favourably to him by ASHENDEN (JWEL: p215).

Holmes, Roy A 15 year old and living at 29A Witney Street, BURFORD. He attends Burford Secondary School, is aptly described as 'appalling' (REMO: p269), and unwittingly shares a birthday with HOUSMAN (the 26th of March).

---

[4] WOOD p178 gives 'protegée'. No, the heavens will not shake nor the earth shudder but please recall just how (very) pedantic Morse could be.
[5] Brownie-point – this is not hyphenated in Chambers (2003), which gives 'a notional good mark or commendation for doing well'. The New Shorter Oxford (1993) suggests its origin in the Brownie (junior Girl Guide) movement; colleagues have suggested a cruder origin (without foundation) – from 'brown-nosing' as in 'he was so far up his boss's backside' …

Holmes, Sherlock (1854-1957) The first consulting detective and, some might argue, the greatest detective ever. His exploits are now the stuff of legend. His name has become common currency – for example, after Morse accurately analyses the history and life of a beautiful dietitian (unbeknownst to her, he has inside information), she asks: "Is your name Sherlock Holmes?" (WOOD: p78). His appeal is wide reaching (being read, for example, by Gaye McFEE). See, in particular both Bunson (1994) and Tracy (1977) for encyclopaedias which detail his cases and biography; see also Ashley (1997) for an amusing collection of 26 pastiches and, most usefully, a comprehensive list of other such works and collections (pp494-517). Baring-Gould (1975) wrote what many regard as the 'standard' life. The debate on whether or not Holmes attended Oxford or CAMBRIDGE University is briefly rehearsed in Hibbert (1988) under 'Holmes' but with sufficient references for the interested reader to follow – one of which, apparently, argues for ST JOHN'S, Morse's old college. Morse has many passages of Holmesian dialogue off by heart including 'the curious incident of the dog' (from *Silver Blaze*) with which he somewhat baffles Lewis (SERV: p225-6). He is also (of course) aware of the 'trick' in *A Case of Identity* (REMO: p93) and jokes to Lewis, while seriously ill in hospital, that he hopes his presence there is just a 'case of mis-identity' (REMO: p412). A Holmesian pastiche (*A Case of Mis-Identity*) appears in Dexter (1994). Morse has had occasion to rein in his train of thought with "Steady, Sherlock!" (NICQ: p170). Also see John WATSON.

Holywell Cemetery This may be found next to St. Cross Church in St. Cross Road. Among those buried here are Walter Pater, James Blish, Maurice Bowra, Kenneth Tynan, H.V.D. Dyson, Theodore and Sibley, John Stainer, and Jimmy BOWDEN (JWEL: pp12, 51). Kenneth Grahame is also buried here; his tombstone reads: '... who passed the river on the 6th July 1932, leaving childhood and literature through him the more blest for all time' (p52). Morse is somewhat touched by a quatrain that he finds in the cemetery: 'Life divided us from each other, Depriving friend of friend, Accept this leave-taking – with my tears – For it is all I have to bring'. There is every good chance that these are the words left by ASHENDEN at the grave of BOWDEN (JWEL: pp52/346). **Map E5**

Holywell Music Room This room, for music, is in HOLYWELL STREET and is referred to, briefly, in both JWEL (pp50/346) and CAIN (p78).

Holywell Street The location of the KING'S ARMS (WNCH: p78); other brief references may be found in JWEL (p103) and, as 'Holywell', in NICQ (p24). **Plate 28, Map D5**

Homelessness Not a recurring theme of the WORKS but there a number of references, particularly in SERV which mentions the Church Army Hostel (p36). Those interested are referred to Dexter (2004) or, rather, the contributors who join him in that book. A certain Ronald Armitage – idle, dirty, feckless, cold, hungry, semi-drunken – appears in ANNX pp216-218.

Horlicks According to its makers 'a delicious and nourishing malted food drink which can make you sleep better at night'. Morse is an occasional user of the product (combined with alcohol unless when hospitalised) but his sleep is far more often induced by alcohol alone.

Horse and Jockey A pub on the corner of the WOODSTOCK ROAD and OBSERVATORY STREET (JERI: p134).

Horse and Trumpet A pub on a corner of the WOODSTOCK ROAD and used by certain staff from the SYNDICATE. QUINN originally mishears its name as the Whoreson Strumpet (NICQ: p28). Morse intends to visit the pub having first enquired of Lewis "What swill do they slop out ..." (NICQ: p103).[6]

Hospital A number of such institutions appear in the WORKS. See, in particular, the entries for the CHURCHILL HOSPITAL, the RADCLIFFE HOSPITAL, the RADCLIFFE INFIRMARY, and the OXFORDSHIRE HEALTH AUTHORITY. The Littlemore is mentioned in NICQ, the Oxford Eye hospital in REMO, and Swindon General in MILE (p236). Brenda JOSEPHS works, for a short time, at the Shrewsbury Hospital and Lucy DOWNES spends some time, in bed in the St Pancras Hospital.

Housman, A. E. (1859-1936) Housman (the classicist) ended his days at Trinity College, CAMBRIDGE where he was, according to Howarth (1978), 'the greatest textual critic of the day' (p88); Sparrow has, in his introduction to the *Collected Poems*: '... at his death in 1936 he was perhaps the most learned Latin scholar in the world' (Housman 1956; p7); and Morse recalls him as being the "... greatest Latinist of the twentieth century" (JWEL: p70). The Master of LONSDALE is recorded as saying (of BROWNE-SMITH) that "... there was never a man, apart from Housman, who was so contemptuous about any solecism in English usage" (MILE: p52). Lines of his verse are obviously very well known to Morse and appearances in the WORKS are far from rare. For example, Chapter 4 of JERI opens with:

> 'I lay me down and slumber And every morn revive.
> Whose is the night-long breathing
> That keeps a man alive?'
> *More Poems (XIII)*

Chapter 47 of WOOD is headed by a verse from *A Shropshire Lad* (XLI); and Chapter 40 of WEAR has:

> 'For she and I were long acquainted
> And I knew all her ways.'

Chapter 44 of NEIG has lines from XXI. The following lines from the same poem (XLI):

> 'And like a skylit water stood
> The bluebells in the azured wood.'

These lines are ones that Morse has long carried in his mental baggage (WOOD: pp264-265), and also appear as the heading to Chapter 9 of CAIN and a postcard in NEIG (p69) shows '... a pool of azured bluebells.'

---

[6] The phrase 'whoreson strumpet' may be found in some translations of Don Quixote (Part II Chapter 13).

Morse recalls the line '… the orange band of eve' (from *More Poems XXXIII*) in REMO (p359) and an extract from *A Shropshire Lad* heads Chapter 76 of REMO. The couplet:

> 'And wide apart lie we, my love,
> And seas between the twain.'

is found on the back of a postcard (STOR: p175) and Morse remembers further lines from the same poem. It is from *Last Poems XXVI*.

Denis CORNFORD's *slight* misquotation of a Housman verse slightly worries Morse (NEIG: pp280-281). A further quotation is the heading to Chapter 9 of REMO and another to that of Chapter 54. Housman, like Morse, failed his GREATS at ST JOHN'S COLLEGE (JWEL: p70; NEIG: p305); unlike Morse, he was later to become (1911) the Kennedy Professor of Latin at CAMBRIDGE University and a Fellow at Trinity College there. Housman is recorded as saying: "This great College, of this ancient University, has seen some strange sights. It has seen Wordsworth drunk and Porson sober." ANDREWS recalls these words when talking to Morse about BROWNE-SMITH (MILE: p117). The quotation is recorded in Chesterton (1936: p283) and he has it continue: "And here am I, a better poet than Porson, and a better scholar than Wordsworth, betwixt and between." According to Morse, Housman had composed some of his loveliest lyrics while walking around the Backs at Cambridge after a couple of lunchtime beers (CAIN: p120). Morse has a first edition (1896) of *A Shropshire Lad* (WNCH: pp169-170). Assuming it is the London edition (published by Kegan Paul Trench Trubner) it could sell for well in excess of £2,000. If Morse has a signed copy, the value rises to some £40,000 at today's prices. Although they are not individually listed, Morse has an '… earnestly assembled collection of first editions …' (NEIG: p305).

There is a reference to the dish Barbue Housman (WOOD: p32). According to the very helpful Housman Society, the official recipe is to use brill or turbot (or any white fish – but turbot preserves the 'barbue' element), and make a stock of white wine, mushrooms, fines herbes, a little butter, and the bones of the fish. Strain the stock and poach the fish in this. Remove the fish and keep warm while the stock reduces and make a sauce Mornay. Lightly butter a serving dish, pour on a layer of the sauce Mornay, and place the fish on this (arranging small boiled potatoes around it). Pour the reduced stock over the fish and cover with the rest of the sauce Mornay. Lightly brown in the oven or under a grill. Eat and enjoy. See also The REMORSEFUL DAY. **Plate 29**

HQ A shorthand for KIDLINGTON Police Headquarters (where Morse is based). **Plate 30**

Hythe Bridge Street The location of the terminus of the OXFORD CANAL and a main route into Oxford from the west and the train station. The terminus of the canal was formerly known as Hayfield Wharf (WNCH: p58). **Map C5**

Plate 25 (Left) Folly Bridge (p64).
Plate 26 (Right) Gloucester Green (p69).

Plate 27 (Left) Part of Hertford College – the Bridge (p73).
Plate 28 (Right) Holywell Street (p75).

Plate 29 (Left) A. E. Housman (p77).
Plate 30 (Right) Thames Valley Police Headquarters in Kidlington (p77).

I

Iffley Road To be found running south from Oxford and notable for two reasons – Roger Banister ran the first sub-four-minute mile at the University Athletics Track there in 1954 and Morse took a 'flighty nurse' back to his digs a few years earlier when they enjoyed WHISKY (then, his favourite drink NICQ: p152) and, apparently, some companionship. **Map E6-E7**

Inside Story, The Morse and Lewis are called to investigate the murder of, according to Lewis, a "lovely-looking girl" – in fact, a young woman who has written a short story which is reproduced in the notes to the case. The characters in this piece of (interesting) fiction are not recorded in this Companion. The anagrammatically inspired Rex DE LINCTO makes a brief appearance. **(STOR).** *Main personnel* Paul BAYLEY, Sheila POSTER.

Interpol The largest police organisation in the world, founded in 1923, and currently with some 186 member countries. Morse contacts the organisation to thank them for their assistance in returning a fugitive from justice (JERI: p277).

In-tray Morse's in-tray often held material that helped to progress criminal investigation (such as reports from the forensic laboratory) but it usually held such uncongenial items as *The Drug Problem in Britain*, *The Police and the Public*, and *The Statistics for Crimes of Violence in Oxfordshire* (LBUS: p78). The contents of his tray led him to suspect that some 95% of the written word was never read by anyone.

ITV The accepted abbreviation for Independent Television (on which Morse has appeared when making an appeal for information in the case of the murdered Sylvia KAYE). One of their flagship programmes is *News at Ten* (WEAR: p205).

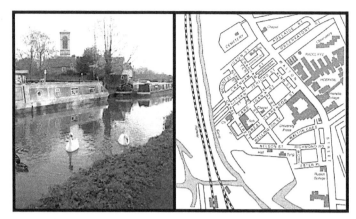

Plate 31 (Left) Jericho from the canal (showing the tower of St. Barnabas) (p82).
Plate 32 (Right) Map of Jericho (p82).

Plate 33 (Left) Jesus College from Turl Street (p82).
Plate 34 (Right) Keble College – the Chapel (p85).

Plate 35 (Left) The King's Arms: '… that square cream-painted hostelry …' (NEIG: p293) (p86).
Plate 36 (Right) The Lamb and Flag (p89).

J

Jackson, George (Alfred) A keen fisherman who (for money – which he banks with the Post Office) assists a number of his near neighbours with minor building jobs (including brickwork). As with so many men in the WORKS, he also has an interest in pornographic material. He is 66 years old and lives, for a time, in CANAL REACH. (JERI). Could he have caught two rainbow trout (JERI: p42) with equipment from the Walton Tackle Shop (p188); could he really have caught them in the OXFORD CANAL?

Jackson's Oxford Journal A source for the case recorded in DENISTON (1978). Details concerning this publication can be found under Newspapers in Hibbert (1988).

Jaguar A make of car; the 2.4 Mk II six-cylinder model (from 1960, registration 248 RPA) is now irretrievably linked with Morse. The reason for changing the faithful LANCIA is not entirely clear but the Jaguar has certainly become Morse's car of choice in the February 1990 DODO case (p81) and in the slightly later JWEL case (where it is described as 'red' on p268). It remains his car in subsequent cases (confirmed by any number of references e.g. WOOD: p161) but sometimes appears as 'maroon' (e.g. WOOD: p12; CAIN: p212; NEIG: p66). It has a car-phone (NEIG: p142) and is off the road for repairs in the MYST case (p46). A Jaguar kills AINLEY (WEAR: p19) and Lewis, rarely not concentrating on his driving, is blasted by a Jaguar's imperious horn (MILE: p183).

James, Rachel She is a freelance physiotherapist born in 1965 (the year that British Rail was formed); she is on a train when thinking of her age.[1] Her ponytail hairstyle has dramatically unfortunate consequences. She lives at 17 BLOXHAM DRIVE (NEIG) and works with a partner at their Oxford Physiotherapy Centre – in a 1901 red-brick house in the WOODSTOCK ROAD.

Jarman, Mabel A widow with two married children. She lives alone (in a semi-detached house) in YARNTON but takes some comfort and company from her television set. She is one of the last people to see Sylvia KAYE alive (LBUS).

JCR See JUNIOR COMMON ROOM.

Jericho An area to the west of WALTON STREET and bounded by the OXFORD CANAL. One learns much of its history in JERI. The area is characterised by mid-nineteenth century terraced houses, originally populated by general labourers (and those who worked for the OXFORD UNIVERSITY PRESS). The area was a centre of activity by the OXFORD MOVEMENT and an early lodger was Jude Fawley (from *Jude the Obscure*, by Thomas HARDY, wherein the area is known as Beersheba). The area is certainly not unknown to the

---

[1] NEIG: p29 gives her year of birth as 1965. On p66 she is described as being 'twenty-nine'. As the NEIG case took place in 1996, clearly there has been a (very) non-essential misunderstanding somewhere.

police – apart from their activity described in JERI there has also been trouble with squatters (SERV: p118). Some of the streets and buildings appear under their own names elsewhere in this Companion; others are simply listed here. For example, Wellington and Nelson Streets (JERI; p20), Juxon Street (p21), and Victor Street (p149). There is a synagogue in Richmond Road (p21) and ST BARNABAS church (**Plate 31**); The Residents' Working Club, The Jericho Testing Laboratories, and Welsh and Cohen (dentists) are all mentioned (p192).

Further places of interest are Cardigan Street and Albert Street (p225), the Jericho Clinic (p248), and the Jericho Tackle Shop (p294). According to the WORKS, some mystery surrounds the origin of the name of Jericho (JERI: p21); Hibbert (1988) claims it is from the Jericho Gardens which lay to the west of the RADCLIFFE INFIRMARY (which only gets one so far). Jericho is liberally festooned with double yellow lines (p23). **Plate 32**, **Map C4-C5**

Jericho Arms A regular haunt of George TAYLOR and where he enjoys membership of the darts team. Other (and more occasional) customers are Joe Morley, Alf, and Len. Outside the inn, the legend 'Tarry ye at Jericho until your beards be grown' (referred to in JERI: p170) used to be seen; a photograph of it may be found in Yurdan (2009; p36).

Jericho Street A street in (one is happy to record) JERICHO (JERI: p22). **Map C5**

Jesus College A CAMBRIDGE college, founded in 1496 (JWEL: p99). Coleridge attended the college but, like HOUSMAN and Morse (at ST JOHN'S), left without a degree.

Jesus College An Oxford college, founded in 1571 and with a strong Welsh connection. T.E. Lawrence graduated in 1907 and DOWNES many years later (JWEL: p98). **Plate 33, Map D5**

Jewel That Was Ours, The A death occurs shortly after a party of American tourists arrive at the RANDOLPH. Superintendent BELL would normally have jurisdiction over the case but he is short staffed and requests that Chief Superintendent Strange uses Morse. One of the tourists is the owner of the ancient WOLVERCOTE TONGUE, which is to be presented to Dr KEMP of the ASHMOLEAN. The tongue disappears and a second body is discovered in the river; Morse seeks to establish a link between the first death, the disappearance, and the second death. A fair amount is revealed about the attractions of Oxford, a little about the affliction of deafness, what some Americans did during the Second World War, and something of the love lives of academic (and other) Oxonians. Quotations head the Chapters and Lilian Cooper (of whom little is known or has been discovered) wrote the poem from which the title has been taken. A helpful map of Oxford is included in the notes of the case. See, in particular, HISTORIC CITIES. (JWEL). *Main personnel* ALDRICH, ASHENDEN, the DOWNES, the KEMPS, ROSCOE, the STRATTONS, Sheila WILLIAMS.

John Radcliffe See the entries under RADCLIFFE.

Johnson, DCI Harold He is a recently-married member of the THAMES VALLEY CID and was once the lead officer in the WOOD case. His passing of the SWEDISH MAIDEN verses (on Strange's instructions) to *The TIMES* leads to much activity on what was almost a dormant investigation. Johnson explains all (well, not quite all) about the 1991 disappearance of Karin Eriksson to Strange (WOOD: pp56-72). There is, at first, some bad blood between Johnson and Morse but sweetness and light prevail (pp284-285). He remains interested in the case – so interested, in fact, that he discovers another body. He holidays in North Wales and drives a Maestro car (WOOD: p39). See also Sergeant WILKINS.

Johnson, Malcolm He is a professional burglar, a drinker of Beamish (for breakfast), a consumer of PORNOGRAPHY, and useful to Morse for the first of these attributes (NEIG). Morse, somewhat bending the law, arranges with him for a burglary (pp163-165). His nickname of 'JJ' arose from his accidental drinking, while young, of some Jeyes Fluid – a brand of lavatory cleaner. He also has a part to play in the REMO case (pp180-182) where he is described as being in his late forties and a car thief.

Jonstone, Sarah A woman of some forty summers (in 1985) who works at the HAWORTH HOTEL and lives in MIDDLE WAY. While first appointed as the receptionist, she has now taken on a number of managerial duties which include dealing with correspondence; she is well aware that letters beginning, for example, 'Dear Madam' should not be signed off with 'Yours sincerely' (ANNX: p46).

Jordan Hill The scene of a police interview (REMO: p305). There is a Jordan Hill Road (and a like-named bus station) off the northern stretch of the BANBURY ROAD. **Map C1**

Josephs, Brenda A soberly attractive woman in her mid- or late-thirties (SERV: p6) married to Harry; they live together in Portmeadow Drive WOLVERCOTE. She works as a nurse, originally at the RADCLIFFE INFIRMARY and, for reasons too explanatory to include here, latterly at Shrewsbury General Hospital.

Josephs, Harry Aged 50 and Warden to the Rev. Lionel LAWSON (SERV), found guilty of a drink-driving offence early in 1977 (and banned), and a former captain in the Royal Marine Commandos (and he still has the tie to prove it). Harry has been made redundant from a job with the Inland Revenue, worked for a short while for a chemist in SUMMERTOWN, but now spends much of his time following the horses – even backing 'Poor Old Harry' at Lingfield Park (SERV: p16).

Jowett Place A street somewhere east of the centre of Oxford and past the shops along the COWLEY ROAD. At number 14 live, in separate flats, Paul BAYLEY and Sheila POSTER (STOR). It cannot be too far along the Cowley Road – Morse walks from it to the BROAD (p177) and he is not one to exercise (even gently) to excess. **Map F6**

JR1 The first building of the John RADCLIFFE HOSPITAL; it covers women's services and neonatology (CAIN: p256).

JR2 A common name for the John RADCLIFFE HOSPITAL. '… Morse drove up to the J.R.2 in Headington …' (JERI: p231) is a rare exception from the more usual 'JR2'.

Junior Common Room This may be literally and physically a 'common room' (for the use of undergraduates) or a group existing to represent the interest of undergraduates. At CAMBRIDGE University, the phrase (sometimes) used is Junior *Combination* Room.

K

Kaye, Dorothy Her husband works on the night-shift at the COWLEY car plant; their daughter is Sylvia KAYE. The family live in a neat three-bedroom semi-detached house in Jackdaw Court, a few minutes from the WOODSTOCK ROAD (LBUS).

Kaye, Sylvia A young girl and a blonde; her body is discovered in the car park of the BLACK PRINCE. Her likely murder (and possible rape) is the first case to be investigated by Morse and Lewis in tandem. She had worked for the TOWN AND GOWN ASSURANCE COMPANY as a copy typist (LBUS).

Keble College Morse drives past here on one occasion (WOOD: p186) and has also been known to walk in its vicinity (CAIN: p119). An undergraduate from this college (who sings the counter-tenor parts from the Handel operas like an angel) provides the piano accompaniment to a production of *The Mikado* in WYTHAM (WOOD: p272); PC KERSHAW gained a First here. **Plate 34, Map D5**

Keble Road Almost traversed by both Brenda BROOKS (CAIN: p109) and Howard BROWN (JWEL: p207); and almost traversed by Morse as well (REMO: p313). Nobody seems to walk along it. **Map D5**

Kemp, Marion She is confined to a wheelchair following an accident when her husband (Theodore) was driving and in which a thirty-five-year-old woman was killed; Marion was pregnant at the date of the crash (1988) and lost both the child she was carrying and the use of her legs. She is rumoured to have come from wealth (JWEL: p79) and this may, of course, have been a factor in her marriage to the less than pleasant Theodore (though he does bring her a cup of OVALTINE and a digestive biscuit; p81).

Kemp, Dr Theodore S. MA, DPhil Oxon, The possessor of a Vandyke beard and a lisping accent; also '… artistic, flamboyant, highbrow, selfish, aloof, rakish …' (JWEL: p78). He is the Keeper of Anglo-Saxon and Mediaeval Antiquities at the ASHMOLEAN and expects to receive the WOLVERCOTE TONGUE on its behalf. He lives with his wife Marion in a ground-floor flat at 6 Cherwell Lodge, WATER EATON ROAD (**Map D2**). Morse is somewhat unimpressed by "we-are-an-Oxford man" Kemp (JWEL: p58) and calls him an "inflated bladder of wind and piss" (p61). He is rumoured to have fathered several illegitimate offspring.

Kempis Street To be found somewhat west of CARFAX, a road of 'quietly senescent terraced houses' (WEAR: p133) – one of which houses BAINES. **Map D5**

Kershaw, PC An officer with the THAMES VALLEY force. He has a First in History from KEBLE (REMO: p274) and one guesses that he will be marked for promotion or a transfer to the CID as a DC.

Kidlington A satellite of Oxford and some 5 miles to the north. As well as being the location of the THAMES VALLEY POLICE HQ (where Morse, Lewis, and Strange are based) it also houses a small police station (and its own History Society – NEIG: p340). Mr Evans (MINOR) attends the Kidlington Health Centre (NICQ: p109) as does Paul MORRIS (SERV: p155). Morse encourages Lewis to buy him some second-class stamps ("... no need to go wild, is there?") at the sub post-office here (STOR: p217).

Kidlington Road Unsurprisingly, a road leading between Oxford and KIDLINGTON and traversed a good number of times by Morse and Lewis. It is called the Kidlington Road in SERV (p17) but is more often known as either the BANBURY ROAD or the Oxford Road.

Kilkearnan A small town in Connemara with 14 pubs and only one road (the High Street). Morse, one guesses, feels rather at home (WNCH). It has a large cemetery, which overlooks BERTNAGHBOY BAY.

Kilroy A name found in the phrase 'Kilroy was here' (a popular example of graffiti, commonly assumed to have originated with American troops during the Second World War). The character is often shown peeking over a wall and has also been known as 'Chad' in Britain. (WEAR: p3).

King Charles, The '(Morse) seldom passed through the village without enjoying a jug of ale at the King Charles.' (WEAR: p22). The village is WOLVERCOTE.

King's Arms A pub on the corner of HOLYWELL STREET and Parks Road, allegedly visited by Donald MARTIN (NICQ: p199), certainly by six members of the marks-meeting panel for GREATS (MILE: p12), and also certainly by Christine GREENAWAY (WNCH: p78). Morse offers to buy one of the BODLEIAN curators a drink next time they met there (MILE: p122) and ASHENDEN enjoys a pint of Flower's BITTER in the back bar on his return from HOLYWELL CEMETERY (JWEL: p53) – and had Morse known, he would have been quietly proud of his choice. Indeed, Morse has a pint of Flower's himself there while thinking of Sheila WILLIAMS (JWEL: p346) and while on a health kick has but two pints and a vegetable lasagne (NEIG: p293). It is clear that the landlord (David) knows him. The CORNFORDs live near enough to be regular visitors (NEIG). Morse enjoys several pints of Best Bitter here with a number of Oxford dons while discussing burglaries (WATC). **Plate 35**

King's Arms (Dorchester) Morse spends the last three days of his 1992 holiday here and uses the time to explore the area made so memorable by HARDY. He starts (naturally enough) in Casterbridge (Dorchester itself) and on foot but then drives past Max Gate (Hardy's house and one mile east) and Talbothays (the dairy in *Tess of the d'Urbervilles*) towards Wool, passing through Moreton (WOOD: p85).

King's Arms (Summertown) This pub may be found in the BANBURY ROAD. McCLURE often has his Sunday lunch here (CAIN: p14) though not on the day of his death. Even though the pub is 'open all day' (p54), Morse declines Lewis's invitation to a drink here (he has just heard some bad news about PHILLOTSON's wife). Honey has: '... the exterior is attractive and at night is floodlit giving a warm inviting feeling.' (1998: p74). Morse has a 'Lewis-purchased pint' here in the GOLD case (p15).

King's Weir A popular fishing location on the Thames and one used by Simon ROWBOTHAM and George WESTERBY (MILE: pp154 and 183). It is a few hundred yards north of the TROUT INN and at the far western end of Duke's Cut – which links the Thames (or Isis) to the OXFORD CANAL.

Kipling, (Joseph) Rudyard (1865-1936) Poet and author (along with *much* else) of Morse's favourite short story, *Love-o'-Women* (WEAR: p165; shown there as *Love O' Women*). Apart from demonstrating that he knows that it was published in the nineteenth rather than the twentieth century (1893 to be exact), he also discusses the story with Sheila WILLIAMS (JWEL: p134-135) and agrees that the soul is rotten when one can't get drunk. Quotes from two Kipling poems form the headings to Chapters 7 and 38 of ANNX. While surveying the front living-room of 17 BLOXHAM DRIVE, Morse notices a copy of Craig Raine's *A Choice of Kipling's Prose*. This selection includes *They* (which Morse appreciates as the work of a genius but never fully understood himself), *On Greenhow Hill*, and *Love-o'-Women* (shown accurately as hyphenated in the notes to the case: NEIG: p111). And Morse confirms, to himself, that this last short story is the greatest in the English language.

Kleenex A brand of tissue paper (ANNX: p84). Only included here rather than in MINOR as the sort of name that one imagines Morse would not be best pleased with.

Plate 37 (Left) A Lancia Flavia saloon (1969) (p89).
Plate 38 (Right) In Woodstock, a bus heads for Oxford; the bus in LBUS was red (p89).

Plate 39 (Left) Only the gates to Lucy's Ironworks remain (p101).
Plate 40 (Right) Magdalen Tower (p103).

Plate 41 (Left) Magdalene College (Cambridge) (p103).
Plate 42 (Right) The Martyrs' Memorial (p105).

L

Lady Margaret Hall An Oxford college founded in 1878 for women (but since open to men). Anne SCOTT was here (JERI: pp9/55) and an unnamed girl on a train wears the college scarf (ANNX: p146). **Map D4**

Lamb and Flag There are two Oxford pubs of this name but the one in CAIN (p109) is that in ST GILES'. The pub is owned by ST JOHN'S COLLEGE and retains many original features (such as uneven floors). There is no official record of Morse having drunk here but its proximity to his old college (a matter of yards if not feet), and its central location, strongly suggest that he has done so (and on much more than one occasion). **Plate 36**

Lancaster Gardens An address in London known to Jennifer COLEBY.

Lancia 'The faithful old Lancia' (LBUS: 176) is Morse's car of choice, being both powerful and reliable (and relatively economical at 300 miles per tank of fuel). It is usually garaged at his flat in NORTH OXFORD and taxed by Morse at the Post Office in SUMMERTOWN (WNCH: p199). Lewis remarks: "He's got a Lancia. He's had a Lancia ever since I've known him." (MILE: p176) and is impressed by the car's road-holding qualities (WNCH: p233). It is a little difficult, for some reason, to avoid the link between Morse and the JAGUAR model of cars – because '… he never drove anything other than his privately owned Lancia'. (MILE: p242). The model of Morse's car is unspecified in the WORKS. **Plate 37**

Last Bus to Woodstock The body of a young girl (Sylvia KAYE) is found in the car park of a public house (The BLACK PRINCE at WOODSTOCK). The police are called and the subsequent investigation is both the first recorded case in the WORKS and the first occasion when Morse and Lewis work together. The case is accurately dated (by the chapter headings) and a reference to RYAN'S DAUGHTER (p25) to 1971 but, thankfully, the dreadful crash at Heathrow Airport (p79) appears not to have occurred and is, presumably, an example of a rare error in Morse's memory (or a confusion with the 1972 crash when 118 people – rather than the 79 mentioned – died). During the course of the investigation one learns a great deal about the personal habits of Morse and, to a lesser extent, of Lewis. A map of the WOODSTOCK roundabout (reproduced under Karin ERIKSSON) is of some slight relevance (LBUS). *Main personnel* COLEBY, Bernard and Margaret CROWTHER, Sylvia KAYE, Mr PALMER, John SANDERS, and WIDDOWSON. **Plate 38**

Last Call A body is discovered in a room at the RANDOLPH and Morse and Lewis investigate. One learns something of DIABETES, a little of the hotel (particularly Room 231) and the potential perils of affairs, and why it used to be cheaper to make telephone calls after 6.00p.m. (CALL). *Main personnel* Mr and Mrs SHERWOOD.

Last Seen Wearing Morse and Lewis investigate the disappearance, in 1973, of a schoolgirl (Valerie TAYLOR). The trail is cold (but is warmed up) and the solution is only realised in 1975 as verified by the many dates, such as 'Tuesday 2nd September' or 'Sunday 31st August', mentioned in the text (but see the entry under DATES). The case becomes, in due course, a murder investigation. The record of this case (and of so many others) has quotations heading every chapter (and they indicate the breadth and depth of Morse's knowledge of literature and poetry); a few of these QUOTATIONS, along with those from other cases, are explored further in this Companion (WEAR). *Main personnel* The ACUMS, BAINES, Yvonne BAKER, MAGUIRE, Donald PHILLIPSON, the TAYLOR family.

Lawrence, Janis A not unattractive cleaner at the PITT RIVERS. She lives with her 4-year old son, Jason (*not* named after the leader of the Argonauts), on the CUTTESLOWE Estate.

Lawson, Rev Lionel Peter MA Cantab, A bachelor, aged 41, who has been at ST FRIDESWIDE'S for 10 years (SERV: pp61/233). There are rumours about his sexual orientation but his religious leanings are High Anglican, perhaps from his years at CHRIST'S College, CAMBRIDGE and St Stephen's House, Oxford. He attended a public boarding school some 10 miles from Stamford (one guesses Uppingham?) followed by a few years of National Service in the army. His evangelism and kindness (one hopes) means that he sometimes puts up a few men from the Church Army Hostel at the Vicarage (SERV: p281).

Lawson, Philip Edward The younger brother of the Rev Lionel LAWSON. Much the same as his brother in terms of school and the Army but he did not quite have the religious calling of his elder sibling.

League of Light, The This is, presumably, a campaigning religious organisation; if it ever existed (apart from in Morse's imagination), it does not appear to exist now (WEAR: p146).

Letts The name of a company that has made diaries since 1796 (being founded then by John Letts). Inspector AINLEY has one and the entry for the September 1st 1975 proves interesting to Morse; Nicholas QUINN has another, which also promises to reveal something. Anne SCOTT has at least two, one of which contains the potentially incriminating initials 'E.M.'.

Lewis, (children) Sergeant and Mrs LEWIS have (at least) three children – two daughters and a son – but details are rather thin on the ground. The eldest daughter (probably Georgina) is aged 13 in 1971 (LBUS: p201 and there are references to 'kids' later in the same case – p276); a reference to her sister definitely - "two daughters", says Lewis in reply to a question about his family – occurs in 1975 (NICQ: p213); and 'teenage daughters' appear in SERV (p113) making them, one guesses, aged about 16/17 and 19 years in 1978. Their homework is mentioned in 1975 (WEAR: p175) and both girls took the eleven-plus exam and O LEVELS (MILE: p125). The fact that Lewis recalls feeling very happy at the announcement of his *elder* daughter's pregnancy (ANNX: p289) confirms, grammatically, that there were only two of them. Except that, in late November 1979, the *eldest* daughter gives birth to a baby girl, making Lewis a grandfather (JERI: p302). Chambers (2003) is quite explicit: the adjective *eldest* simply means oldest while the same word as a noun only refers to the oldest of three or more. Clearly, more research is needed into the offspring of Lewis. Of the (probably only) son, all that is revealed is that he is sitting his A LEVEL in French in 1998 (REMO: p33) and this makes him a likely 18 years old in that year; Lewis, of course, has insufficient knowledge of the language to help him.

Lewis, George A Detective Sergeant in the THAMES VALLEY POLICE and the usual (though, in many ways, unequal) partner of Morse through a large number of cases. Morse has a neat summary of his character: 'Lewis was placid, good-natured, methodical, honest, unassuming, faithful, and … a bit *stolid*, too.' (MILE: p80). There has arisen an unfortunate misconception that his Christian name is Robbie (or, one guesses, Robert or Robin); for example, Goodwin gives Robert and Robbie (2002: p141) as do Bird (1998) and Bishop (2006, 2008). Although his forename is *never* mentioned in the WORKS, there is (fairly) clear evidence that it is George (JWEL: p332). Here, Morse explains how common it is for a father to choose the feminine equivalent of his own designation when naming a daughter ('"Georgie', 'Georgina', 'Georgette'"). Lewis's glance at Morse suggests that someone has hit the spot. It appears that MRS LEWIS may well call him by his surname (WNCH: p189). He does not like the name George much (NICQ: p214).

Childhood and Education It us unknown exactly where he was born or educated. It is also uncertain even *when* he was born – he is 'several' years older than Morse (LBUS: p90), which would give a birth date in the 1920's but, mysteriously, is seen to be younger than Morse during a number of cases (for example, Margaret BOWMAN thinks him a few years younger (ANNX: p183). DEXTER certainly thought he was Welsh (2006b) but a number of details imply some sort of origin or background in the north-east of England. For example, he knows of Washington in County Durham (NEIG: p345), he prefers Newcastle Brown ale to champagne (WOOD: p407), and he swaps reminiscences about the north-east with Laura HOBSON after having first 'correctly' pronounced Newcástle (WOOD: p282). A few more details are known about his schooling. He left statutory education aged 15 years and then gained some technical skills through day-release courses and night schools (JERI: p165). Before the age of 15, he had attended an establishment where ties were not worn (NEIG: pp82/106), a production of *The Mikado* was put on (WOOD: p251), and he learned no foreign languages (WOOD: p211). Indeed, he feels a little envious of the '... white-tied, SUBFUSC-suited students' (MILE: p97). It has been confirmed that he does not have a degree in English (LBUS: p80). Sadly, he was never near the top of any subject (JWEL: p321) and believes even now that he has '... a second-class mind'. (STOR: p217). For no reason of which one is aware, he felt like running away from home as a late teenager (WEAR: p313).

Knowledge of Literature and the Classics The extent of Lewis's knowledge seems to have been somewhat limited by his education. He passes to a hospital-bound Morse what he regards as a family heirloom (*Scales of Injustice: A Comparative Study of Crime and Punishment as Recorded in the County of Shropshire, 1842-1852*) together with the more salacious *The Blue Ticket* (WNCH: pp17/21). He has heard of Chesterton's *The Man Who Was Thursday* (CAIN: p50) and also *The Wind in the Willows*, but it is unclear whether this latter is a favourite book or simply a favourite title (CAIN: p51). He has never been inside the ASHMOLEAN and only knows, of Alfred the Great, the story of 'burning cakes'

(JWEL: p61). He does have an encyclopaedia at home (in which he looks up 'Tragedians'; JERI: p244) to try to get an insight into Morse's exposition of the Oedipus myth. As Lewis admits, we "... didn't have any of that Greek and Latin stuff when I was at school" (JERI: p 243) though he does recall Thomas Babington Macaulay and *Lays of Ancient Rome* from that education (JWEL: p282). His reference to Oedipus brings Morse's rejoinder: "The things I've taught you, Lewis, since you've been my sergeant!" (WOOD: p351). He has never read *Little Dorrit* but he has read *The Beano* (REMO: pp33/77). Although a slow reader (STOR: p197), he is particularly skilled at reading upside down (NEIG: p106).

Spelling and Grammar It must have been quite hard for Lewis to live up to the great expectations of Morse. He has trouble with the words schizophrenia (NICQ: p215), corroborate and desperate (JERI: p192), checks a spelling in *Chamber's Dictionary* (note the apostrophe; MILE: p241) or in the *Pocket Oxford Dictionary* (WOOD: p257), and has 'leizure' for 'leisure' until self-corrected (REMO: p216). His pretence to identify only two spelling mistakes in a document is seen through by Morse (JWEL: p198). Lewis has never really mastered the full stop (CAIN: p102) and needs reminding about an OXFORD COMMA (NEIG: p115). His use of pronouns can be excessive – one report back to Morse contains a "veritable plethora" (NEIG: p105); there are thirteen in all (not including the nominative singular). He has, though, learned from Morse – if his use of *ad hoc* raises the latter's eyebrows (NEIG: p313) who can predict the reaction to "Numquam animus, sir, as you tell me the ancient Romans used to say" (CAIN: p374); well, never mind. And, when Morse says: "I've never done it quicker", Lewis's response of "Shouldn't that be 'more quickly'" brings the appropriate remark of "Good man! You're learning at last" (REMO: p380). He has a '... painstakingly slow long-hand ...' (MILE: p170) but is a semi-competent typist (WOOD: p408).

Knowledge of Pornography and Attitude to Sex His interest is not as substantial as that of Morse and reflects only a passing acquaintance. He enjoyed the film *Grub Screws* – as seen on DIXON's stag-night – though Lewis wouldn't want to see it twice (NEIG: p273); ignores a Scandinavian porn magazine (ANNX: p115); and feels generally cheapened by erotic videos (GOLD: p30). Indeed, Lewis would rather have egg and chips than watch a sex video (WOOD: p342). When asked whether he would ever leave his wife or have a fling, Lewis replies: "I've never given it a thought ..." (ANNX: p171), but there is the merest suspicion that he may, once, have had an affair. In WEAR (p145), Morse asks Lewis: "Have *you* ever had another woman?" Lewis smiles and an '... old memory stirred and swam to the surface of his mind like a bubble in still water'. He is certainly susceptible to flirtation – his 'sluggish libido' is quickly aroused by Lucy DOWNES (JWEL: p184) and he enjoys the advances that Irma ERIKSSON gently makes (WOOD: pp215-218). He thinks Laura HOBSON is a "smasher" (WOOD: p283), prefers Princess Diana to Kim Basinger (NEIG: p5), and has not considered an affair with the Lewis's fat milk-lady (NEIG: pp356/363). Incidentally, Lewis swears, at the outside, only once a fortnight (ANNX: p168).

Family background Little is known of this beyond the fact that he had an uncle whose toes were run over by a barrel (LBUS: p118), his parents were blessed with neither wealth nor privilege (JERI: p165), and he had a brother or a sister (or brothers, sisters, or both) (WNCH: p223). There is a brief reference to his father, who advised him on his career, telling him '… to keep his mouth mostly shut and his bowels always open' (WOOD: p158).

Physical appearance As has been proved on many occasions, different witnesses may give different descriptions of the same incident or person.[1] Thus, we are told that Lewis is *not a big man* (WEAR: p80), but also that he is 'placid-looking, rather thick-set' (SERV: p268), 'rather thickset' (JERI: p13), has a 'burly figure' (WNCH: p124), and is either five foot eleven (WNCH: p224) or six-foot tall (WOOD: p214). He also has large feet, described by Morse as 'megapodic', (but Morse will be disappointed when he checks for that word in his recently purchased *Shorter Oxford*; CAIN: p125). At one point, Lewis says to Morse: "… you're a bit fatter than I am round the middle …" (MILE: p133).

Leisure Lewis follows horse-racing but rarely, having the occasional bet on major races such as the Derby and the Grand National (CAIN: p342); he has, also, bet on *The BLACK PRINCE*. He seldom gambles (JERI: p207) but regularly checks his football pools (SERV: pp188-189). He has played cricket as an amateur (NEIG: p227) and occasionally watches football at Oxford United (SERV: p107). His crossword of choice is that in *The DAILY MIRROR*.

Music From his close association with Morse, Lewis has picked up just a *little* of the former's interest in classical music though possibly less of the tastes: 'The one Strauss he knew was the 'Blue Danube' man. And he'd only recently learned there were two of *those*, as well – Senior and Junior; and which was which he'd no idea.' (NEIG: p43). Of Richard Strauss, there is no mention. Lewis does, however, enjoy the Prelude to *Parsifal* (REMO: pp160-161) even though his pronunciation of the conductor Knappertsbusch as Napperbush is later and pedantically corrected by Morse (pp164-165). He enjoys Gilbert and Sullivan, certainly in preference to WAGNER (WOOD: p250).

Smoking "I've never smoked, myself." (BURG: p288). He does have a slight concern about the possible dangers of passive smoking – being sure that it must have *some* effect (CAIN: p71).

Food and Drink On the former there is really little more to say than EGG AND CHIPS. References to this meal, clearly the favourite of Lewis, are legion (including ANNX: p138, NICQ: p235 with the '… thrice-blessed clatter of the chip pan', and REMO: p266). One might have thought that simply listing other citations would be enough but in each of the following a little more is learned about the exciting world of Lewis's staple diet. For example, sausages make an occasional appearance by way of addition – at least two (JERI: p202) and a rather staggering six in WOOD (p275). Further, Lewis demonstrates his ability to manage the proper ratio of consumption, wiping up the last of the last of the yolk with a

---

[1] The literature is vast but centres on two main theories – a bare smidgeon of that of 'cognitive dissonance' (Festinger 1957) and a little more of 'selective perception' (Broadbent 1958).

'final, solitary chip' (JERI: p204); presumably, years of practice have helped. He eats egg and chips on Mondays, Wednesdays, and Fridays (CAIN: p243) and tends to follow his preference even when away from home – in London, he has the meal once or twice (MILE: p240) and, most notably, in Bath orders egg and chips in the ROYAL CRESCENT. When reminded by Morse that it's a cordon bleu establishment, he replies, "Should taste good then, sir." (NEIG: p373). And does Lewis ever tackle eggs (plural) and chips? Most probably (CAIN: p348). One particular question is unresolved in the WORKS – Lewis's preferred condiments. In NEIG (p239), the kitchen red Formica-topped table carries cutlery, a lacy doily, bread and butter, a glass of milk, and a bottle of tomato ketchup whereas REMO (p33) sees Lewis using brown HP sauce. Perhaps he has hidden depths.

Lewis happily drinks both tea and coffee, particularly the latter when in the police canteen. While he enjoys 'real' coffee (NEIG: p210) he prefers tea to the instant variety (NEIG: p350) and takes one sugar in the latter, occasionally having a second cup (SERV: p200). His hopes are raised when he sees Morse bearing a coffee and a digestive biscuit (ANNX: p167) but, of course, they are for Morse himself. His consumption of alcohol pales into insignificance compared to Morse but he does drink the odd beer – a half pint in the BOAT INN (MILE: p180), a pint in the HORSE AND TRUMPET (NICQ: p108), and a quite amazing three pints in the BULLDOG (SERV: pp171-173). Of wine and spirits, his moderation is quite exceptional – a rare bottle of red wine (JERI: p302) to accompany egg and chips, some Beaujolais Nouveau and brandy (ANNX: p170) when entertaining Morse, and some Schnapps (WOOD: p215) when in Sweden. He enjoys a glass or two of GLENFIDDICH with Morse (REMO: p321) but cannot be said to enjoy finishing, in silence, the bottle after Morse's death (REMO: p431). Although he would have refused it, he is a little miffed that he is not even offered a dram of Glenfiddich when Max and Morse are getting stuck into the same (MILE: p73). He is, in fact, largely temperate and certainly tends to abstain when on duty (to the benefit of Morse who may then indulge, knowing he has a driver); for example, he usually drinks orange juice but has been known to order the slightly more exotic St Clements (WNCH: p232).[2] The tendency for Lewis to be in the chair when buying drinks runs consistently throughout the WORKS. Occasionally, he rebels and reminds Morse that it might be Morse's turn to pay (for example, JERI: p204 or WOOD: p397) and he has calculated that on half the salary, he buys three quarters of the drinks (CAIN: p79).[3] Lewis, after all, only has a small bank account (JWEL: p103).

Driving Lewis patently has two weaknesses and a love of fast driving is often yoked with that of his desire for egg and chips (for example, MILE: p91, WNCH: p217, and CALL: p273); these twin passions are notably recorded thus: '… the only blemishes on a life of unexciting virtuousness were a gluttonous partiality for egg and chips, and a passion for fast driving' (ANNX: p52). According to Morse, Lewis once managed the 'thirty-seven or thirty-eight miles to Stratford (upon Avon)' in half an hour. Equally, according to the AA, the journey is a little over 51 miles and should take a law-abiding driver a few minutes

---

[2] St Clements is a mixture of orange juice and lemonade. It is also drunk by Cathy MICHAELS in the WHITE HART (WOOD: p259).
[3] This figure appears as three fifths of the salary and three quarters of the drinks in JWEL: p64.

under the hour (JWEL: p212); perhaps Lewis knows a short-cut. Similarly, he takes 65 minutes from Leicester (CAIN: p79) for a journey of some 80 miles. It is clear that he often drives at 90mph or above (SERV: pp136/226, and ANNX: p162) though he never goes above 45mph in a built-up zone (JWEL: p143), where the speed limit is 30mph. At home, he has an old Mini but goes to work on the bus (MILE: p176). He is a 'wizard' at parking (REMO: p173) and using the police siren is one of his greatest joys – not, one assumes, on his Mini (REMO: p352).

Home life He lives with Mrs Lewis (and, at various times, their children) in a modest semi-detached house in HEADINGTON (ANNX: p73) with a neat garden (WEAR: pp199-200); they have two daughters and a son – see LEWIS (CHILDREN). Little is known of the property beyond the facts that it was redecorated in 1994 (CAIN: p342) and that, thankfully, the big crack in the kitchen may not be too much of a problem (STOR: p201). The exact location of the big 1942 Utility wardrobe – that Lewis is trying to give away – has not yet been firmly established (WATC: p128). Lewis appears to be a home-loving man – since his marriage, Christmas and the New Year have always been spent at home (ANNX: p73) and, in recent years, it has been rare for him to spend two nights or more away from Oxford (MILE: p237). Indeed, Lewis could hardly be called well-travelled – he has been to Sweden, Australia for three weeks, Italy for two, and Calais for an afternoon of shopping (all WOOD: p211). He has not, for example, been to Greece (MILE: p221).

Career Confirmation that Lewis was in the Forces is given in LBUS (p53) – he was glad to receive lifts as a member of the Armed Services – and one guesses that his enrolment lasted but a few years. It is clear that he left school at the age of 15 years, carried out a succession of training courses, and joined the police when he was aged 20; the JERI case is reliably dated to 1979 and Lewis became a sergeant, therefore in 1969 (JERI: p165). There is the slightest of confusions as to when he first met Morse – obviously, he knew him in 1971 (LBUS) but JERI records that he first came into Morse's orbit in 1973 (p165). Attempts to clear this matter up have, so far, failed miserably.

Detective Skills Lewis is, without doubt, a hard and conscientious worker. He works best when given a task (NEIG: p263), stays after office hours (ANNX: p254), and is usually happy to let Morse do the thinking while he carries such donkey work as telephoning The War Office (and the Ministry of Defence, Wiltshire Regiment, and Territorial Unit at Devizes) trying to track down some information (MILE: p169). He sees, at one point, his main task as building up evidence into '… an impressively documented pile that could be forwarded to the DPP' (REMO: pp265-266). The DPP is, of course, the Director of Public Prosecutions. While he is not the sharpest knife in the drawer (for example, he needs the NICQ case explained to him in some detail; pp284-291), he genuinely believes that he usually does provide some help (JWEL: p322). He is quite proud of his rank and status, announcing on at least three occasions that he tracks down Morse (at the PEEP OF DAWN, in hospital, and the RANDOLPH) by announcing that "I'm a detective …" (respectively, ANNX: p156, WNCH: p15, and JWEL: p120). He is, however, misguided when he thinks that Morse is going to resist the temptation of going to the GARDENER'S ARMS – which

Morse, of course, does not (ANNX: p77). He even tries to unravel one case by using his own version of Socratic dialectic (REMO: pp167-170). His office, which he probably shares, is up a flight of stairs from Morse (NEIG: p126) and in the WOOD case he finds himself back in uniform helping with a riot (p118). While he seems quite happy giving a television interview (NEIG: p63), he is unsure and tongue-tied when faced with leaving an answerphone message later in the same case (p267).

Health (Physical and Mental) As befits an ex-boxer (light middleweight champion in the Army: WEAR: p81, JWEL: p269, CAIN: p145), and apparently in spite of his diet, Lewis retains a good overall level of fitness (REMO: p62). This is certainly demonstrated more than once when Morse is under violent attack (NICQ: p284 or SERV: p265 for example). On only one occasion – during the WEAR case – is he laid up in bed with a high temperature and feeling weak – and his intake of medicine is limited to Vitamin C and Nurofen Plus (REMO: pp426-427). He can feel nervous (while bending the law over a typewriter in LBUS: pp157-8), is not scared of spiders (WEAR: p187, SERV: p161), feels like crying (with some justification) at a singular event and does so later (REMO: pp422/448), has cried before when learning Morse's Christian name (NEIG: p413), and has donated blood fifty times (at least) with a gold badge to prove it (MILE: p247). While not quite as sensitive as Morse, he hates the sight of death and has '... felt his stomach turning over' (WEAR: p174). He believes himself to be in the top 25% of the population in terms of intelligence (LBUS: p129) but readily admits that memory is not his strongest asset (LBUS: p248). He is not renowned for his sense of humour and only one, fairly feeble, attempt at a joke has been recorded (CAIN: p261). Of his religious beliefs little is known – apart from a reference to his belief in the Resurrection (MILE: p134) no other traces have been found bar his knowledge that John Bunyan came from Bedford (CAIN: p137). Some might argue that his punctuality (CAIN: p128) has an element of religious fervour; some might not. His attempt to lie to Strange over Morse's alcohol consumption is easily seen through (REMO: pp249-250) but this need not indicate any particular moral or ethical stance.

Relationship with Morse Though much appears elsewhere, it may be sensible to gather a few examples here. Somewhat optimistically, he sees his partnership with Morse in the same terms as those of Gilbert and Sullivan, Moody and Sankey, and Lennon and McCartney (JERI: p166). More pessimistically, he has seen Morse like some '... inexperienced schoolmaster ... anxious to parade his own cleverness (rather) than to elicit any halting answer from his dimmer pupils', (MILE: p124) but he is always happy when the 'Chief' is on to something (MILE: p91) and he is prepared to, then, suffer the bouts of irascibility. Even when Morse snaps at him, Lewis rarely takes offence: '... for he and Morse were long acquainted, and Lewis knew all his ways' (CAIN: p310). In fact, it seems very easy to make Lewis happy – the occasional 'my old friend' from Morse (for instance, ANNX: p255), a congratulation that makes him feel he has won Wimbledon (MILE: p125), or when his superior intimates that his brain functions better with Lewis by his side (WNCH: p217). On many occasions, indeed, does Lewis (usually unwittingly) act as a prompt to a chain of thought – a set of the initials 'DC' in NEIG (p307) or a suggestion concerning fingerprints bringing the response: "Bloody 'ell! You've done it again, Lewis. You've done it *again*!" (CAIN: p348).

On the negative side, it is also clear that the common bouts of near hero-worship are tempered with realism – Lewis finds Morse to be crude (NICQ: p78), conceited (CAIN: p9), is prepared to have a real go at him over his lifestyle (NEIG: pp181-183), and sees him as irredeemably tight-fisted (too often to be individually listed), neatly summarised by his words: "You probably know you haven't got a reputation for being too generous with money ..." (CALL: p279).[4] But while he recognises that Morse can often be universally unpleasant, he does admit to his wife that: "I'm the only one he's ever treated well". (NEIG: p239). Although he has been trusted with a key to Morse's flat (REMO: p410), he is by no means a regular visitor; he has not been inside it for two years before the NICQ case (p90) and is not overly welcome there in MYST (p45). Further references appear for Lewis, of course, throughout many other entries.

Lewis, Mrs[5] The wife of Sergeant Lewis, a source of great comfort and support to him, and the provider of copious meals of egg and chips. A most sympathetic person and one is relieved, on her behalf, that the crack in the family kitchen does not appear to be serious (STOR: p202).

Background She was born in Wales (JERI: p167) and raised in the Rhondda Valley (NEIG: p238). Her mother is 'ancient' (SERV: p130).

Appearance and Attributes She has down on her upper lip, fair hair (ANNX: pp161-162), is right-handed (NEIG: p239), and has false teeth, (SERV: p206) which she wears in bed. She speaks with '... an attractive Welsh lilt' and has been known to, unwittingly, discourse in anapaestic pentameters and hexameters (CAIN: p346); she also drops her aspirates (NEIG: p238; WOOD: p276) and has occasionally produced a slightly unladylike whistle (CAIN: p347). Unlike some, she would not wear a black bra with a white blouse (LBUS: p26). Her health appears to be good though a touch of flu is recorded on one occasion (LBUS: p276).

Culinary Skills Apart from cooking an 'excellent egg and chips' (SERV: p187), she has provided the more exotic bacon and eggs (JERI: p167) and, on one occasion at least, a more substantial meal comprising '... lightly undercooked beef, horseradish sauce, velvety-flat Yorkshire pudding, and roast potatoes ...' (ANNX: p170; and please note the OXFORD COMMA).

Tastes and Beliefs She is very keen on television (SERV: p188) and probably has a favourite soap opera (REMO: p34). She listens to *THE ARCHERS* and enjoys Gilbert and

---

[4] His view of Morse's miserliness is mollified when he sees him putting money into a charity bottle (JWEL: pp123-124) but Lewis is sadly unaware of the true circumstances.

[5] Goodwin (2002) has her as Valerie, born in the Rhondda Valley (p144). He also gives the two Lewis children the names of Lyn and Ken. These cannot be traced in the WORKS. It's almost as if someone has re-invented them for another public.

Sullivan (WOOD: p250); she reads Agatha Christie but Lewis has not yet taken her to CHOLSEY (NEIG: p85) to see the grave. Like Morse, she believes in coincidences – or, rather, that things 'come in three's' (JWEL: p281); she somehow knew she was pregnant before confirmation at the ante-natal clinic (JERI: p195). She does not appear to gamble but does have just the one Premium Bond (and wins £50 with it – NEIG: p115).

Relationship with Lewis His happiness means that she is happy too (JERI: p167; ANNX: p139; JWEL: pp126-127). While they are not unknown to have rows these are patched up (JWEL: p181), she provides his breakfast (NEIG: p1), and cleans his shoes (ANNX: p221). In the absence of a dishwasher, they split the duties of washing up and drying (ANNX: pp170/174) and it is unclear whether or not the planned purchase of the said item ever comes to fruition (NEIG: pp166-167). Her wants seem to be fairly undemanding – a set of knives (CAIN: pp385-386), for example – though she is fairly insistent upon the matter of new kitchen curtains (JWEL: p178). While she stays up after Lewis has gone to bed (ANNX: p279) she is not beyond trying to use her charms on her husband: on one occasion, '… she quietly breathed the prospect of egg and chips into (Lewis's) ear …' (JWEL: p277) – though this time, he remained unaroused.

Home Life No doubt much of her time involves raising the children but other duties include feeding the birds (REMO: p424), hosting a Tupperware party (WATC: p125), leaving keys with a neighbour (ANNX: p220), and arranging a 'get well' card for Morse (CAIN: p205). In all she does, she is '… immaculately methodical …' (BURG: p292).

Lincoln College The only reference traced is in NEIG (p91) and then only in connection with the BEAR pub. Well done, Lincoln. **Map D5**

Listener, The Once a weekly magazine (until its demise in 1991), its notoriously difficult CROSSWORD was saved and now appears on a Saturday in *The TIMES*. Morse has had the rare privilege of appearing as a theme not only once but twice in particularly rewarding examples – 3612 *Goo Goo G'Joob* by Franc (2001) and 3715 (2003). The latter is reproduced in APPENDIX A. A further crossword (2476) was titled 'Last Seen Disappearing from the Last Bus to Woodstock'; while there was no grid, clue, or answer connection to Morse, the puzzle was dedicated to DEXTER, Morse, Lewis, DIXON, and The THAMES VALLEY police. Morse, while trying to get through a few days of sickness, tries to occupy the time with thoughts about an old murder case. He realises that he is simply amusing himself with a happy little problem – '… like a tricky cryptic crossword from *The Listener*' (WNCH: p103). And it is by analogy to the same type of crossword that Morse's approach to any problem in detection can be expressed: 'One clue unfinished in a *Listener* puzzle, and he would strain the capacity of every last brain-cell to bursting point until he had solved it' (JWEL: p288). A most helpful website exists (easy to find through any search engine on *Listener* and *Crossword*) and there one may find details of many relevant guides and publications. Puzzle 3906 (December 2006) recreated the first crossword – that of Arthur Wynne from 1913. Needless to say, the clues were a trifle harder. The edition of 23rd March 1989 contained an article (*Code Books*) exploring some of the links between Morse and the magazine. In 2007 a series of occasional and, usually, encouraging guidance notes started to appear beneath the crossword (including, on the 13th October 2007, the daunting: 'Only in exceptional circumstances will two very hard puzzles appear in consecutive weeks'). Unfortunately, both the website and the series were a little too late for Morse (as was the incredibly complex 4000th crossword published in September 2008).

Literae Humaniores The phrase appears in MILE (p17) and is the name of the OXFORD UNIVERSITY classics course lasting four years. At the end of five terms, Moderations (MODS) are sat; at the end of a further seven terms there are final examinations (GREATS). The course involves a detailed study of Roman and Greek history and philosophy and successful completion leads to a Bachelor of Arts degree. It is the course that Morse went up to read in 1950.

Literary Curiosities See APPENDIX C.

Locals, The An affectionate name for the University of Oxford Delegacy for Local Examinations. It occupies a large building (developed 1965) in SUMMERTOWN and can be reached via Ewert Place (ANNX: p198) from the BANBURY ROAD. Gladys Taylor, no doubt with many colleagues – including Margaret BOWMAN, Mrs Bannister, and Mrs Webster – works here (ANNX: p176; p180). The offices overlook the playing fields of Summerfields Preparatory School (from the first floor). On the ground floor can be found the slightly forbidding office of The Secretary – Miss Gibson. The Locals issues identity pass-cards to its staff (ANNX: p229). Also see A LEVELS.

Lollipop man (or woman) A guardian of a pedestrian crossing (or other regularly used stretch of road where people – usually schoolchildren – need to get to the other side). The name is derived from the warning disc ('Stop – children') placed on top of a pole, the whole resembling a 'lollipop' (WEAR).

Longwall Street Running north from the HIGH and to the west of MAGDALEN. The street is mentioned in both JWEL (p50) and CAIN (p241). **Map E5**

Lonsdale College A college founded in the fifteenth century. NEIG (p19) helpfully gives the date as 300 years before Gibbon wrote of Popes and Prelates. *The History of the Decline and Fall of the Roman Empire* was first published between 1776 and 1788 and this gives an approximate date of 1480 or so (which, if nothing else, distinguishes it from BRASENOSE to which it has often been compared architecturally). The college, of course, admits women and has done so since at least 1975 (MILE: p47) but only to a number of reserved places (NICQ; p251).

> **Features** It has a PORTER's Lodge that shuts at 11.00pm (WEAR: p160; MILE: p26) but over the years this has become known as the Porters' Lodge (WOOD: p225; NEIG: p335). The Lodge is in the HIGH (MILE: p135). It has a 'front quad' (WOOD: p309) and a 'second court' (LBUS: p161). The Master's rooms are in the 'first quad' (MILE: p47) and the Old Staircase in the 'inner quad' (NICQ: p137). The Master's lodge itself is 'wisteria-

clad' (NEIG: p18).[6] The SCR is 'smallish' and the Chapel (NEIG: pp150/193) a little difficult to describe. The Great Hall has a fine table of oak plank (NEIG: p286) and, in Hilary on Sunday evenings, the lights are switched off and dinner is by candlelight (NEIG: p283).[7] Morse has attended guest evenings (LBUS: p97; MILE: p136), presumably on a Thursday – the usual night for such events (NICQ: p250) – though he has also refused lunch with the Master (JERI: p125) despite being on friendly terms (MILE: p54). There are four guest evenings per term (NEIG: p150). Sweet sherry is never served in Hall (NEIG: p151) but Madeira may be offered, together with port, after the meal (p155). The Stamper Room (named for William Leslie STAMPER) is a convenient location in which to hold an Extraordinary General Meeting of the Fellows (NEIG: p402).

Staff The college is (uniquely, it seems) headed by either a Principal (LBUS: p164) or a Master (for example, MILE: p63), respectively supported by a Vice-Principal or Vice-Master. The essential rules governing the election of a new Master form the heading to Chapter 2 of NEIG and on pp17-20. In brief, they require that the new Master should be of sound mind and good health, that they shall not have taken Holy Orders, and that they should not have a criminal record. There is no mention of any need for academic achievement beyond exercising 'Skills of the Arithmetick' (NEIG: p79). These rules are slightly amplified in MILE – the Master must be layman, elected by the 8 Senior Fellows with minimum of 6 votes in favour (p136). When necessary, a Fellows' Appointment Committee is convened (NEIG: pp18-19). In 1996, Sir Clixby BREAM is the Master. Under the rules (or, more properly, the Founders' Statutes) any Master shall not continue in his post beyond the age of sixty-seven – and Sir Clixby is 68 years old. Lonsdale has a Visitor (usually an archbishop) – a dignitary who periodically inspects and reports on college matters (NEIG: p402). Other positions in the college include the Senior Tutor and the Senior Tutor's Secretary (WEAR: p137), the Tutor for Admissions and Domestic Bursar (NEIG: p78), Investments Bursar and Senior Fellow (MILE: p99), college secretary (MILE: p112), probably an otherwise-unqualified Bursar (MILE: p136), a Dean (NICQ: p94) and a Chaplain (NEIG: p195).

Members These include ANDREWS, BRADLEY, BREAM, BROWNE-SMITH, CORNFORD, CROWTHER, HARDINGE (with rooms in the front quad), NEWLOVE, STORRS, TOMPSETT (with rooms on the Old Staircase), and WESTERBY. Dr Clive Hornsby is Senior Reader in Social Sciences, and an unnamed Professor of Arabic is also a member (NEIG: p79). In MINOR, brief references are made to these others – Jennifer Bennett, Donald Franks, Professor Liebermann, Gareth Llewellyn-Jones, David Mackenzie, Melhuish, Plummer, 'Rosemary', and Jane Summers.

Other matters It is, surely, a coincidence that a certain Mrs Lonsdale is a housekeeper at the fictional Jordan College in Philip Pullman's Oxford in his trilogy, *His Dark Materials*. The exact location of Lonsdale College has, for some reason, long puzzled tourists and other

---

[6] See 'wistaria' under LITERARY CURIOSITIES.
[7] See MAGDALENE.

visitors. On one occasion, even Morse asks Lewis: "You're not going to ask me where Lonsdale is, I hope!" (with a very large dose of sarcasm). In fact, the directions are simplicity itself – starting from BLACKWELL'S in the BROAD, walk through RADCLIFFE SQUARE (across the cobbles) and into the college (WOOD: p309). Some of the college windows look directly out into HOLYWELL STREET (NEIG: p218). If still in doubt, find the cobblestones outside the college and listen for the striking of the clock on ST MARY'S (NEIG: p195). Or do as Morse does – and walk out of the college into RADCLIFFE SQUARE (NEIG: p282) or into the college from that Square (p335). The college may also be reached from the HIGH (through the back door, for Senior Fellows only; MILE: p13). For further guidance on location, see CATTE STREET. **Map D5**

Lonsdale Road Running east from the BANBURY Road towards the Cherwell (JWEL: p77). It is not the location of LONSDALE COLLEGE but does provide a residence for Cedric and Lucy DOWNES. **Map D3**

Lower Road The route from Marine Parade to the COOMBE STREET garage parking – for those staying at the BAY HOTEL, Lyme Regis (WOOD: pp12, 15).

Lower Swinstead A village that is central to the REMO case. While there is a Swinstead in Lincolnshire, the exact location of the Lower variety is slightly problematic (although it is clearly in Oxfordshire – REMO: p14) and may be approached along the Windrush Valley (p400). It is, according to Debbie RICHARDSON, about 3 to 4 miles from BURFORD (p114); a good guess would put it in the vicinity of Swinbrook (some 2 miles east of Burford). The HARRISON family live here, there is a church, the only pub is the MAIDENS ARMS, and there is an unsuccessful cricket team.

Lucy's Ironworks Properly known as Lucy's Eagle Ironworks, this can either be found in Juxon Street (JERI: p21) or in WALTON WELL ROAD (Hibbert 1988); perhaps it lies between them. George JACKSON used to work here and presumably passed the 'green gates' (JERI: p192) a good number of times; Edward WILKINS was an apprentice here (ANNX: p260). For further information on the history of the company, feel free to browse Andrews and Brunner (1965). The site was converted into a sheltered scheme of flats in 2008. **Plate 39**

Plate 43 (Left) The William Dunn School (p108).
Plate 44 (Right) Girl Reading (p110).

Plate 45 (Left) Merton College (p110).
Plate 46 (Right) The Mitre (p112).

Plate 47 (Left) Captain Cook (p113).
Plate 48 (Right) The *Endeavour* (p114).

M

Maclean, Sheila Known to many as Nessie, she is a sister at the John RADCLIFFE HOSPITAL (WNCH) before her transfer to Director of Nursing Services at the Derby Royal Infirmary. Morse refers to her, unkindly, as the Dragon of the Loch (p172). She appears, literally, in a different light at an Oxford Christmas party and Morse meets her again (in Derby) to cement their relationship (WNCH: p233).

Macnutt, Derrick See XIMENES.

Madrid Capital of Spain and meeting-place of the RICHARDS brothers (one of whom flies here on a British Airways DC10). A number of places are mentioned in the WORKS including the Calle de Alcatá, the Cafe Léon, the Palace Hotel, and a rather fine statue of Neptune (JERI).

Magdalen Bridge This links the HIGH to the PLAIN and thus onto the suburbs. Morse knew it as a 'Bridge Too Far' in his undergraduate days (CAIN: p172) from, presumably, the comment made by Lieutenant-General Browning of the Battle for Arnhem in 1944. The police (and others) frown on the traditional practice of jumping off the bridge on May Day. **Map E6**

Magdalen College Founded in 1448 by the then Bishop of Winchester, the college still retains extensive grounds. ASHENDEN claims to know little of it but enthuses about the deer-park, the walk along the Cherwell, and the architecture of the Tower (JWEL: p68). Morse believes that his descriptions have simply been lifted from the book Oxford by Jan Morris. Morris (1978) has many references to Magdalen. The likeliest begins: 'Magdalen has a deer park. Magdalen has a walk along the River Cherwell, and 100 acres of meadow and garden ...' (p131). **Plate 40, Map E5**

Magdalene College One of the smaller of the CAMBRIDGE Colleges (re-founded in 1542) but with an extensive river frontage. Its alumni include QUINN, ROOPE (both NICQ: p72), the actor Michael Redgrave, and Samuel Pepys, the diarist.[1] Its members still meet by candlelight when dining in the Hall (for the practical reason that nobody ever managed – or bothered - to create an electricity supply there). Honorary Fellows include some of Morse's favourite poets and authors – T. S. Eliot, HARDY, and KIPLING. **Plate 41**

Magdalen Road A street in East Oxford (pronounced M-a-g-dalen) (JWEL: p89). **Map E6**

Magdalen Street Running south from St GILES' (pronounced 'maudlin'; JWEL: p89). **Map D5**

Magistrates' Court Morse is expected to appear in this court on the 13th October 1971; one hopes to further some police business rather than for any misdemeanour (LBUS: pp163/175). It

---

[1] Pepys provides a quotation for the heading to Chapter 60 of WOOD.

is also to such a Court that parking fines issued by the Fixed Penalty Office should be paid (JERI: p168). The court is immediately opposite ST ALDATES police station.

Maguire, John A fairly unpleasant (and ginger-haired) young man who was at school with Valerie TAYLOR. He now lives in SOUTHAMPTON TERRACE, London and works in SOHO. His reading includes *The Goon Show Scripts*, Dracula comics, and porn from Denmark (WEAR).

Maidens Arms The only pub in LOWER SWINSTEAD (REMO: pp45/122). It is low-roofed, built in Cotswold stone, has an office above the bar, and keeps traditional OPENING HOURS. Tom BIFFEN is the landlord and he allegedly keeps about the best pint of bitter in Oxfordshire. The pub is also known as the 'Maiden's Arms' (p111); one guesses the correct title depends on the number of maidens involved though the fact that the landlord has a T-shirt emblazoned with 'The Maidens Arms' may be conclusive.

Malplaquet Last of the four great battles (1709) won by John CHURCHILL, Duke of Marlborough; the victory is celebrated, along with that of OUDENARDE in a tapestry at BLENHEIM PALACE (LBUS: p10). The campaign order of battles was known for years by schoolchildren as B R O M (BLENHEIM, RAMILLIES, OUDENARDE, and Malplaquet) and is so recalled by JOHNSON (WOOD: p312).

M & S A common shortening of MARKS AND SPENCER.

Manning Terrace A road to the east of BANBURY ROAD (SERV: pp37-38). Number 14 appears to have been divided into 14A and 14B with Mrs RAWLINSON and her daughter Ruth occupying the former. **Map D4**

Manor Hotel A pub close to Manor House underground station in London. Its open doors prove irresistible to Morse (MILE: p208).

Mansfield College Mansfield was granted full college status within the University in 1995. It is unclear whether Dr McBryde (MINOR) or his friend is a member of this college (or, indeed, both of them; WOOD: p190). **Map D5**

Marks and Spencer A chain of stores that sells clothing (including ties) and groceries – the former under the brand name of St Michael (NICQ: p211). The Oxford shop in QUEEN STREET is Morse's 'favourite store' (LBUS: p175). They may also have supplied socks to a body found in the canal (MILE: p128) though this is by no means certain. The stores are often known as 'Marks and Sparks' (CAIN: p274).

Marsh Harrier A public house in Marsh Road (a turning off the COWLEY ROAD). Honey (1998) calls it a '... pleasant pub for a quiet drink and a read, the landlord even had a small library'. Morse and Lewis review progress in the CAIN case over several pages (pp173-177) and, in Morse's case, two pints of Fuller's London Pride (both bought by Lewis).

Marston Ferry Road A street running into the BANBURY ROAD from the east; at their junction, sits the Summertown Health Centre. Morse witnesses a fatal accident here between a car and a motor-cyclist and his physical reaction – nausea and sweating – coupled with his thoughts of inadequacy and cowardice lead him to ponder the 'Lucretian business about the random concourse of the atoms ...' (SERV: p64). Lucretius (95-51 BC) promotes an atomist theory in his *De Rerum Natura* – in a nutshell, that the universe is formed by the chance interaction of atoms. It must be a dangerous road – a further fatal accident occurs (JWEL: p281); it is one that eventually sets Morse on a fruitful chain of thought. **Map D3-E3**

Martin, Angie Apparently, a toffee-nosed little tart (NEIG: p207). She has been a nude model and worked as a stripper – occupations she would now, understandably, rather forget in her married life.

Martin, Donald J BA. A tall, lank-haired man and a member of the SYNDICATE. He maintains a crucial ALIBI by claiming to visit several pubs at the relevant time (good for him) and also prowls round a paved yard 'like a hyaena' – which spelling is certainly recognised (NICQ: p218).

Martin, Mrs The wife of Donald, she is plain-looking and has dandruff (NICQ: p37). One rather wishes one could say something nice about her but the WORKS are otherwise silent.

Martyrs' Memorial A rather fine and imposing statue which commemorates the immolation of the English Protestants Latimer and Ridley (1555) and Cranmer (1556). The memorial, compared by some to a church spire, was designed by George Gilbert Scott (based on the 13th century Eleanor Cross at Waltham Cross in Essex). The monument was erected between 1841 and 1843. Taxis are known to wait in the shallow lay-by beside the Memorial (SERV: p5) and the deaths of Latimer and Ridley are recalled in the same case (p268) in a description of a crowd outside BALLIOL. Margaret BOWMAN reads a leaflet (in ST MARY'S) about the Martyrs (ANNX: p210). The leaflet recalls '... when Mary became Queen and England reverted to Roman Catholicism, Archbishop Cranmer and two of his fellow bishops, Latimer and Ridley, were tried in St Mary's for heresy. Latimer and Ridley were burned at the stake. Cranmer himself, after officially recanting, was brought back to St Mary's and condemned to death. He was burned at the stake in the town ditch, outside Balliol College, holding his right hand (which had written his recantation) steadily in the flames ...' The Memorial is in ST GILES' and is clearly visible to tourists (and other people) staying at the RANDOLPH HOTEL (JWEL). **Plate 42**

Master A common title given to the head of an Oxford (or CAMBRIDGE) college. Hibbert (1988) gives a full list of such heads (under 'Colleges') and the variety covers Warden, Rector, Principal, President, Dean, and Provost. To some extent, though they may deny it, both the Provost of QUEEN'S and the President of ST JOHN'S are both Masters.

Max His full name is Maximilian Theodore Siegfried de Bryn but to Morse he is 'Max' and thus he is entered here. He and Morse have known one another since about 1960; Morse always calls him Max, he has never addressed Morse by anything other than his surname (ANNX: p58). He is a police surgeon based at the William Dunn School of Pathology (**Plate 43**) in SOUTH PARKS ROAD (WNCH: p200) and his most distinguishing feature is a hump-back. Unless there are two hump-backed police surgeons working in Oxford (a coincidence that might even amaze Morse), he first appears (unnamed) in WEAR (p171) and is not named as Max until JERI (p84) – some three cases and four years later. He plays parts (some of them major) in NICQ, SERV, JERI, MILE, ANNX, WNCH, JWEL, and WOOD. Little is known about his private life or history though his use of the word 'forrader' (SERV: p244) – meaning 'more forward' – may indicate some Scottish links. His reference to: "... some of the bodies they used to fish out of the water at Gravesend" may hint at previous work in or near London (SERV: p116).

Physical Appearance and Public Habits A little more is known of these. Unflatteringly (though no doubt accurately) he is described as: '... one of the more unusual specimens of humankind ... a thin-lipped, mournful mouth, and with the few remaining strands of his lank, black hair plastered in parallels across a yellowish dome of a skull ...' (ANNX: p58). His skull is described as being dolichocephalic (ANNX: p78) – a shape shared with Phil ALDRICH (JWEL: p22) and, if Dr Mortimer is to be believed (on a first meeting) in the Baskerville case, also with HOLMES. Originally thin (NICQ: p219), he has become overweight by the date of the JWEL case (p222), and he is plagued by lumbago "mid-*every*-bloody-season" (MILE: p68), linked (no doubt) to the curvature of his spine. He wears ancient spectacles, hooked behind his large ears (WOOD: 144), a black waistcoat (ANNX: p77), and has spidery handwriting (ANNX: p100). His taste in cars includes a big, battered old Ford (MILE: p67) and a BMW (JWEL: p115). He is fond of (or addicted to) both alcohol and tobacco. He drinks at home – and allegedly before breakfast (JERI: pp84-85). In company, his preferred drinks are gin and Campari (ANNX: p78) and GLENFIDDICH (JWEL: p55).[2] He is a chain-smoker and lets the cigarette droop at an angle of 45 degrees from his lips (ANNX: pp77/58); his cigarettes are 'long-ashed' (ANNX: p74). Although he dies from a heart attack no clear link is suggested here with these fairly common activities.

Intelligence He seems to have enjoyed a classical education (ANNX: p78), is au fait with the works of Shakespeare (JWEL: p116), has a *Chambers Dictionary* on his shelves (WOOD: p257), and is consulted by Morse on the height of Victorian women (WNCH: pp193-194). Morse doubts, however, that Max knows anything about DNA (WOOD: p147).

Work Max is rather thorough and when examining a body claims that: "I always look everywhere" (JWEL: p104). He has also developed, as a pathologist, a keen sense of smell – detecting alcohol in the presence of Morse from a distance (JWEL: p55). He often has to give evidence in Court and this he gives at such a speed that it has been compared, in terms of comprehensibility, to reciting the Russian creed to a class of the educationally subnormal (NICQ: p219). Or, indeed, with: '... the exhilarating rapidity of an Ashkenazy laying into

---

[2] If one adds dry vermouth to gin and Campari, the cocktail is known as a Cardinal. Add some bitters and make the vermouth sweet and one has the classic Negroni.

Liszt.' (JERI: p83). When asked for his opinion on the possibility of suicide as the cause of death, his inevitable answer (given for the last 20 years) is: "That is for the jury to decide, sir." (JERI: p83).

Relationship with Morse There is certainly a great feeling of mutual respect: 'There was only one policeman he'd ever met for whom he had a slight degree of admiration, and that was Morse.' (JERI: p84). And that was only because Morse had told him of his contempt for the twaddle produced by pathologists. They are also close enough, for example, and equally dismissive of sentiment to have a bet on the time of a particular death (JERI: pp144-145). The exchanges between Max and Morse are, by and large, a delight. They tend to be a mixture of wit, friendly contempt, verbal sparring, and erudition. A long example may be found in MILE (pp109-112) – too long to quote in its entirety here and too flowing to use mere extracts. A shorter conversation may, however, illustrate their banter:

Morse: "Do you think whoever murdered *name* was left-handed or right-handed?"
Max: "If he was a right-handed tennis player it must have been a sort of backhand shot: if he was left-handed, it must have been a sort of smash."
Morse: "You're not very often as forthcoming as that!"
Max: "I try to help."
Morse: "Do you think our tennis player was right-handed or left-handed?"
Max: "Don't know." (ANNX: p107)

Max does (eventually) give Morse an unequivocal answer (WNCH: p200): '... the very first such answer, in fact, in their long and reasonably amicable relationship'. No doubt though, that for much of their relationship, Morse would have thought of Max as one of "... those prevaricating pathologists". (NEIG: p62).

Death As a pathologist Max is only too aware of the frailty of the human condition: "You know, Morse, don't you, that every single person ever born has at least one serious illness in life – the last one?" (SERV: p267). Max dies early in the morning of Sunday 19th July 1992 (in the John RADCLIFFE HOSPITAL) after a heart attack in his laboratory; his remains are to be left to medical science. Morse visits him the previous Saturday evening and their last conversation is poignant indeed; it also allows Max to tell Morse that the sex of the bones from a discovered body are not as expected (WOOD: pp180-182). On hearing from HOBSON of Max's heart attack, Morse says: "Max and I – well, we ... let's say we don't either of us have too many friends and...I want to see the old sod again if he's going to die." (WOOD: p178). And he weeps, silently, when he hears of his death (p183).

McClure, Felix Fullerton MA, DPhil. He is a retired (66-years old) former Ancient History don from WOLSEY College (where dons are known as Students). He won a scholarship to Oxford in 1946 and took a First in both MODS and GREATS. Once married, his SOMERVILLE-educated wife chose the time of her Junior Fellowship at MERTON to run off with an undergraduate from TRINITY (a typical story of everyday Oxford folk ...). He lives in a two-bedroomed flat at 6 Daventry Court, DAVENTRY AVENUE (where he is Secretary of the Residents' Action Group) and shares Morse's taste in Sunday papers – the coarse and the cultured (CAIN: 14). His flat is tastefully decorated and contains many pictures – including the head of Theseus in the Pittura Pompeiana series – and busts of Homer, Beethoven, Thucydides, and Milton. It is unclear whether his taste in low-class prostitution or his past attempts to address drug-dealing (including helping to form OUCH – Oxford University Counselling and Help) lead to an early end.

McFee, Gaye Hostess (and barmaid) at the BLACK PRINCE; she prefers to be known as 'Mrs'. She is red-headed, divorced, and lives with her son and mother (LBUS).

McPherson A Constable with the THAMES VALLEY POLICE, both intelligent and observant (LBUS: p136).

McQueen, Janet An amply bosomed Sister (with dark, wavy hair) at the RADCLIFFE INFIRMARY (NEIG). She first meets Morse when he is under her care following his diabetes diagnosis in 1996 and it is she who discovers Morse's Christian name (from old hospital records) – alerting him to the fact on a postcard showing *Girl Reading* (**Plate 44**) by Perugini (pp343-344). She spends an interesting time with Morse at the ROYAL CRESCENT HOTEL (pp407-411) and buys the postcard that Morse sends to Lewis – signed 'Endeavour' (p413). Unfortunately she is away in Carlisle (looking after her mother) when Morse is seriously ill (REMO: pp410-411). She is clearly very special to Morse and is named as a beneficiary under his will. The lovely Janet once leaves a saucy message on Morse's Ansafone (REMO: p152).

Meadow Lane This runs south from DONNINGTON BRIDGE ROAD and parallel to the Thames (but at a distance). It provides access to a number of buildings, including those of the Sea Cadet Corps, the Riverside Centre, the Falcon Rowing Club, and the Riverside Club (CAIN: pp306/311-12). The Riverside Club may be based at the Riverside Centre (or *vice versa*). **Map E6-E7**

Meiklejohn, Rev Canon Keith D. MA. He follows Lionel LAWSON as vicar of ST FRIDESWIDE'S and mistakenly thinks that Morse has come to the church for confession. Morse's response is worth recording: "I'm afraid I've not been sinning much today. In fact there's many a day when I hardly get through any sinning at all" (SERV: p190). Meiklejohn misses an appointment at PUSEY HOUSE to allow Morse and Lewis access to the crypt. He is originally from Dorset, unmarried, aged 41 years at the time of the case, and knows something of each St Augustine (SERV: p239).

Merton College Only one reference has been traced to this college – CAIN (p15) records that MCCLURE had a Junior Fellowship here (as did his wife). Although GARDNER was the Merton Professor of English Literature (the college and the professorship both being named after Walter de Merton) she was based at ST HILDA'S. **Plate 45**

Metropolitan Police The name (often reduced to 'The Met') of the police force responsible for the London area (with the exception of the small area covered by the City of London Police).

Michaels, Cathy The beautiful young wife (much younger) of David MICHAELS; she claims to have been born in Uppingham (Rutland) and may have been married before, as Catharine Adams (but it is all rather confusing). She is concerned that, perhaps, her husband is being a little too helpful to the police. Her performance as one of the three little maids in *The Mikado* in the WYTHAM village hall has a hint of eroticism about it (WOOD) and, during an interview, Morse looks '… unblinkingly at the lovely girl seated opposite him' (p362).

Michaels, David He is the head forester at WYTHAM WOODS but unavailable when Morse and Lewis first want to seek his help (his wife advises them that he is away on a National Trust conference in Durham). He is about 50 years old, bearded with blue eyes, and has been in the post for some 15 years (WOOD).

Michaels, Mrs The landlady of the GEORGE. She is auburn-haired, a smoker, and married with a daughter (WATC).

Middle Way A road running between SQUITCHEY LANE and SOUTH PARADE, with the BANBURY ROAD to the east and the WOODSTOCK ROAD to the west. It is the home of the SUMMERTOWN Bridge Club (JERI) and the North Oxford Conservative Association (WNCH: p199), and has a post office at its southern end (ANNX: p28). **Map C3**

Mikado, The A light opera by Gilbert and Sullivan. Lewis saw a production at school, and it features prominently in the WOOD case, and selections from it are also performed in SERV (p74).

Milk of Magnesia A branded medicine, taken in either liquid or tablet form to combat indigestion, marketed by the company Phillips'.

Milk tokens Both PHILLOTSON and Lewis use these (CAIN: p76 and WOOD: p275 respectively). The primary use of such tokens was as a welfare benefit but they could also be used to 'pay' the milkman (or woman) without leaving cash outside.

Minor (Individuals, Firms, and Organisations) See APPENDIX D.

Minster, The A PUBLIC HOUSE in the HIGH; it is notable for possessing a 'gentlemen only' bar at the back. In common with many Oxford pubs, witty graffiti can sometimes be found in its toilets; in common with almost all pubs, less than witty graffiti may also be found (LBUS: pp28/110).

Mirror, The See *DAILY MIRROR, The*.

Mitre, The A public house on the corner of the HIGH and TURL STREET (which Morse *once* walks past without entering) and is therefore notable for that fact alone (JERI: p125). It is some 100 yards from LONSDALE College; Morse arrives here early (for a meeting with Lewis) '… but a thirty–minute wait in a pub was no great trial of patience …' (MILE: p139) and contemplates leaving a supper in LONSDALE so he could spend half an hour alone there (p275). Margaret BOWMAN drinks two large BELL'S here while contemplating her future (ANNX: pp208-9) and Ashley DAVIES has taken and entertained a girlfriend there (CAIN: p146). **Plate 46**

Moat Hotel Found at the top of the WOODSTOCK ROAD. Mr PALMER moves here after a murder at the HAWORTH HOTEL (ANNX: p125).

Mods The first of two public examinations in some subjects at OXFORD UNIVERSITY (and taken by Morse in 1952). Also see GREATS.

Momigliano, Arnaldo (1908-1987) Italian historian whose 1966 book *Studies in Historiography* (published by Weidenfeld and Nicholson) is purchased by PHILLIPSON from BLACKWELL'S (WEAR).

Morris Bar, The An unremarkable place to drink (for both Lewis and Morse) in the motel on the roundabout at the junction of the WOODSTOCK ROAD and the A34.

Morris, Paul Organist at ST FRIDESWIDE'S (SERV) and a music teacher at the ROGER BACON Comprehensive School. He has been widowed since 1974 and lives at 3 Home Close (a rented semi-detached house) in KIDLINGTON. His nickname from some of the pupils is 'Dapper', from his habit of wearing suits and ties – one of which is light-blue (SERV).

Morris, Peter Only son of Paul MORRIS, a choirboy at ST FRIDESWIDE'S (SERV) and a schoolboy at ROGER BACON. His mother died in 1974 in a car accident.

Morse, Endeavour (1930-1998) Morse appears *throughout* this Companion (as indeed he must). The sections and comments below merely attempt to bring some focus to certain of his attributes and practices; other entries contain information, for example, on such matters as Morse and CROSSWORDS or his relationship with Max. A potentially vain attempt has been made in this Companion to omit nothing of Morse that is known from the WORKS.[3]

'A lover of classical music and an enthusiast for crosswords, Inspector Morse is a problem-solving detective, delving into the minutiae of a case rather than psychoanalysing his suspects

---

[3] Boswell has, of Johnson: 'Let me be not censured for mentioning such minute particulars. Every thing relative to so great a man is worth observing.' (1930: p458). Earlier, Boswell records Johnson as saying: "Sir, there is nothing too little for so little a creature as man. It is by studying little things that we attain the great knowledge of having as little misery and as much happiness as possible." Rather oddly, this is Johnson speaking of Boswell's private journal (in the entry for 16th July 1763 in Boswell 1950). No claim is made here to Boswellian skill or intimacy with one's subject.

… Spiritually a loner, he has never married although he enjoys the company of women. He has a sound working relationship with his sergeant, Lewis, but finds his superiors unaccommodating … He is very squeamish, a problem for a man who has to deal with corpses and attend autopsies. This, and his distaste for much of his job, has meant that his need for alcohol has seriously affected his health …'

This succinct summary captures the essential Morse in but a paragraph. The quotation is from Chambers (2004); the title of the work ('Dictionary of Literary Characters') is most apt – Morse is certainly a 'literary' 'character' being both 'knowledgeable about literature … bookish … (of language) formal' and 'a person especially noted for eccentricity or distinctive personality' (Chambers 2003). Although Morse is, of course, dead it seems a little harsh to always write about him in the past tense and the following mixes and matches tenses at will.

A Brief Chronology

1930	Birth
1935-1948	School
1948-1950	National Service
1950-1954	Oxford University
1954	Joins police
Pre-1971	Rises to rank of Detective Chief Inspector
1971	Leads the investigation in the LBUS case
1971-1998	A number of recorded cases
1998	Death

Family and Background The origins of the surname 'Morse' are probably from the personal name Morris, itself from the French Maurice or Latin Maurus meaning 'Moorish' i.e. dark and swarthy; there are a variety of spellings. Examples of 'Morse' as a forename are rare.[4] There is only one E. Morse, living in North Oxford, in the local telephone directory (SERV: p100). Both his parents had left school early and were keen for the young Morse to try as hard as he could; he loved them both with a particular fondness for his father (NEIG: pp409-410). His father had been a taxi driver (JERI: p161) who drank and gambled far too much but could recite, by heart, Macaulay's *Lays of Ancient Rome*; he also read everything about Captain James Cook (**Plate 47**) (NEIG: p410). His gambling appears to have been hidden from his wife but not from Morse (REMO: p128). Morse was beside his father when he died and heard him reciting the *Lord's Prayer* (REMO: p415); he died in 1954 (MILE: p62). He recalled his mother as 'loving and kind' (SERV: p91); she was a Quaker (NEIG: p410). The only books he could remember belonging to his parents were *Chambers' Dictionary*, *A Pictorial History of the Great War*, and *The Life of Captain Cook* (REMO: p128). A black and white photograph of them (his parents rather than their books) was found in Morse's desk drawer after his death (REMO: p429). His great-aunt Freda (or Gladys) lived in Alnwick but died, aged 92 years, before or during the 1996 NEIG case

---

[4] A Morse Hudson appears in the HOLMES' case *The Six Napoleons*.

(LBUS: p165; NEIG: p183; REMO: pp393/410); oddly, this aunt appears to have been aged 97 years in 1989 (WNCH: p16) unless, of course, this reference indicates the presence of another and previously *undiscovered* relative. A pair of Northumbrian sisters perhaps, mistakenly recalled by Morse as a single entity? But by 1989 (WNCH: p56), and confirmed elsewhere (REMO: pp21/267), Morse has no next of kin nor living relatives.

Birth There is some evidence in The WORKS to enable Morse's birth to be pinpointed but with only a small degree of accuracy. Needless to say, efforts to track down a birth certificate have (so far) been in vain, even knowing that Morse was born under the sign of Libra (CAIN: p32) and therefore narrowing the months to September or October. As to the year, well ... Morse is aged 50 years in JERI (p4) – more precisely, '... he was only just past his fiftieth birthday' (p130) and the case is October-based. With a case date of 1979, his birth year is therefore limited to 1928 or 1929. The MILE case of 1980 has Morse aged 52 years (p46) and the case runs through July and August which agrees with 1928 or 1929. In the 1975 WEAR case, he is in his 'mid-forties' (p193) and this *may* suggest a preference for 1929; NICQ, dated to 1975, has him in his mid- to late-forties (p254). However, the date of the SERV investigation is indubitably 1978 (and around about Easter – pp211-212); similarly, Morse is definitely 47 years old (p47) – which gives 1930 as the only possibility (and confirms the existence of numerical coincidences).

Goodwin (2002), in his lavishly illustrated book, has provided a list of dates (and places) for Morse's life prior to 1971 (or, as he has it, 1975 – but see DATES). For example, he gives his birth-date as '... in the final days of September, 1930' in Stamford, Lincolnshire (p136) and his entry into ST JOHN'S as October 1950 (p26). If Morse had been born in the same place and at the same time as DEXTER, this must surely rank as one of the more amazing coincidences to which Morse was so susceptible (see also *Coincidences* under LITERARY CURIOSITIES). ANNX adds a further twist. The case begins shortly before Christmas in 1985 and Morse is precisely aged as 54 years old (pp149-150); so 1931 is the year of his birth. He is, unfortunately, mistaken for a pensioner in 1980 (MILE: p88) but he is suffering somewhat at the time. With a date range of 1928 to 1931, explicable no doubt by Morse's faulty memory or the odd slip by DEXTER, little can be done but accept that coincidences do occur and plump for 1930 as a tentative answer.[5]

His father's hero was Captain Cook (NEIG: p122) and he was christened Endeavour after the name of Cook's ship (**Plate 48**) and in a parental spirit of encouraging effort. Morse '... had never quite forgiven his parents for christening their only offspring as they had' (JERI: p109); and is, for example, unwilling to tell Ellie SMITH any more about his forename beyond that it begins with an 'E' (CAIN: p282). Perhaps he should be grateful that his father did not have such an interest in Nansen or da Gama.

---

[5] The implication that Morse is aged 55 years in the JWEL case of 1990 – giving a birth year of, say, 1935 – may (one hopes) be safely ignored (p201).

Childhood "I've never known your first name, and I don't give a sod what it is. For all I know it's "Eric" or "Ernie" or something" (Max speaking); Morse '… had ever sought to surround his Christian name in the decent mists of anonymity …' (MILE: p75). There is no clear evidence but it is likely that this particular reticence to reveal his name started early in childhood. It is, one guesses, unlikely to be connected with his fear of the dark as a boy (WOOD: p195). The young Morse grew up in a house with a tiny kitchen; the house is now demolished (WNCH: p221) but may well have been in Oxford for Morse used to watch steam trains from a bridge near the WOODSTOCK roundabout (WEAR: p22). And this interest in railways (and model trains) was cemented by the *Meccano Magazine* that he read each month until the age of 12; he also read the weekly *Dandy* (NEIG: p204). Other activities included visiting archaeological sites (WNCH: p147), singing in a choir (SERV: p164), listening to the radio and Raymond Glendenning (SERV: p105), and going to a music-hall with his parents (SERV: p165). The family had no pets (WOOD: p82). Whether or not he had a camera is a moot point: Lewis is sure that Morse had told him (WOOD: p83) that he had a 'Brownie' camera given to him (that he failed to master) but Morse himself is quite adamant: "I've never had a camera myself …" (REMO: p131 and confirmed in NEIG: p53). It is also a little unclear when his interest in CROSSWORDS started – CAIN: p22 gives early teens while NEIG: p274 has mid-twenties.

An eating habit was formed early in life – how to properly tackle EGG AND CHIPS (WNCH: p153); he started drinking alcohol aged 14 years (REMO: p303) and appears to have rather liked it, if later practice is a true guide. While he later admired the Boy Scout movement he was never a 'tenderfoot' himself (WEAR: p40; WOOD: p161).

Early Education No examples of Morse's school reports have been found but it is likely that at least one recorded his failure to 'make the best of his limited abilities' (WEAR: p50). Nor is it easy to split exactly his activities at his junior school from his grammar days beyond knowing that the following are from the former. For example, he remembered history books from his first school and drawings of skulls of *Eoanthropus dawsoni* and *Pithecanthropus erectus* (MILE: p87), and at '… the age of eight he had known – and still knew (with the exception of South Dakota) – all the capital cities of the American States' (WNCH: p51).[6] Why would Morse forget 'Pierre'? At the age of 10 he had memorised lists of American presidents and the kings and queens of England (REMO: p46), starting at William the First (JWEL: p60). He had also been fascinated by a picture of an American slave-ring without understanding the caption (NEIG: p49). He sat the eleven-plus examination (in, probably, 1941) and recalled that the stupid boy next to him was far quicker at solving anagrams (SERV: p158). He passed and moved up to a single-sex Midlands Grammar School (CAIN: p41; WNCH: p87; MILE: p48). He was taught Latin early and, by all accounts, taught it well; he remembers his old Latin master but whether he was an aged teacher or simply from the past is a matter of conjecture (WEAR: p167). He appears to have retained a fondness and admiration for traditional methods of schooling; he

---

[6] Morse has been known to try and retrieve a name or word that has proved elusive by the diversionary tactic of reciting the State capitals (LBUS: p74).

is certainly dismissive of a subject such as 'Environmental Studies' and expresses a sour contempt for sociology (WEAR: p69). He did not thrive in the 'hard' sciences and grew to distrust the 'soft' ones. He was taught French, remembering many years later that 'donne, donnes, and donnent' are pronounced the same way (WEAR: pp70/305). It seems he had some basic German (JERI: p102) but both this subject and Geography were dropped in favour of Greek (WNCH: p51; STOR: p171); his knowledge of Geography may be described as 'minimal' (WNCH: p51) and he has, in later life, no instinct for which is east and which is west (ANNX: p122).

Science was not, apparently, a favourite. Physics was largely a closed world to him but Heisenberg and his 'uncertainty principle' stuck with him (WOOD: p385) and while he remembered the Wheatstone Bridge it '… had ever remained a deep mystery to him.' (WOOD: p385; CAIN: p341); in fact, he hated the subject (WOOD: p185). He was later to claim that he had no medical or scientific qualifications (WNCH: 102). In History he obtained a School Certificate with credit (WNCH: p84) but his main academic direction was to the Classics: "I was a Classic in my youth …" (JWEL: p297). As a boy, he was moved by Socrates' final words about the long, unbroken, dreamless sleep of death (WOOD: pp207/260).[7] He read Catullus but was advised to ignore poem LVIII (CAIN: p42) – which is relatively tame compared to some others – and he spent many hours with Plato (NEIG: p181); he also mastered the rule that 'if' introduces the pluperfect subjunctive in Latin (NEIG: p15). He had always wanted to know answers (WNCH: p193): in Sunday School he pondered about the creation of God, the location of Heaven, and the limits of space (NEIG: pp273-274) and this curiosity was only partly satisfied by his progress in algebra and translating Greek texts.

Interests during his school-days included a short-lived one in church architecture (SERV: p50; REMO: pp205-206), reading the *Naturist Journal* while in the Lower IVA (NEIG: p173), and a first experience of love – aged 15 years – which lasted some three years (CAIN: p41). He also learned the etymology of the names of flowers and any associated mythology (REMO: p8). He is able, for example to use the Latin name *Asphodelina lutea* (more often *Aspholdeline lutea* or, commonly, King's Spears) as an excuse to examine a garden (WOOD: p156). Though it is also recorded that he would not recognise an asphodel if it '… flashed across a Technicolor screen' (REMO: p8). He left the sixth form in 1948 (WOOD: p10).

National Service Before going up to ST JOHN'S, Morse was called up and spent 18 months of National Service with the Royal Signals Regiment (MILE: p56; CAIN: p41). It was during this period that he discovered he had sensitive skin (NICQ: p50), crossed a river in harness (REMO: p260), and was tested – successfully it seems - for colour blindness (WEAR: p164). It may have been at this time that he started to develop his knowledge of ties (for example, recognising a Royal Marine Commando one in SERV). Morse

---

[7] The words may be found in *The Apology* and the speech to the jurors. Morse recalls them shortly before his own death (REMO: p338).

occasionally uses slang associated with the armed forces – Egyptian P.T. for sleep, especially a nap in the afternoon (SERV: p291; REMO: p154). Puxley (2004) gives its origins as the Second World War when serving British soldiers mocked the supposed laziness ascribed to Arabs. Morse's reference to the 'Egyptian Civil Service' (ANNX: p170) may fall into the same category (but then again may not).

University Morse went up to ST JOHN'S (Oxford) in the Michaelmas term in 1950 with an exhibition in Classics (MILE: p48). The date is relatively certain – although MILE (p48) gives '… just after the war …', the 1971 LBUS case has him at university '… twenty years ago …' (p188) and 1950 matches with the established dates for his early life. He followed the dress code of the time – a college scarf, a tie, and sometimes a blazer (NICQ: p-145) and, presumably, explored for the first time many of Oxford's pubs. Little would be known of his four years at college were it not for the lengthy recollections recounted in MILE (particularly pp56-62). His first two years were the happiest and most purposeful and he was awarded a first in Classical Moderations in 1952 but in the middle of his third year he met Wendy SPENCER and began a deep but ultimately disastrous love affair. He had moved from his college rooms to a college-owned property at 24 ST JOHN STREET (not at first knowing that Wendy lived at 22). He had gone to see an Oxford University Dramatic Society production of Marlowe's *Doctor Faustus* at the NEW THEATRE (in February 1953) and in the interval Morse had managed to get to the front of the crowded bar and had been served his pint when Wendy, behind him, took the opportunity to ask him to order for her. Morse, of course, obliged and (understandably) took her pound for two GINs AND TONICs. Joining her – and her friend Sheila – Morse suggested that they all meet at the RANDOLPH for a post-play drink and although only Sheila turned up it was then that he discovered he and Wendy were neighbours.[8] After some four days of mooning listlessness, he plucked up the courage to knock at her flat door and impetuously declared his love. They spent almost all their time together (often in bed) but with an awful impact on both their academic activities. Despite warnings to improve his performance, Morse made little effort and his exhibition was rescinded and he was forced to apply to his county authority for funds. Wendy had left Oxford to look after her ailing mother and despite visiting her twice (Wendy that is, though perhaps he saw the mother as well) the affair was terminated despite a desperate plea from Morse. And this but three weeks before his final exams. Predictably, he failed GREATS and left the university without a degree. Only in later years did Morse come across the theory that one may revise while drunk and achieve decent results if the exam is sat in a similar frame of mind (JERI: p113); perhaps he had read *The Mystery of Edwin Drood* by DICKENS – '… thus, if I hide my watch when I am drunk, I must be drunk again before I can remember where' (Chapter 3). He remembered his university time as '… dark, disastrous days' (MILE: p47) and sometimes '… he thought again of his own sad days at Oxford' (MILE: p50;) or, while examining a room in WOLSEY COLLEGE, '… his own unhappy, unsuccessful days at Oxford …' (CAIN: p88). Perhaps BROWNE-SMITH was close to the mark when he wrote (some years later) to Morse: 'You were a fool

---

[8] Morse later recalls a 'girlfriend' called Sheila from his days at university (JWEL: p70). This otherwise unidentified Sheila is unlikely, for any number of reasons, to be either POSTER or WILLIAMS.

when you were an undergraduate – wasting, as you did, the precious talents of a clear, clean mind' (MILE: p166).

Police career Morse's father suggested the police as a career after Morse had failed to obtain a degree (MILE: p62); Morse obviously took the first steps and joined the force, presumably, as a constable. By 1971, at least, he had achieved the rank of Detective Chief Inspector (LBUS: p36) but he did not progress above this despite a further 27 years of service (REMO: p7). On various occasions he gave lectures to colleagues on good practice and procedure (LBUS: p89; JERI: p22) though he himself rarely followed such advice (for example, WOOD: pp161-162 and the GOLD case); he also claimed to know nothing about the law (NICQ: p216). He was seconded to West Africa for 8 weeks in late 1977 (SERV: p48). Although he had known Lewis slightly, the two had never worked together until the LBUS case (pp15-17). It is almost certain that they worked together on a far larger number of cases than have been recorded – Morse comments at one point: "We've been on a lot of cases together, Lewis …" (ANNX: p250) – as solving one case every few years or so would not really justify their salaries and might suggest a drastic misuse of police time.

Physical appearance[9] No photographs exist but from descriptions in The WORKS one can almost imagine him looking rather like the late actor John Thaw. We certainly know him, in the early 1970s, to be lightly built and dark haired (LBUS: p15) and to be concerned about his thinning hair and tendency to put on weight; 'he wasn't a tall man' (LBUS: p220) nor was he 'a big man' (WEAR: p80), he was 'medium height' (WEAR: p227) and just over medium height (SERV: p57). But he does not need to duck to get into the TURF pub (CAIN: p78). He has been described as 'pleasant-looking' (NICQ: p254), with nice ears (CAIN: p281), a pale olive complexion (REMO: p178), and with a Jewish nose (ANNX: p71). He is, at one time anyway, slimmer than Lewis (SERV: p268) and remains shorter (WOOD: p152); his weight in 1996 is almost thirteen stone (NEIG: p235) though this is after he has been losing it because of his DIABETES. His nails are well-manicured (ANNX: p182) and he claims, with what justification is not apparent, to have nice feet (WNCH: p145).

> **Hair** The WORKS accurately (one hopes) chart the changing thickness and colour of his hair from a bald patch (NICQ: p217) and thinning hair (SERV: 261; JERI: p31) to 'thinning grey-black' (MILE: p177) to balding and whitish (WNCH: pp74/76) and prematurely white (NEIG: p243). If he has been correctly identified in the 1992 BAGG case, his hair is then still grey (p241). Morse has his hair cut professionally – on one occasion by the great Gerrard himself who offers him: "The usual, sir?" (NEIG: p88). On this occasion, Morse perceives his hair as turning from ironish-grey to purish-white. 'He was never happy when his hair began to grow in untidy, curling profusion just above his collar, and he wondered sadly why it now failed to sustain such luxuriance upon the top of his head' (NICQ: p50). His post-haircut ritual involved washing his hair and changing

---

[9] See the comments under LEWIS and *Physical appearance*; they may help to explain inconsistencies in the physical description of Morse.

his shirt – to protect what he felt was rather sensitive skin (NEIG: p103). His eyebrows are dark (MILE: p67) and he is invariably clean-shaven, using an old electric razor (JWEL: p155).

Eyes 'To an observer, Morse's eyes would have appeared slightly 'set', as Shakespeare has it ...' (MILE: p55). According to Onions (1911), one of the ten meanings of 'set' is '(of the eyes) to be dimmed by drink'. They have also been described as 'fanatical' (ANNX: p57) by comparison to the politicians Tony Benn, Keith Joseph, and Enoch Powell. His eyesight is reasonably good but he does wear National Health Service half-lens glasses, at least by the time of the ANNX case (p71). Bizarrely, his eyes may either have been blue or 'light-grey' (WEAR: p91 gives light-grey, WEAR: p114 and 157 give grey) but blue is the predominant description in later cases. One guesses their description relies on the testimony of different witnesses.[10]

His Voice No known recordings have been traced but by all accounts Morse's singing voice is a baritone (WEAR: p234); its tenor has been described as '... bleating, uncertain ...' and '... unmusical ...' (NEIG: p250; CAIN: p194). Of his accent, one must remain silent.

Clothing Morse does not seem to have an extensive wardrobe (by any stretch of the imagination). Three pairs of pyjamas (CAIN: p162), at least one of which is 'gaudy' (WNCH: pp1/76; REMO: p401) and is possibly the exciting mauve and Cambridge Blue pair (NEIG: p225); tweed trousers (ANNX: p128) and a 'rumpled slate-grey suit (REMO: p178). And a scarf – useful when one has toothache (MILE: pp85/89) – which can, Morse realises, also be useful as part of a disguise (CAIN: p180 and MILE: p105). Almost certainly Morse has another suit (or suits) and probably a selection of ties but the evidence is rare if not non-existent; he can certainly recognise a number of ties, including that of the Oxford Magdalen School (JERI: p125). He does, apparently, little better with shirts – an off-white one (JWEL: p322) and a pink 'un (WOOD: pp95/109) - and one of these may well have a tight and slightly frayed collar (CAIN: p17) – and a clean white one which goes rather well with a pair of grey flannels (NEIG: p249). His size 8 feet (LBUS: p177) are accommodated in bedroom slippers (LBUS: p39) and probably only two pairs of shoes (WNCH: p81). He has at least one plimsoll '... and a dangerously low supply of suitable socks ...' (LBUS: p175) and is forced to buy a pair of otherwise useless size 10 shoes to accommodate a damaged foot (LBUS: p177). He owns a light fawn raincoat (JERI: p179) and an expensive-looking dark grey overcoat (ANNX: p150) or greatcoat (ANNX: p300). Of his sole handkerchief (ANNX: p105), it may be best to be a little reticent. It is 'grubby' in 1994 (CAIN: pp161-162) but washed – and ironed! - by himself by 1998 (REMO: p193).

---

[10] References to the colour of his eyes may also be found at LBUS: p17; WEAR: pp288/321; NICQ: pp52/152/235/256; SERV: pp67/123/170/231/240: JERI: pp5/107/116; MILE: 53/177; ANNX: p53; WNCH: pp76/79/226; WOOD: p350; CAIN: p9; REMO: p30; and CALL p275.

His Flat In Oxford There are many 'clues' as to the location of Morse's bachelor flat – it is at the 'top' of NORTH OXFORD (NICQ: p50), about 100 yards from the BANBURY ROAD roundabout (MILE: p149), it is 'just south' of the A40 road (JWEL: p75), some directions are given in REMO (p148), and details of Morse's route when posting a letter (WNCH: p198) narrow down the address even further. However, from a combination of JERI (p74) and WOOD (p107) the address is made certain as 45, The Flats, Leys Close, BANBURY ROAD (**Map C2**). He has lived there for many years and owns it, originally with the aid of a mortgage (ANNX: pp17/24) which has been paid off by 1998 at least (REMO: p430) and should have been by 1991 (WNCH: p196). Visitors to the location should, of course, respect the privacy of the current occupant(s). His flat is in a two-storey, yellow-bricked (with white woodwork) block of newish properties and reached through a courtyard marked 'Residents Only: No Public Right of Way'.[11] It has its own entrance hall (DODO: p84) and his front door has some frosted glass, a small letterbox, loud doorbell, and may be bolted and locked (WOOD: p108; WNCH: p2; REMO: pp10/360/409; NEIG: p173). Here are left, in the porch, a daily pint of semi-skinned Co-op milk, purchased with milk tokens (SERV: p65; WOOD: p108; REMO: p428; WATC: p129). On the ground floor may be found a lounge and a kitchen, with two bedrooms and bathroom facilities upstairs (WOOD: p381). On the landing, sits a nest of Chippendale tables from 1756 (WATC: 129).[12] He also has an upstairs room, used as a study (REMO: p428). His flat has partial central heating (WNCH: p172) and he has not had a coal fire since 1977 (WOOD: p164). Most of these rooms are briefly discussed further below. The flat is very much Morse's retreat – to drink, to read, to listen to music and the radio in these '… book-lined, Wagner-haunted rooms …' (MYST: p45) – and guests are few and far between; he rarely speaks to his neighbours (NEIG: p305). Morse has a garage (WEAR: p141) and a garden (LBUS: pp174/177), his own '… little patch of greenery …' (REMO: p21), from which he has, on occasion, improperly disposed of grass-cuttings (REMO: p119), perhaps because he believes that dustmen do not take garden waste (WOOD: p358). The location of his 'small window-box' can only be guessed at (NEIG: p402).

Lounge This is large and has two settees – both leather, one honey-coloured and a smaller one in black – with a sophisticated bank of musical equipment (WOOD: p108). There is also a writing-desk (LBUS: p119), an armchair (WNCH: p181), and a low coffee table (WOOD: p108). Morse's rented television may be found here, and only after 1996, a video recorder (NEIG: p273; REMO: p13) together with a CD player and, one guesses, a record and tape player (REMO: p252). Morse keeps his bills on the mantelpiece (LBUS: p199) behind a clock. A French window opens onto the garden (REMO: p8). Three of the pastel-coloured walls are lined with books, there are stacks of records everywhere, and at least four pictures including reproductions of Rembrandt, Vermeer (*The Milkmaid*), Atkinson Grimshaw, and a water-colour of the Oxford skyline in a bluey-purple wash (WOOD: p110; CAIN: p285; REMO: p252). Morse looks

---

[11] See *Apostrophes* under LITERARY CURIOSITIES for the sign in the parking area.
[12] This nest – a family heirloom – appears neither in Morse's will nor in his own 'list' of valuable items (REMO: pp430-431; NEIG: p305); Morse does not see the need for a burglar alarm (NEIG: p305).

closely at his only water-colour after a romantic meal when clouds are discussed – for he '… had never consciously contemplated a cloud …' before (CAIN: p285).

Study Here are a white carpet, a Scandinavian oak desk, and a black leather armchair (WEAR: p116). On the desk sits an ancient portable typewriter (WOOD: p408) and a red angle-lamp; the walls are sun-bed tan, terracotta, and white and only one – bearing a Matisse reproduction - is free of books (REMO: p428). In one of the desk drawers, Lewis finds six personal photographs (listed in REMO: p429).

Kitchen It is unclear whether or not the hole in a wall of this room was ever repaired as Morse fell from his set of household steps during the proposed DIY attempt (LBUS: p115); it somehow seems likelier that he would simply have hung a picture over it some time after his return from hospital. The bottle of Persil on the draining board (WOOD: p108) is only a temporary fixture.

Morse's bedroom The view from his curtained (and double glazed) window is over the BANBURY ROAD (MILE: p149; JWEL: p19). On his bedside table may be found a portable radio, a telephone, and an alarm clock; the room has a mantelpiece above, one guesses, a redundant fireplace (LBUS: pp174/176). His bedroom is also the likely location for his late mother's walnut suite (MILE: pp198-199) and has a single chair (NEIG: p306). Lewis is, apparently, the only person to have a key (other than Morse) to the flat (NEIG: p305; REMO: p410) which rather repeats the question, raised by Bishop (2006: p84), of how does Mrs Green, the cleaner, gain access.

Possessions Morse is not unduly materialistic beyond books and music. His collection of 6 expensive cut-glass tumblers (from his mother) is down to 3 glasses after Strange breaks one (REMO: pp22-23) and he has a pair of binoculars of unknown make (WOOD: p24) replaced years later by a second-hand 8/50mm pair (REMO: p9). His wallet contains a BODLEIAN Library ticket, a phonecard, cards for Lloyds, the blood donor service, BLACKWELL'S Bookshop, Oxford City Library, and the RAC (NEIG: p43); he also has an OXFORD UNIVERSITY diary (REMO: p148). His silver Parker pen (perhaps won as a CROSSWORD prize) makes an appearance in several cases (NICQ: p116; JWEL: p200; WOOD: pp40/147; and REMO: p361).

His Office Morse is based at KIDLINGTON HQ and is of sufficient rank to have his own office (where, seated in his black leather armchair (ANNX: p289) he has been known to do the odd CROSSWORD or two). Morse has personalised the office to the extent that he has a bottle of GLENFIDDICH (GOLD: p25), a copy of *Chambers* (NICQ: p215) and Fowler's *Modern English Usage* (LBUS: p155), and six pint bottles of beer – together with glasses and an opener – in a wall cupboard (NICQ: p216). His office overlooks the car park (GOLD: p25), has a fluorescent light and no curtains (NICQ: p126), and a large map of Oxford City to the left of the door (ANNX: p256). The office carpet is off-white (GOLD: p26) and finishes six inches short of the skirting-board (REMO: p74). The office also has, somewhat obviously, a desk – and a filing cabinet (LBUS: p156).

Smoking Morse is '… not an addictive smoker' (LBUS: p54); a few years later 'he either smoked addictively or not at all …' (SERV: p316); he goes through very many bouts of giving up and restarting. When he does smoke, it always seems to be cigarettes and he rapidly finishes a packet before deciding to give up again (or buy another packet); no references to cigars or pipes appear, for Morse, in the WORKS. Sometimes, he 'was glad to find he had one last cigarette left' (WEAR: p112). On rare occasions he smokes 'cigarette after cigarette' (WEAR: p309; JWEL: p268) – he smokes '… at an extravagantly compulsive rate or not at all' (JERI: p167). His brand of choice is Dunhill International; he smokes at the rate of about 30 a day (WNCH: p8). He certainly smokes during all the thirteen major cases.[13] He tries to give up in most of them with, of course, little permanent success – for example, he has given up for the thousandth time during the ANNX case (p64) and manages to last from Christmas to New Year before succumbing in the ROYAL OAK (p220). In the NEIG case he appears to succeed – reaching for the 'cellophaned packet', he resists but it is, perhaps, the CAIN case that explores most fully the patterns of his addiction. Having given up in the morning, he refuses an offered cigarette only to change his mind seconds later and then accepting a further one during the same (short) interview (pp68/71); in the afternoon of the same day he borrows money from Lewis to buy a packet in the TURF and, surprisingly, pays him back (pp80/85). During a bout of illness (pp159-163) he is still smoking but has again given up (p210) before succumbing once more (p211). At Lewis's urging, he smokes a final cigarette before throwing the rest of the packet in his office bin but retrieves it when Lewis has departed (pp225-227). A little later in the case, Morse refuses a cigarette from Ellie SMITH (who does notice that his car's ashtray is full) but is soon smoking again having given up for a remarkable 3 or 4 days (pp252-253/262). At the end of the case he determines that he will permanently renounce nicotine on the first of November 1994; he is certainly smoking two years later (NEIG) until late in the case when he merely fumbles with the cellophane wrapping on a packet (p327). One benefit for Morse of smoking is the usefulness of matchboxes. Some of his thoughts on suicidal tendencies come from the back of such a box (SERV: p206) and his knowledge of Pythagorean Triplets is from a similar source (CAIN: p263). As Morse himself says, "I've learned quite a lot in life from the back of matchboxes" (NEIG: p148). And finally, a clue (perhaps) to his behaviour and addiction as Morse recalls that smoking was a vice '… but one which had given him almost as much pleasure as any other vice in life' (REMO: p149).

Food In common with many middle-aged people (particularly men, perhaps), Morse has mastered the art of food estimation – that rapid and continuous calculation that begins with the first examination of a meal, proceeds throughout the eating of the various elements in combination, and ends with the last triumphant mixture. Morse, for example carefully mounts: '… the last segment of his fried egg on the last square of his fried bread' (WOOD: p76). While he enjoys the roast beef of the Lewis family, he is not averse to the somewhat more exotic – considering, and finally eating (for example) a Chinese takeaway meal (WEAR: pp118/231) and he is even prepared to eat a hamburger from a stall (SERV: p109).

---

[13] For example – LBUS: p54; WEAR: p112; NICQ: pp94/242; JERI: p26; MILE: p50 and 55 when he stocks up on supplies; ANNX: p220; WNCH: p8; JWEL: p293; WOOD: p22; CAIN: pp68/71; NEIG: pp119/209; and REMO: p253. He also smokes in BURG (p288).

Although he claims to have only the culinary skill of boiling an egg (CAIN: p374) he has certainly cooked himself a large percentage of an ENGLISH BREAKFAST; on occasions, in the morning and when rather unwell, he has to weigh up the benefits and consequences of a single Weetabix cereal (WNCH: p1). When particularly unwell, he is unable to find his emergency Mars Bar (REMO: p223). When dining out he has been known to eat sparingly (he would prefer more to drink than to eat) but enjoys, at least, Stilton cheese (WOOD: pp17/19). His lunch at the Swedish Embassy in Montague Place is but the '… thin pale slice of white-pastried quiche, the half jacket potato, and the large separate bowl of undressed salad' (WOOD: p266). He escapes as soon as he is able – to a pub in Holborn and Ruddles County BITTER. Pub meals include a vegetable lasagne in the KING'S ARMS in the BROAD (NEIG: p277) and a packet of plain crisps in the FRIAR BACON (ANNX: p278). On many occasions, he prefers to take his lunchtime calories in liquid form (for example, CAIN: p241; WOOD: p254; STOR: p176) and this leads here, inexorably, to the subject of Morse and alcohol.

Drink Morse has been known to be happy without the presence of alcohol but these occasions are rare. His first recorded drink during a case is a WHISKY in the BLACK PRINCE (LBUS: p17) and his last, a Scotch, very shortly before his death (REMO: p419). Between those two occasions the records show a varied but regular intake in what may be termed either a heroic or an excessive devotion. Bishop (2006) has listed, on a case by case basis, Morse's consumption and it is unnecessary to repeat such detail here, informative as it may be. Rather, this section is broken into types of drink, views on practice and consumption, and a final section on drinking habits (a slight emphasis on beer) with a few relevant quotations involving Lewis and the whole subject of Morse and alcohol.

Whisky Morse invariably drinks doubles (e.g. LBUS: p18, MILE pp59/187) in pubs and, almost certainly, larger measures at home (such as SERV: p80; REMO: p368) or in private company (for example, WEAR: p246; REMO: p401), where units are not subject to Licensing Acts. Preferred brands include BELL'S, GLENFIDDICH, and TEACHER'S but he has been known to drink Glenmorangie (and water, to look after his liver; REMO: p149 or NEIG: p384 where ice is used) with CORNFORD (NEIG pp276-277); a large Glenlivet is drunk at the RANDOLPH (JWEL: p119); and a Macallan is shared with Strange (GOLD: p3). Whisky is often drunk after beer (for example, ANNX: pp277-278, CAIN: p60, or REMO: p314) and, occasionally, before (JWEL sees Morse have four pints after several Glenfiddichs (pp49/55-56/71); on this occasion he wisely decides not to drive, commenting: "Funny lot the police, you know" (p71). On another occasion, Morse maintains that the '… sole trouble with Malt Whisky (is that) it left one feeling rather thirsty …' – and encourages Lewis to buy him a post-Scotch beer (GOLD: pp14-15). He drinks whiskey (rather than whisky) in the COTSWOLD HOUSE (NEIG: p405) and also buys three bottles of Irish malt when acting as a chief mourner (WNCH: p203) in Ireland. The record shows that, once (and perhaps only once), he had refused the offer of a whisky (NEIG: p341); his early interest in the spirit goes back, at least, to his University days when it was declared to be a 'favourite' (NICQ: p152).

Beer Morse's staple diet. Named favourites include BRAKSPEAR's (NEIG: p163), GUINNESS (REMO: p184), Morrell's – with a large Bell's in the FRIAR BACON (ANNX: pp277-278), Burton Ale (REMO), and London Pride (NEIG). He also drinks Cask Flow Beamish (CAIN: p347) at Lewis's home and two cans of Courage which have been found in OWENS' flat (NEIG: p269). Readers may wish to pause here and contemplate how far it is to their nearest pub and what range of beers they offer. If it's the right time of day, the distance a stroll rather than a hike, and the available options acceptable, why not exercise your body and mind and raise a glass or two to the memory of Morse. Also see BEER and REAL ALE.

Wine Morse only seems to drink red wine and then only on a few occasions – for example, Quercy claret (WOOD: p97), Beaujolais (ANNX: p170), and a bottle of Médoc (despite being offered a half; WOOD: p17). Red wine makes him sentimental – and thirsty (MILE: p275).

Other alcoholic drinks Morse occasionally drinks champagne (LBUS: p184; REMO: p256) and entertains Strange, JOHNSON, and Lewis to a mid-price variety in his flat (WOOD: pp406-407). It is clear that he enjoys it but with the common caveat that he reserves for most drinks other than beer: "Champagne's a lovely drink, but it makes you thirsty, doesn't it?" (WOOD: p409). He knows how to open a bottle correctly (REMO: pp252-253) though it is unlikely that this has come from extensive practice. He is dismissive of sherry: "Bit like drinking lemonade, isn't it, Lewis?" (NICQ: p92) and it is probably more from the absence of an alternative that he drinks the same with a Headmaster (SERV: p123); he is keener on gin and French, drinking three of them on one occasion (MILE: p47). He drinks brandy (ANNX: p170) and gin and Campari (ANNX: p79). Of the latter mix, Morse comments that "... I could develop quite a taste for this".

Practice and Consumption Morse drinks at home and in pubs, in his office and restaurants or hotels, at work and on holiday, alone or in company (and 'Morse was usually reasonably tolerant about fellow-tipplers ...' (JWEL: p122). He has been known to fancy a large Scotch at 8.35am (CAIN: xxvii), certainly drinks before the sun is over the yard-arm (WOOD: p109), complains that they've "already been open five minutes" (REMO: p97), and (on a particular occasion) one learns that '... it had never occurred to Morse that he might be drinking tea at 9pm' (SERV: p77). And (on another occasion): 'It was now 11.20 a.m., and Morse felt thirsty. Perhaps he was always thirsty' (NEIG: p90). He has no time for other than the traditional serving: '... a pint of beer, for he would never lend his lips to anything less than that measure' (SERV: p322). So, how much Morse drink? When questioned (while in hospital) about his intake, Morse divides the true amount by three. From the false figures, his actual consumption seems to be between 6 to 9 pints of beer a day and a bottle of Scotch every 3 days or so (WNCH:

p8).[14] There is no mention of wine or other alcoholic drinks and these must, inevitably, somewhat bump up the average; for example, one evening meal involves two pints before dinner (and one after), a bottle of wine with, and a large malt after (WOOD: p22). In fact, Morse often regards eating while drinking as an interruption and likely to interfere with the consumption of alcohol; he considers lunchtime drinking without food as normal. He certainly has a reputation – not least with Lewis and Strange - for drinking and is happy to admit to the former that he is a 'secret drinker' (ANNX: p221); others have also recognised his reputation (e.g. WPC WRIGHT; WNCH: p127).

Drinking habits and (a few) relevant quotations Morse does occasionally drink just the one pint – usually when it his round next (e.g. REMO: p161) but the normal range is between two and four pints (e.g. a pair in CALL: pp264/266; a trio in WNCH: p232 and JERI: p206; and quartets in ANNX: p128 and JERI: p124). As Morse puts it: "… there have been some thousands of occasions in my life when I've looked forward to a third pint of beer …" (MILE: p263). Rare are the times when Morse can recall that it '… was already half past nine, and he hadn't drunk a pint all day' (JERI: p137) or that he had an almost unprecedented alcohol-free lunch (WOOD: p287). And even rarer: '… Lewis had never known Morse so apparently uninterested in his beer, over which he lingered like a maiden aunt sipping homemade wine at a church social' (NICQ: p107). The main excuse that Morse gives for drinking (as if one were needed) is to be able to *think* more clearly and to find the necessary links between seemingly disparate events or people: 'He had long since recognized the undoubted fact that his imagination was almost invariably fired by beer, especially by beer in considerable quantities' (NICQ: p67). Thinking and drinking, drinking and thinking are intrinsically bound together (NEIG: p65; JWEL: p68 – though later in this same case Morse recognises that while he often needs drink to think, on this occasion he just needs a *drink*; p289). In one case, though, he recognises that he has '… a mind so often dulled these days by (cigarettes and) alcohol' (JERI: p28). Once, when Lewis feels concerned enough to remind Morse about his liver, he receives the reply "… my medical advisers have warned me it may well be unwise to give up alcohol at my age" (NEIG: p65). Again, it is Lewis who notices that '… it was quite clear that for once in a lifetime (Morse) had *not* been drinking' (NICQ: pp215-216) – and it is Lewis who issues the (surely unnecessary) reminder: "Don't forget your beer, sir!" (JERI: p300). Let Morse have a few final words here. "I'm the only person in Oxford who gets more sober the more he drinks" (CAIN: p241) and, accurately, "… a mind like mine that's mainly motivated by thoughts of booze and sex …" (MILE: p261).

Non-alcoholic Drinks Morse drinks both tea and coffee (for example LBUS: pp42/175; NICQ: p235) and normally has sugar in the latter (MILE: p90) until a later health kick when he takes it without (NEIG: p313). His preferred tea is, one guesses, of the basic English breakfast variety (he has not heard of Darjeeling: NICQ: p137) and his favoured coffee is instant (WNCH: p173; WOOD: p112). But, 'seldom had tea as a meal, never

---

[14] A discussion between two doctors (REMO: pp36-37) confirms that the medical profession tends to multiply by three what a patient tells them.

had tea as a beverage, assumed any great importance in Morse's life' (WOOD: p267). Only three other non-alcoholic drinks need to be mentioned – an empty can of alcohol-free lager found during a police search (ANNX: p219) though one doubts if he would have been tempted by a full one, orange juice in place of coffee during the NEIG case (p210 and unsweetened p306), and copious amounts of water – early in the morning (JWEL: p75) and at night (CAIN: p244) though rarely during the day.

Telephones There is a single entry in the local telephone directory for an 'E. Morse' (WNCH: p178; WOOD: p107) but it also appears that his home number is ex-directory (and subject to change) – and given out to only a few (such as Lewis, Strange, and Ellie SMITH – CAIN: pp256/273). His ex-directory status is confirmed on a number of occasions (including NEIG: p336 and REMO: pp127/250). Perhaps he has two phones (as well as an Ansaphone machine: CALL: p271). He carries a phonecard in his wallet (NEIG: p43) and has been known to use Directory Enquiries (ANNX: p69). Morse's use of the telephone does raise one interesting possibility – that he is, in fact, left-handed. In the SERV case (p197), he drums the fingers of his left hand on the desk-top while bellowing into the mouthpiece of the phone. While by no means a certainty, the majority of right-handed people hold the receiver in their left hand to free up the right for taking notes, doodling, or whatever.[15] It seems that even in the later cases that Morse does not possess a mobile phone (though he does have a car-phone: NEIG: p331).

Language Morse revels in the correct use of the English language and his slips are rare (for example, 'you and me'; LBUS: p23).[16] He was educated in a system where errors of punctuation, spelling, and sentence construction were severely punished. He is pedantic, fussy, and happy to correct grammatical slips in others; he has been known to find 12 such errors in a 10-line report by Lewis (LBUS: p33) and to correct a statement concerning a witness seeing 'the murdered girl' to 'the girl who was later murdered' (LBUS: p39). And when dictating a press release, he is prepared to dictate a comma – not for the avoidance of doubt but for the sake of good form (MILE: p128). He has a large number of *bête noires*. These include the words 'womb' and 'kid' (CAIN: pp9/376), 'parameters' (JWEL: p74), 'scenario' (although he uses it; CAIN: p336), and (a particular favourite hate) 'actually'. He fears he will scream if he hears this last one again (NEIG: p7) and criticises Lewis for using it, calling it a weasel word (BURG: p288).[17] Although Lewis is often the source of the particular target of Morse's criticism – he has a go at him for using the cliché about flies and ointment, especially as Lewis says 'potential fly' (CAIN: p101) – MAX is also in his sights: "Why do you say 'affixed', instead of just plain 'fixed'?" or, when the medic refers to a

---

[15] In JERI (p206), Morse idly joins splashes of beer with the little finger of his left hand; perhaps, a further indication, though little need be made of the fact that he strokes his nose with left index finger (NICQ: p255). A contra-indication is that he camouflages the shake in his *right* hand when pouring drinks (REMO: p192).

[16] In a similar vein, Morse says, "We're partners, aren't we? We do things together, you and me. Or 'you and I'" (SERV: p135). An extended version of this is in CAIN (p10): "You see, we take a bit of beating, don't we, Lewis? Don't you reckon? Me and you? Morse and Lewis?"

[17] See under QUOTATIONS (from JERI) for further comments.

corpse having had 'flat feet', "... you mean he *has* flat feet?" (ANNX: pp76-77). And the traffic with Lewis is not always one-way: when Morse comments, in connection with a typed witness statement, that the word 'bad' should be the adverbial 'badly' Lewis corrects him (a little later) over his use of the word 'different' rather than the appropriate 'differently' (ANNX: pp288/293). Perhaps because of (appropriately) different educational experiences and because of Morse's need to correct, the following exchange has been recorded:

Lewis: "... due to modernization."
Morse: " 'Owing to' modernization, Lewis."
Lewis: "I've never known the difference."
Morse: "No need. Just say 'because of' and you'll always be right." (JWEL: p164).

It is almost certain that Morse knows the correct usage i.e. that *due* is an adjective and that *due to* is an adjectival phrase and must therefore qualify a noun. He is very much at ease amending a notice on a church by crossing out 'due' and substituting 'owing' (SERV: p120); STORRS, too, is accurate about such usage and is critical of a railway conductor's use of 'due to' instead of 'owing to' (NEIG: p131). What else does Morse correct? It is a relatively short list and may as well be taken in chronological order starting with 'penance' rather than 'pennance' (SERV: pp281/288/291) followed by, in a specific context, the preferred 'replicate' to 'duplicate' (MILE: p250). "Who to?" elicits Morse's response of "'To whom', do you mean?" though he does admit that "Nor I" rather than "Nor me" would be a little pedantic (ANNX: pp64/66). A reference to a 'post-graduate researcher' should be to a 'graduate researcher' (JWEL: p80) and, on being told he has a 'temperature', Morse's response is: "I thought *everybody* had got a temperature" (WNCH: p6). Even Lewis's talk of "... an empty plate of eggs and chips ..." – fairly common usage one might think – brings out the pedant in Morse: "I think you mean a plate empty of eggs and chips ..." (CAIN: p348). There are a few gaps in his comprehension. He is unsure whether or not 'calibre' refers to the diameter of a bullet or of the barrel (NEIG: p134); it can mean either. While he knows what dreadlocks look like he needs to be told what they are called (ANNX: pp74-75). He admits to having problems with spelling 'proceed' (REMO: p317) but this seems to be the only such word. Would he let a spelling mistake through a police report? *"Never!"* (MILE: p53).

Pornography There are fewer references in the WORKS to pornography than there are to ALCOHOL but a substantial body exists, nonetheless. Morse takes the subject seriously and believes that '... he had probably missed the boat in life and should have been a very highly paid and inordinately successful writer of really erotic pornography' (JERI: p 145). His consumption is irregular – looking at a Scandinavian example ignored by Lewis (ANNX: p115), twice reading 'the lewdest' book (MILE: p251) found in a flat, and twice again with a similar magazine (JERI: pp144/188) – but apparently not bought by himself. In the WOOD case, for example, he is too embarrassed to make a top shelf purchase at a newsagents (p35) and later in the same case pretends that he is uninterested in such material (pp201-202), presumably to protect his reputation while with colleagues. He claims never to have watched a pornographic video (GOLD: p30) but does so later in that case and he turns down the offer to watch a 'red-hot' example as '... a considerable sacrifice' (NEIG: p164). See also the entry for PORNOGRAPHY.

Women 'He thought, as he often thought, of the attractiveness of women. There had been women, of course; too many women, perhaps' (WEAR: p193). It would be impossible (if not a touch unseemly) to provide a complete list of Morse's affairs here but it is fair to say that an active interest in women ranks somewhere in any list of his addictions. It is also impossible to determine with any measure of certitude whether or not such an interest is simply a wish to fulfil the needs of companionship or lust. He is, of course, a bachelor but some affairs seem to be embarked upon with a view to some sort of longer term relationship; if that were the aim, then none succeed. Mention is made elsewhere (under SPENCER and *University* herein) of an early entanglement but the no doubt charming Wendy was not unique for '... lovely young girls. There had been so many of them, once ...' (NICQ: p92). And a particular interest in nurses (first noted in LBUS: p151) is maintained with a certain predictable frequency – from a 'flighty little nurse', taken by Morse back to his student digs in IFFLEY ROAD (NICQ: p152), through WIDDOWSON and Eileen Stanton (MINOR) to (at least) MACLEAN and MCQUEEN. Morse does not, however, necessarily direct his amours just to the medical profession – he has a rather unfortunate habit of also falling for some of the suspects or participants in a number of cases such as RAWLINSON, SMITH, and WILLIAMS. With many he enjoys a degree of success – including Winifred Stewart (MINOR; MILE: p216) – but not, alas, Philippa PALMER when thwarted by the twin problems of the unavailability of a suitable room and an intrusive phone call (ANNX: pp128-129).

One affair in particular needs a little consideration. At the end of the WOOD case (pp409-410) an unnamed female calls to Morse's flat late in the evening. We know that she has not driven there – in the expectation of both drinking (and staying). The only likely suspects are Laura HOBSON or Claire OSBORNE and the only written clue is that 'she' knows at least a little of MOZART K numbers and identifies K 467; Hobson has previously indicated some such knowledge but Osborne has expressed an interest in Mozart to Morse (particularly on the *Requiem*) and may be assumed to have learned a little. Both women certainly find Morse attractive (and Morse has agreed with Lewis's estimation of Hobson as a 'smasher'; p283). The plump here, however, is for Claire and for four (potentially) simple reasons. Firstly, shortly before the visitor arrives, Morse is contemplating a visit to Salisbury (Claire's home town) and her arrival would fit well with his belief in the prevalence of coincidences in life. Secondly, Morse turns off his music when Claire arrives on an earlier occasion in the case (p108) because he can never do two things at the same time (that is, listen to music and devote himself to Claire). When the unnamed visitor arrives this time, Morse also decides to turn off his music: "I *will* turn it off ... I've never been able cope with two beautiful things at the same time" (p409).[18] The question here is whether Morse would use a similar line

---

[18] A chapter heading in NEIG (p331) has a quote from a book about the publishers Mills and Boon and contains the lines "I will turn this Mozart off, if you don't mind, my love. You see, I can never concentrate on two beautiful things at the same time."

twice with the same woman – on the basis that it proves to her that he clearly remembers their previous meeting – or whether he is so bereft of imagination to use it with a second party. A difficult question: one knows how parsimonious Morse can be but that is surely only in terms of money rather than words, phrases, and intellect. Thirdly, when Morse next meets Laura (in 1993, during the STOR case) his amatory feelings are merely ambivalent – sometimes he thinks '… he could fall in love with (her), sometimes he thought he couldn't' (p173). Finally, a year later, any thoughts of love have completely evaporated (CAIN: p314) – and given a choice between this being post-coital rejection or a case of there never having been anything between them, the latter is preferred here. Indeed, by the time of the REMO case, their relationship appears to be entirely professional (pp155-157).

The years occasionally take their toll on Morse and sexual ambition but they run a very uneven course. In 1975: 'There were times (not very frequent, he admitted) when he seemed to lose all interest in the female sex …' (NICQ: p155) but by 1980, he is willing to tell his colleague that: "I'll let you into a secret, Max. My sexual appetite grows stronger year by year" (MILE: p256). The WOOD case of 1992 sees Morse close to tears as he compares his present and previous sexual activity (p370) and a mere four years later, although (according to Strange) his secretary is a '… a pretty little lass …', Morse is losing his lust (NEIG: p157). Not completely though – he still demands the right to interview Della CECIL on the grounds that she is attractive (NEIG: p132) and that case does end with a rather glorious romp with Janet McQueen (pp407-411). It is somewhat regrettable that, despite all the highs of his numerous liaisons, Morse considers himself '… not unacquainted with the agonies of unrequited love' (JERI: p282). Indeed, on the subject of love, he does not feel particularly lucky at all (REMO: p17) and, on more than one occasion, Morse realizes just how lonely he is (NICQ: p195, while contemplating the desirability of Monica HEIGHT).

Reading It is absolutely clear that Morse has an excellent grounding in English literature (and the classics) and he appears comfortable with most poetry including Keats, Gray, Wordsworth, Coleridge, KIPLING, Eliot, and HOUSMAN (and Dante; WEAR: p145). Exactly how many books Morse has on his shelves is a matter of pure conjecture but it is suggested here that the great majority are hardback – his 'decimation' in 1979 produces 30 paperbacks for resale by the OXFORD BOOK ASSOCIATION, giving a literal (and Morse is usually very literal) total of 300 paperbacks; these would hardly cover half a wall, let alone the hundreds of square feet of books that line his flat (JERI: p22). One knows a number of the books that he possesses (and can easily guess at many others). Of the known, are editions of HOUSMAN (and first at that – NEIG: p305), KIPLING, DICKENS, HARDY, and *Chambers*; a World Atlas (on his large-book shelf; WNCH: p181) together with *The Collected Works of Swinburne* and *Extracts from Victorian Pornography* (WEAR: p26); and a London map plus the *AA Hotels of Britain* guide (SERV: p69). At one point, his bedside reading includes *The Road to Xanadu* (presumably the book by John Livingston Lowes where the sources of imagery in Coleridge's poetry are explored), *A Selection of Kipling's Short Stories*, *The Life of Richard Wagner*, and *Selected Prose of A.E. Housman*

(WEAR: p165).[19] A fairly recent purchase is the first volume of Sir Steven Runciman's *History of the Crusades* (NEIG: p337) and one hopes that *The Transmission of Classical Manuscripts* – ordered from the OUP – has now been delivered (WNCH: p81). He has a copy of the Penguin *Oxfordshire* (Buildings of England series) and an anthology of modern verse; in the latter, he looks up *Five Ways to Kill a Man* by Edwin Brock (WOOD: p176; CAIN: p181). As a matter of interest, the first four ways are crucifixion, mediaeval battle, gas in trenches, and a bomb from the air. The fifth is to let him live in the middle of the twentieth century.

Morse has his favourites – as a classicist, Ovid among the Latin poets (REMO: p222) and the passage recounting the burial of Sarpedon from *The Iliad* (WOOD: p207); if all the classical texts bar one were to be destroyed Morse would keep Book XVI of the *Iliad* – the death of Sarpedon, where Sleep and Death carry the dead hero to Lycia – and after that, Socrates on death as long painless sleep (CAIN: pp244-245). It is unclear which editions he has of the classics but he certainly recognises those in the Penguin Classical Authors series (JERI: p101). He determines to re-read *The Odyssey* while on holiday (WOOD: p28). He is very well aware of the Oedipus myth and recounts it, at some length, to Lewis who learns, possibly for the first time of King Laius and Queen Jocasta (JERI: pp242-244). His favourite short story is Kipling's *Love-o'-Women* (WEAR: p165), and *BLEAK HOUSE* his choice of novel.[20] Charlotte Brontë has a special place in Morse's heart (WNCH: p107). He turns to Burton's *Anatomy of Melancholy* when ill (CAIN: p160) and starts *The ABC Murders* (he had always enjoyed Agatha Christie) in hospital (NEIG: p246). During another stay in hospital, Lewis brings a copy of *Scales of Injustice: A Comparative Study of Crime and Punishment as Recorded in the County of Shropshire, 1842-1852* (a sort of family heirloom to be left, at Lewis's request, in the hospital library (WNCH: p17)). Morse consults it to look at '... the misdeeds of Old Salopians ...' (WNCH: p132) and notices a reference to the Shropshire Union Canal, which proves to be of much interest. The reference to the proceedings of the *Canal and Navigable Waters Commission* (WNCH: p135) is of much less interest. Lewis also brings him a thriller – *The Blue Ticket* (WNCH: p21).

One knows he has read *Catch 22* but not *Zuleika Dobson* (WOOD: p45; JWEL: p70) and he is *au fait* with the King James version of *The Bible* (NEIG: p277). His comments on finding a copy of Stevenson's *Travels with My Donkey* are clearly a reminiscence ("Well, well, well"; WEAR: p66), he recalls Poe's *The Premature Burial* (SERV: p188), and (of course) knows Gibbon well – "Any man who reads Gibbon has got my vote for a start" (JERI: p281) – as he does *Jude the Obscure* and *Tess of the d'Urbervilles* (WNCH: pp100/117). He has a good knowledge of *The Rubaiyat of Omar Khayyam* and also of Baudelaire (CAIN: p11; SERV: p82), a passing knowledge of *The Guinness Book of Records* and its reference to Daniel Lambert (BAGG: pp253-254), and it may be strongly suggested that he has a deep grasp of the works of Shakespeare though direct references are rare (for example, *Macbeth*;

---

[19] *The Road to Xanadu* by Lowes provides a quotation as the heading to Chapter 44 of WOOD. The Wagnerian biography has been suggested, by Bird (1998: p93), to be that by Ernest Newman.

[20] 'He remembered when he'd first read Bleak House (still to his mind the greatest novel in the English language) ...' (WNCH: p87); he even slows his reading down to make it last.

JERI: p227). The speed at which Morse reads seems to vary. He is quick in 1971 (LBUS: p32), and reads about five times faster than Lewis in 1975 (WEAR: pp49-50) though with some loss of comprehension. However, he '... had always been a slow reader ...' (ANNX: p100), knows that '... one gift had never been bestowed on him – that of *reading* quickly' (WNCH: p146), a slow reader (REMO: p335), and is also a sluggard in the CAIN and STOR cases (p64; p197). He does, however, read CROSSWORD clues quickly (REMO: p70) and may be described as a 'slow reader but a quick thinker' (JWEL: p197). Morse does not enjoy reading when listening to music (WNCH: p152); he is also a 'dipper-in' rather than a systematic reader, also marks books (WEAR: pp164-165) though not, one hopes, those he borrows from the library (LBUS: p73).

Newspapers Morse's daily paper of choice is *The TIMES* (which he has delivered); on a Sunday, he usually purchases *The NEWS OF THE WORLD* or *The SUNDAY TIMES* (or both). At some point, he decides to stop the deliveries – in the REMO case (p226) his excuse is that he needs the exercise of the walk to the newsagents (in SUMMERTOWN) but as early as the JWEL case he has been known to buy *The Times* (p217) beyond his flat. In fact there is also some confusion over his Sunday papers – they are delivered, for example in 1989 (WNCH: p172) and so, on occasions (NEIG: p178), is *The Observer* (mainly for AZED's contribution). Morse takes *The Times* for three reasons – the CROSSWORD, the letters page, and the obituaries (ANNX: p149; WNCH; p38; WOOD: pp112-113; REMO: p12). Morse's interest in the obituaries is just to check the dates that the dead were born and to compare them to his own age (CAIN: p224). In the absence of *The Times* on a train journey, Morse is reduced to reading *The SUN* (ANNX: p149); he vainly tries to forgo *The Times* when on holiday (WOOD: p16). See also NEWSPAPER and various titles.

Religion and Religious Beliefs At some point during his life, Morse went from an 'early ebullient' belief in a God (SERV: p251;CAIN: p386) to the state where he '... had long ago, albeit unwillingly, discounted the existence of any supernatural agency' (LBUS: p154). Indeed, he has convinced himself that death is '... just a process of chemical disintegration' (CALL: p269). Morse undergoes a process of reverse conversion – from belief, to being a low-church atheist via agnosticism, the rejection of the placebos of conventional religion (WNCH: pp2/79/117), and a confirmation that he has no belief in God (WOOD: p181) nor in an afterlife (NEIG: p188). Should he be reincarnated, however unlikely that may seem or that he believes, he would wish to come back as a part-time Quaker with lots of spare time for ornithology (REMO: p9). His early faith appears to have given him a fair knowledge of some of the more popular hymns – he knows the first verse of *Lead Kindly Light* (WEAR: p234) and most of the hymns at a particular service (SERV: p85); also, he is no stranger to the rituals of a church (SERV: p237) even though he has not attended for more than a decade (SERV: p83). One rather guesses that he was raised, for a time, as a (High) Anglican though he does remember going to a Methodist service in his youth (MILE: p210) if only to look for a particular girl. His knowledge of the Bible is obvious though he does need to check – in a Gideon version in a hotel room – to confirm what he recalls about a sermon on 'The Religion of the Second Mile' (MILE: pp219-220). A fairly precise exposition of Morse's 'beliefs' occurs in JERI (pp241-242). Here, he summarises (for the benefit of Lewis) that

"There are three basic views about human life …" These are, briefly, that all things happen by chance, that one's own character helps to determine the way things turn out, and that the future is fixed and firm; of these, Morse favours a mixture of the second and third. He certainly is no believer in an ineluctable fate (or the 'fates'; JERI: p13). Before deciding to forbid any religious service in connection with his death (REMO: p430), he had chosen at least three pieces of music for his funeral – the hymns *The Day Thou Gavest Lord* and *O Love That Will Not Let Me Go*, and *In Paradisum* from Fauré's *Requiem* (WOOD: p208; REMO: p325; DODO: p85).

As a mere by the by, he thinks the Church Commissioners are 'mean-minded' (SERV: p297), is not unknown to blaspheme (WNCH: pp23/32/33), thinks of archangels (Michael, Raphael, and Gabriel) as his patrons (MILE: p191), and lights two candles in the Oratory in a vague sort of groping towards a miracle (REMO: pp206/7). He (once) reads his horoscope (WEAR: pp52-53) but without much conviction; somewhat strangely, he knows that the amethyst is the birthstone for February (CAIN: p280). He is, of course, a firm believer in 'coincidences' (for example, DODO: p87; also see that subject under LITERARY CURIOSITIES).

Sport and Leisure Activities This section is simply split into three and details Morse's interest (or relative lack of it) in sport and also how he occupies some of his leisure time (which, to be fair, appears to have been mainly taken up with listening to *THE ARCHERS* on the radio and to various composers, reading, drinking, and doing CROSSWORDS); the third part looks at Morse and gambling.

Sport and Games While a youngster he played both cricket and tennis (WNCH: p87; WOOD: p323) and had a reliable backhand at the latter. Although he professes to Lewis that cricket is a 'ridiculous game' (NEIG: p227), he still keeps his old batting scores somewhere (WEAR: p42) and asks Eddie ANDREWS about how Northamptonshire Cricket Club are doing (REMO: p239). He also uses his common knowledge (of tennis) to lay a trap for Dorothy EVANS (WOOD: pp321-322). Of football, there appears to never have been much interest, he never wants to watch it again (NEIG: p6), and could not care if the game had never been invented (CAIN: p6). He has some knowledge of the card game Bridge – at least as far as trumps, finessing, and playing aces off the top is concerned (LBUS: p87; JWEL: p209); he is also skilled at cribbage (REMO: p348). Of chess, BELL says: "Morse? He's never pushed a pawn in his life! Spends most of his free time in the pubs – or listening to his beloved Wagner" (JERI: p38). Of course, HOLMES was also rather dismissive of the game, believing it to be one mark of a scheming mind (*The Retired Colourman*).

Leisure Morse seems to watch television but a little (looking at the Shi'ite and Christian militias in Beirut on a news programme is a rare example; ANNX: p84) and only later in life has he obtained a video recorder. He has seen the film *Casablanca* a few times (NEIG: p6), possibly at the cinema. He is probably a member of a quiz team at the FRIAR BACON – but freely admits to large gaps in his knowledge of 'pop' and 'sport' questions (ANNX: p51); he thinks narrow-boating to be 'grossly overrated' (WNCH: p52) and is, in principle, against hunting (REMO: p40). He knows nothing of photography nor trees (WOOD: p175) which is rather surprising as these two interests would both match well with his late-developed (say, from the 1990s) interest in ornithology. He knowingly refers to the Lesser Spotted Woodpecker as *Dendrocopus minor* (WOOD: p70; though the more common is *Dendrocopos*); he also subscribes to the magazine *Birdwatching*, and goes as far as to borrow the RSPB *Birdwatcher's Guide* from SUMMERTOWN library, and to buy a pair of binoculars from OXFAM (REMO: p9). Shortly before his death he buys an RSPB video and just about manages to watch it (REMO: pp314/361).

Morse is not a natural holiday-goer – not the least hampered by his fear of flying (WOOD: pp6/149). He has only flown once – and not on British Airways - during the decade before 1996 (NEIG:p11) and, of course, his trip to west Africa was way back in 1977. Where he flew must remain, for now, a mystery. His fear contributes to, no doubt, his failure to visit the Greek Islands (SERV: pp47/322) and any thoughts of trips to Bayreuth, Salzburg, or Vienna (REMO: p8) are also thereby deferred. His holidays in England include a week at the SWISS LODORE (SERV), a week's rest spent in Oxford (REMO: p73), and a break in Dorset (WOOD); this last giving him the opportunity to brush up some of his knowledge that has gone a trifle rusty (p35). Despite his poor DIY skills (LBUS: p115), one Christmas break is spent largely decorating rather than celebrating (MYST: p45). When he complains to Strange that he does not take his fair share of holidays (WOOD: p5), Strange wryly counters by pointing out the time that Morse does spend in pubs.

Gambling Morse has an occasional bet on the horses (see *The BLACK PRINCE*) and reads the *SPORTING LIFE* when readily available. He also checks his football pools (LBUS: p74; WEAR: p49) and has been known to beam like a Treble Chance winner (WNCH: p227). If he has a local bookie, it is that in SUMMERTOWN (ANNX: pp30-31). It is hard to tell whether he is bluffing or not when he tells ASHENDEN that he has lost 'much money' on the horses (JWEL: p212), especially as one knows that he rarely gambled (REMO: p78); perhaps he is remembering his father's addiction. He is aware of the National Lottery (NEIG: p67) but it is doubtful if he plays it though he does win a magnificent £50 in a Police Charity Raffle (MYST: p46).

Music Morse is, pure and simple, devoted to classical music (although he does, once, ask in a pub for some Irish music to be turned up (REMO: pp188-189) – much to the surprise of Lewis. He has a number of favourite composers, a smaller favourite number of their compositions, and a number (smaller still) of favourite versions of their recorded work. He listens mainly at home (but also while in cars) to either vinyl or CDs and to the radio; his attendance at live concerts is, apparently, rare. He bought a new CD player in 1992 (WOOD: p380) but later envies the Revox CD-cassette player of OWENS (NEIG: p272); late in life, he joins a Music Club Library just to get some free CDs but also orders

Janáček's *Glagolitic Mass* recorded by Simon Rattle (NEIG: p43). At least four composers feature prominently in his life:

Bruckner While puzzling over some early information in a case, Morse anticipates returning to his flat and listening to the Second Movement of the seventh symphony; a little later, and still somewhat puzzled, he treats himself to the first two movements before going to bed (JWEL: pp57/75). He also listens to the Seventh on his car radio (REMO: p132). Bruckner's Eighth is mistaken for Mahler (or Wagner) by Claire OSBORNE (WOOD: pp108/115); Morse knows them both well. He admires the works of Gustav Mahler, immediately recognising *Das Lied von der Erde* when played in OWENS' flat (NEIG: p272) and listening to his Eighth in an unmarked police car (REMO: p106). Morse believes, and tells Strange the same, that Bruckner was "… a very small man …" (JWEL: p341).

Fauré For the *Requiem*, Morse has two (at least) listening attitudes – with eyes closed and in ecstasy (SERV: p124) or with eyes open (or, indeed, closed) and with awesome reverence (GOLD: p35); reluctantly turning the CD off on the latter occasion – to deal with a visitor – Morse turns it on again for the *In Paradisum* (pp36-37). The *In Paradisum* is played at (and Morse attends) the Service of Thanksgiving for the Life of Ambrose WHITAKER (DODO: p87); on hearing Dvořák's *American Quartet* (JWEL: p113), Morse considers whether or not this should edge out the *In Paradisum* from the eighth spot in his *Desert Island* choices.

Mozart After almost an hour of deep thought (prompted by what he discovers in a telephone kiosk), Morse deliberately chooses the Barenboim recording of the Piano Concerto number 21 (JERI: p36).[21] He wrongly identifies the Clarinet Concerto K622 as K662 (DODO: pp87-88) and has several versions of the *Requiem* (WOOD: p126).

Wagner He is a member of the Wagner Society (WNCH: p81) and owns (of course) the complete RING cycle, presumably on vinyl (LBUS: pp74-75) and definitely on CD (NEIG: p305). He has a cassette tape of *Die Walküre* in his JAGUAR (CAIN: p164) and listens, in his flat, to Birgit Nilsson in *Götterdämmerung* (WOOD: p102) after a phone conversation with Strange. *Parsifal* is heard twice by Morse on a short holiday (JWEL: p344) and induces the look of a man sublimely satisfied with life when played in a car driven by Lewis; the cassette, rather surprisingly, has been bought by Lewis (REMO: pp160/164).

Other composers and artistes His proposed start to a holiday at home – listening to *Vier Letzte Lieder* (Four Last Songs) by Richard Strauss – is postponed because of a sudden train of thought (SERV: p65). He has a number of versions of that work (with different sopranos) but is happy to add that sung by Jessye Norman (NEIG: p43); later in

---

[21] BROWNE-SMITH believes he recognises a recording of Barenboim playing another Mozart work while sitting in The FLAMENCO TOPLESS BAR (MILE: p22).

the same case he recognises that STORRS is humming *September* from the lieder (p381). His only knowledge of the German language stems from his addiction to Strauss – and to Wagner (ANNX: p60). He varies in his appreciation of Bach – listening lovingly to the *Brandenburg Concerto No 5 in D* on Radio 3 (WEAR: p221) but asking Lewis to turn off the *No 2* from Classic FM radio (NEIG: p359). In the REMO case, Morse identifies some favourites (apart from Wagner) as the clarinet compositions of Mozart and the Lieder of Schubert, especially with Schwarzkopf singing (REMO: pp7-9). When about to be discharged from hospital, he looks forward to luxuriating in Wotan's farewell from the last act of *Die Walküre* and Pavarotti singing a Puccini work (WNCH: p169). It is unclear whether familiarity or aesthetic considerations lead to his temporary dismissal of (rather than contempt for) such works as Mozart's *Eine Kleine Nachtmusik*, *The Four Seasons* of Vivaldi, *The Lark Ascending* of Vaughan Williams, or *The Ride of the Valkyries* (REMO: p247). The dismissal of the Mozart piece is, one guesses, rather more than temporary – along with *Hark the Herald Angel Sings* it is one composition that Morse never wants to hear again (NEIG: p7); he also fears that a Schoenberg string quartet might be a little above his head (WEAR: pp221-222).

See also *DESERT ISLAND DISCS*, MOZART, and WAGNER.

Health As a snapshot of his health (during a bout of illness necessitating a stay in Ward 7 of the JR2 Hospital in 1994), it is easiest (and more exact) to quote Morse. He is explaining his symptoms to Strange, who has asked what is wrong with him: "I'm suffering from bronchi-something beginning with 'e'; my liver and kidneys are disintegrating; my blood pressure isn't quite off the top of the scale – not yet; I'm nursing another stomach ulcer; and if that wasn't enough I'm on the verge of diabetes, because my pancreas, they tell me, isn't producing sufficient insulin to counteract my occasional intake of alcohol. Oh yes, and my cholesterol's dangerously high" (CAIN: p194). Strange thinks he should have asked what is right with Morse. Morse's long decline into permanent (and terminal) ill-health, though occasionally put on hold through bouts of abstinence and exercise, is recorded in a large number of cases. But first, the good news.

When checked by Dr. Blair (MINOR) he is told that he is ("surprisingly") fit (CAIN: p253). His eyesight remains remarkably good and although he has a little trouble in 1992 (WOOD: p20), and states a year later that the "… old eyes are not as sharp as they were" (STOR: p215), it is not until 1998 that he thinks he will soon have to see an optician (REMO: p106). Also, his hearing is in fine fettle – it is extremely acute (WEAR: p119), he hears well (WOOD: p357), and he is able to detect the rustle of tissue paper on a bottle of BELL'S (WNCH: pp20-21). Despite no regular exercise routine, he has retained considerable physical strength (SERV: p256), his teeth are '… reasonably regular, if rather off-white …' (WNCH: p18), and his bladder has held up remarkably well over the years – drinking, for example, 4 pints before needing the gents (ANNX: p128). His sporadic fits of trying to live a healthier life couple gentle exercise (usually of the walking variety) with differing degrees of cutting back on smoking and alcohol. Of walking, Morse has: "They tell me walking is the secret of perpetual middle age" (LBUS: p81), and "I sometimes walk down to

Summertown for a newspaper. Just to keep fit" (NEIG: p296). His unaccustomed exercise includes a walk from his flat to the railway station (WEAR: p323), one from JERICHO to home (JERI: p36), from the RANDOLPH to his flat (SERV: pp63-65), and both from and to ULLMAN's flat (WATC: pp128/132). During one of his 'get fitter' phases he even resorts to using stairs – "Lift? We're not climbing the Empire State Building!" (JWEL: p31) he tells Lewis – and (just) succeeds in tackling three flights. Plans to improve are also notable in CAIN (pp210/387) including a change of diet to take in plenty of fresh fruit and salad, performing a dozen press-ups, and cutting back or forswearing alcohol altogether; in WNCH (p56) for weight loss; and, rather dramatically in MILE: '... and now, at the age of fifty-two, he had once again decided that a few days of virtually total abstinence was urgently demanded by stomach, lungs, and liver alike' (p46). On one of the many occasions when he decides to give up alcohol – 4th March 1996 – he has a GLENFIDDICH in the evening while listening to The *ARCHERS (N*EIG: pp304-305/309). His last attempts to reform (in REMO) by adding water to his whisky for the sake of his liver (p149) and abjuring alcohol altogether after a particularly horrendous hangover (p196) are somewhat doomed to ultimate failure. Probably the factors that mitigate most in Morse's favour is an odd mix of realism, optimism, and a failure to take his health too seriously; the apparent hypochondria he suffers in the WEAR case (pp196-197) does not last long and rarely, if ever, resurfaces. He is prepared, for example, to massage his blood-sugar figures or extrapolate them from a small sample (REMO: pp149/198), and later makes a very unlikely offer to leave his body to science and the RADCLIFFE (**Plate 49**) (p313). He also clearly recognises his own limits – after a row with Lewis about his failure to look after himself, he says "I don't want to die, not just yet" (CAIN: pp178-179) – and thinks that any doctor who predicts when someone is going to die is "a bloody fool" (NEIG: p241).

Mental Although the ultimate reaction is often physical, Morse's common response to a dead body probably has a mental origin or cause. He has stood beside such a body without feeling squeamish (for example, LBUS: p16) but a little later he gladly skips reading the gory parts of a forensic report (p79) and as the years progress his reaction to corpses and carnage becomes more pronounced. In the NICQ case, he '... turned his head away, closed his eyes, and felt the nausea rising in his gorge' (p183); his stomach tightens, sweat breaks out, and he feels he is about to vomit at the sight of a traffic accident (SERV: p64). Other examples include being squeamish (NICQ: p183), recoiling from a corpse (ANNX: p61), lurching as if to vomit (JWEL: p115), and keeping his eyes shut in a morgue (SERV: p219). He is physically sick in both MILE (p70) and REMO (p183). In summary, he was '... used to death of course; but accident, and terrible injury, and the sight of much blood – such things he could never stomach' (WOOD: p326). But Morse, for all his classical education, is unable to coin an accurate term for this phobia – his fear of being sick at the sight of bodies (CAIN: p309). Of his other phobias, the fear of heights (acrophobia) is high on any list – even to the extent of feeling a clammy sweat on the 3rd or 4th rung of a ladder (ANNX: p207) – and features prominently in the SERV case (pp102/232/259-260) where, at one point, '... his head reeled vertiginously, his gut contracted, and twice he retched emptily ...' (p112). He has always been frightened of the dark (CAIN: p223), has a fear of flying (WOOD: pp6/149), and suffers from a number more including arachnophobia, ornithophobia, myophobia, and necrophobia (MILE: p66).

Physical Only a few of Morse's problems are not wilfully self-inflicted – such as a fall from a ladder with no permanent damage (LBUS: pp97/115-116), needing stitches after a fight (NICQ: p284) and possibly more had Lewis not assisted, incipient spondylosis (WOOD: p15), and a touch of lumbago (NEIG: p306). He has been known to sometimes lapse into aphasia when driving (DODO: p81) and realises that he is getting old when he has to sit in order to pull on his trousers (CAIN: p98). It is probably fair (though hardly kind) to blame Morse for the state of his teeth. The MILE case has some details: he does not have many teeth left (pp86-88) but seems to have avoided dentures; a nagging toothache is eventually shown to have been caused by decay with an extraction as the solution (pp80/245). It is almost certainly fair (and only a trifle unkind) to blame Morse for the state of his enlarged liver and a perforated ulcer, both of which feature in the WNCH case (along with a first hint at subsequent DIABETES). While alcohol no doubt has played its part, it appears that his frequent attempts to lead a healthier life are both not frequent enough nor sustained for any length of time. A bout of vomiting blood (and unconnected to any nausea at the sight of corpses) leads to a lengthy stay in the JR2 of over a week (pp4-170) when he endures an endoscopy, his ulcer is soothed, and his liver given a little respite despite the best efforts of Lewis and medical staff to keep a gentle supply of whisky going. He is back in hospital in 1994 for 'observation' and four nights (Sunday to Thursday) for another stomach ulcer (CAIN: pp194-209) and a depressing diagnosis of what else is happening to his body. Morse learns from a book that his tiredness, weight loss, and thirst may well indicate diabetes and this is rapidly confirmed (NEIG: pp233-236) by Dr Paul Roblin (MINOR) at the SUMMERTOWN Health Centre (**Plate 50**) and – after an ambulance ride – subsequent tests at the RADCLIFFE INFIRMARY (Geoffrey Harris Ward). His blood sugar level is horrendously wrong and his pancreas has stopped functioning; his blood pressure and blood sugar levels are still too high two years later (REMO: p15). The inexorable deterioration in his physical condition is hardly helped by an increasing reluctance to exercise – he is unwilling to walk '... even a hundred yards or so ...' (WNCH: p232), not prepared to walk fifty yards (JWEL: p223), and is a little out of breath from an ascent of sixteen steps (CAIN: p10).

Medication Morse, medication, and mathematics are intertwined. When speaking to medical staff he tends to halve, or otherwise divide, the things that are supposedly bad for him (WNCH and NEIG); when self-dosing, he tends to double the recommended amount. He advises Lewis that a double dose has always been "... the secret for me" (CAIN: p162) and takes, for example, six Aspro tablets (MILE: p84). As his health deteriorates, his nightly routine involves visits to the lavatory, frequent glasses of water, and doses of Nurofen and Paracetamol (sic), indigestion tablets, and a tumbler of Alka-Seltzer (NEIG: p178). During a particularly bad night the routine is slightly varied – Nurofen Plus tablets are used and black coffee accompanies the water (NEIG: pp304-305). He is no stranger to Alka (no hyphen) Seltzer tablets (CAIN: p160) and has been known to carry them regularly on his person (JWEL: p162). By the time of his last case, he has been prescribed diuretic pills (REMO: p107). Details of medication related to DIABETES appear under that entry.

Money The WORKS are benevolently littered with references to Morse's parsimony, especially when it comes to buying drinks. 'Morse never seemed to think it was *his* round …' (JWEL: p64) and Lewis calculates that he buys about three-quarters of the alcohol consumed during any case. Indeed, 'Morse was not renowned for his generosity in treating his subordinates – or his superiors …' (WNCH: p231). He also seems to have a particular thing about the cost of postage – getting Lewis to buy him (second-class) stamps (STOR: p217); 'borrowing' a first-class one from Lewis (NEIG: p44); and, rather than risk the minimal additional cost of first-class for a postcard, queues for an inordinately lengthy time to buy a second-class in the High Street Post Office, Dorchester (WOOD: p88). All he recalls of the pleasant seaside town of Tenby is that he once found a ten-pound note there (ANNX: p62). It would reveal rather too much of the MYST case to offer any evidence as to Morse's potential for generosity.

Cars and Other Transport Morse is a reasonably regular traveller on the railways but it is by car that the great majority of journeys are made, either as driver or passenger. As the latter '… he was invariably a taciturn companion' (JERI: p210) being usually quiet (WNCH: p223; WOOD: p317), and morose (MILE: p135) and although he does appear to be quite chatty on a scant few occasions (CAIN: p164; NEIG: p75; REMO: p399) the usual conversation tends to consist of a question to Lewis about the location of the nearest pub or if they are open yet. He is not at all knowledgeable about technical aspects of motoring (CAIN: p230) and carries an RAC Breakdown Service card in his wallet (NEIG: p43). If going from his flat into town he may catch a bus (NEIG: p88) and has an account with a firm called Radio Taxis (REMO: p256).

See also JAGUAR and LANCIA.

Methodology Morse is not a forensic detective as such and rather relies on his powers of deep mental analysis (fuelled by alcohol), determined application – working, for example, on a Sunday in the WOOD case (p18) – and flashes of intuition and inspiration. These flashes are often unwittingly prompted by Lewis, leading to the typical exclamation of "Lewis, my old friend, you've done it again!" (STOR: p202). He often comes to quick and wrong conclusions but rapidly rethinks when new facts come to light: 'One of the most extraordinary things about (Morse's) mind was that any check, any setback, to some sweet hypothesis, far from dismaying him, seemed immediately to prompt some second hypothesis that soon appeared even sweeter than the first.' (JWEL: pp172-173). Sometimes these checks or setbacks need to be fairly dramatic – for example, a 'cataclysmic shift' to change his fixed ideas (WEAR: p101) – but he is always being driven to find the correct solution: 'For all his wayward unpredictability, there was at the centre of his being an inner furnace of passion for truth, for logical analysis…' (WEAR: pp279-80). He exhibits this passion when interviewing suspects (and, occasionally, witnesses) and while he usually has an idea of the answers to the questions he has posed, this is not always the case (JERI:

p191). He has a number of rather illogical beliefs – he has little faith in fingerprints (ANNX: p62), thinks that jealousy is the most powerful motive for murder (REMO: p392), and declares (for a short while at least) that the person who finds the body is the prime suspect (STOR: pp215-216) – though there is a certain logic to his pronouncement that "We think of anything that's unlikely … any bloody idiot can tell you what's *likely*" (CAIN: p82). These (perhaps) apart, it is sensible to agree with Lewis that Morse has a 'thoroughbred' mind (WEAR: p128).

Dreams Morse recalls a number of his dreams and these include: a long cross-country race where a topless blonde sits at the finishing line holding '… a pint of beer with a head of winking froth' (WNCH: p27); a beautiful girl slowly undressing before revealing an unwelcome face (WEAR: p126); and a mildly erotic dream involving a woman wearing a large Elastoplast on one ankle (ANNX: p146). Other dreams involve an architect and a girl in the RANDOLPH (WEAR: pp194-195), one of a scantily clad siren in lavender-hued underclothing (WNCH: p89), a disturbing experience in CAIN (pp367-368), and one involving a young Margaret DALEY (WOOD: p279). The majority of his dreams have two things in common – eroticism and a link to a woman in the case under investigation (for example, Philippa PALMER has previously met Morse while wearing an Elastoplast: ANNX: p123; the siren is called Joanna FRANKS). Morse indulges in daydreams as well – they are usually erotic (WOOD: p279), occur most of the time (WOOD: p181), and he feels he needs them just as a diabetic may need a balance of insulin (JWEL: p127). Whether or not his half-conscious sight of the Angel of Death (REMO: p412) is a (less than erotic) daydream is a moot point.

Some Likes and Dislikes … Morse has, of course, many of these and only a few less obvious will be highlighted here. For example, he admires Isambard Kingdom Brunel (NEIG: p207) and both laughed and cried at the film, *The Full Monty* (REMO: pp390-391); he enjoys storms (REMO: p360) and prefers to carry out any interviews held in London rather than delegating them to Lewis (ANNX: p113). He is a lifelong addict of puzzles and cryptograms (MILE: p82) and likes his food plates to be appropriately hot (REMO: p392). He does not like Christmas cake (MYST: p45) nor is he is keen on either the Welsh (WEAR: p300) or dogs (WOOD: p130) and he hates litter (GOLD: p34). He is a little worried by rats (SERV: p194), terrified of spiders (WEAR: p187), but is squeamish about even killing insects (WOOD: p135). He has a phobia about form-filling (CAIN: p5) and affects to despise 'psychology', showing little respect, for example, in the works of Freud (MILE: p260; LBUS: p284; JERI: p130). Occasionally, his dislikes are rapidly formed: 'Seldom was it that Morse took such an irrationally instant dislike to one of his fellow men …' (of Dr Swain (MINOR); JWEL: p33). He has a fear of corpses (WNCH: pp205-206), hates traffic accidents (JERI: p29), and thinks of his town planners as '… Oxford-City-Council Vandals …' (WNCH: p222). He has a particular distaste for facial jewellery: "Rings in her nose, Lewis? Pretty tasteless, isn't it? Like drinking lager with roast beef" (CAIN: pp35/257).

… and Some Aspects of His Character Morse is aware of his own strengths and weaknesses (as are others) and these can be fairly easily grouped. Perhaps foremost, and clearly obvious, is the fact that he has a basic honesty and integrity (LBUS: p226) which only bends on the odd occasion; he firmly believes in the principle that people are innocent until proved guilty (WNCH: p151). Further, he is a seeker after the truth – it always bothered him not to *know* (WNCH: p223) – whose brain goes into an overdrive of fertility '... when faced with some apparently insuperable obstacle ...' (JWEL: p268). As befits one of his occupation and rank he exudes an air of authority and, according to Dr MOULE (JWEL: p297), more so than Lewis; on one occasion, he says, "What's that?" with such quietly massive authority that VICKERS' forearm hairs stand on end (ANNX: p231). Other marks in his credit column include his enviable capacity for discounting disappointments (ANNX: p146) and his recognition that life is full of them (NEIG: p224), his extreme competence as an administrator (MILE: p79), and his earliness if not punctuality for appointments (JWEL: p344; NEIG: p161). He also has a good short-term memory (WOOD: p10). It is suggested here that he exhibits another characteristic that may be classified as a strength: he has small, neat, and scholarly handwriting (**Plate 51**), with an upright script (WOOD: p89; NEIG: p412; REMO: p332) which may be disguised for the purposes of forgery (WEAR). The fact that he considers himself an accomplished liar (REMO: p96) is not necessarily a strength but it seems harsh to call it a weakness when there are a number of others from which to choose.

Regrettably, he has been known to have a bit of a temper – sometimes with Lewis as the target (and thought by Lewis after one particular outburst – LBUS: p270 – to be 'frightening') but also with others (as an unnamed bank employee could no doubt testify; MYST: p45). His ill-humour is particularly vented in the ANNX case (p73 for example) when he feels the need to declaim that: "I'm *not* bloody cross ..." (p271). He does, however, have the good grace to either regret his intemperate behaviour – hoping that he would feel remorse after tearing a strip off staff in front of others (WNCH: p30) – or actually apologising after he has bawled out EDWARDS (NEIG: p197). When angry, he has the soothing secret of counting up to 'however-many' (see QUOTATIONS for *Little Dorrit* under the entries from REMO). Other weaknesses include a '... deprecatingly conceited look on his face ...' (NICQ: p118); his acceptance of loyalty with no appreciation of any sacrifices made (WNCH: p147); his difficulty in giving thanks when due and a failure to express his deeper feelings (JWEL: pp62/288-289). And his impatience, certainly when awaiting a hotel breakfast (WNCH: p5). He admits to Lewis that he has never known anyone very well (BURG: p288) and is, by temperament, a loner 'if only because, although never wholly content in the solitary state, he was almost invariably even more miserable in the company of others.' (MILE: p80; this is confirmed by parallel wording in WNCH: p181). Despite his occasional wish for a wife and slippers (NICQ: p126), he seems predestined to remain a bachelor – though his late liaison with McQUEEN promised much. His inclination to remain distant has been aptly expressed metaphorically: '... the mask that he ... invariably wore for most occasions before his fellow men' (ANNX: p130). Morse thinks that the masks are real and the faces beneath, the pretence. Although Morse has his own recipe for contentment – "The secret of a happy life, Lewis, is to know when to stop and then go that little bit further." (NICQ: p67) – a more accurate summary appears to be that he has endured a '... lifetime of muted laughter and occasional tears ...' (NEIG: p304).

And a man who knows him better than most has: 'Like his beloved Hardy, he is probably more of a pejorist than a true pessimist' DEXTER in Bird (1998: p7).[22]

Death All references in this section are to the 1998 REMO case unless otherwise indicated and start with his chest pain (p144) and Morse, a day or so later, going to bed at the unprecedented early hour of 9.30p.m., suffering from severe indigestion (p222). The chest pain resurfaces briefly (p403) a good few days later while with Lewis and, after separating, Morse eventually returns to his flat. Early next morning (p409), the chest pain is so bad that he calls for an ambulance; having suffered '… a hefty anterior myocardial infarct', he is admitted to the Coronary Care Unit in the RADCLIFFE HOSPITAL (p409-413). He dies between 4.20p.m. and 5.00p.m. with his last words, to a nurse, being "Please thank Lewis for me …" (pp419-420). It is suggested here that this takes place on Wednesday the 12th of August; the reasoning for this choice of day and date is based purely on internal evidence in the REMO case and a hint of guesswork. Firstly, the death of a leading participant is confirmed as the third of August (p422 for example); this was a Monday in 1998. Following the report of his death (p272), the sequence of references followed here run as:

P272	Death of A.N. Other	Monday 3rd August
P273	'The following morning …'	Tuesday 4th
P279	'… the following morning.'	Wednesday 5th
P285	'… the following day …'	Thursday 6th
P304	'… the following morning.'	Friday 7th
P323	Funeral of A.N. Other	Tuesday 11th

Lewis speaks to a number of professional people on '… the previous day' to the funeral (pp326/329) and also visits a nun; while one of these calls was made at the weekend of the 8th to 9th (p334) – TURNER is '… clearly not a Monday-Friday medic …'), the range of occupations contacted suggests a weekday. If the funeral had been, as is just about possible, a week or so later – say, on Tuesday 18th – the conversations noted below at pp345/350 would be a nonsense. P332: 'I'm out to lunch and shan't be available till tomorrow morning – no **Monday** morning.' Thus reads part of a note left by Morse for Lewis; the note was probably left by him on Saturday the 8th and indicates that Morse feels he has done enough for now – or reached a dead end and needs the Sunday to drink and think. P337: 'Anyone wishing to take up Morse's earlier promise of being available the following Monday would have been disappointed …' but he responds to a call from Lewis to his flat and appears in the afternoon at HQ Monday 10th. P345: '"What were you doing **last** Monday morning …"' (emphasis added). This is Morse questioning a potential suspect on Monday 10th. P347: A bill is reproduced showing the hotel stay of Frank HARRISON as the 3rd of August. P350: Lewis asks Sarah HARRISON (Monday 10th), "Did you see your father while he was staying at the RANDOLPH **last** week?" (emphasis added). P358: Morse listens to the evening *ARCHERS* on Monday 10th. P359: A thunderstorm hits NORTH OXFORD. Despite

---

[22] A pejorist is one who believes that the world is becoming worse. The noun appears in *The New Shorter Oxford Dictionary* but not in *Chambers*.

(a few) enquiries, this storm has not been verified as being on the 10th. P373: 'The following morning … is Tuesday 11th. P389 'It was 6.10 p.m.' on Tuesday 11th. P400: Morse and Lewis visit a pub; Lewis drives him back to Oxford and drops him at another pub (p403) – Tuesday 11th. P409: 'Morse awoke at 2.15 a.m …' with a chest pain – Wednesday 12th.

And his will?[23] Morse has made a draft (p267) which suggests he has no living relatives and this draft is finalised with a certain Mr Daniel of Lloyds Bank (pp312-313). The will confirms that there are no known next-of-kin (and even if there were, it would not make any difference), his flat is mortgage-free and contains many rare first editions, he has two insurance policies, and two accounts with Lloyds Bank; the sum of his estate is estimated to be in the region of £150,000 (pp430-431). This sum is to be divided (like Gaul) into three parts, of equal amounts (unlike Gaul), and the beneficiaries will be the British Diabetic Association, Janet McQUEEN, and Lewis. Typically, Morse exhibits reticence when asked (on an earlier occasion) by Strange whether or not he has made a will; his reply of "Not much to leave, really" (WOOD: p210) rather understates the case (even in 1992). Morse's wishes, expressed in his will, to have no formal services (religious or memorial) to mark his death are observed (p437).

Morse and Lewis Much information on this pivotal relationship may be found elsewhere; only a little is added here. For example, of the few references to their relative ages, it is worth noting that Lewis is '… by several years the older man …' (LBUS: p90; this marries with DEXTER's recollection 2006b); appears – how rapidly Morse must age – to Margaret BOWMAN to be '… slightly younger …' (ANNX: p183); and is thought, by Della CECIL to be a bit younger (NEIG: p137). Morse's criticisms of Lewis have, by and large, been noted elsewhere but it is worth adding one more: "No, Lewis. You didn't miss one vital clue, at all. You missed two." (ANNX: p251). And following that, from here nothing but praise and bonhomie will be found. For example, Morse has been pleased enough to accord Lewis a certain rare status: "We're a team, we are – you realize that, don't you?" (JERI: pp237-8) or commend his essential assistance: "You are – not for the first time in your life – a bloody genius, Lewis!" (ANNX: p231). It is, perhaps, in the NEIG case that Morse most realises and recognises the value of his sergeant: "You're indispensable, old friend. Absolutely *indispensable!*" (p229) and the poignant: "Thank you, my old friend." (p144). The case ends, of course, with an emotional Lewis reading the card sent by Morse (even if purchased by McQUEEN): '… let me thank you for everything, my dear old friend. Yours aye, Endeavour (Morse)' (p413). But Morse has remembered Lewis's home address (p412) – unlike a previous occasion (WOOD: p89) when he has to write to Lewis and addresses a card to HQ. Finally, and from the CAIN case, what is patently an honest sentiment from the commonly acerbic or sarcastic Morse. He is talking to Lewis about retirement: "You just asked me if I'll miss things and I shan't, no. Only one thing, I suppose. I shall miss you, old friend, that's all." (p139).

---

[23] He has neither 'dependants' nor made a will in 1989 (WNCH: p196). The existence after 1989 of an aunt is briefly explored under *Family and Background* above; she seems to have died 'recently' (REMO: p410).

Morse's Greatest Mystery Morse and Lewis investigate the theft of £400 charity money from the GEORGE pub at Christmas time. (MYST). *Main personnel* Mrs MICHAELS.

Moule, Dr Barbara She is an expert on Romano-British archaeology (in Somerset) and addresses most of the members of the HISTORIC CITIES tour during their stay at the CHESTERTON HOTEL in Bath. She seems to be fairly astute – without having really met Morse she thinks, on sight alone, that he drinks too much and is (but of course) instantly attracted to him (JWEL: p322).

Mozart, Wolfgang Amadeus Child genius and prolific composer. A number of references are dotted throughout this guide; some are also collected here. The second movement of his Piano Concerto in C major (K467) became known as the 'Elvira Madigan' (at least in the FLAMENCO TOPLESS BAR) from its extensive use in the film of the same name. See also the entry for Alfred GILBERT (MILE). It may be his version of the *Ave Verum Corpus* ('Hail, True Body') that Margaret DALEY recalls (WOOD: p244). Morse sends Claire OSBORNE a number of typed sheets, one of which details five different versions of the *Requiem* (K626). These are (with recording companies in brackets) those conducted by Rilling (Master Works), von Karajan (Deutsche Grammophon), Scmidt-Gaden (Pro Arte), de Sabata (Everest), and Richter (Telefunken). The inclusion of this list here may seem unnecessary *but* this guide does seek to be exhaustive and it should be a matter of record that Morse has all these versions on old-fashioned vinyl (or record, for that matter).[24] An otherwise unidentified visitor to Morse appears at the end of the WOOD case (and she certainly knows some K numbers). He is listening to Lipatti play the slow movement of K467 (piano concerto no. 21) when the pleasant and erotic interruption takes place (WOOD: p409). This visitor has been identified as Laura HOBSON by Bishop (2006: p69) though a case could be made for Claire OSBORNE (see *Women* under MORSE). Mozart's works have, of course, been catalogued by reference to Köchel (K) numbers. Claire OSBORNE listens to the *Tuba Mirum Spargens Sonum* ('the trumpet casts a wondrous sound') from the 4th movement of the *Requiem* after speaking to Alan HARDINGE on the telephone (WOOD: p355). The *Requiem* has been sent to her by Morse (on a cassette); his note advises her that the *Recordare* is his favourite 'bit'. At Morse's prompting, Lewis has a cassette of the Clarinet Concerto in his car (CAIN: p234) – to educate his musical tastes. A cassette of either this Concerto or Quintet is found in Rachel JAMES'S car (NEIG: p109).

'M' Roads The common designation for motorways. Of particular interest, in as far as any motorway can be thought interesting, is the M40, which runs from London to its junction with the M42 (just south of Birmingham) and conveniently has two junctions for Oxford (8 and 9). In NEIG, Lewis may (as usual) be found driving too fast from KIDLINGTON to the Chieveley junction on the M4 (p360).

---

[24] Morse does move with the times (albeit slowly) and buys a copy of the *Requiem* on CD (WOOD: p307).

Muldoon, Kieran Dominic A prisoner on remand in the recently re-opened Oxford Prison. He is aged about 36 years at the time of the STOR case and has a history of involvement in terrorism. The prosecution against him hinges on certain specific evidence and such evidence appears to have been mislaid. His addiction to erotica (from the age of 13 years) is crucial to the case and he rather (simplistically) hopes that the BODLEIAN LIBRARY carries a copy of every pornographic video. **Plate 52**

Mulvaney, Inspector A policeman with the Irish Garda (and probably no relation of KIPLING's hero of the same name). He gives what appears to be an accurate description of Morse: 'mid-fifties, losing his whitish hair, putting on just a little too much weight, and exhibiting perhaps, as was to be hoped, the tell-tale signs of liking his liquor more than little.' (WNCH: 202).

Mumbles, Viscount Little, if anything, is known of this author beyond his dates (1797-1821; NEIG: heading to chapter 10); that he wrote *Reflections on My Life* (CAIN: heading to chapter 29); that he also wrote *Essays on the Imagination* (REMO: heading to chapter 30). Bird's suggestion (1998: p62) that Diogenes SMALL was ennobled as the said Mumbles may reflect the degree of uncertainty about the confused dates of the former. DEXTER appears to be one of the few people who have access to the Viscount's works.

Murder 'the act of intentionally and unlawfully killing a person ... with malice aforethought' (Chambers 2003). It would make tedious – and rather revealing – reading to list the methods and victims in The WORKS. Suffice it to say that Morse gets "... on better when we've got a body – a body that died from unnatural causes. That's all I ask." (WEAR: p157).

Murdoch, Edward Aged 17, he is getting to grips with the short stories of Franz Kafka (particularly *Das Urteil/The Judgement)* with the aid of Anne SCOTT. The 'final, awesome, terrifying sentence' (JERI: p49) may be translated as 'At this moment an unending stream of traffic was just going over the bridge'. He is due to sit A LEVELS in French, German, and Latin at the Magdalen College School.

Murdoch, Michael He is aged 18 or 19 years and about to sit his A-LEVELS. It is unclear, at first, whether he will be able to take up his prospective place at LONSDALE (JERI: p98).

Myton, James (Jamie) William A jack-of-all-trades with a major interest in the PORNOGRAPHY industry. Once living at 24 Hickson Drive, Ealing (west London), he has been on Scotland Yard's missing-persons list since 1991 – along with another some 30,000 people (WOOD: p289). He has had a chequered past – taken into care by the local authority, some time being fostered in Brighton, and a spell in HM Borstal prison on the Isle of Wight. An interest in photography and some work in a television studio in Bristol[25] appear to have provided the necessary aptitudes and attitudes to give entry to a career (if such it can be called) in porn.

---

[25] Possibly the ITV Zodiac production team (WOOD: p296).

N

Nag's Head A pub at which Donald Favant stayed in 1859 (WNCH: p92). It is likely to be the one in HYTHE BRIDGE STREET; according to Honey (1998) the pub has been known as the Antiquity Hall since the 1980s.

Neighbourhood Watch Morse and Lewis discuss strategies to defeat an anticipated burglary (WATC). **Main personnel** Eric ULLMAN.

New Bodleian See BODLEIAN.

New College ASHENDEN walks past the back of this college (JWEL: p50) and Eddie STRATTON notes it on a street map (JWEL: p69). The TURF nestles under its walls (CAIN: p78). The college is 'New' because (although founded in 1379) its proposed title of the College of St Mary had already been taken by ORIEL College (founded 1326). Hence, it became the New College of St Mary. **Plate 53**, **Map D5**

New College Lane It runs east from CATTE STREET and is spanned by the Bridge of Sighs (which links the Old and New quadrangles of HERTFORD COLLEGE). Many members of Oxford University (and a good few tourists and townsfolk) have passed this way to gain eventual entry to the TURF TAVERN (CAIN). **Plate 54**, **Map D5**

Newlove, Peter A senior fellow with rooms in LONSDALE COLLEGE and an interest in Gaye MCFEE. Little is known about him beyond the facts that he was originally from Gloucestershire and enjoys a game of golf (LBUS).

New Road Home to the Oxford Register Office mentioned in CAIN: p276 (and also see LITERARY CURIOSITIES). It runs between Oxford Castle and Nuffield College. Shelly CORNFORD garages her car here (NEIG: p280). **Map D6**

News of the World, The A Sunday NEWSPAPER (now defunct) with a high circulation but rather low tastes. Morse is a regular reader. Geoffrey OWENS has his own copy delivered (NEIG: p261).

Newspaper(s) See *The DAILY MIRROR*, *The DAILY TELEGRAPH*, *The NEWS OF THE WORLD*, *OXFORD MAIL*, *OXFORD TIMES*, *SPORTING LIFE*, *The TIMES*, *The SUN*, *The SUNDAY MIRROR*, and *The SUNDAY TIMES*. Also see the entry *Newspapers* under MORSE. It would be tedious (in the extreme) to list all references to publications; usually, only one reference (and that of first appearance) is given. Publications mentioned include the *Financial Times* (NICQ: p233), *The Independent* (WOOD: p25; NEIG: p177), *The Independent on Sunday* (NEIG: p258), *The LISTENER*, *PUNCH*, *Woman's Weekly* (NICQ: p27 and p105 – obviously once a popular magazine), *Playboy* (NICQ: p67), *Pravda* (NICQ: p30), *The Daily Express* (SERV: p20; JERI: p278; WOOD: p25), *The Times Educational Supplement* (SERV: p23), *Sporting Chronicle* (SERV: p104), *The Guardian* (SERV: p149), *Chinese People's Daily*

(SERV: p153), *The Sunday Express* (SERV: p188), *The Angler's Times* (JERI: p64), *Bridge Monthly* (JERI: p123), *Lilliput* (JERI: p130, a magazine from Morse's youth wherein stately nudes could be glimpsed), *The Oxford Journal* (JERI: p189), and *On The Move* – a magazine concerned with adult literacy (JERI: pp189/222). To continue – *Country Life* (JERI: p270, WNCH: p131), *Evening Standard* (REMO but referred to as the London Standard (ANNX: p122), *Wireless Weekly, Amateur Photographer,* and the *Angling Times* (all 3 ANNX: p151), *Socialist Worker* (JWEL: p11), *Herald Tribune* (JWEL: p164), *Railway Magazine* (JWEL: p183), *The Observer* (JWEL: p84), *Property Weekly* (WOOD: p195), *TV Times, Oxcom, Oxford Today, Daily Mail, The Star* (all WOOD: p202), *Good Housekeeping* (CAIN: p286), and *The Star* – a free paper distributed throughout Oxford (CAIN: p299; known as the *Oxford Star* in NEIG: p61). Others include JACKSON'S OXFORD JOURNAL (WNCH: p60), *Court Registers* of the Oxford Assizes 1860 (WNCH: p60), the *University Gazette* (CAIN: p123; NEIG: p108), and the *Oxford Gazette* (STOR: p177). A few of the less savoury magazines are listed under PORNOGRAPHY.

New Theatre Formerly known as The Apollo, this is the theatre where Morse heard (and saw), from row J (seat 26), Die WALKÜRE in September 1975 (WEAR: p16). Somewhat (but only slightly) confusingly, *Aladdin* could be seen at The Apollo in 1985 (ANNX: p 22). It can be found in GEORGE STREET. **Plate 55**

NHS The standard abbreviation for the National Health Service (the staff of which provide – apart from diagnosis and care – for many of Morse's sexual fantasies and occasional successes).

Norham Gardens The name of a street leading to LADY MARGARET HALL and forming part of the northern border of the PARKS (JWEL: pp18, 183). It also allows a mistress to park her car prior to a meeting at The RANDOLPH (CALL: p271). **Map D4**

North Oxford A loosely defined area of the City but one that is well known and defined by its residents. It has been suggested that the development of the area was accelerated by the decision, in 1877, that FELLOWS need no longer be bachelors (Bradbury 1996 p112). Accordingly, a sudden rush of hormonal college members apparently caused many villas to be built to house their new spouses and children. Morse has his bachelor flat here and a number of the personnel involved in the various cases live here or hereabouts. As a snapshot of the area: 'A traveller who visits Oxford today, and who walks northward from St Giles', is struck immediately by the large, imposing houses, mostly dating from the latter half of the nineteenth century, that line the Woodstock and the Banbury Roads and the streets that cross their ways between them' (NICQ: p25). The area is referred to as either north or North Oxford in the WORKS though it is most definitely the North Oxford Golf Club to which Cedric DOWNES belongs (JWEL: p263). **Map C2-3, D2-3**

North Parade A turning off the BANBURY ROAD and location of the ROSE AND CROWN pub (WOOD: p192). Rather bizarrely, it lies to the south of SOUTH PARADE. **Map D4**

North Sea gas The high carbon monoxide percentage in domestic gas used to contribute to some 40% of suicides in the United Kingdom. Changes in the supply – to 'natural' North Sea gas in the late 1960s and early 1970s were not quite in time for one particular suicide (LBUS). Ironically, perhaps, Morse picks up a letter from the Southern Gas Board from the doormat of Anne SCOTT (JERI: p296). Also see SUICIDE.

Nuffield French (experiment) An attempt by the Government of the day to encourage bilingualism in schools (WEAR: p160). The experiment is discussed at a conference held in LONSDALE COLLEGE attended by, inter alios, David ACUM.

Nurses Morse seems to have met more nurses than the average middle-aged man. Rather than list and describe them here (which would involve an excessive concentration of lustful adjectives and epithets), they are dotted about (as they were in Morse's life) under their surnames. The heading to the Prolegomenon of REMO quotes some lines of Edmund Raikes from *The Nurse*. The opening two seem so apt for Morse (and how clever of DEXTER to record them):

> 'As o'er me now thou lean'st thy breast,
> With launder'd bodice crisply pressed ...'

Plate 49 (Left) The John Radcliffe Hospital (JR2) (p134).
Plate 50 (Right) Summertown Health Centre (p135).

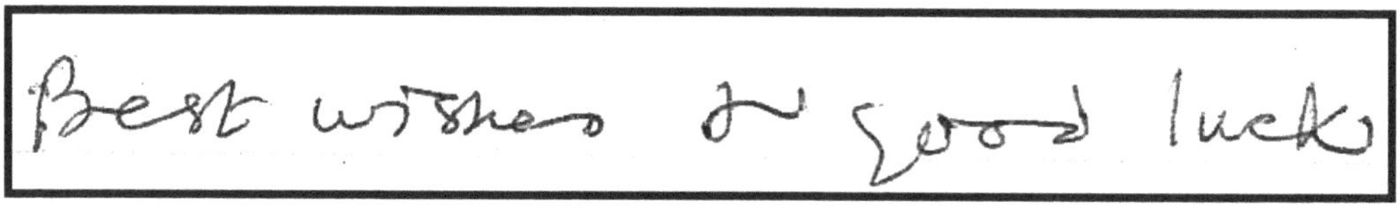

Best wishes & good luck

Plate 51 A rare example of Morse's hand (p138).

Plate 52 (Left) Oxford Prison (once a castle, now a hotel) (p142).
Plate 53 (Middle) New College – the Chapel (p143).
Plate 54 (Right) New College Lane (p143).

O

Observatory Street This may be found at the bottom of the WOODTOCK ROAD and is the home of Mr PALMER. It also appears in JERI (p134 and p294 – the latter advising that it is one-way). **Map D4-C5**

Ogleby, (Arnold) Philip MA, The Deputy Secretary of the SYNDICATE, specializing in Mathematics, Chemistry, and Physics (but with a sideline in the Welsh and Russian languages). He is 53 years old in 1975, lives in WALTON STREET, and a bachelor with interests in travel. The prospects promised by his 'brilliant first' (NICQ: p31) from CAMBRIDGE did not materialise; despite a number of interesting pubs in the area, he has been known to lunch at a Berni Inn (NICQ: p122).

Old Bull A pub in Deddington (some 20 miles or so north of Oxford) enjoyed by Paul MORRIS (SERV: pp41-42).

Old Marston This still retains the elements of a village despite its proximity to the suburbs of Oxford. Monica HEIGHT lives here as do Michael Woods and Karen Jones (JWEL: p107). **Map F3**

Old Orleans A Restaurant and Cocktail Bar – and only mentioned in an advertisement in the back of a taxi (CAIN: p104).

Old Parsonage Hotel To be found at 1 BANBURY ROAD (and dating from 1660), it describes itself as a 'haven of tranquillity'. Julia STEVENS plans to meet Brenda BROOKS here but finds that the latter is unavoidably detained; Julia enjoys a solitary glass of Bruno Paillard Brut Premier Cru in the Parsonage Bar (CAIN: p104). They do meet, however, the following day and enjoy what reads like a fairly tasty lunch. Morse meets Ellie SMITH here for a drink (or two); he is forced to switch to claret in the absence of a suitable BITTER (CAIN: pp278-284).

Old Tom A pub in ST ALDATES since 1335. It was re-named in 1865 to Great Tom (after Great Tom, the famous CHRIST CHURCH bell) and Old Tom in 1878. Ted BROOKS may, or may not, have drunk here (CAIN: p84).

O Levels The usual name for the 'ordinary' level of examinations taken by students at the age of about 15 or 16 years. See A LEVELS.

Opening Hours A quaint English tradition (dating from the First World War when the Government were keen to have at least some sober munitions' workers). Various Licensing Acts have determined the hours during which a PUBLIC HOUSE could remain open and how much 'drinking-up time' was allowed. Morse is as keenly aware of such restrictions as he is to flout them whenever possible or necessary. The cry of 'Last orders' does not seem to have overly chilled Morse's heart though various relaxations in the Licensing Laws (and extended opening hours) may have come a little too late to allow Morse a number of deserved freedoms.

The key change affecting Morse came under the Licensing Act 1988 (c. 17). Prior to this, public houses were forced to close for '... a break of two and a half hours beginning at three in the afternoon' on weekdays and 'five hours beginning at two' on Sundays. The Act also allowed pubs to open at 11.00am and close at 11pm (with shorter hours on the Sabbath). The Act was not prescriptive and a number of pubs (such as the MARSH HARRIER) chose to close for Sunday afternoons (CAIN: pp176-177). Morse did not have many reasons to like the then Conservative Government but, perhaps, this enlightened legislation softened his heart a little – he feels: '... a wholly unprecedented sense of gratitude to the Tory Government ...' (NEIG: p282). Luckily, his trip to Wales (WEAR) is not on 'a dry Welsh Sunday' (p222) when all public houses were closed and his 1989 trip to Derby refers to opening hours as being a thing of the past (WNCH: p231). In 1990, Morse offers to give Lewis the names and addresses of three pubs between OXFORD STATION and the RANDOLPH that are open all day though is slightly surprised to learn (from Lewis) that the latter has a bar open at 10.30am – where Morse repairs a short while later (JWEL: pp163, 167-8). Morse recognises that different pubs, under a more liberal regime, may have welcomed recent freedoms under the Licensing Acts – he is keen (in 1992) to find '... one of those open-all-day places ...' (WOOD: p323). His body clock seems keenly attuned to opening hours – challenging Strange's guess of about an hour until the pub is open with 'fifty minutes' (REMO: p274). And one guesses that Morse's suggestion is fairly accurate.

Oriel College There is a reference to this college (NEIG: p91) in connection with the BEAR pub. **Plate 56**, **Map D5**

Osberton Road A street running between MIDDLE WAY and the WOODSTOCK ROAD and home to Mrs Gerrard, a charity volunteer (REMO). **Map C3**

Osborne, Claire It is, at first, a little unclear whether Louisa HARDINGE is her pseudonym (and it is not one's role here to clarify such obfuscation). She is aged 39 years (WOOD: p278), stays at the COTSWOLD HOUSE (despite its ban on smoking), and (apparently) coincidentally (which would please Morse) sees him from her bedroom window carrying two bags from Oddbins, a local off licence. She later visits Morse at his flat (WOOD: pp107-115). She gives Morse a number of details about her history in a letter (pp150-151) but has trouble spelling 'preferable'.

Osney Mead estate An area of industrial and residential properties in west Oxford (WOOD: p286). It is also the location of the employers of OWENS – Oxford City and County Newspapers. **Map C6**

Ottery St Mary The birthplace of Samuel Taylor Coleridge (1772); this East Devon village is of some interest, because of that connection, to Morse. He takes a holiday here and also visits the immediate surrounding area (WOOD).

Oudenarde Third of the great battles won (1708) by John CHURCHILL, Duke of Marlborough (LBUS: p10). Also see BLENHEIM, RAMILLIES, and MALPAQUET.

Ovaltine The brand name of a drink supplement, usually made with hot milk (SERV: p20), and occasionally confused with Horlicks. Morse has been known to make himself a 'rare cup' (WOOD: p385); Julia STEVENS has at least two (one with Nurofen painkillers) in fairly quick succession (CAIN: p245).

'Over-beered' A little more precise than 'over-liquored' (ANNX: p278). On one occasion, when Morse is over-beered, he walks like a 'diffident funambulist' (WOOD: p259). He is also over-beered shortly before having to call an ambulance (REMO: p406). See UNDERBEERED.

Owens, Geoffrey (Gordon) A journalist and senior reporter with a number of desk-bound skills, living in BLOXHAM DRIVE at number 15. He is in his mid-forties, wears his hair in a ponytail, and works for Oxfordshire Newspapers (referred to as 'Ox and Cow' by Lewis) in OSNEY MEAD. His past experience of SOHO, his current rapacious nature, and his intimate knowledge of many of the secrets of a number of people are crucial to the NEIG case.

Ox, The A pub in CARFAX which holds no appeal for the Rev LAWSON (SERV: p5).

Oxbridge The word is both a noun and an adjective, combining the universities of Oxford and CAMBRIDGE. This portmanteau use is often used pejoratively to suggest a certain upper-class kind of education or as a way of obtaining unfair advantage in life after the joys (and usual excesses) of attendance at either university. However, the term also connotes a certain diligence and expertise in all matters academic as in the phrase 'You can always tell an Oxbridge man but you cannot tell him much'. There is also a presumption that some particularly bright schoolchildren will '... assume their natural Oxbridge birthrights' (WEAR: p159). The word appears to have been coined, according to Bradbury (1996), by Thackeray in *Pendennis* (published in 1850). See also CAMFORD (though not necessarily CAMELFORD).

Oxfam There are several references to this charity, founded in Oxford in 1947, in the WORKS and these are briefly recapped here. Max flippantly suggests sending a pair of a corpse's trousers to an Oxfam shop (MILE: p70); JERI (p117) notes a then-current Oxfam appeal on behalf of refugees; the second-hand bookshop is mentioned in SERV (p321); and Morse envisages his neighbours doing good works for the charity in WNCH (p169). A person claiming to be Karin ERIKSSON writes to the police on Oxfam recycled paper (WOOD: p55) and, finally, ASHENDEN asks for his gambling winnings to be donated to Oxfam (JWEL: p279). **Plate 57**

Oxford A city in the East Midlands, first recorded in 912AD; the name is (unsurprisingly) derived from 'ford for oxen' (**Plate 58**) (Ekwall 1960). Brewer's (2005) usefully describes Oxford as '(a city) of the well-worn 'dreaming spires': ancient buildings of mellow golden stone, secluded ivy-clad courtyards and quadrangles, Gothic pinnacles, gowned dons, bicycling undergraduates and so on ... the dreaming spires are not the whole picture, however. There is an industrial side to Oxford, too ... Britain's first mass-produced cars came from the car-plants of Cowley, in southeastern Oxford, in the 1920s ... and deprivation is in evidence in Blackbird Leys.'(pp842-843). Only brief comments will be given here – Oxford permeates the WORKS and a very large number of entries herein reflect that fact. Of the antipathy between Town and Gown, it is a pity that no notes of the session given by DOWNES, KEMP, and WILLIAMS on that subject have been traced (JWEL: p87). And although Morse has a foot in both camps, he is accused (by Ted BROOKS) of not really understanding or appreciating the difference (CAIN: p167).

Many, many writers have enthused about Oxford. Some appear to have gone a little overboard: 'When one strays through those aisles and under those arches, one fancies them almost as conscious of their sacred eld as one is one's self. Then suddenly one comes out into the vivid green light of a grassy quadrangle, or the flowery effulgence of a garden, where the banks of blossomed bushes are pushed back of the beds of glowing annuals by the velvety sward unrolled over spaces no more denied to your foot than the trim walks that wander beyond their barrier, under the ivied walls, and to and from the foot-worn thresholds.' (Howells 1906: pp202-203). Oxford has long been subject to the motorcar – Morton (1942) has: '... it is now difficult to cross the road except at a hunted run. No other town of its size in England leaves upon the mind such an impression of congestion' (pp152-153). According to Lewis (NEIG: p130), Monday morning traffic is the busiest. See also BLACKBIRD LEYS, DREAMING SPIRES, and WATERWAYS. There are now some helpful, if uninspiring, ring roads. But the attractions outweigh any disadvantages and for Morse, '... he could now imagine few if any places closer to his heart than Oxford ...' (REMO: p7).

Oxford Avenue A street in ABINGDON and home to Charles and Celia RICHARDS.

Oxford Book Association A society that holds its sessions in the Clarendon Press Institute (in WALTON STREET). Morse is a member and provides some thirty paperbacks from his bookshelves to assist their secondhand sale (JERI: p23). His is an irregular presence at their meetings but he does hear Dame Helen GARDNER and one of the RICHARDS brothers speak (JERI) and, in 1987, heard Malcolm Muggeridge propound a disturbing philosophy (WNCH: p79). In 1993, the Chairman is Rex DE LINCTO (STOR) and a short story competition is being organised. The nine entrants are Ian Bradley, Emma Skipper, Valerie Ward, Jim Morwood, Christina Collins, Una Broshola, Elissa Thorpe, Richard Elves, and Mary Ann Cotton. Of these, Morse recognises Cotton as the name of a Victorian criminal (hanged in Durham) and Collins as the name of a murder victim from Staffordshire.[1]

Oxford Brookes University Established as a university in 1992 (from Oxford Polytechnic) and with several sites around and about Oxford. For a reason yet to be established, they have written to Morse (REMO: p429). Its roots go back to the nineteenth century and its origins in the Oxford School of Art.

Oxford Canal The canal was first developed between 1769 and 1790 as an outlet for the industrial produce of the Midlands. In 1789 the Duke of Marlborough arranged for a cut to be

---

[1] WNCH is partly dedicated to John Godwin, author of *The Murder of Christine Collins*. Christine Collins does not appear in Brindley (2006) though many other 'Oxford' murders do. The similarity between Christina and Christine may, of course, be coincidental.

made (Duke's Cut) linking the canal to the Thames north of Oxford; in 1796 a link to the south was made by building Isis lock. The canal runs to the west of JERICHO (see CANAL REACH and JERI generally). In one particular case, a body is discovered at Aubrey's Bridge (THRUPP) in MILE (p80). It is of some relevance that the bridge is on an elbow bend – meaning that boats are prohibited from mooring and, therefore, there is less likelihood of witnesses (p260). The archives of the Oxford Canal Company Registers are, apparently, in existence (WNCH: p58) and the Oxford Canal Authority – who published Regulations (WNCH: p92) – once managed the canal.

There are, no doubt, more pleasurable activities than cruising most of the Oxford Canal (in good company), spending 3 days in Oxford, and getting as far down The Thames as one can before turning back in order to return one's hire boat. There are fewer such activities when one is re-reading WNCH at the same time. The canal is central to the 1859 case recorded in WNCH. Here we learn that Morse has limited experience of narrow-boating (which he regards as grossly overrated). His only known trip was from the terminus at HYTHE BRIDGE STREET to the PLOUGH at WOLVERCOTE and it is detailed in WNCH (p52). Morse's recollection of this nightmarish trip (which only left 5 minutes for drinking) is somewhat faulty – the crew member who kept 'hopping out for locks' would have found none at all on this stretch of the canal (unless they went through Isis Lock onto the Thames – which seems unlikely). The trip is a little over 2 miles and should take approximately three quarters of an hour or so (depending on the passage under the three lift bridges that cross this stretch). Morse seems to have felt that it took much, much longer than this.

The book, *Murder on the Oxford Canal* (DENISTON 1978) recalls the southward-bound trip of the boat, the *Barbara Bray*, from Preston Brook to Oxford in 1859. The crew were Oldfield, Musson, Towns, and Wootton and their passenger was Joanna FRANKS. As Deniston records, the trip from Preston Brook (the northern terminus of the Trent and Mersey Canal) to Hawkesbury Junction was '... comparatively uneventful ...' but from Napton Locks (**Plate 59**) 'the story appears to change ... dramatically' (WNCH: p60). The former section includes the very real Harecastle Tunnel and what may be a mythical Northwich Tunnel (the latter certainly does not exist today though there are differently named tunnels in the vicinity according to a reliable guide: Nicholson 2003). As such, this entry will ignore the Atherstone locks and tunnels and concentrate on the last stage of the journey – from Napton Locks to the end of the canal (not least because it has been most recently travelled). In 1859, the *Barbara Bray* cruised from Napton, through BANBURY, to King's Sutton Lock (where a wharfinger's wife, Agnes Laurenson, disembarked) and thence to Aynho. At Somerton Deep Lock, the Robsons – lock keeper and wife – heard a disturbance on the boat and vaguely tried to intervene. Later, it appears that Joanna walked along the towpath towards Gibraltar Lock, re-joining the boat at some unspecified point. There is, now, no lock called Gibraltar – it has been renamed Baker's Lock in honour of an early landlord of the Rock of Gibraltar pub (**Plate 60**). A crew-hand from the boat *Isis* gave evidence that he had seen her on the towpath. Between Gibraltar and Oxford lie the village of Hampton Gay (away to the east of the canal and deserted) and THRUPP (**Plate 61**). Here, the canal has a sharp elbow bend (and under a lift bridge); Morse reconstructs the conversation that may have taken place near here between Joanna and the young crew member, Wootton. Passing the terrace of cottages at Thrupp, the *Barbara Bray* passed through Roundham and Kidlington Green locks. Shuttleworth's lock (now, perhaps, known as Duke's lock – for there is no Shuttleworth at present) was next – the last lock before the Cut where entry may be gained into the Thames. The body of Joanna FRANKS was discovered in Duke's Cut on the 22nd June 1859 by Philip Tomes who was assisted by John Ward in removing it from the water. Later, the Barbara Bray had to negotiate Iffley Lock on the Thames (which lock is also briefly mentioned in CAIN: p302).

Oxford Cathedral See CHRIST CHURCH.

Oxford Central Library Morse is, obviously, aware of this facility to be found in Westgate (or BONN SQUARE; NEIG: p199). He recalls that Jackson's Oxford Journal can be found on microfiche there (WNCH: p106). Christine GREENAWAY carries out research here on Morse's behalf (pp121-124) and, unplanned, meets Lewis. The library has a Local History section (STOR: p211).

Oxford Classical Texts Otherwise known as *Scriptorum Classicorum Bibliotheca Oxoniensis*, this series of books (published by the OUP) seeks to include the works of all the principal classical writers (WEAR: p167).

Oxford Comma Trask (2001) usefully explains this usage: '... most Americans prefer The Three Musketeers were Athos, Porthos, and Aramis. This style is also preferred in certain quarters in Britain, notably the OXFORD UNIVERSITY PRESS ...' As an example, the OUP claims that it '... furthers the University's objective of excellence in research, scholarship, and education by publishing ...' (from the ISBN details in Roberts 2005). Without the Oxford comma, the Musketeers would, of course, be Athos, Porthos and Aramis. Fowler recommends its use but only for the sake of clarity rather than form and gives the example of: 'The smooth grey of the beech stem, the silky texture of the birch, and the rugged pine. If there is no comma after birch, the pine is given a silky texture' (Originally 1926; 1968: p588). A further example from Fowler is given as the heading to Chapter 18 of NEIG – here the example is 'French, German, Italian and Spanish' where there is little chance of ambiguity – but Morse suggests a preference for its use to add clarity to a newspaper report (p115) and to a report by Lewis (REMO: p140). Fry (2005: p23) suggests that '... Oxford commas (are now an) archaic usage'. It may be best to follow Truss who advises: 'There are people who embrace the Oxford comma and people who don't, and I'll just say this: **never** get between these people when drink has been taken' (2003: p84). Gowers usefully has, of commas in general: 'The use of commas cannot be learned by rule ... good writers of the same period differ among themselves' (1977: p242). REMO has a dedication by DEXTER: 'For George, Hilary, Maria, and Beverley (please note the Oxford comma)'.

Oxford Crown Court Despite being the eventual destination, one assumes, of several characters in the WORKS, there are scant references to this arm of the judicial system (SERV: pp305-315 gives some details of a case heard there).

Oxford Disease '… that tragic malady which deludes its victims into believing they can never be wrong in any matter of knowledge or opinion' (JWEL: p187). The ex-husband of Sheila WILLIAMS (an English DON) is (or was) a sufferer – as are many others found in the WORKS.

Oxford Mail A newspaper with a circulation local to Oxford. It carries details of certain police investigations (for example SERV: p320, MILE: p118, and WOOD p263).

Oxford Movement A religious movement arguing for a return of Anglicanism to such principles of Catholicism as faith in the Early Fathers. Founded (in effect) by John Keble in 1833, its leading proponent was John Henry Newman. The Movement was concerned by increasing liberalism in the Anglican Church and wished for a catholic sense of unity coupled with Gothic style. MEIKLEJOHN is attracted to the Movement's doctrines and comes 'within a communion wafer of conversion to the Roman Church' (SERV: p228).

Oxford Pike Anglers' Association An association in Oxford for anglers who specialise in (one hopes) fishing for pike in (one guesses) a number of areas including the OXFORD CANAL at THRUPP (MILE: p93). Tom BIFFEN has been the Secretary since 1993 (REMO: p294).

Oxford Playhouse Claiming to be one of Britain's leading theatres, it has long enjoyed a close relationship with the University. It can be found in BEAUMONT STREET (**Map D5**). PHILLIPSON claims to have seen *Saint Joan* there on a crucial evening (in seat M14). **Plate 62**

Oxford Probation Service An organisation that is responsible (among a few other things) for ensuring that Supervision in the Community (under the Criminal Justice Act) is properly enacted. They are based in PARK END STREET (REMO: p85).

Oxford Railway Station Once upon a time one needed a platform ticket to either reach the platforms (LBUS: p218) or have a drink in the buffet (NICQ: p151); STRATTON claims to have had a drink in the latter (JWEL: p162). Morse catches the Cathedral's Express from here (WNCH: p234) to PADDINGTON; the Turbo Express covers the same route (NEIG: pp30/86). For anybody who may be interested, some details of how the Railcard scheme operates may be found in NEIG (pp32/87). The car park is not as extensive as it used to be but still might (or might not) be a good place to abandon a car that has been involved in a crime (REMO: pp171-75). It is bounded by the BOTLEY ROAD on one side. **Plate 63, Map C5**

Oxfordshire Health Authority The organisation that, in the mid-1970s at least, oversaw the work of both 'Radcliffe' hospitals (NICQ: p 104). It also appears that it has organised a British Medical Association dinner at which Max is a guest speaker (JWEL: p114).

Oxford Story An entertainment to be found at 6 BROAD Street and one that is undertaken by several members of the HISTORIC CITIES tour (JWEL). It is, effectively, a ride – one sits (in a pair) at a sort of desk and are then transported slowly past a number of tableaux, pageants, and exhibits (with, in 1990, a recorded commentary by Sir Alec Guinness; 2006 has Magnus Magnusson). The exhibits include, according to Ginger Bonnetti, Roger BACON, Thomas Bodley, Charles the First, Hobbes and Locke, John Wilkins, Wren, Boyle, and John Wesley *et al*. Much is made of Lewis Carroll and Alice; the ride lasts about 25 minutes. Lewis thinks the attraction is 'brilliant' (JWEL: p146). The Oxford Story also has an extensive (though not necessarily expensive) Gift Shop where one may buy, among other things, Cheshire cats, jigsaws, and jugs (JWEL: p93). **Plate 64**

Oxford Times A paper of record – well, at least recording a name or two (SERV: p320). It is read by DICKSON (MILE: p154) and carries advertisements for kung-fu classes (MILE: p192) as well as CROSSWORDS by QUIXOTE.

Oxford Town Hall No doubt notable for many reasons, it is only mentioned here as the venue for a dance in 1944 (JWEL: p204).

Oxford Union A famous debating society (but rarely mentioned in the WORKS; WOOD: p150 being the only example traced here).

Oxford United A football team enjoying varying degrees of success and popularity. The club was founded in 1893 as Headington United; its fortunes during the period of the WORKS were rather up and down and only the intervention of the late millionaire publisher Robert Maxwell saved the club from bankruptcy. Lewis is reasonably interested in their progress. Their ground is at Manor Road in Headington (until 2001) and Morse parks in nearby Sandfield Road on a rare visit (SERV: p108). The Chairman of the club has discussed football hooliganism with BELL over lunch (JERI: p57) and the club's game against Everton was postponed, because of bad weather (a shame), in 1986 (ANNX: p50).

Oxford University The academic year is split into three terms – Michaelmas (Autumn), Hilary (Spring), and Trinity (Summer). After Trinity, comes the Long Vacation (CAIN: p91). The University is a separate legal entity from the 38 self-governing colleges (and a number of Halls) of which it is constituted; one cannot be a member of the University without being a member of a college. The figure of 38 is current for 2007; it has, of course, been less and there is every reason to believe that it may eventually increase. The University issues blue diaries (NICQ: p185; JWEL: p3) and employs a Marshal who is advised of the theft of a knife (CAIN: p219). The Registry (NICQ: p145; SERV: p135) is responsible, inter alia, for administrative tasks. The University has (rather more than) two museums but note is made here of the History of Science (in BROAD Street) and the Natural History (in PARKS ROAD). It is clear that it is the latter of these which is referred to in JWEL: p149 – '... the dodo, Darwin, and the dinosaurs'. See also ASHMOLEAN and PITT RIVERS.

Oxford University Press Housed in a most impressive building in WALTON STREET (but looking somewhat out of place – '... like some dowager duchess at a discotheque' JERI: p20). A number of responsibilities reside in the Delegacy of the Press including, it would seem, control of parking; Lewis has to scrape off the obstinately glued notice that has been affixed to the windscreen of Morse's LANCIA (JERI: p52). The Press also publishes the results of examinations (MILE: p97), the *Oxford Almanack* (CAIN: p20), and has an Atlas Department (STOR: p202). OGLEBY visits the OUP in NICQ (p98). **Plate 65**

Oxpens A campus in Oxford where a number of educational courses are run (WEAR: p307). In 1975, the lip-reading classes are transferred from here to HEADINGTON (NICQ: p80). These lip-reading classes seem to have moved back to Oxpens by 1988 (REMO: pp319/369). **Map C6**

Plate 55 (Left) The New Theatre (p144).
Plate 56 (Right) Oriel College (p148).

Plate 57 (Left) A poignant reminder – the plaque outside the first shop (in the BROAD) (p149).
Plate 58 (Right) Seal of the City of Oxford (p149).

Plate 59 (Left) Waiting for one of the Napton Locks (p151).
Plate 60 (Right) The Rock of Gibraltar public house (p151).

P

Paddington The mainline station in London for trains to Oxford. The 3.05pm train from Paddington is a rather important one in terms of ALIBIs (NICQ: p261) but this need not be confused with the *4.50 from Paddington* by Agatha Christie. Morse travels by first-class on a '125' from here (MILE: p218) and also admires the statue of one of his heroes, Brunel (NEIG: p207).

Paddington Station Hotel Its toilets are noteworthy simply because they are used to facilitate a disposal (MILE: pp228-229).

Palmer, F A guest at the HAWORTH HOTEL. He lives, perhaps, with his wife (perhaps), at 29A Chiswick Reach London, W4. Because of late booking, they can only be accommodated in the Annexe (Room 1). (ANNX).

Palmer, Mr Manager of the TOWN AND GOWN ASSURANCE COMPANY and only male employee. Josephine Palmer, his wife, attends WEA classes on Headington Hill; they live in OBSERVATORY STREET. (LBUS).

Palmer, Mrs The wife of F. Palmer (perhaps) and known as Philippa or Pippa. There seems to be some confusion about her address in Chiswick – she looks up at the ceiling of her first-floor flat (ANNX: p110) but also entertains in her own discreet flat on the eighth and top floor (p124).

Park End Street This runs east from the BOTLEY ROAD, provides access to OXFORD RAILWAY STATION, splits and branches just about south-east into the city centre. Also see the entry under QUEEN STREET. **Map C5**

Parks Road This runs from a little north of KEBLE COLLEGE down to a junction with the BROAD and HOLYWELL STREET. **Map D4-D5**

Parks, The An area of some 70 acres of parkland, with many varieties of trees, on the west bank of the Cherwell. It contains the Oxford University Cricket Club ground and pavilion and an island known as Mesopotamia. The Parks is gated and fenced and access is, supposedly, controlled (JWEL). The Royalist artillery was quartered here during the Civil War (JWEL: p107). The Parks may be reached from the village of OLD MARSTON by a path crossing Rainbow Bridge (formally High Bridge) over the Cherwell. **Map D4**

Park Town An area of Oxford between the BANBURY ROAD and the River Cherwell (ANNX: p17; JWEL: p183). It was laid out in 1853 with a North and a South Crescent enclosing an oval of gardens and all the houses are now listed as Grade II. The Dragon School moved to Park Town in 1895 - and James Hughes (MINOR) has his name down for it (CAIN: p304). **Plate 66**

Morse brushes up on the area from his Penguin copy of Pevsner's *Oxfordshire* (Buildings of England series) to help him find the location of a photo (WOOD: pp176-177). In Park Town one may also find the property known as Seckham Villa (WOOD: p190); the architect Samuel Lipscomb Seckham designed Park Town. **Map D4**

Parson's Pleasure The famous and infamous bathing place (where once male nude swimming was positively encouraged). It is found on a bend of the Cherwell and provides (at the time of the JWEL case) changing cubicles. **Map E5**

Pater Street Named after the essayist and Fellow of BRASENOSE, Walter Pater. Morse remembers his description of the *Mona Lisa* as the 'woman who'd learned the secrets of the grave' (the line is from *The Renaissance*). Pater Street is in COWLEY. (CAIN). **Map G8**

Pear Tree Inn A pub at Hook Norton (where Sarah HARRISON intends to meet pro-hunting colleagues in organising a Countryside March).

Peep of Dawn, The A public house in Reading and '... as engagingly named a pub as Morse could remember ...' (ANNX: p154). It has only one bar and wooden wall-seats, and Morse is content to sit here philosophising about whether he thinks more lucidly when and after drinking. As a classicist he does, of course, consider whether or not this is a *post hoc, ergo propter hoc* fallacy – 'after this, therefore because of this' – but comes to no firm conclusion.

Pembroke College This college does not feature heavily in the WORKS. The only mention appears to be a reference to a rather dishy undergraduate (NEIG: p12). **Map D6**

Penguin Classics A series of paperback books, published since 1946, with notable (and noticeable) black spines. Anne SCOTT has an extensive collection of them: many such are listed (in JERI: p190) and they are kept in alphabetical order, from Aeschylus to Xenophon (including Seneca and Suetonius). Morse recognises that a volume appears to be missing and obviously knows the series well (JERI: p101).

Penthouse Club A fairly seedy establishment in BREWER STREET, which employs John MAGUIRE as a 'receptionist'. It has, allegedly, eighteen gorgeous girls and the entrance fee (with no other charges) was a mere 95p in 1975.

Peters, 'Old' He is employed in the forensic laboratory of the THAMES VALLEY POLICE, having previously worked for the Home Office (NICQ: p171), is in his early 60s (in 1975), and is an expert in handwriting analysis. His manner is as clinical and dry as Morse's is creative and 'wet' (he does seem to think rather better after a glass or two). Peters '... thought at the speed of an arthritic tortoise and acted with the decisiveness of a soporific sloth' (NICQ: p172). He also appears in the WEAR case (pp98-100).

Peter's Pence The practice in the Roman Catholic religion of earmarking a percentage of the lay money (usually raised by a special collection) to send to the Vatican. While ST

FRIDESWIDE'S is High Anglican it is not quite 'spikey' (i.e. Anglo-Catholic) enough to get that close to Rome (SERV: p83). Chambers (2003) prefers 'spiky'.

Phillips, Sergeant A police officer, from the City CID, on the scene at the HAWORTH HOTEL investigation (ANNX: pp39/55) and used in enquiries concerning Margaret BOWMAN (p219).

Phillipson, Donald The headmaster of the ROGER BACON school (once attended by Valerie TAYLOR). After attending public school, he studied History at CAMBRIDGE. A short spell in the Army preceded a career in teaching. He is in his mid-thirties at the time of Morse's investigation (WEAR) and lives, with Sheila (his wife), and their primary school age children (Andrew and Alison) at The Firs, BANBURY ROAD, Oxford (with a very pleasant garden). He drives a Rover car. Phillipson is still at the school during the course of a later case (SERV).

Phillipson, Sheila Married to Donald (for over 12 years by 1975); they keep their own financial affairs in order (though she does have a key to the drawer where he keeps his). One knows little about her appearance though she does have light-brown eyes and is a non-smoker (WEAR: p212).

Phillotson, Detective Chief Inspector He is originally in charge of a murder case (CAIN) before Morse is put in charge by Strange. The official reason for the switch is that his wife is ill but Strange has his doubts about Phillotson's competency; the latter is unfavourably compared to Sherlock HOLMES (p36).

Phillotson, Mrs Morse shows a sensitive (and sensible) side of his nature on hearing of Mrs Phillotson's death (at the age of 46 years) – he leaves a note for the new widower which, being honest, brings the latter some comfort (p76). Mrs Phillotson is sent off at Oxford Crematorium to the hymn *O Love that wilt not let me go* – a favourite of the absent Morse (CAIN: p194).

Phoenix Cinema A picture-house in WALTON STREET (JERI: p20) showing, for part of 1979 at least, *Sex in the Suburbs*. **Plate 67**

Pitt Rivers Museum The main entrance is from PARKS ROAD with access gained through the Oxford University Museum (of Natural History).[1] The museum, founded in 1884, has over half a million exhibits of Oxford University's archaeological and anthropological collection (including displays of knives). Of some relevance to the CAIN case is the display of artefacts collected by Captain Cook in 1772 from the South Pacific; of less relevance are the Japanese, Burmese, Siamese, and Indonesian display-cases. The museum also runs temporary exhibitions such as that of the desert photography of Wilfred Thesiger (NEIG: p107) – where Julian STORRS and Morse briefly met. Ted BROOKS works here and Morse enjoys a little verbal fencing with the Administrator, Jane COTTERELL (CAIN: pp121-125), before wandering through the galleries. Janis LAWRENCE makes an interesting discovery while cleaning the

[1] Morse thinks of the 'Dodo and the Dinosaur' when entering the University Museum grounds (CAIN: p119); a permanent exhibition so entitled was set up in 1999, some 5 years later.

Upper Gallery (CAIN: p218); this discovery is not wholly unconnected with an example of a Barotse knife (Northern Rhodesia) from some 75 years ago. A diagram of the same (with label) appears in CAIN (p220); part of the label appears later (p315). An annual lecture is named in honour of Lieutenant-General Augustus Henry Lane Fox Pitt Rivers; in 1995 Julian STORRS delivered it – on Captain Cook. **Plate 68**

Pixey Place A road in Upper Wolvercote (ANNX: p256). **Map B2**

Place names See APPENDIX E.

Plain, The A roundabout and the location of the CAPE OF GOOD HOPE pub. ASHENDEN walks round it (JWEL: p209) and it is briefly mentioned in WOOD (p346) and STOR (p177). **Map E6**

Plough, The Almost a canalside inn – the walk is a few hundred yards – at WOLVERCOTE. Morse has visited it, briefly, as recorded in WNCH (p52). The pub has one room set apart, almost, as a library with hundreds of books on yards of shelves. In 1859 the body of Joanna FRANKS was brought here (WNCH: p91). **Plate 69**

Poirot, Hercule A Belgian fictional detective created by Agatha Christie. His exploits are known to Gaye McFEE (LBUS).

Police There are two main branches of the British police, the uniformed and the detective (the CID i.e. Criminal Investigation Department). There are also a number of specialist units (such as the Gatwick Security Police (ANNX: p286), traffic officers, frogmen or divers (JWEL: p309),[2] and dog-handlers. All police personnel are known as officers and their relative importance, powers, experience, toadyism, or good luck are confirmed by their RANK. Morse is a Detective Chief Inspector, at least from the date of his first recorded case (1971) but this rank is also commonly called 'Inspector'. All officers, uniformed or otherwise, should carry a badge and their WARRANT CARD, which certifies their identity and their entitlement to use police powers. See also SOCO and THAMES VALLEY POLICE.

Police Welfare Fund Most, if not all, police forces (certainly including the THAMES VALLEY) operate a charitable fund. Common calls on the funds are from widows, widowers, and orphans of police officers. Morse suggests, ironically one hopes, that Mrs PALMER may wish to make a contribution (ANNX: p123).

Pollard, PC A constable detailed to look after a site in WYTHAM WOOD. He appears to be relatively oafish (WOOD: pp226-229) – and is described as '… rather less-than-dedicated …' (p283). One hopes, of course, that he is more-than-well-intentioned.

---

[2] The Underwater Search Unit is based at Sulhamstead (CAIN: p307).

Polstead Road A thoroughfare linking the WOODSTOCK ROAD to ARISTOTLE LANE and home to Julian and Angela STORRS. A plaque commemorating T. E. Lawrence (who lived here on and off between 1896 and 1921) may be seen (NEIG: p354) at 2 Polstead Road. The road may well have been named after a village in Suffolk. **Map C4**

Pornography This is defined as the portrayal of prostitutes or prostitution[3] but is commonly held to refer to books, magazines, and films dealing with sexual acts in a more or less explicit manner. Bertrand Russell, according to the heading to Chapter 36 of WOOD, suggests that nine tenths of its appeal is due to the indecent feelings concerning sex which moralists inculcate in the young. Morse may be found reading the *Naturist Journal* at the age of 12 years (NEIG: p173) and, as a boy, glancing at demure nudes in the barber's copy of *Lilliput* (JERI: p130). Morse reveals a certain fascination for pornography but despairs of the halfway house kind found in salacious NEWSPAPERS: 'he liked it hot or not at all' (WEAR: p39). Exactly how 'hot' the Fabulous Fiona, Sexy Susan, Sensational Sandra, Voluptuous Vera, and Kinky Kate were at the PENTHOUSE CLUB is, perhaps, hard to imagine but Morse was reluctant to leave the strip show when Fiona made her reappearance (and did, indeed, return to the Club) (WEAR: pp82-84). Morse does not regard himself as totally beyond the pale – thinking to himself, he muses: 'He was a lecherous old man too, wasn't he? Very nearly, anyway. Just a sediment of sensitivity still. Just a little. Just a little' (WEAR: p335).

References to pornography include such magazines as *Lush* and *Lust*, *Flesh* and *Frills*, and *Skin* and *Skirt* (LBUS: p105); MAGUIRE has a collection of imported Danish material, which briefly occupies Morse, and SANDERS has an interest in porn magazines and films such as *Danish Blue* and *Hot Pants* (LBUS: pp105/148). BROWNE-SMITH, on a visit to London, sees serious porn ('wilder by a dozen leagues') than he had seen at the ABC in Oxford (MILE: p35). Morse finds a book (*Sex Parties*) in the BOWMANS' house (ANNX: p223) but a brief glance at its contents confirm it as the kind of anti-climactic pianissimo porn for which he has no time. He is, for example, not tempted by *On the Game* at the Moulin Rouge: 'an X-trailer, no doubt, advertising a U film' (SERV: p108) but may have been tempted by *Sex in the Suburbs* at the PHOENIX (JERI: p21) had he not other things to do. He does, however, (after reading a brief review: NICQ: p128) see *The Nymphomaniac* at STUDIO 2 with Lewis (NICQ: pp291-292). Morse is reasonably familiar with the titles *Men Only*, *Escort*, *Knave*, and *Video XXXX* (JWEL: p128) that he sees in a garage.

Morse enjoys the performance of the Fabulous Fiona in the CORN DOLLY (a different stripper to that employed by the PENTHOUSE CLUB, one guesses, unless she works very long hours) but finds that anticipation may grow as cold as the experienced reality (JERI: p130). He also knows that there is a Private Sex Shop at the city-centre end of the COWLEY ROAD (CAIN: p173). An anonymous diary writer traces his descent into pornography (WOOD: p32) and notes, correctly, that kleptolagnia – the practice of achieving sexual arousal through stealing – is not in Chambers Dictionary (though it is in the 1993 New Shorter Oxford). The

---

[3] Young (1969) has: 'Licht [in his detailed analysis] found the word *pornographos* – a writer about whores – only once in his reading of classical literature.' (p60).

same writer suggests that it is 'process' that arouses – not the nude but the anticipation of the nude through the removal of clothing (p41). A telling description of the process of addiction to pornography may be found in WOOD (p222): '... private film clubs; imported videos and magazines; live sex-shows; 'hostess' parties ... the *anticipation* of such occasions! The extraordinarily arousing words that became the open sesame to such erotic entertainments: 'Is everybody known?'' Seckham Villa in PARK TOWN is the scene of much (very much) pornographic activity (WOOD: pp200-204), Kevin COSTYN's bedroom rather less so; OWENS has videos called *Grub Screws* and *Sux and Fux* (NEIG: pp272-273).

Porter A COLLEGE worker. Porters need (and exhibit) a blend of servility and officiousness (MILE: p99). Bowler hats are traditionally worn.

Porter's Lodge Invariably sited at the main entrance to a COLLEGE and a key point for the exchange of information, telephone calls, and correspondence (via pigeonholes). 'Porter's Lodge' is the most common spelling (e.g. LBUS: p211) but 'Porters' Lodge' is not unknown (see LONSDALE).

Portland Road Running east from the BANBURY ROAD to the Cherwell (JWEL: p77). **Map D3**

Port Meadow A fairly pleasant area to the west of the City. It is officially controlled and inspected by the 'Conservator and Sheriff' (WEAR: p110) who has the power to fine unauthorised users. The area was originally gifted by William the Conqueror and is currently owned by the Freemen of the City of Oxford who may depasture on it any cattle and horses; the Freemen also retain the right to fish in that section of the River Thames which runs along the entire length of the Meadow. **Plate 70, Map C4**

Poster, Shcila (Emily) A graduate of ST HILDA'S with a second-class honours degree in English. She is an only child and her parents are either dead or in a home. It is unclear (at first) how her work in the University's Geology Department might impact on a short story she has written. Her notice board contains a wealth of information (STOR: p174) – some of which is recorded elsewhere in this Companion.

Prestige A brand of kitchen knife with large sales, particularly (it would seem) in Oxford and, perhaps, North Wales. One such knife, at least, is used as a murder weapon (WEAR: p173).

Priestley Grammar School A school in Bradford; Nicholas QUINN taught there after graduation.

Prince of Wales, The Morse spends a happy lunchtime (from 11.05am) in this pub in Bont-Newydd – the local brew is good and helps him decide whether or not to call at the ACUMs' home (WEAR).

Princess Street Off the IFFLEY ROAD (CAIN: p235) and home to Ellie SMITH at number 35. **Map E6**

Prince William Hotel McBryde (MINOR) stays here (near PADDINGTON) after a rapid departure from Oxford (WOOD: pp252-253).

Principal An alternative title of the Master of a COLLEGE (and used at, for example, BRASENOSE and HERTFORD).

Printer's Devil The name of a pub in JERICHO frequented every evening by the occupant of 1 CANAL REACH (JERI: p92). It is also here that Morse, parking on the double yellow lines outside, fortifies himself with a couple of large Scotches (p99) before undertaking some illicit nocturnal activity. It has a saloon bar (p134).

Proctor Proctors are involved in disciplinary and administrative work on behalf of the University. Their history and changing roles is admirably described in Hibbert (1988).

Proctor Memorial School A secondary modern school in East Oxford. One of its teachers is Julia STEVENS and one of its pupils is Kevin COSTYN (CAIN).

Publications An alarming variety of published works are mentioned in the WORKS, particularly in a large number of Chapter headings. A list of those in headings would be otiose here (though many appear elsewhere in this Companion or under NEWSPAPERS). A few, which do not appear elsewhere, include: *Kubla Khan* (LBUS: p124); *Know Your Köchel Numbers* (MILE: p25) and also see MOZART; a range of books owned by the BOWMANS includes works by Jackie Collins, *Brideshead Revisited*, *A Passage to India*, and a *Concise Oxford Dictionary*. One may also find Dr KEMP's *Pre-Conquest Craftsmanship in Southern Britain* (Babington Press 1991); *Cambridge History of Early Britain* (JWEL: p132); *Persuasion* (Austen) and *The French Lieutenant's Woman* (Fowles) – both in WOOD: p7; *The Oxford Companion to Music* (with its page on 'MOZART on the Billiard Table') (WOOD: p35); *The Bitch* by Jackie Collins (WOOD: p36); *Catch 22* – with its profusion of Majors (WOOD: p45); and *The Good Hotel Guide* (WOOD: p92). Further works are the *Model Year Book* produced by the Elite Booking Services agency (WOOD: p231); *The Great Plague at Athens* (abbreviated title) by McCLURE (CAIN: p15); *Distinguished People of Today* (CAIN: p32); *Gray's Anatomy* (CAIN: p105); *Good Pubs of Oxford* (CAIN: p173); and *Youth Employment Schemes and Opportunities* (CAIN: p187). And a few more: *Who's Who* and Debrett's *People of Today 1995* (both NEIG: p20 and the former also on p329); *Debrett's Peerage* (NEIG: p104); *The Masters* by C.P. Snow (NEIG: p104) – about shenanigans in a CAMBRIDGE College; *The Seventh Scroll* by Wilbur Smith (NEIG: p167); *Topless in Torremolinos* by the pseudonymous Ann Berkeley Cox (NEIG: p170); unnamed works by P.D. James, Ruth Rendell, Minette Walters, Jack Higgins, and Wilbur Smith (all NEIG: p273); *RAC Handbook*, Pevsner's *Oxfordshire*[4], a *World Atlas* (also NEIG: p273); and *Egon Ronay Guide*

---

[4] As *Pevsner's Oxfordshire* in the WORKS.

1995 (NEIG: p293); *The Ringer* by Edgar Wallace and *The Beano* (REMO: p77); the *Highway Code* (REMO: p138); *Family Walks in the Cotswolds* (REMO: p211); *Joys of Jogging*; *The Jungle Book* and *Cooking with Herbs* (both videos, both REMO: p433).

Public Houses See APPENDIX F.

Punch A once well-loved and humorous magazine; a few people in various Oxford waiting rooms glance at outdated copies (LBUS: pp150, 273).

Purvis, Mrs The occupier of 7 CANAL REACH and the eventual supplier of important information (JERI).

Pusey House A building in ST GILES', originally housing the library of E.B. Pusey. It encourages theological scholarship within the aims of the OXFORD MOVEMENT.

Puzzle Corner This appears to be a regular feature in the *Police Gazette* (as published by the THAMES VALLEY force). One brain-teaser lists operas by Verdi – *Tosca*, *Aida*, *Nabucco*, *Don Carlos*, *Ernani*, and *Macbeth* – and asks the readers to make an intelligent link. Morse has been known to contribute items for the Corner (REMO: p374).

Q

Quadrangle of the Schools Sometimes known as 'The Golden Heart of Oxford', it can be reached by The Great Gate (the tower of which is sometimes known as 'The Tower of the Five Orders of Architecture'). The quadrangle contains the Proscholium, sometimes known, presumably, just as the Proscholium, which is the entrance to the BODLEIAN LIBRARY and the Divinity School. The area is well known to Christine GREENAWAY who admires, in particular, her favourite sign – *Schola Naturalis Philosophiae* (The School of Natural Philosophy) (WNCH: p75). **Plate 71**, **Map D5**

Quality supermarket A general store in KIDLINGTON and purveyors of general goods (including extra butter, it seems) to, among others, Nicholas QUINN and Brenda JOSEPHS. It is open until 9pm on Friday nights.

Queen Street Leading west from CARFAX, this street changes its name to New Road and then, effectively, to Park End Street. From this latter address can be found KEMPIS STREET, home of BAINES and the occasional Antiques Fair (JWEL: p36). **Map D5**

Queen's College, The An Oxford College founded in 1341 by the Chaplain to Queen Philippa, wife of Edward the Third. Not to be confused, unless you want to rile residents of either institution, with Queens' College, CAMBRIDGE. And just to show how touchy some people can be, some members of the University still ignore the definite article (introduced in the 1890's) and refer to the college as Queen's College. An aerial photograph can be found in the upstairs lounge of the CHERWELL MOTEL. **Map E6**

Queen's Street Presumably an error (WNCH: p121) for QUEEN STREET. 'Queen's Street' also appears in CAIN (p189).

Quinn, Nicholas MA, He has worked, since 1st September 1975, in the Humanities Department at the SYNDICATE (where his DEAFNESS causes him a few problems, particularly with the telephone but his beard does not). He is in his thirties, a skilled lip-reader, and has a North Country accent (which may be linked to his birth some 20 miles from Bradford and where his parents still live). He read History and English at MAGDALENE, and lives at 1 Pinewood Close KIDLINGTON in a semi-dignified, semi-detached house. Crucially, he is a car-owner (a dark-blue Morris 1300, kept in a garage) and driver; not crucially, his birth sign (born on the 23rd October 1944; NICQ: p145) is either Libra or Scorpio (p82) and he eats Polo mints (p126). Philip DALEY's preferred brand of mint is also Polo (WOOD: p273).

Quixote A pseudonym employed by the CROSSWORD setter, Don Manley. Morse certainly enjoys his setting style in *The OXFORD TIMES* (WNCH: pp136-137) and elsewhere (for example, *The Independent on Sunday* (NEIG: p259). As Don Manley, he has identified and listed a great number of clue types (Chambers 2000: ppxvi-xix).

Quotations See APPENDIX G.

Plate 61 (Left) Thrupp elbow bend from the north (p151).
Plate 62 (Right) Oxford Playhouse (p153).

Plate 63 (Left) Main entrance to the railway station (p153).
Plate 64 (Right) Outside the Oxford Story (p154).

Plate 65 (Left) The Oxford University Press (p155).
Plate 66 (Right) View of South Crescent (p157).

R

RAC The Royal Automobile Club is an organisation providing a variety of services to motorists. Their contact number appears in the personal telephone directory of BAINES (and QUINN has a membership card – as does Morse).

Radcliffe Camera One of the most famous (and photographed) of Oxford buildings. Building started in 1737 and the Camera was formally opened in 1749. Its original purpose was to house the Radcliffe Science Library (relocated to PARKS ROAD) but it is now used to provide additional reading rooms for the BODLEIAN LIBRARY. Beneath the Camera there is space for well over half a million books. **Plate 72, Map D5**

Radcliffe Hospital A general hospital set in Manor Park, HEADINGTON and properly known as the John Radcliffe Hospital (with different areas commonly called the JR1 and the JR2). The first phase (the maternity unit where Joyce GREENAWAY gave birth to Nicholas John), was opened in 1971 and the main hospital in 1979. It is also here that Morse learns (while hospitalised under a chart headed 'MORSE, E.') of the Oxford Canal murder that forms the spine of the WNCH case. He also finds copies of *Victorian Banbury* and *OXFORD (Rail Centre Series)* on a hospital bookshelf; both provide him with some lines of enquiry. The hospital has a Nurse's Hostel on Headington Hill where Morse attends a Christmas party with some unexpected consequences (WNCH: pp212-215); it also has a Coronary Care Unit (WOOD: p169) and a Major Trauma Ward on Level 5 (CAIN: p270). **Map G4**

Radcliffe Infirmary The main hospital serving the City of Oxford. It is found between WALTON STREET and the WOODSTOCK ROAD and provides an accident and emergency facility as well as a variety of wards (including Dyne Ward – JERI: p269 – as part of the Eye Hospital). It has been known as the 'Old Radcliffe' (ANNX: p81), contains a morgue (and a Chapel of Rest - JWEL: p63), and has a fountain based on Neptune in its forecourt (NEIG: p248). It is a matter of opinion, but the statue of Neptune in MADRID is arguably somewhat finer. Morse is admitted here in 1996 when his diabetes is confirmed (NEIG); all is not bad news, however, as he also meets Sister Janet MCQUEEN. **Plate 73, Map C4**

Radcliffe, John (1652-1714) He graduated from UNIVERSITY COLLEGE and became royal physician to William and Mary. A number of buildings are named after him – Radcliffe Quad in his old college, the Camera, both the Hospital and the Infirmary, and the following entry. **Plate 74**

Radcliffe Square For many, the heart of the splendid architecture of Oxford. MARTIN calls at 'several pubs near' to it (NICQ: p188) and Margaret BOWMAN stands here while thinking about her future (ANNX: p209). The area is well known to Christine GREENAWAY (WNCH) and is the planned location for a twilight stroll by Eddie STRATTON and Shirley BROWN (JWEL: p325). Alan HARDINGE parks his car near here, on the double-yellow lines in CATTE STREET (WOOD: p353). **Map D5**

Radio Morse occasionally listens to Radio Oxford (part of the BBC local radio network) which is based in a yellow-bricked building in the BANBURY ROAD (JWEL: p77). Morse hears an interview with the Rev MEIKLEJOHN on it (SERV: p48). Radio Oxford also broadcasts weather news – informing its listeners, for example, that the snow had stopped falling (ANNX: p94) and thus raising a question mark over the absence or presence of footprints; Morse also learns (WNCH: 234) of black ice on the M40 which confirms his decision to take the train to London rather than drive (with the possibility of a few drinks an added attraction). Morse listens to Classic FM – a radio station unsurprisingly devoted to classical music – while in hospital (NEIG: p246). Oxford is also served by Radio Oxon (a commercial enterprise) and Fox FM (CAIN: p261; NEIG: p16). Also see the entry under BBC.

Ramillies Second (1706) of the battles in the campaign begun at BLENHEIM. Also the name of a style of wig made popular at the time.

Randolph, The The name of a very grand hotel in BEAUMONT STREET, Oxford (and, in 1990, part of the Welcome Trusthouse Forte group – known as THF), standing almost directly opposite to the MARTYRS' MEMORIAL. It displays the Union flag and the flags of the EEC and USA to underline its international appeal. Morse knows it well but it would be tedious to list his numerous visits though perhaps mention should be made of that in REMO (pp161-163) when he declares that the view of the ASHMOLEAN is possibly the best view (from any bar) in Britain. The Hotel was built in 1864 and has some 150 bedrooms (some of which have been occupied by members of the HISTORIC CITIES tour). It has renamed the Chapters Bar (where Morse has certainly drunk) as the 'Morse Bar' though there is, as yet, no 'Lewis Lounge' or 'Strange Saloon'. In JWEL Morse relocates his temporary headquarters to the Chapters Bar Annexe for reasons not totally unconnected to its OPENING HOURS (p169). REMO (pp258-262) gives details of The Spires restaurant and recounts a meal there between members of the HARRISON family. There are a number of function rooms – such as the Lancaster and the Worcester – and the St John's Suite can be found on the first floor; it has a Ball Room and has been known to allow collections for the Leukaemia Fund (to which Morse donates £20; JWEL: p123). It has a grandly wide staircase leading from Reception – where guests are invited to complete a Guest Registration Card on arrival (CALL). In 1952 the hotel commissioned Osbert Lancaster to paint twelve scenes from BEERBOHM's *Zuleika Dobson*. It is on looking at one of these that Morse recalls he has neither read the book nor is sure how to pronounce 'Zuleika' (JWEL: p70). The Hotel is central to the JWEL case but is referred to elsewhere: for example, McCLURE and Ellie SMITH have met here (CAIN: p55) in the Chapters Bar, and DAVIES and she meet in the vaults Bar (p301); perhaps she likes the place. Paul BAYLEY and Sylvia Grainger meet at a bar here, somewhat surreptitiously (STOR: p216) and Peter SHERWOOD books into Room 231 (CALL). In 1994, Roy Harden is the Senior Concierge and Bamber Goodall the Manager (CALL) and, in 1998, personnel include Tony Marrinan as Manager, Ailish Hurley as a barmaid, and C.M. as a waiter (REMO). **Plate 75, Map D5**

Rank English police forces are organised on a regional basis. A regional force outside London, such as the THAMES VALLEY POLICE, has the following ranking structure: Chief Constable,

Deputy Chief Constable, Assistant Chief Constable, Chief Superintendent, Superintendent, Chief Inspector, Inspector, Sergeant, and Police Constable. Criminal Investigation Department (CID) officers do not usually wear uniforms.[1] They have equivalent ranks to their uniformed colleagues: Detective Chief Superintendent, Detective Superintendent, Detective Chief Inspector, Detective Inspector, Detective Sergeant, and Detective Constable. The internal unity of the ranking structure means that a Detective Sergeant is junior to a uniformed Inspector, and so on. Further, during the period of much of the WORKS, female officers were identified by a letter W for 'woman' ("We'll need a WPC ..." JWEL: p125); the abolition of the 'W' is noted by Strange (REMO: p20). Senior ranks are differently entitled in London. The City of London Police is headed by: Commissioner, Assistant Commissioner, Commander, and Chief Superintendent. The Metropolitan Police (covering all of London bar the City) are headed by: Commissioner, Deputy Commissioner, Assistant Commissioner, Deputy Assistant Commissioner, Commander, and Chief Superintendent. 'The Force had always retained its obstinately hierarchical structure, and friendships between the higher and lower ranks would perhaps always be slightly distanced' (WNCH: p126).

Rawlinson, Mrs Alice Mother of Ruth, she is largely confined to a wheelchair at 14A MANNING TERRACE. Her daughter views her as grumbling, demanding, and generally unpleasant; Morse comes to share some of those views. She manages to spend some three weeks at an expensive clinic in Switzerland (overlooking Lake Thun) but a cure does not appear to materialise either here or at her short stay at the Old People's Home in COWLEY (SERV: pp278-279; 320).

Rawlinson, Ruth (Isabel) At first sight her age is indeterminate (anywhere between her mid-thirties and late forties; she is, in fact almost forty-two according to SERV: p66). She cleans at ST FRIDESWIDE'S mainly, it seems, to get away from her "demanding, discontented, self-centred" mother (SERV: p39) though she can be motivated by more spiritual urges, including the music of Palestrina, dry Martinis, and the desire to recycle, for example, a Sainsbury carrier bag (p142). From Oxford High School (where she sang the Stainer *Crucifixion* with the choir), she attended the Marlborough Secretarial College in the HIGH before joining the OXFORD UNIVERSITY PRESS as a secretary (pp273-274; 280). Morse feels an affinity with her (such as he has only ever felt once before); that affinity is later taken to a somewhat higher level (pp317/324).

Reading University Julian STORRS is known to have been invited to a Brains Trust here (NEIG: p219). It was the only university to be granted its Royal Charter between the two world wars; it has other claims to fame not recorded here.

Real Ale A term coined by CAMRA (The Campaign for Real Ale) in the early 1970s to draw a distinction between the bland, processed beers that were then being promoted and the traditional beers that were under threat of extinction. There are many subtle differences between real ale and other beers but the main one is that the latter are served by gas pressure

---

[1] Lewis is in uniform when there are riots to be faced (WOOD: p118).

from a keg. CAMRA produce an annual *The Good Beer Guide* and the 1991 edition appears in JWEL: p214. Morse has been known to express a very real preference for real ale and to shun other forms of beer; indeed, he occasionally talks of the 'wickedness' of lager-brewers (WNCH: p232).

Redbridge The name of the main Waste Recycling Centre for Oxford (in the ABINGDON ROAD). It is considered as a disposal site for a body (CAIN: p288) but rejected though it does serve that purpose in REMO. It may (or may not) be worth mentioning here that Oxford dustmen are properly known as Waste Disposal Operatives (REMO: p119).

Red kite (*Milvus milvus*) A splendid bird of prey, recently in decline but now finding some success. Once confined to Wales it has now been reintroduced to a number of areas (including Stokenchurch in Buckinghamshire; REMO: p384). The bird features quite prominently in the WOOD case and tangentially in REMO in challenging a statement by Simon HARRISON (pp321-322). **Plate 76**

Red Lion Little is revealed of this pub beyond the fact that Strange seems to regard it as a regular haunt of Morse (NEIG: p109): "In your office? I almost rang the Red Lion." There is a Red Lion at 5 Oxford Road, KIDLINGTON – a short walk, even for Morse, from HQ. According to Dunkling and Wright (1987) the pub name is the commonest in Britain (at least 600 examples) and appears to be linked, heraldically, to both John of Gaunt and the arms of Scotland.

Regis, Lionel A pseudonym adopted by Morse when writing to *The TIMES* on the SWEDISH MAIDEN verses (WOOD: pp120-121). Morse uses the address of 16, Cathedral Mews, Salisbury and, confusingly, refers to both Whytham and Wytham. His letter is the first to understand much of the significance of the verses. See also the footnote to Louisa HARDINGE.

Remorseful Day, The It is with a heavy heart that one writes of these last words in which the record of Morse's singular gifts comes to an end. Lewis's last words to the living Morse are "… and what I really want to say is thank-you for …" (REMO: p419); and to the dead Morse: "Goodbye, sir" (p427). An old murder case is re-opened at Strange's insistence (Morse is, at first, reluctant to be involved). Both Morse and Lewis were on another case at the time of the original murder (although Morse was briefly active in the latter; REMO: p75). Further deaths confuse matters and, unsurprisingly (though rather surprisingly in the case of one person), sexual shenanigans have their part to play. And the case demonstrates that not all families are nuclear. Before his untimely death, Morse is able to grant a substantial favour to Strange; after, his Will may provide some (little) comfort to Mr and Mrs Lewis. In notes left for Lewis, Morse anticipates that this will be his last case before retirement (p436). The notes of the case are dedicated to 'George, Hilary, Maria, and Beverley' with an aside drawing attention to the use of the OXFORD COMMA. The origin of the title appears to be Housman rather than Shakespeare. Housman's lines (from *More Poems* XVI):

'… How hopeless under ground
Falls the remorseful day.'

170

appear before the notes of the case. Shakespeare has the Captain speak these lines (from *Henry VI Part II*, Act 4 Scene 1):

'The gaudy, blabbing, and remorseful day
Is crept into the bosom of the sea ...'

The same lines appear as the heading to Chapter 34 of CAIN (where they are misattributed to *Henry IV Part II*). Some suggestions on the Prolegomenon to this case appear under DATES (REMO). ***Main personnel*** The BARRONS, FLYNN, the HARRISONS, REPP, and Debbie RICHARDSON.

Repp, Harry A recent prisoner (for handling stolen property) but now 'free' (1998). He is aged 37 years at the time of the REMO case, an occasional burglar, of medium build, and has a tattoo of a naval design. His common-law wife is Debbie RICHARDSON and they live at 15 CHAUCER LANE, BURFORD.

Rhadamanthus The Lord Chief Justice of Appeal in the Underworld (NEIG: p7) and a pseudonym employed by Morse. He was the son of Zeus and Europa and his brothers were Minos and Sarpedon (though not the same Sarpedon of the Trojan War fame recalled by Morse in WOOD: p207).

Richards, Celia Wife of Charles RICHARDS and aged 37 years old (JERI).

Richards, Charles A publisher (with his younger brother Conrad). He is married to Celia RICHARDS and they live, in some harmony (despite his having an affair), in a posh-addressed and well-appointed bungalow on the outskirts of ABINGDON; he drives to his office in that town (JERI: p43/p76). He reads *The TIMES* (p76) and his thoughts about his affair are full of Biblical imagery: 'healing stream', 'balm of hope and grace', and 'robe of honour' (p77). No wonder that he takes Opas tablets (designed to cure heartburn and acid indigestion).

Richards, Conrad A publisher (with his elder, by some 18 months, brother Charles) (JERI: p78). When interviewed by Morse (p281) he reveals a love and knowledge of Gibbon (which Morse appears to share if not exceed).

Richardson, Debbie (Deborah) Common-law wife of Harry REPP and occasional visitor to BURFORD Public Library (REMO: p101). She is blonde and in her mid-thirties and wears very little indeed on a visit by Morse, the bearer of potentially bad tidings (pp190-194). She wears about the same on a later occasion.

Richards Press A small publisher at 14 White Swan Lane, ABINGDON and managed by Charles and Conrad RICHARDS (JERI: p147).

Richmond Arms A public house (near East Putney underground station in London) in which Morse consumes two large whiskies (BELL'S) in anticipation of meeting an old flame (MILE: p210).

Richmond Road In a poetic (and curiously disengaged) frame of mind, Morse sees the ill-lit houses here present '... a huddled, almost cowering appearance, as if they somehow feared the night.' (JERI: p30). **Map C5**

Riddle of the Third Mile, The A slight knowledge of Gilbert and Sullivan may assist in understanding this case (only slight, mind) but the initials W. S. are well woven within. Does an incident from the Second World War have any bearing on the discovery of a body (and, this is literally a body without the head, hands, and legs) in the OXFORD CANAL?[2] Morse splits his time between Oxford (particularly LONSDALE College) and London (the latter the scene of further deaths). The record of the case dispenses with quotations as Chapter headings; in their place are brief summaries of what follows (such as 'Like some latter-day Pilgrim, one of the protagonists in this macabre case is determined to rid himself of his burden' Chapter 31). Morse's summary refers to the case as running its course like a tragedy by Aeschylus (MILE: p269). Many details are revealed about Morse's personal life in this case (particularly pp56-62). The title is taken from *Matthew 5,41* '... And whosoever shall compel thee to go a mile, go with him twain'. An alternative reading is 'If a man in authority makes you go one mile ...' which resonates with *Matthew 8,9* and a 'man under authority' (see SERV under QUOTATIONS) (MILE). *Main personnel* BROWNE-SMITH, anyone called GILBERT, and WESTERBY.

Ring Cycle Der Ring des Nibelungen (The Ring of the Nibelung) is a cycle of four operas by WAGNER – *Das Rheingold*, *Die Walküre*, *Siegfried*, and *Götterdämmerung*. Morse has bought the Wilhelm Furtwängler recording of the Ring in 1989 (WNCH: p207) but he listens to an early Bruno Walter recording with Lauritz Melchior and Lotte Lehmann singing the title roles of Siegmund and Sieglinde in *Die Walküre* (REMO: p150). He discusses the merits of the Furtwängler and Solti recordings with Richard BARTLETT (NICQ: p176). Lovelock (1959) gives a brief introduction to the musicality of *The Ring*. For further information on, and background to, the myths see any number of sources; McSpadden (1905), Mackenzie (1934), and Picard (1953) have been used here (in anticipation of a need – unwarranted, as it so happens – to expand either this entry or the bibliography).

Robertson, Bill A 75-year old bachelor who returns from a holiday to a suspected burglary at his house in CHAUCER CRESCENT. He once showed Morse his cigarette card collection – which Morse thought was 'very fine' (BURG: p288).

Rodway, Mary The mother of Matthew; she lives at 14 Evington Road South, Leicester (alone, since the departure of her husband on the 5th November 1990). She is interviewed there by Morse (with Lewis driving him) and has had some dealings with McCLURE in the past. Morse is interested in the décor of her living room and notices, inter alia, the prints by Braque, Picasso, and Matisse and the photographs of BLENHEIM and Versailles (CAIN).

---

[2] Gerasimov (1971) has some pertinent comments on the identification and reconstruction of mutilated bodies (but these appear to be unknown to Morse).

Rodway, Matthew An undergraduate at WOLSEY COLLEGE. His death – a fall from a third-floor window – may be a straightforward suicide or a drunken accident (or something else altogether) though appears to be unconnected with his viola-playing for the National Youth Orchestra. What seemed certain at the inquest is that he was involved with drugs (CAIN).

Roger Bacon Comprehensive School Opened as such in 1972; the school had formerly been a 'secondary modern'. It is based in KIDLINGTON, the headmaster is Donald PHILLIPSON, supported by his secretaries, Mrs Webb and later Mrs Clarke, and the second master is Reginald BAINES. The teaching staff includes (or included) David ACUM (WEAR) and Paul Morris (SERV); pupils include Valerie TAYLOR and John MAGUIRE (WEAR), and Carole Jones (SERV). The school tie is red and grey (SERV: p162).

Rogers, Chief Inspector He is based at New Scotland Yard in London and is a tall, military-looking man. His letter to Morse – concerning, among other matters, the East Chelsea Nursing Home – rather threatens to undermine one of Morse's solutions to the case (WEAR: p270).

Rogers, Sergeant He is based at New Scotland Yard in London (in 1996 at least) and works for the Porn Squad. One rather hopes that he is somehow related to Chief Inspector Rogers though there is nothing in the notes of the case to suggest this (NEIG: p205).

Roope, Christopher (Algernon) A bearded chemist from CHRIST CHURCH where, while a FELLOW, he is known pedantically as a 'student'. He is 30 years old in 1975 (NICQ: p145), a member of the SYNDICS, lives 'up the WOODSTOCK ROAD' (p149), and has worked in the past for the Anglo-Arabian Oil Company. It is possibly irrelevant to the solution of a murder that he is left-handed, smokes, likes a drink, and graduated from MAGDALENE after attending a public school in Bradford (NICQ).

Roscoe, Janet A diminutive septuagenarian from America who sometimes exhibits a keen intelligence but always a strict diet – eating, at The SWAN HOTEL, a '… concoction of beans so splendidly bleak as to delight the most dedicated Vegan' (JWEL: p247). She shares the same church in California as Phil ALDRICH and has an interest in *A Midsummer Night's Dream* (pp213/258) and, one learns, the plays of Arthur Miller (p334).

Rose and Crown A pub in NORTH PARADE where Morse enjoys two pints (WOOD: p194).

Rosie O'Grady Having just avoided the temptation to place this pub under 'O'Grady, Rosie', there is little else to say about it beyond the fact that it is usually known as Rosie O'Grady's, was the first Irish theme bar in Oxford (Honey 1998), and may be found close to GLOUCESTER GREEN (REMO: pp174/179). Its interior is briefly described (pp184-185).

Rowbotham, Simon Morse states, "… that's an unlikely sounding name" (MILE: p75) and believes it is made up. He prefers what he believes to be the more natural-sounding unions of an aristocratic Simon Carruthers or a proletarian George Rowbotham). The name also suggests a relevant – though not necessarily accurate – anagram. Simon Rowbotham lives, with his mother, in BOTLEY and is a fairly successful angler, particularly at King's Weir (MILE: p154).

Royal Crescent Hotel A superior establishment in BATH at number 16 in the Royal Crescent. It features quite prominently both in that city and the NEIG case (and its awards – RAC Blue Ribbons, AA Rosettes, and Egon Ronay Stars confirm its superiority). Its breakfasts are particularly praiseworthy and it has been claimed that it has a wider selection of cereals (including Ricicles and Weetabix) than Sainsbury's (pp368-369). George IV stayed here in 1799 (while Prince of Wales) and a fine portrait of Lord Ellmore may be found in the lounge. Recreations for guests include a swimming pool and a croquet-green. The Dower House is sited in its grounds – an elegant annexe containing suites and bedrooms, the restaurant, main lounge and bar; the Beau Nash suite is inside (NEIG: p382).

Royal Oak A pub in the WOODSTOCK ROAD and opposite to the RADCLIFFE INFIRMARY. According to Honey (1998), it was owned by the hospital until 1956. Morse sits (and drinks, one guesses) here with Lewis (ANNX: p220) and despite efforts over Christmas and the New Year succumbs to temptation and buys a packet of cigarettes. Sarah HARRISON (REMO) has also drunk here.

Royal Oxford Hotel An imposing building which PHILLIPSON claims to have visited for 'bed and breakfast' (WEAR: pp139/148). Morse thinks about a beer at the hotel but settles for the buffet at OXFORD RAILWAY STATION instead (NICQ: p151). **Plate 77**

Royal Sun A pub on a slip-road off the A44, a short way south of WOODSTOCK (WOOD: p61). It seems to be known to regulars as the Sun. Morse appears to be very interested (during the 1991 part of the case) in what beer it serves (p70) although Lewis knows the answer (Morrell's) having bought Morse several pints there (p81). George DALEY has a pint here most evenings (WOOD: p243). The pub name does not appear in Dunkling and Wright (1987); there is another Royal Sun in Beckley, north east of Oxford, and one (as a matter of limited interest) in Crook, County Durham. No derivation can be suggested here for the name beyond the obvious link between the sun, agriculture, the harvest, and the ingredients of beer.

Running Horses Inn This pub stood on the corner of UPPER FISHER ROW by Hythe Bridge (WNCH: p58). It was here that a Coroner's inquest was held into the murder of Joanna FRANKS in 1859 (and charges laid) with the accused being committed to Oxford Gaol until their trail at the Oxford Summer Assizes in August that year. According to Honey (1998) it was closed in 1939 and is now a private house; perhaps Morse has wistfully wandered by it.

Ruskin College There does not appear to be a direct reference to this relatively modern college in the WORKS; but, perversely it is included here to try and gather the references to the Ruskin Room in the Clarendon Institute (JERI: p124) in WALTON STREET and the 'Ruskin-influenced' architecture of NORTH OXFORD (JWEL: p18). It may have been simpler to have had an entry for John Ruskin. **Plate 78**, **Map D5**

Ryan's Daughter A film directed by David Lean (1970). According to her diary, Sylvia KAYE saw it in January 1971 (LBUS: p25).

S

St Aldates As a church, St Aldates appears to be the preferred spelling; as a street, St Aldate's has also been recognised (particularly by Hibbert 1988). Oxford Police Station is based here (and they give their address as St Aldates and if they do not know, who does?). The buildings were extensively renovated in the 1980s (WNCH: p126). There is also a courtroom behind the police station (NICQ: p218), the City Museum (JERI: p21), a mortuary (JWEL: p214), and Courts opposite. A plaque has been placed on the police station – part of the central text reads: '… where Chief Inspector E. Morse *settles cuckoo-like to pursue his unofficial enquiries …*' Colin DEXTER unveiled the plaque on the 23rd of July 2006. **Plate 79**, **Map D5-D6**

St Anthony Morse buys a (tiny) pendant of this saint (CAIN). It may be that the saint is Anthony the Great, the Egyptian Father from the 4th Century. Morse hopes it is Anthony of Padua, one of the Patron Saints of lost property. Ellie SMITH has some belief in the saint and Jane EDWARDS experiences what may be a miracle linked to him (NEIG: pp197 and 203 respectively). In the Oratory, Morse looks at a statue of this Saint and subsequently lights two candles (REMO: pp206-207) with a minor result (p223).

St Barnabas' Church Consecrated in 1869, its tall Italianate campanile tends to dominate JERICHO (JERI: p23). The church has been celebrated in a poem (of the same name) by John Betjeman.

St Benedict A church (location unknown but spoken of in Oxford), which is notable for a story about how the solution to an electric clock problem spurred Morse into further action (WEAR: pp201-203).

St Catherine's A modern college at Oxford (founded 1962). Its architect was Arne Jacobsen and not, Arne Johansen as DOWNES mistakenly suggests before being corrected by Janet ROSCOE (JWEL: p41). A college with a similar name (give or take a vowel) and of an earlier foundation may be found in CAMBRIDGE. **Map E5**

St Clement's Street This short street leads east from the PLAIN towards HEADINGTON (CAIN). It is referred to as St Clements in REMO (p216). **Map E6**

St Ebbe's A street in central Oxford. Much of the St Ebbe's area was redeveloped during Morse's era; it seems he was not in favour (WNCH: p69). See also DEAFNESS. **Map D6**

St Edward's School To be found in the WOODSTOCK ROAD (JWEL: p213). It is an independent boarding school with many famous old boys – including Kenneth Grahame and Laurence Olivier – and, one hopes, since going slightly co-educational in 1983, the prospect of as many famous old girls.

St Frideswide's A church in CORNMARKET (SERV: p48) and not, presumably, to be confused with the church of the same name in the BOTLEY ROAD, for which see Hibbert

(1988). It has a font dated 1345, a graveyard, and an impressive, if somewhat crumbling, tower. Recent incumbents include the Rev Lionel LAWSON and the Rev Keith MEIKLEJOHN. The contents of the collection are eventually transferred from a Huntley and Palmers biscuit tin to an account held with BARCLAYS BANK in the HIGH. The Vicarage (a fine building of three storeys) is in nearby ST EBBE'S. St Frideswide was supposedly born in Oxford (or Berkshire). Lewis recalls learning about her at school as the Patron Saint of Oxford and curing someone of blindness – to which Morse adds that she had caused that blindness in the first place (CAIN: p50). Even accepting that there is little clarity about where Lewis was educated – with Oxford a rank outsider in the field – she does seem rather an odd saint about which to learn. But, presumably, the story that Lewis heard is when a certain Prince Aelfgar besieged her in Oxford, she prayed to a number of saints and the Prince was struck blind. She was able to restore his sight on his promise of repentance. The site of her monastery was built over when CHRIST CHURCH was founded.

St Giles' A street wherein one may find, at the very least, both the EAGLE AND CHILD and ST JOHN'S COLLEGE. Somewhat bizarrely, the street appears as St Giles in a number of entries – most oddly at SERV: p247 just a few pages after Morse carefully dictates an item for the *OXFORD MAIL* using the words: "I don't want any sub-editor buggering about with so much as a comma." One guesses that Morse would show equal concern for an apostrophe (SERV: p242) and there is a suggestion (ANNX: p16) that the street should properly be called St Giles's'. The street is marked by several cast-iron street-plaques that were wrought at LUCY'S IRONWORKS and has a War Memorial (**Plate 80**) at its northern end (ANNX: pp16-17). The War Memorial contains no individual names; it commemorates all the dead of Oxford in both World Wars. **Map D5**

St Giles' Church This stands at the north end of ST GILES' (JWEL: p207). Possibly the most famous vicar was William Juxon (1610-1615) who later became the Archbishop of Canterbury.

St Giles' Fair Held in September each year in, unsurprisingly, ST GILES'. It was originally a commercial market but elements of entertainment have crept in (WEAR: p352); also see Roud (2008: pp391-393) for some details of the history of the Fair. Kevin COSTYN attends the Fair in 1994 (while considering his recent criminal activities) and has a pint of Burton in the EAGLE AND CHILD (CAIN: pp186-188). Morse compares his worried mind to a '… whirligig at St Giles' Fair …' in REMO (p361).

St Helen's Passage A (very small) turning off NEW COLLEGE LANE and one way to access the TURF TAVERN (CAIN: p84). **Map D5**

St Hilda's College Dame Helen GARDNER is a Fellow and Sheila POSTER is a graduate; Morse admires a painting of this college (by Sir Hugh Casson RA) in the 1993 *Oxford Almanack* (CAIN: p20). The College has an Old Girls' society (STOR: p174). See also Wendy SPENCER. **Map E6**

St John's College Morse was an undergraduate at this Oxford (rather than Cambridge) college between 1950 and 1954. The college Dean is briefly referred to in MILE (pp56-57). Its sports ground lies between the BAINTON and the WOODSTOCK ROADs (ANNX: p256). The College has been a major player in the design and use of modern buildings in Oxford (see Tyack 2005); Lang (1909) enthuses about the '… garden-front, perhaps the most lovely thing in Oxford.' (p124) and Alden (1948 i.e. shortly before Morse went up) calls them '… a favourite resort of visitors who are much impressed …' (p115). Anthony Blair went here and HOUSMAN and Philip Larkin. **Plate 81**, **Map D5**

St John Street This runs parallel to ST GILES' to the west. It was once the home of Wendy SPENCER and of Morse in the early 1950s. **Map D5**

St Mary Magdalene A church in CORNMARKET (occasionally known at St Mary Mags). Its railings provide a useful place to chain a bicycle (CAIN: pp261/272).

St Mary's Often known as the University Church, this imposing building has a highly Decorated Gothic steeple ('… the more spectacular when we climb to wander among the pinnacles on top and look down on central Oxford' (Jenkins 2002: p547) and the nave saw the trial of Latimer, Ridley, and Cranmer (see the MARTYRS' MEMORIAL). It can be found in the HIGH (between BRASENOSE and ALL SOULS) and may also be entered from RADCLIFFE SQUARE. Its tower has been climbed by Margaret BOWMAN who passes the Old Library – the very first one belonging to the University – and over the roof of the Lady Chapel (ANNX: pp209-210). **Plate 82**

St Paul's A church in WALTON STREET noted for its 'fluted columns supporting the classical portico' (JERI: p61). It was begun in 1835 (JERI: p90).

St Peter's College A mere 10 minutes walk away from LONSDALE (NEIG: p218), this college opened as a Permanent Private Hall in 1929 and became a College in 1961. It may be found in New Hall Inn Street (**Map D5**). It aims to provide an education that matches rather than slavishly imitates that of its longer-established and richer neighbours.

St Peter's Road A street in Upper Wolvercote (ANNX: p256). **Map B2**

Sanders, Amy The mother of John SANDERS; she does rather worry about her son and may, or may not, be aware of his keen interest in PORNOGRAPHY (LBUS).

Sanders, John The discoverer of the body of Sylvia KAYE (LBUS). It is, at first, a little unclear why he happened to be in the BLACK PRINCE on that particular evening.

Scenes of Crime Officer See SOCO.

Schools A large number of references may be found to various schools in The WORKS. These include The Dragon, New College School, Oxford High, and Headington (all in Oxford;

WEAR: p91), the Cherwell School, also in Oxford (NICQ: p242), and Magdalen College School (JERI: p125). Other schools mentioned are the Frederic (sic) Delius School in Bradford (NICQ: p82), Rochdale Grammar School (JERI: p55), Winchester College (JERI: p 165), the Summerfields preparatory School (ANNX: p180), Eton College (JERI: p221), Harrow (CAIN: p269), and the CHIPPING NORTON Comprehensive School (attended by Margaret BOWMAN; ANNX: p203). And the list may be expanded by Hobson Road primary and Oxford Boys' (both attended by Edward WILKINS; ANNX: p259); Bishop Kirk Middle School in SUMMERTOWN (WNCH: p198); Cheltenham Ladies' College (WOOD: p78); the PROCTOR MEMORIAL – where the National Curriculum is taught (CAIN); CUTTESLOWE Primary School (CAIN); and the East Oxford Senior School (Head C.P. Taylor) where Ellie SMITH gained a Prize for Art (CAIN: p375). NEIG: pp20-21 adds another three – Christ's Hospital, Dartmouth Services, and Wyggeston GS – while the later p67 introduces Torquay Comprehensive. Della CECIL went to – one might have guessed – Roedean (NEIG: p138). Bethlehem Tech (JWEL: p99) is, one sincerely believes, fictional. Also see the entries for ROGER BACON, and the PRIESTLEY GRAMMAR SCHOOL. An unnamed public school features large in the lives of the LAWSON brothers (SERV) and the Sisters of the Covenant run a preparatory boarding school for girls in REMO.

Schools Mathematics Project The name of an educational charity, which develops textbooks and other material. Some of its works could be found on the bookshelves of BAINES (WEAR: p175)

Schools, The Properly, the Oxford University Examination Schools (on the HIGH). Its primary responsibilities are the organisation and administration of examinations but it is also used as a major lecturing facility (LBUS: p191).

Scott, Anne She meets Morse at a party (where much of her background is revealed; more is revealed in JERI: pp55-56). She was born in Rochdale, read modern languages at LADY MARGARET HALL, and worked for a time for Charles and Conrad RICHARDS. Married at the age of 19 years to John Westerby, but now single (and reverted to her maiden name); she earns some money from private tuition (JERI: pp9-13) and sits on the committee of the OXFORD BOOK ASSOCIATION (p118).

Scout The title of someone employed as something more than a cleaner; most of the Oxford COLLEGES have a pack of them. They usually have responsibility for a single staircase (or a set of staircases – rather depends how many rooms there are) and have been known to be encouraged by the college authorities to keep an eye on students. At WOLSEY COLLEGE the ratio is simply one scout per staircase (CAIN: p86) and there are more females than males in this occupation (only fair, really, especially as the college is 'mixed'). See Ted BROOKS and Susan EWERS. Hibbert (1988) dates the use of the word to the beginning of the eighteenth century but gives its origin as 'obscure'. Of the other kind of scout (boy), it may be simply noted both that Morse never was one (WOOD: p161) and that Max jokes about sending truncated trousers to that organisation rather than OXFAM (MILE: p70).

SCR See SENIOR COMMON ROOM.

Scrubs, The The common nickname for Wormwood Scrubs prison in West London (ANNX: p242). The name derives, in part, from its location in an area that was originally scrubland.

Secret of Annexe Three, The Morse and Lewis are told to investigate a body discovered at the HAWORTH HOTEL where New Year's Eve has been celebrated with more than a fair degree of vengeance. A fancy dress party offers enough opportunity for disguise and deception and something is learned of Rastafarianism (including dietary matters) and the common (but regrettable) habit of people signing into a hotel under false names and misleading addresses. The seasonal weather has provided a blanket of snow, giving Morse the opportunity for a (fairly rare) witticism: "The snow, my old friend, is a complete white herring" (p96). Chapter headings are dated and provide quotations relevant to the following text. The hotel has been, and is being, extended while the case takes place and Annexe Three is part of that extension. The building works are, for Sarah JONSTONE, reminiscent of pictures of Passchendaele (p26). (ANNX). *Main personnel* The BALLARDS, the BOWMANS (Bowmen?), Sarah JONSTONE, F and P PALMER, and WILKINS.

Senior Common Room Commonly found in Oxford as the meeting-place of FELLOWs of a COLLEGE. A rather fine clue appeared in *The TIMES* (18th April 2007): 'Examiner can always join academics' room at university' (10) with the answer as 'scrutineer'.

Senior Wrangler The student achieving the highest marks in the final mathematical tripos at CAMBRIDGE University in any one year (JWEL: p197).

Service of All the Dead Through a coincidence or two (and, of course, his natural dedication to seeing justice done) Morse becomes involved in a crime committed the previous year. Inspector BELL (SERV: p94) suggests, "The case is closed – and it's got nothing to do with you." However, it is soon clear that the case is open again. The investigation covers a murder in a church (ST FRIDESWIDE'S), an apparent suicide, lots of liturgical detail, and permanently disappearing witnesses. Lewis really proves his worth, physically if not mentally (SERV). *Main personnel* Harry and Brenda JOSEPHS, a couple of LAWSONs, Paul MORRIS, and Ruth RAWLINSON.

Seth, Mrs Chairman (sic) of the Science Committee of the SYNDICS. Her father was deaf and she has a certain sympathy for Nicholas QUINN.

Shakespeare, William See the references under LITERARY CURIOSITIES and STRATFORD-UPON-AVON. He has also provided, as one might expect, a number of QUOTATIONS.

Sheep Street A road in BURFORD (REMO). Richards (2008) notes that its name is a reflection of the town's links with the wool trade (and its Chamber of Trade have remarked that wool revenues – somewhat aptly – cushioned the town in the Elizabethan era).

Sheldonian Theatre Built in the 1660s after a design by Wren. The Theatre is used for lectures, recitals, and various university ceremonies. Christine GREENAWAY walks *sub imperatoribus* (under the emperors – the nickname of the sculptured heads on the railings) and up the steps leading into its gravelled courtyard (WNCH: p74). **Map D5**

Sheridan, The It is, perhaps, 'The most fashionable of the Oxford hotels' (LBUS: p181). It hosts, in the upstairs Evans Room, a regular dinner with dancing; Morse attends, with Sue WIDDOWSON, on one of these occasions. The hotel plays host to five emissaries from the Sheikdom of AL-JAMARA (NICQ) in 1975 (who themselves host a party in the Disraeli Suite – with, apparently, no sense of irony). It can be found just off the bottom of ST GILES'.

Sherwood, Pamela She is aged 45 years at the date of the CALL case and has a son and a daughter. She has a Chemistry degree from CAMBRIDGE and works part-time in a pharmaceutical laboratory.

Sherwood, Peter He is in his forties, well built, with frizzy hair. He might well have booked into The RANDOLPH for extra-marital purposes though his official reason for visiting Oxford is to attend a conference on Computer Technology at Rewley House (**Plate 83**).[1] He is an insulin-dependent diabetic and this is central to the CALL case. He lives with Pamela at 53 Leominster Drive, Shrewsbury.

Ship Street This links TURL STREET and CORNMARKET STREET; the exit from the OXFORD STORY runs into it (JWEL: p94). **Map D5**

Silent World of Nicholas Quinn, The The third of the cases investigated by Morse and Lewis of which details have been made available. The FOREIGN EXAMINATIONS SYNDICATE, in Oxford, is the setting (a room layout is provided which, thankfully, assists) and much relies on how Morse finally understands how the DEAFNESS of Nicholas QUINN impacts upon the solution. The book is dedicated to the now late Jack Ashley, an MP who was both deaf and very active in the cause of all affected by disability. Whether or not QUINN is present at a fire drill (and, if not, who marks him 'present') is a bit of a puzzle (NICQ). ***Main personnel*** Thomas BARTLETT, BLAND, HEIGHT, Donald MARTIN, OGLEBY, QUINN, and ROOPE.

Small, Diogenes A provider of many quotations and a prolific writer; the dates given (1797-1812) either suggest a tragically short life or represent the period over which his *Reflections* were gathered. It appears that the full title of this work is *Reflections on Inspiration and Creativity* (Macmillan have issued an edition with uncorrected spelling) and a substantial quotation (on personal experience and fictional matters) is given in STOR (p171). The first one hears of him is in JWEL when a 'reflection' is given as a heading to Chapter 7: 'Almost all modern architecture is farce.' A further 'reflection' seems to appear in STOR (p181): 'Yet always it is those *fictional* addenda which will affect the true alchemy' (*Reflections on*

---

[1] The location of Rewley House is given, in CALL, as '... just up at the top of St John Street ...' (p262). Its correct address is 1 WELLINGTON SQUARE.

Inspiration and Creativity). In WOOD (heading to Chapter 28) he opines from his *Obiter Dicta*: 'Be it ever so humble there's no place like home for sending one slowly crackers.' *Small's English Dictionary* gives a definition of 'thanatophobia' (WOOD: Chapter 55) and the *Enlarged English Dictionary* (12th edition) gives a definition of 'pension' (CAIN: Chapter 1), which has some echoes of Dr Johnson's with the common use of the word 'hireling'. The 12th edition also defines 'U-turn' (GOLD: p19). The *Enlarged* (1812) defines 'Examination' (CAIN: Chapter 17) and *Small's Enlarged English Dictionary* (13th edition 1806) defines 'prosopagnoia' (NEIG: Chapter 16)[2] and 'hypoglycaemia' (NEIG: Chapter 64) in the 17th edition. Small was, no doubt, prolific. His *Latin-English Dictionary* has a definition of ALIBI as '(adv.): in another place, elsewhere.' (NEIG: p263). His *Autobiography* provides another Chapter heading (40 of CAIN). In this, he relates that while Thursday is a bad day, any day is worse when he has to return to his labours after idleness. A quotation from *An Irreverent Survey of Saints* by Simon Small heads Chapter 59 of CAIN. It has been a little difficult to trace this volume and the suspicion is that Simon may be a relative of Diogenes. If this is not the case, then sincere apologies to Simon Small. And a quotation from *A Most Complete Guide to the Hostelries of the Cotswolds* heads Chapter 24 of REMO. It is by D. Small and has yet to be traced. A substantial quotation from Small's *The Joys of Occasional Idleness* heads Chapter 43 of REMO. Alarmingly, his dates are given there as 1797-1805. Finally, his *Enlarged English Dictionary* (18th edition) has a definition of 'character' (REMO: p332). Little (if anything) is known of his private life.

Smith, (Kay) Eleanor (Ellie) Noticeable features include her nose-rings; her dull green eyes have been described as being coloured like the OXFORD CANAL (CAIN: p99) and as a faded version of glaucopis Athene (pxx).[3] She is aged about 25 years (p58) and, as 'Kay Blaxendale', currently earns her money in a somewhat immoral fashion (not so much from choice but a combination of redundancy, negative equity, and a fondness for the bottle). The purpose of her visit to Birmingham (by train, to New Street station) is for medical advice. Her usual perfume is the exotically entitled *Mimosa Pour Moi* (p153) and her 'Barely Black' stockings have the desired effect on Morse (p279). Perhaps she could have become deeply involved with Morse – all the signs were there – and she declares her love for Morse after he had given her a chain (CAIN: pp339-340). But she moves a little out of his ambit and eventually writes to him with the closing words: 'Why didn't you look for me a bit harder ... ?' (NEIG: p197). Unfortunately, Morse has already burned the photograph of her that he had kept (between pages 88-89 of his *Collected Poems of A.E. Housman*; and this is revealed, coincidentally, on p89 of NEIG). Her deep involvement with the BROOKS family is not, at first, apparent. Her dislike of the name Kay may well stem from the surname of the first husband of Brenda BROOKS (CAIN: p380), assuming that he was a Mr Hunt.

Smoking It used, once, to be allowed to smoke on the upstairs of buses (LBUS). BROWNE-SMITH is a particularly heavy smoker ('forty-plus a day for fifty years' MILE: p15) and

---

[2] *Prosopagnosia* appears in both Chambers (2003) and The New Shorter Oxford (1993) – but not *prosopagnoia*.
[3] Glaucopis Athene is a common epithet for the goddess since Homeric times. It means 'bright-eyed' or 'blue-green eyed'.

Margaret BOWMAN heroically smokes three cigarettes in each of her twenty-minute breaks from work (ANNX: p179). ASHENDEN – a former smoker but now abstinent – is sickened at the sight of tourists lighting up between courses (JWEL: p9). See CIGARETTES and the section under MORSE on *Smoking*.

SOCO The usual abbreviation for a Scenes of Crime Officer. His or her role is to attend the scene of a crime and identify and record forensic material which may support the overall police investigation in identifying the culprit or providing corroborative evidence. Typical tasks include taking fingerprints from surfaces or objects, preserving foot or shoe prints, and photographing the scene. There is a Fingerprint Department at ST ALDATES. Thanks are recorded by DEXTER to Eddie ANDREWS in the acknowledgements to REMO and a few named officers may be found under MINOR etc.

Soho An area of central London, running mainly north and east from Piccadilly Circus. It has long been known as a focus for the sleazier kinds of activity and entertainment. It is an area, which, somewhat to Lewis's surprise, Morse appears to be fairly – if not intimately – conversant with (WEAR: p78). OWENS also has a deep knowledge – having lived in Soho Square and tramped around Brewer Street, Greek Street, Old Compton Street, and Wardour Street – 'a litany of seediness and sleaze' (NEIG: p36). BROWNE-SMITH is drawn 'into the cesspool that is known as Soho' (MILE: p18); there are echoes here of WATSON's description, in *A Study in Scarlet*, of London as 'that great cesspool into which all the loungers and idlers of the Empire are irresistibly drained'. In Soho one may find, amidst many others, such clubs as the PENTHOUSE, the FLAMENCO TOPLESS BAR (MILE: p19), the Striporama Revue Club (ANNX: p124), and Le Club Sexy (NEIG: p37). Should one wish to telephone the Flamenco, DEXTER has kindly provided the number – 01-417-8088 (MILE: p94). Morse believes that Dawn CHARLES – with her legs right up to the armpits – would have adorned the stage of the Windmill but is advised by Lewis that that famous club was now shut (NEIG: p353).

Somerville College There are brief references to this (once, all female) college in JWEL (p213) and CAIN (p111). The former wife of McCLURE was educated here (CAIN: p15). Its name is shown, in capital letters on Donnington Bridge, to indicate its boathouse (CAIN: p304). **Map C4**

Sorbonne, La A restaurant in the HIGH where the chef Raymond Blanc once worked. Regrettably, the restaurant closed in the 1990s.

Southampton Terrace A road in London, SW12. John MAGUIRE lives at number 42 and is visited there by the police. He commutes to work in SOHO.

Southdown Road A street in NORTH OXFORD, home to Bernard and Margaret CROWTHER. **Map C2**

Southey, Robert (1774-1843) Morse finds his poem, *The Cataract of Lodore*, banal (SERV: p71). The opening lines are:

> "How does the water
> Come down at Lodore?"
> My little boy asked me
> Thus, once on a time;
> And moreover he tasked me
> To tell him in rhyme.

The poem was written while Southey was Poet Laureate; Morse's judgement appears sound.

South Parade The location of a public library and various shops in SUMMERTOWN. Apparently, Oliver Cromwell had once arranged his Roundheads here (SERV: p37). The Oxford Animal Sanctuary Shop is on the corner shared with MIDDLE WAY (REMO). **Plate 84**, **Map C3**

South Parks Road This runs east from PARKS ROAD (JWEL: p153). It is the location of the William Dunn School of Pathology (where Max is based) and the Department of Human Anatomy (who issue the donor form completed by Morse; REMO: p430). **Map D5**

Sparrow A common enough bird (though with a number of varieties). Morse, in a rash of untutored ornithological enthusiasm, believes the specimen in his garden may be a totally different species. Strange corrects him by identifying the bird as a female *Passer domesticus* – the house-sparrow (REMO: p22).

SPCC An abridged form of the Royal Society for the Prevention of Cruelty to Children – a charity for which Jennifer COLEBY collects (LBUS: p222).

Spencer, Wendy A graduate of Leicester University, she starts to study for a DPhil at ST HILDA's in 1953. Originally living in digs in the COWLEY ROAD, she moved to the top floor flat at 22 ST JOHN STREET – and Morse moved to number 24, meeting her at the bar of the NEW THEATRE shortly thereafter. Love blossomed and both their academic careers nose-dived, her DPhil being terminated. Wendy took a job at the RANDOLPH before moving to the West Country to look after her ailing mother and the affair was, eventually, terminated by her. When Morse meets her, she is blonde with large but regular teeth (MILE: pp56-62, 211).

Sporting Life A daily newspaper devoted to the world of betting with an emphasis on horse racing.

Springs Hotel A cut above Morse's usual watering holes, this swish hotel in Wallingford offers coarse fishing on the Thames, an adjoining golf course, and a croquet lawn. Morse has plans of his own in inviting a woman of some forty summers out for a meal (ANNX: p301).

Spring Street Once the Derby home (at number 12 – which stands on the corner with Burton Street) of Joanna FRANKS. Morse and Lewis visit the house (which is just still standing) to try and lay a ghost (WNCH). Morse also hopes to lay, later that day, with Sheila MACLEAN.

Squitchey Lane A short road joining BANBURY ROAD to WOODSTOCK ROAD. **Map C2**

Stamper, William Leslie (1880-1985) A long-lived member of LONSDALE College; its Stamper Room is named after him. He graduated in 1903 in Classical Moderations, lamented his absence from the fields of Flanders and Passchendaele because of ill health, and subsequently refused to stand for the Mastership of the college. His death, at the age of 104, may have been linked to excess alcohol consumption (NEIG: pp76-78).

Station Hotel Close enough to OXFORD STATION to allow drinkers to wait for trains (or to indulge before going home); this establishment has a small lounge bar sometimes used by BAINES and, on at least one occasion, by PHILLIPSON. "The beer there's bloody awful" according to Morse (WEAR: p151). It may have improved (or, of course, deteriorated), since.

Statutory Instruments (SI) There is, one hopes, only one reference in the WORKS to these examples of secondary legislation. In WOOD (p166) Morse bluffs the DALEY's into revealing (some) information by threatening to rely on quoting – just quoting – Statutory Instrument 1991 No. 1531. This SI covers, in fact, the control of explosives and the regulation came into force on the 1st of November 1991. Morse could have relied more accurately, in this instance, on the Firearms Acts 1968 to 1988.

Stevens, Julia A Titian-haired teacher with a life-threatening illness. She has been divorced for some 8 years and has just reached 46 years of age (1994). She lives in a two-bedroom terraced house in Baldwin Road, EAST OXFORD (CAIN: p211) and employs Brenda BROOKS as a cleaner. Morse attends her funeral at the Oxford Crematorium and leaves a tribute in the Garden of Remembrance.

Storrs, Angela Miriam (née Martin) The wife of Julian since 1974; they live in POLSTEAD ROAD. While still attractive to most men, she has aged rather badly in certain bodily parts (NEIG: p95), at least according to her husband, Julian. She, like Morse, is diabetic.

Storrs, Julian Charles A Senior Fellow, and one of the candidates for the Mastership, of LONSDALE (NEIG). Many details about him are set out on p20; suffice it to note here that he took his BA and MA at Emmanuel College and has been a Captain in the Army; he is aged a little over sixty at the date of the case. His knowledge that Stephenson's *The Locomotion* (rather than the *Rocket*) was the first engine to pull a passenger train on the Stockton to Darlington railway in 1825 (and his interest in railways nationalisation) fail to impress Rachel JAMES (little wonder) but she is still prepared to spend more time with him than, perhaps, she ought.[4] His interests appear to be wide – in 1995, for example, he delivered the PITT RIVERS lecture with the subject of Captain Cook (NEIG: p122), attended the opening of the Polynesian Art Exhibition (at the same place) with Angela (p176), and he is active in the Conservative

---

[4] His knowledge of Nuneham Park (p29) is correct insofar that Capability Brown landscaped the gardens. It is unclear why he links 'Somebody' Adams to the house (which was designed by Stiff Leadbetter).

Party as a local Vice-President (p139). He has, to his credit, a Lloyds Bank Gold Card and drives a blue BMW (p265).

Strange A Chief Superintendent with the THAMES VALLEY force, he is first mentioned (though not named) in LBUS (p130); his surname, though never his Christian name, is revealed on p288. He is Morse's immediate superior in the CID and is either 6 months (REMO: p358) or one year older than him (WOOD: p8). He joined the force in 1964 (NEIG: p186) and was a PC (number 734) in, at least, June 1968 (REMO: p446). His plans to retire are a constantly shifting set of sands – from 1995 (CAIN: p4) to September 1996 (NEIG: p186) and, finally, August 1998 (REMO: p437) when he is presented with a lawnmower and Sir David Attenborough's *The Life of Birds*.

Physical characteristics The most obvious thing is his shape and size. He is heavily jowled (JWEL: p341; NEIG: p156 – 'great jowls') and is grossly overweight (GOLD: p4). He tends to lumber into a room (CAIN: p293), struggle to his feet (p296) and Claire OSBORNE – on only a short sighting – subsequently thinks of him as '… that fat slob of a man …' (WOOD: p127). It is not clear how he has become so fat; he rarely visits the police canteen (GOLD: p40) and he is not known to drink heavily beyond the odd large single-malt Scotch – no ice, no water, and downed in one – in the CHERWELL ARMS (NEIG: p253) and a malt on his birthday (GOLD: p3). 'It was certainly not that he enjoyed walking up the stairs, for he had no pronounced adaptability for such exertions …' (WOOD: p53). He is slightly deaf (by the time of the WOOD case (p357) and exhibits both dandruff and hair in his ears and nose (REMO: p54). He is generally in good health – despite his being overweight – and only complains of piles, being bald, a little deaf, and (one guesses, high) blood pressure (NEIG: p188). Exactly what the "endocrinological dysfunction" was (from which he suffered in about 1995) remains a mystery (REMO: p15). He wears glasses with half-lenses (NEIG: p187).

Mental attributes Strange manages to exhibit a fair degree of learning – he knows the Ancient (Bloody) Mariner (WOOD: p8) and *Cynara* by DOWSON (REMO: p393) but he also thinks Lyme Regis is in Devon (WOOD: p7) and has some trouble with spelling (REMO: pp27-28). Although he is able to correct Morse's 'skeleton in a sideboard' to 'cupboard' (NEIG: p156) he does have the reputation of being neither an ARISTOTLE nor an Isaac Newton (REMO: p52); but he also (probably correctly) believes that the phrase 'as good as gold' is related to the Gold Standard (GOLD: p4), taking 'good' to mean genuine, for example, rather than well-behaved. He appears to have a mental block in sorting out his pension forms (NEIG: p333), is 'penny-pinching' (JWEL: p288), and can be emotional – over, for example, the death of someone's daughter (JWEL: p343). He is, unlike Morse, a quick reader (WOOD: p69) and his handwriting is 'spidery' (REMO: p27) and large, semi-legible, and leaning to the right (REMO: p332). Strange is not without a sense of dry wit: Morse asks him "Have I ever let you down, sir?" Strange replies "Frequently" (NICQ: p218). Also, for example, his reply to JOHNSON (who wants more officers for a body search) is "Look, Johnson! You find *me* a body and I'll find *you* all the bloody personnel you need, all right?" (WOOD: p71). And he thinks that PHILLOTSON is as much use as a "dyslexic proofreader" (CAIN: p10). He is often somewhat grumpy:

Lewis (of Strange):	"He won't be very happy about that."
Morse:	"He's never very happy about anything." (WEAR: p341)

While facing near riots on the BROADMOOR LEA estate, Strange recalls being tempted to throw a brick in his youth (WOOD: p100). His later views are more conservative – he favours hanging and fining tearaways or their fathers (WOOD: pp146/188).

Musical and Other Interests Much is discovered about Strange during the REMO case. He knows The *RING CYCLE*, as conducted by Solti, and recommends it to Morse (p28), correctly recognises Schubert on one occasion (p11), but mistakenly identifies Bruckner as Schubert[5] on another (WOOD: p119). He is not a churchgoer (REMO: p58) but wants *Praise, My Soul, the King of Heaven* at his funeral (p324), plays golf (p154), and is a knowledgeable birdwatcher (pp22/321). It is unclear how widely travelled he may be beyond a week's holiday to the West of Scotland, a short break in Eastbourne for a Superintendents' Conference (CAIN: p293), and a trip to Cork (REMO: p189).

Relationship with Morse and Others Strange is astute, without a doubt. He recognises the bond that has developed between Morse and Lewis – and that their joint working (eventually) seems to produce results. At an early stage in a particular case he asks Morse: "You'll want Lewis, of course?" (MILE: p79); he also suspects the true identity of Lionel REGIS (MINOR; WOOD: p122). He has known Morse for a number of years and had '... marvelled many times at the exploits of this extraordinary and exasperating man' (MILE: p223) and believes, of Morse, that "... he had the most brilliant mind I ever encountered in the whole of my police career ..." (REMO: p438). Their relationship is characterised by (usually gentle) verbal sparring and banter (WOOD: pp7-9; CAIN: p3). There is also a fair degree of mutual respect – Morse advises Lewis to "Never under-rate that man, Lewis!" (REMO: p371) and thinks, not for the first time, that Strange should not be underestimated (CAIN: p4). And Strange says, to JOHNSON: "Morse may be an idiot ... but he's never been a fool" (WOOD: p68). Of Lewis, Strange has, "Don't you underestimate yourself, Lewis! Let others do it for you" (REMO: p32) – remarkably reminiscent of an earlier comment of Morse: "Don't underestimate yourself, Lewis – let me do it for you!" (MILE: p247). 'Strange and Morse had never really been friends, but never really been enemies either ...' (CAIN: p3); they were '... friends without being friendly' (REMO: p23). And what a subtle shift from Strange calling Morse "matey" in a derogatory sense (NEIG: p157) to "old mate" when Morse is in hospital (REMO: p418).

Strange, Mrs Wife of Chief Superintendent Strange and President of the Kidlington Women's Institute in 1994 (CAIN: p195). She is slim and fit; '... outwardly timid and inwardly bullying ...' (REMO: p16), and makes Strange promise to take more exercise (WOOD: p53; CAIN: p3).

---

[5] Schubert does not feature much in the WORKS – though Rachel JAMES does imagine her body being played like a Schubert melody (NEIG: p30).

She has a brother (WNCH: pp2/181), owns a King Charles spaniel (WOOD: p70), and a two and bit years old grandson in 1994 (GOLD: p3). Their telephone number is ex-directory (REMO: p25). She died in 1997 from a coronary thrombosis and it might have been a mistake for Strange to carry on working after her death (REMO: p16).

Stratford-upon-Avon A town in Warwickshire, much favoured by tourists and celebrated as the birthplace of William Shakespeare. It is some 52 miles distant from Oxford. The HISTORIC CITIES tour has it in its itinerary (though they do not have enough time to hear the planned speaker from the Royal Shakespeare Company); Janet ROSCOE reminds DOWNES that the town is properly known as 'upon-Avon' rather than 'on-Avon' (JWEL: p41). The town contains many sights worth visiting including the Swan Theatre (p42); the pillar-box in Bridge Street – where ASHENDEN posts a letter (p245) – may safely be omitted from a tourist perspective, as may the Coach Park (CAIN: p198). Pupils from the PROCTOR MEMORIAL SCHOOL, shepherded primarily by Julia STEVENS, are regular visitors (by coach) and see *Twelfth Night* at the Shakespeare Theatre in 1994.

Stratton, Eddie In 1990 (the date of the JWEL case) he is 66-years-old (p16). He gives his date of birth as 1922 (p200); perhaps he is vain by two years or there has been a simple error. He is the (second) husband of Laura and is tall and bronzed (p62). He has worked as a mortician (i.e. an undertaker) and in this occupation met his future wife as a disconsolate widow. He is interested in railway steam engines and claims to have seen *The Flying Scotsman*, the *Cornish Riviera*, and the *Torbay Express*. He has also, apparently, been photographed on the footplate of *The Cornishman* (JWEL: p277).

Stratton, Laura (Mary) The 70-year old wife of Eddie and owner of the WOLVERCOTE TONGUE (which she intends to present to Dr KEMP). Her desire to get into a bath quickly in room 310 has certain unforeseen consequences (JWEL). Her main interests in life appear to be smoking and playing contract bridge (at the same time; JWEL: p314).

Studio 1 and 2 A cinema in WALTON STREET (and on the corner of Cranham Street; HEIGHT parks her car in nearby Cranham Terrace NICQ: p157/8). It has shown in Studio 2, doubtless among other such films, *The Nymphomaniac* starring Inga Nielsson (not, one hopes, to be confused with the Danish soprano Inga Nielsen nor the Swedish Birgit Nilsson).

Subfusc The term occurs as an adjective (SERV: p39) meaning 'dusky, sombre'. As a noun, subfusc refers to the dark and formal clothes worn (with an academic gown) at Oxford when attending examinations or other formal occasions. Venables and Clifford usefully quote the Proctor's memorandum where *subfusc* is described as: 'For men: a dark suit, dark socks, black boots or shoes, a white shirt, white collar and white bow tie. For women: a white blouse, black tie, dark skirt, black stockings, black boots or shoes and, if desired, a dark coat' (in Douglas (ed) 1973: p211).

Suicide 'the act of killing oneself intentionally' (Chambers 2003). Methods (successful or otherwise) encountered by Morse appear to include NORTH SEA GAS (LBUS), jumping

(SERV, MILE, and CAIN), shooting oneself through the brain (MILE), hanging (JERI), tablets (JWEL), throwing oneself under a Central Line train in London (WOOD), carbon monoxide fumes (NEIG), and slashed wrists (REMO). One is not, at first, sure whether suicides such as these are, in fact, MURDERS. Of course, it is not unknown for a murder to be so disguised as a suicide and vice versa. "It's not always easy to tell suicide from murder," muttered Morse (to Lewis) on one occasion (SERV: p131). On suicides by jumping, and according to *Murder Ink*, 'Myopic jumpers invariably remove their eyeglasses and put them in a pocket before jumping' (SERV: p321).

Inspector BELL has his own thoughts on the subject (shared with WALTERS): "And just let me tell you one thing, my lad. That woman committed suicide – you can take the word of a man who's been finding them like that for the last twenty years" (JERI: p58). John Collins, quoted as the heading to Chapter 9 of JERI, has the following: 'Suicide is the worst form of murder, because it leaves no opportunity for repentance'. Camus, in the heading to Chapter 50 of WOOD has: 'There is but one truly serious philosophical problem, and that is suicide. Judging whether life is or is not worth living amounts to answering the fundamental question of philosophy'. Margaret BOWMAN recalls the death of Socrates by hemlock when considering her own future (ANNX: p203) – as does Morse (REMO: p226) – and a quote from ARISTOTLE (that suicides seek to escape some ill rather than from a noble object) heads both Chapter 12 of CAIN and 67 of REMO. Sir Clixby BREAM recalls that latter Greek thinking of suicide as a form of cowardice (NEIG: p342). Both Max and Morse know that nothing '… could be quite as sombre and sickening as suicide' (JWEL: p221).

Summertown A district of Oxford. It has, among other attractions, a health centre on the corner of BANBURY ROAD and MARSTON FERRY ROAD, a car park (SERV: p38), a Newsagents (SERV: p245; and run by a flattering lady councillor – ANNX: p149), the Summertown Curtaining Company (JERI: p296), and a public library in SOUTH PARADE used by Jennifer COLEBY (and as a meeting place for Margaret BOWMAN and what her husband suspects to be her lover). Further shops and buildings include the RAC, Budgens, the Straw Hat Bakery, Allied Carpets, Chicken Barbecue (MILE: p142 and, for some of these, ANNX: p199), Ladbrokes (ANNX: p30; JWEL: p279), and the Greek Taverna (JWEL: p44). When Morse realises the value of birds and their song, he purchases a pair of binoculars from the OXFAM shop here and calls at the Summertown Pet Store for suitable bird-feeding provisions (REMO: p9). Of some importance to solving the case in JERI is the interrogation of several members of the Summertown Bridge Club. The Summertown Parish Churchyard was largely redeveloped in 1963 and a number of tomb-stones moved; that of Joanna FRANKS was still in place (and decipherable) in 1978 (WNCH: pp44-45). **Map D3**

Sun Insurance Company One of the fourteen entries in the personal telephone directory of BAINES belongs to this company.

Sun, The See the ROYAL SUN.

Sun, The A daily NEWSPAPER read by, among others, Sylvia KAYE and George JACKSON. It has the highest circulation in England, which has been achieved, critics suggest, by pandering to the lowest of popular tastes. It is relentlessly brash, arrogant in tone, and unapologetic; it carries, particularly on its third page but often elsewhere as well, pictures of topless women.

Sunday Mirror, The A weekly NEWSPAPER read by Lewis for its sport coverage (among, one guesses, other things).

Sunday Times, The A weekly NEWSPAPER, usually credited with introducing the type of supplements now found with most Sunday papers. A letter published in the paper prompts Morse to current action in an old case (WEAR) and Denis CORNFORD reads the Books Section (NEIG: p192).

Sunderland Avenue A road in NORTH OXFORD (JERI: p104), lined with hornbeam trees (WOOD: p59). **Map C2**

Sutherland Avenue A street in NORTH OXFORD (LBUS: p139). **Map C2** (probably)

Swan Hotel A place to stay in STRATFORD-UPON-AVON for all the surviving members of the HISTORIC CITIES tour (JWEL: p215). In today's Stratford there exist the White Swan Hotel and the Swan's Nest Hotel – it is not clear if either of these were the intended location.

Swan Inn An inn of this name in BANBURY was a pick-up point for travellers en route to Oxford in the 1850s (WNCH: p139).

Swedish Maiden The name by which a poem of five verses has become known. The verses were sent anonymously to the police at KIDLINGTON (addressed to Chief Constable Smith – and such name seems to have been not just a stab in the dark from the sender as Smith was the name of the previous incumbent). Strange arranges that the Literary Editor of *The TIMES* (Howard Phillipson) is asked to help decipher what appear to be clues to the whereabouts of the missing Karin ERIKSSON. The verses appear in WOOD (pp38-39) and their contents and provenance cause much discussion both within and beyond the pages of that newspaper. Phillipson's analysis appears on pp73-76 and has a few remarkably astute insights far beyond the observation that the writer is no Herrick or HOUSMAN (p75).

Swiss Lodore Hotel A fairly grand hotel (often known as the Lodore Swiss) on the shores of Derwentwater in the Lake District. Morse spends a very wet week here (SERV).

Syndicate, The The name of both the building (in CHAUCER ROAD, not far from WALTON STREET) and the organisation where papers are set for students from abroad (The Foreign Examinations Syndicate). A board such as Oxford Local sets for students, such as Sally Height, sitting exams in Oxford. It supervises some hundred or so overseas centres – in, for example, Bombay, East and West Africa, Geneva, and the Persian Gulf – where O and A LEVELS may be taken (NICQ: p63). In 1975 the main staff were BARTLETT (The Secretary), and Assistant

Secretaries HEIGHT, MARTIN, OGLEBY, and QUINN (who had replaced BLAND). All of the graduate staff must have spent at least five years teaching their subject in schools. The graduates are supported by five secretarial staff (including Margaret FREEMAN). Somehow, the total staff numbers twenty-six (NICQ: p98); apart from junior clerks, perhaps the Secretary's secretary has a secretary?

Syndics Properly, the Foreign Examinations Syndicate (which, slightly confusingly, is also the name of the organisation to which they act as a Board). This body comprises twelve unpaid (bar expenses) members, 'each a prominent fellow of his or her college within the University of Oxford ...' (NICQ: p3). They meet to formulate official examinations policy, oversee the work of the SYNDICATE, and also, crucially, to sit as an Appointments Committee. They are led by TOMPSETT as Dean (supported by the Vice Dean); other members include ROOPE, SETH, and Voss. Thomas BARTLETT acts as permanent Secretary and in this capacity attends meetings (but does not vote).

T

Taylor, George Husband of Grace TAYLOR; they live in a council house in Hatfield Way, KIDLINGTON. George is heavily built and bears a large tattoo on his right arm. He used to work at the COWLEY Steel plant but now works at the main Oxford City Corporation rubbish dump, down a track from WALTON STREET.

Taylor, Grace The wife of George TAYLOR (WEAR) and mother of Valerie. She is aged about 37 (in 1975) and, when wearing full make-up and elegantly dressed, can appear quite attractive (to Morse, at least). She works at a local 'cash and carry', filling shelves, and enjoys twice-weekly sessions of bingo at the Ritz in Oxford (and other forms of gambling).

Taylorian The common name for the Taylor Institute (or Institution – JWEL: p100). It forms the east wing of the ASHMOLEAN (for the less geographically minded, the building on the right as you stand in front) and devotes itself to the study of Modern Languages.

Taylor, Valerie A seventeen-year old schoolgirl who disappears in 1973, believed to have been murdered (WEAR).

Teacher's A brand name of a WHISKY somewhat familiar to Morse. While trying to unravel a certain two problems it takes Morse '… four hours and a bottle of Teacher's …' to come to the solution of the first (JERI: p231). It is distilled in Ardmore, Scotland and made its first appearance as 'reliable spirit' in 1830.

Television See the entries under BBC and ITV.

Thame A pleasant market town (within the area of South Oxon District Council) and one where John BARRON claims an alibi in Cattle Street (REMO: p264).

Thame and District Diabetic Association Morse is invited to speak at one of their events (NEIG: p363). Past speakers have included Dr David Matthews, Lesley Hallett, Professor Harry Keane, Dr Robert TURNER, Willie Rushton, and Angela STORRS.

Thames Valley Police The employer of Morse, Lewis, Strange, and a number of other named officers or civilian support workers; the headquarters are in the Oxford Road, KIDLINGTON and are often known just as HQ. The telephone number given in WOOD (p263) may not be currently accurate (though the description of the building as 'brick-and-concrete' given in CAIN: p369 certainly is). Also based here is the Traffic Comptroller with access to registration number details (DODO: p89). The force dates back, as the Thames Valley Constabulary, to 1968 when the following forces were amalgamated: Berkshire, Buckinghamshire, Oxford City, Oxfordshire, and Reading Borough. The amalgamated force was renamed 'Thames Valley Police' in 1971. The force has the motto *Sit Pax in Valle Tamesis* (Let there be Peace in the Thames Valley) and this appears as the heading to Chapter 13 of JERI; it also publishes its own Gazette (NEIG: pp2-8) including a PUZZLE CORNER (REMO: p373). Morse receives post on a number of occasions at HQ; such post is delivered to The Registry for recording purposes but mail marked 'confidential' (or some such words) is passed unopened to the addressee. Morse receives such a letter – from BARCLAYS BANK – concerning an important enclosure (MILE: p155). The Chief Constable has an international reputation for his handling of terrorist sieges (ANNX: p50).

The Queen's College See QUEEN'S College.

Three Pigeons A pub in Witney where a couple who should not have been together were seen together (REMO: p434).

Three Tuns Inn A canalside pub (in 1859) at Fazely Junction (WNCH: p57). It does not appear in Nicholson (1976) and may be assumed to have closed under that name.

Thrupp A tiny hamlet and home to about twenty cottages, a fairly crucial telephone box, a depot of the Inland Waterways Executive (now British Waterways), and the BOAT INN (MILE: p65). It is here that a body is found in the OXFORD CANAL.

Times, The Commonly regarded as a paper of the establishment, it sought to broaden its appeal in the late twentieth century. Morse, wisely, has his copy delivered to his flat (LBUS: p199) – but it is usually late on a Saturday (WNCH: p2). The celebrated crossword was on the back page which allowed for ease of folding and attempted completion in crowded railway carriages. Louisa HARDINGE has obviously attempted the crossword before – she turns to the back page, and folds it horizontally then vertically before studying 'one across' (WOOD: p14). The paper is not only read by BROWNE-SMITH (MILE: p15) but is also used by a removals firm to wrap items (MILE: p104). The Literary Editor, Howard Phillipson, publishes the SWEDISH MAIDEN verses in 1992 with his own commentary; such publication effectively invites a number of correspondents to advance their own theories by Letters to the Editor (the overall editor, of course, and not Phillipson). The paper used to give a Parker pen as a prize to the winner of their Saturday CROSSWORD competition. And a very fine pen it is. See also CROSSWORDS.

Tompsett, Professor Felix A former Vice-Principal of LONSDALE COLLEGE and the Emeritus Professor of Elizabethan Literature at OXFORD UNIVERSITY. He has made astute property investments on behalf of his College (LBUS) and is Dean of the SYNDICS but due to retire in 1976 when aged 65 (NICQ: p138). He is obviously a man of many talents being also described as a (tall, grey-haired) theologian (p11). He has his own method of interpreting the data given on UCCA (Universities Central Council on Admissions) forms by head teachers about prospective candidates (such as 'vivacious' meaning 'usually drunk' (NICQ: p251).

Tooley's Yard An historic boatyard in BANBURY, which has been in continuous use since 1790. The crew of the *Barbara Bray* (WNCH) almost certainly moored here because Joanna FRANKS made enquiries from Laurenson, a local wharfinger; his wife joined the boat there.

Tower of the Winds A nickname for the Radcliffe Observatory in the WOODSTOCK ROAD (JWEL: p213). The building now forms part of Green Templeton College (for graduate students with a medical bent); the nickname refers to the octagonal structure on the top of the building erected in 1794 (mimicking the horologium in ancient Athens).

Town and Gown Assurance Company, The A business based in the HIGH; it is managed by Mr PALMER and employs Sylvia KAYE (and another 13 women, some of whom are implicated in her death). It is open six days a week but closes at midday on a Saturday (LBUS).

Town and Gown travel agency Morse discusses plans to visit the Greek islands with them in January 1978 but he fails, through a lack of organisation and decisiveness, to put those plans into action (SERV: p47).

Trinity College (Oxford) A college that is much walked past by Christine GREENAWAY (WNCH: p74), by ASHENDEN (JWEL: p50), and by Morse himself, making him feel rather glad to have spent so much time in Oxford (CAIN: p119). There is a passing reference to Trinity in the heading to Chapter 26 of REMO and also to a bearded undergraduate (CAIN: p15) who runs off with McCLURE's wife; for Trinity College at the other place, see HOUSMAN. **Map D5**

Trout Inn A splendid riverside pub between Godstow weir and Godstow Lock. It is (very) near here that police divers search the Thames for the WOLVERCOTE TONGUE. At the time of the JWEL case, the landlady is an attractive and buxom woman. She may (or may not) still be there when Morse spends an hour on the paved terrace overlooking the river (WOOD: p235). Alan HARDINGE and McBryde meet here for lunch (WOOD: p353) but there are, a shame, no further details of the landlady. Morse meets Della CECIL here in March 1996, has a few pints of London Pride (despite knowing of his diabetes), refrains from smoking, and admires her Oxford BLUE blouse (NEIG: p327). **Plate 85**

Turf Tavern A very popular pub in ST HELEN'S PASSAGE (just off NEW COLLEGE LANE) and nestling beneath the walls of that college. It only has one bar (with a busy outdoor area) and is Muzak-free; Morse prefers to drink cask-conditioned beer inside and is well known to the landlord and landlady, Biff and Pam (CAIN: pp78/80-84). Biff is ex-Royal Navy and Pam is a slimly attractive brunette. Denis and Shelly CORNFORD appear to be regulars (NEIG: pp24-25), each enjoying pints of London Pride BITTER. **Plate 86**

Turl Bar A pub allegedly visited by Donald MARTIN (NICQ: p199).

Turl Street A street connecting the BROAD and the HIGH and often known as The Turl (ANNX: p217). **Map D5**

Turn, The Apparently a nickname for a street some 100 yards from LONSDALE College (MILE: p236) and where BROWNE-SMITH has purchased handkerchiefs (or handkerchieves – Chambers 2003 has both). There may be a confusion with TURL STREET or with the somewhat more distant Turn Again Lane; whichever, The Turn is a little tricky to exactly locate.

Turnbull, Robert H. (MB, ChB, FRCS) A consultant at the HARVEY CLINIC (more properly, the Senior Cancer Consultant). Prior to his death (on CUMNOR HILL) he was seeking to assist Julian STORRS with a medical problem.

Turner, Professor Robert C. In 1998, he is in his sixties (and both fair-complexioned and mild-mannered). He is the Professor of Diabetes Studies and the chief-guru of the RADCLIFFE INFIRMARY's Diabetic Centre. He employs, among (no doubt) many others (including the Dr Matthews whose advice Morse has received), Sarah HARRISON (REMO). As Morse appears not to relish reducing his alcohol intake, Turner suggests that Atorvastatin is prescribed (p200).

Typewriter These were once of two main types – portable and 'static' (LBUS: p150) – and it was believed that each model had its own unique characteristics enabling a detective, for example, to trace a typed letter back to a particular machine. In MILE (p102) Morse seeks to test one particular typewriter by typing some, if not most, of a standard phrase ('the quick brown fox jumps over the lazy dog'; this phrase contains all the letters of the English alphabet and is sometimes used to demonstrate fonts). The portability (and substitution) of typewriters has, of course, the potential to cause confusion (MILE: pp123-124). Morse has an 'ancient portable' typewriter; as Lewis discovers, it produces a distinctive (and possibly unique) typeface (WOOD: p408). Morse has never mastered it (REMO: p337).

U

Ulfgar Road A street in Upper Wolvercote (ANNX: p256). **Map B2**

Ullman, Dr Eric A particularly intelligent Oxford don. He is a bachelor, lives in NORTH OXFORD, is fat and balding, and was a refugee from pre-war Germany (WATC: p120). He is also particularly keen on MOZART and antiques.

Unbuttoning A favourite word of Morse (ANNX: p80). Morse recalls that the word comes in one of Philip Larkin's poems (though does not, unfortunately, say which). *The Whitsun Weddings* has the line: 'Displace the reek of buttoned carriage-cloth' but this is of the upholstery in a train and not terribly erotic. Also see the GARDENER'S ARMS. In NEIG, Morse links the word to Plato's idea of progress (p181). The Literary Adviser to the Philip Larkin Society has the following helpful comments: that there is a Concordance of Larkin's poetry (giving every word used in the 1988 Collected Poems); neither unbuttoning nor unbuttoned (nor even unbutton) appear therein; though Larkin may well have used the word in his prose (Booth 2007). There are two further references to Larkin and unbuttoning – in an anonymous diary extract (WOOD: p31) and by Morse himself (REMO: p253) when toying with a seduction.[1]

'Underbeered' An apposite and accurate description of Morse, though only on rare occasions (for example, WEAR: p164 and JWEL: p289; NEIG: p129 has the charming "I'm a bit weary and I'm much underbeered"). The word is yet to appear in Chambers or the Shorter Oxford English Dictionary (but may yet do so – the Senior Lexicographer at Chambers has advised, in a personal communication, that they will keep the word in their database to see if it becomes more widely adopted – which one may, of course, take as a personal challenge). It is not easy for Morse to function in any proactive or investigative sense when in such a condition. The more prosaic 'over-beered' also appears (NICQ: p242; JERI: p172) but, perhaps, there are already enough synonyms for this state of mind and body.

University Arms Hotel A (very) grand building in CAMBRIDGE and where John ASHENDEN sinks a couple of large glasses of GLENFIDDICH. The HISTORIC CITIES tour moves from here to the RANDOLPH but not before certain members of the group hatch a plan (JWEL: p324). **Plate 87**

University Chest Literally, the name of an iron box, 'The Painted Chest', (the current one being that of the seventeenth century) but used more generally to refer to the finance department or treasury of the University of Oxford in WELLINGTON SQUARE. The Board of the Chest manage the University Superannuation Scheme (NICQ: p80).

---

[1] May Morse have been recalling Lord Byron rather than Larkin? Marchand (1974) has the following: 'When one subtracts from life infancy (which is vegetation), sleep, eating and swilling, buttoning and unbuttoning – how much remains of human existence? The summer of a dormouse' (letter 7th December 1813).

University College DOWNES addresses members of the HISTORIC CITIES tour about the stained-glass windows in the chapel (JWEL: pp105-106), pointing out the '… Garden of Eden, where the apples on the tree of knowledge glowed like giant golden Jaffas'. The windows were designed by Abraham van Linge, stored (before their installation) during the Civil War for fear of damage by Puritans, and put into place in the 1660s. The number 2 bus stops outside the college (LBUS: p33); members have been known to frequent the BEAR pub (NEIG: p91). The late husband of Patricia Bayley (MINOR) was an anthropologist here (REMO: p233). **Map D5-E5**

University Parks See PARKS.

Upper Fisher Row A short street beside the OXFORD CANAL. Canal crews occupied, presumably, some of the terraced cottages here (WNCH: p53). **Map C5**

V

Vickers, Sergeant Sam A police officer (based at ST ALDATES). His handling of Lost Property is not quite up to the standards that Morse expects (ANNX: pp226-229). For Vickers, thankfully, Morse does not realise the full extent of his involvement.

Victoria Road Running east from the BANBURY ROAD to the Cherwell (JWEL: p77). **Map C2-D2**

Victor Street A street in JERICHO and somewhat typical of the area. **Map C5**

Plate 67 (Left) The cinema (now known as the Phoenix Picture House) (p159).
Plate 68 (Right) Outside the Pitt Rivers Museum (p160).

Plate 69 (Left) The Plough at Wolvercote (p160).
Plate 70 (Right) Port Meadow (p162).

Plate 71 (Left) The Proscholium (p165).
Plate 72 (Right) The Radcliffe Camera (p167).

W

Wadham A college (founded in 1610). Walking past Wadham makes Morse feel glad to have spent so much time in Oxford (CAIN: p119). **Map D5**

Wagner, Richard (1813-1883) A German composer and probably Morse's favourite (LBUS: pp74-75). He regards *Der Ring des Nibelungen* ('The Ring') as one of the seven great wonders of the modern world; *Siegfried* is his least favourite (CAIN: p272). And of the Ring, *Die Walküre* is probably his favourite; he has and loves the version conducted by Solti, plays the first act (MILE: p129), turns down the mighty volume of the finale (ANNX: p51), and listens to the love duet from Act One with a beatific smile (ANNX: p279). On hearing that he is soon to be discharged from hospital, Morse imagines himself luxuriating in Wotan's Farewell from the last act of *Die Walküre* (WNCH: p169). The correct spelling of *Die Walküre* (or, rather, an incorrect version) causes Morse some concerns in the WATC case. He listens to *Das Rheingold* in LBUS (p75) and again in STOR (p172) when the opening chords stir something in his mind. And he listens to the 'well-worn grooves' of the Furtwängler recording of *Götterdämmerung* (JWEL: p19). He owns a set of Deutsche Grammophon cassettes of *Tristan und Isolde* (CAIN: p210). Morse has compared (perhaps accurately but rather unflatteringly) the works of Gilbert and Sullivan to Wagner: "We don't go in for 'tunes' in Wagner – we go in for 'continuous melody'" (WOOD: p251). Morse and Laura HOBSON enjoy the finale of *Götterdämmerung* (with Brünnhilde riding into the flames and the waves of the Rhine rippling into silence); they also enjoy a glass or two of GLENFIDDICH (WOOD: p380). McBryde (MINOR) softly whistles the Prelude to Act Three of *Lohengrin* while he evades the attention of the police (WOOD: p399). Also see RING CYCLE. Morse knows a little German but only from the works of Wagner and Strauss (ANNX: p60).

Walsh-Atkins, Mrs Emily An 81-year old regular churchgoer (ST FRIDESWIDE'S). She lives in NORTH OXFORD (north Oxford in the text) at the Home for Ageing Gentlefolk and her sight is poor; the former fact is included for completeness, the latter rather more pertinently. When asked her age by Morse she asks him if he can keep a secret (to which he replies, 'yes'). "So can I" is her whispered response (SERV: p79).

Walters A young and newly fledged (though bulky) detective constable. He has been in the force some 18 months and is based at the City police in ST ALDATES. His first contact with Morse is when he listens to him lecture on Homicidal Procedures (JERI: p22) though he has cause to meet him again during the course of the investigation (including a visit to Morse's flat after wrongly, perhaps, 'arresting' him). He is somewhat slow in recognising jokes (JERI: pp59/71) but is, one guesses, appreciated by his young wife at their home in KIDLINGTON. Rather surprisingly, he leaves the police to join the army (JERI: p302).

Walton Street One of the more interesting streets in Oxford. It is home to the OXFORD UNIVERSITY PRESS (since 1832), RUSKIN COLLEGE, a cinema which used to show films of an adult nature (LBUS), and a tremendous variety of restaurants (including Le Petit Blanc; REMO: p202). **Map C5**

Walton Well Road A turning (south from ARISTOTLE LANE) leading (over a humpbacked bridge across the OXFORD CANAL) to the City rubbish dump. **Map C4**

Warrant Card All police officers should, on request, offer proof of their identity – and this is usually provided by a warrant card (which includes a photograph and the name of the officer together with rank and 'warrant number'). Morse, on one occasion when his authority is questioned, gets by with the production of an official-looking letter about pension rights (WEAR: pp74-75).

Warwick Street A car-cluttered turning off the IFFLEY ROAD. **Map E6**

Washerwoman effect A phrase known to forensic scientists and first met in MILE (p68). It indicates the condition of the skin after immersion in water for some time (in this instance, in the OXFORD CANAL) and is typified by the disaggregation of the stratum corneum and the discovery of perinuclear vacuoles in the stratum germinativum (the skin is somewhat wrinkled, one guesses). After some twenty-four hours, the skin goes beyond the washerwoman effect to 'sodden' and then 'blanched' (MILE: p77).

Water Eaton Road A road in NORTH OXFORD and home to Dr and Mrs KEMP. From certain rear gardens it appears that access may be had to the River Cherwell. **Map D2**

Waterways Oxford seems at first sight to be surrounded by four of these – the Isis, the Cherwell, and Thames (all rivers) with the OXFORD CANAL making an appearance as well. Maps do not always make the situation clear. The key to understanding is that all four bodies of water are interlinked; the Thames is known as the Isis (by some) during its course through Oxford; the Cherwell (a separate river altogether) runs to the east of Oxford and joins the Thames (or Isis) a little under half a mile south of FOLLY BRIDGE; the canal links to the Thames (or Isis) in the north at Duke's Cut, via Castle Mill Stream by JERICHO, and in the south at Isis (not 'or Thames') lock. Potentially confusingly, the Thames has those feats of engineering usually associated with canals i.e. locks (and Iffley Lock and Sandford Lock are mentioned in CAIN: p303, along with Green Bank, the Gut, Donnington Bridge, and Haystacks Corner). The Cherwell is pronounced Charwell by a number of Oxford residents (JWEL: p77) though not by all.

Watson, Dr John (1852-1929) He is best known for recording the great majority of the cases of his companion HOLMES. On a particular occasion, Morse decides that he does not need to apply Holmesian intelligence to locate a particular garden: '... a brief Watsonian reconnoitre would have established the spot almost immediately' (WOOD: p189). Watson also appears as a clue (WEAR: p97); see CROSSWORDS.

Watson, PC Barry Robert He accompanies (and drives) Sergeant DIXON to Bath; they are following Morse and Lewis. Watson provides some support, in 1990, for the fact that Lewis is a speedy driver (JWEL: p294). A young PC Watson is on the scene in the BURG case. Assuming this took place in 1995 it is just about possible they are one and the same. Similarly, a PC

Watson appears in BAGG (1992) and here his Christian names are revealed (p241). Mention is also made of a DC Watson (MINOR); he was a DC in the 1990 JWEL case and in GOLD (1994). Perhaps they are related or one and the same person has switched from the uniformed to the detective branch and back again (unlikely in one so young).

Way Through the Woods, The Morse is on holiday but, somehow, an old case rears its pretty head in the shape of the missing 'Swedish Maiden' – Karin ERIKSSON. There is much correspondence and some poetry in *The TIMES*, a body or three, a fair amount of PORNOGRAPHY, a little of ornithology, and Lewis gets to fly to Sweden. There are also a number of initially anonymous diary entries. DCI JOHNSON had originally investigated the case in 1991 but the Chief Constable and Strange pass it to Morse as further developments arise; this is the tenth major case investigated by Morse and Lewis. The investigation is very much out of town for most of its course and the delights and opportunities of the countryside and woodland play a prominent part. Morse demonstrates his love and knowledge of poetry and even turns his hand to composing a stanza or two. The record of the case has two maps (of WYTHAM WOOD and the grounds of BLENHEIM) and most of the Chapters are headed by quotations. The title is taken from KIPLING (and acknowledged as such):

'Only the keeper sees
That, where the ring-dove broods,
And the badgers roll at ease,
There was once a road through the woods.'
The Way Through the Woods

See also the SWEDISH MAIDEN verses (WOOD). **Main personnel** Some members of the ERIKSSON family, the DALEY family, MICHAELS, Alan HARDINGE, Louisa HARDINGE, Claire OSBORNE, and MYTON.

WEA See WORKERS' EDUCATIONAL ASSOCIATION.

Wellington Square Home to OXFORD UNIVERSITY (in terms of administration) and the UNIVERSITY CHEST. Christine GREENAWAY foregoes a cocktail reception here to visit Morse in hospital (WNCH: 120). **Map D5**

Wench is Dead, The Morse is taken by ambulance (after vomiting blood) into hospital (Ward 7C of the JR2 – the John RADCLIFFE HOSPITAL) and receives a copy of a book by Wilfred DENISTON called *Murder on the Oxford Canal*. The book outlines details about a murder that took place in 1859 during the trip of the *Barbara Bray* along the canal. There is sufficient information in the book to convince Morse that some sort of miscarriage of justice took place and he is determined (with the help, of course, of Lewis) to seek out the truth. Further details can be found under OXFORD CANAL. The title, as revealed in the record of the case (WNCH), comes from Marlowe's *The Jew of Malta*:

Friar Barnadine: "Thou hast committed …"
Barabas: "Fornication; but that was in another country,

And besides, the wench is dead."
(Act 4 Scene 1).

This quotation also appears as the heading to Chapter 34 of JWEL and resurfaces in NEIG: pp278-279 when Morse further demonstrates his wide knowledge of literature. The line appears, without attribution and spoken by a suspect, in P.D. James's *Cover Her Face* 1989: p182. Chapters are headed by quotations, much is revealed about Morse's state of health and something of the insurance industry, and Morse travels by his LANCIA to Ireland to visit a cemetery. Adrian Page (2000: pp125-130) analyses the record of this case with some sensitivity (though also with many references to semiotics). Bird (1998) notes that the sentence of transportation, apparently passed on one of the defendants, was abolished 6 years before the 1859 case. (WNCH). *Main personnel* DENISTON, DONAVAN, FRANKS, Christine GREENAWAY, and MACLEAN.

Wentworth Road A street in NORTH OXFORD notable (in this Companion) only for the fact that it was from here that Karin ERIKSSON made a life-changing telephone call (WOOD: p232). **Map C2**

Westbrook, Stephen The Manager of The BLACK PRINCE. He contacts the police after the body of Sylvia KAYE has been discovered and is instructed by Lewis how to secure the crime scene (LBUS).

Westerby, George D A (fairly short) Geography don at LONSDALE College, residing in Room 3, Staircase T, Second Quad (MILE: p17). He has been at the College for some 30 years and is aged 68 years at the time of the MILE case. He plans to move to Flat 6, 29 Cambridge Way, London, WC1 on his retirement (MILE: p108) though it is unclear how he will then maintain his interest in angling at THRUPP. There is some slight confusion about his second initial – given as D or O (MILE: p102 and p195 respectively). The former is preferred (printed above the door of his rooms in College) rather than the latter (appearing as labels on crates – which also declare him to be an MA).

Western Avenue A major thoroughfare leading into London (from, unsurprisingly, the west) and the obvious route for those driving from Oxford (JWEL: p264).

Westgate Central Library See OXFORD CENTRAL LIBRARY.

Westgate Shopping Centre A recent building development (with modern shops and places of refreshment). It was built on the site of the old ST EBBE'S (JERI: p19 which gives St Ebbes). It has car parking – a space of which is occupied for a time by the Smith's (APPENDIX D) BMW (ANNX: p109). **Map D6**

Westminster, The A pub near to New Scotland Yard in London. The beer is drinkable – just (WEAR: p270).

Whisky A favourite drink of Morse. A number of other personnel have been known to like a dram (for example, George JACKSON drinks TEACHER'S (JERI: p41) and BROWNE-SMITH has what may be a GLENFIDDICH (MILE: pp32-33). Morse, on occasions, favours BELL'S as a brand (MILE: p187) – a large one, of course – and the same brand is available in the HAWORTH HOTEL (ANNX: p91). Alan HARDINGE brings a bottle of Skye Talisker malt to an assignation at the COTSWOLD HOUSE (WOOD: p96) and Denis CORNFORD favours a large Glenmorangie in the WHITE HORSE next to BLACKWELL'S. Morse has also been known to drink The Macallan (CAIN: p160) – a fine single malt indeed.

Whitaker, Ambrose Born in 1917 and brother to Dodo. He had an undistinguished record in the Second World War (obtaining two stripes and acting as an artillery trainer in Bodmin). His later career included an MA from Cambridge, a move to 6 West View Crescent in Bournemouth, and Fellowship of the Royal Academy of Music. He died in 1989 (DODO).

Whitaker, Dodo She lived at 14 CROZIER ROAD in the 1940s (and here met Philip WISE who lived beneath her). Wise believes her first name may be Alice (or Angela or Anne or Audrey). Their platonic relationship seems to have been largely based on a shared love of music (DODO).

White Hart A pub at WYTHAM. It is prominent in the WOOD case, serves Burton ale (p171), and, according to David MICHAELS (a regular), has a condom machine in the gents (p135). Morse, remarkably, declines an offer of Max to have a drink there (p145) because of a work commitment. It has a dovecote in its car park (p250) and a small upstairs bar (p396). It is here that Morse drinks Best BITTER in a straight glass (allegedly on the basis of the optical illusion that it holds more); he also engineers Lewis into buying the round (p252). Later in the case, Morse enjoys a further two pints of the same (pp332-333). Simon HARRISON claims to have had a lunch here (REMO: p306).

White Hart According to Sergeant WILKINS there are a number of pubs or inns with this name (including that at WYTHAM entered above). Others may be found at HEADINGTON, Marston, Minster Lovell, and Eynsham (WOOD: p81). He mentions that at WOLVERCOTE – which is further identified in REMO: p434. He also sarcastically suggests (though, one guesses, truthfully) that Morse could no doubt add to the list. **Plate 88**

White Horse, The A public house in KIDLINGTON with both a public and a lounge bar. It is close enough to walk to from the THAMES VALLEY POLICE HQ. It is highly likely that it is the pub described as: 'The cigarette smoke hung in blue wreaths, head-high like undispersing morning mist, and the chatter along the bar and at the tables was raucous and interminable, the subtleties of conversational silence quite unknown. Cribbage, dominoes and darts and every available surface cluttered with glasses …' (WEAR: p192).

White Horse, The A pub in the BROAD (and very convenient for BLACKWELL'S). Donald MARTIN alleges that he visited the pub in connection with an ALIBI (NICQ: p199) and Alan HARDINGE drinks Scotch here (WOOD: p276). Morse, while a little under the weather, drinks a pint of Hook Norton BITTER washed down with a double dose of penicillin tablets (CAIN: p119).

White Horse, The A pub in the London Road, HEADINGTON (and only mentioned as a place where Morse needs to turn while driving) (CAIN: p255).

White Swan The name of a pub in ABINGDON. Charles RICHARDS, with some justification, has three double Scotches here (JERI: p81). After interviewing one or two of the RICHARDS family, Morse offers them a drink here (which is refused). Morse stoically decides to wait for a pint until he gets back to KIDLINGTON.

Whitham Woods See WYTHAM WOODS (though Whitham is the preferred spelling in LBUS: p229).

Whytham Woods See REGIS and WYTHAM WOODS.

Widdowson, Susan A nurse, in her early twenties, with a secret (or two) and a flatmate (or two); Morse is somewhat attracted to her (LBUS).

Wilkins, Edward James A crane-driver and tenor saxophone player (a reasonably unlikely combination) who was born in 1951 (in DIAMOND CLOSE – where he still lives). He attended Hobson Road Primary and Oxford Boys' school and knows of Milton's *Comus* (ANNX). He has, apparently, played at the FRIAR BACON pub (p274).

Wilkins, Sergeant Based at THAMES VALLEY, he appears to work closely with DCI JOHNSON. They jointly interview Lewis (WOOD: pp80-84) about Morse's brief involvement in the 1991 part of the case – and when they snigger, Lewis knows that he hates them both. He plays a reasonable part in the GOLD case (by acting unreasonably).

Williams, Sheila MA, BLitt Cantab, An inhabitant of NORTH OXFORD, living in HAMILTON ROAD. She is divorced and is a guest speaker on the HISTORIC CITIES tour. She manages to give '… the simultaneous impression of vulnerability, sensuality, and mild inebriation' (JWEL: p45). As such, Morse is immediately attracted to her. She is rather fond of Gordon's gin and slim-line tonic and can drink a glass in a single draught – much to Morse's secret admiration (JWEL: p49). She slightly worries about her intake and recognises that she drinks in a morning more than the weekly-recommended average as promoted by the SUMMERTOWN Health Centre (p187). Her knowledge of KIPLING is seen by Morse as an admirable quality (pp134-135); she is also able to lecture on Lewis Carroll's 'Alice' (p307). She finds Morse both 'dishy' and 'sexy' (p66) and although early in the case she makes Morse an offer that he must refuse; he is less professional and more amorous on a later occasion (pp291-292).

Wilmot, John (1647-1680) Second Earl of Rochester. He was a rake and a libertine and also a poet; all of these activities were prominently carried out at the court of Charles the Second. Six lines attributed to him appear in the NEIG case (p69) though Morse believes they are an invention. His analysis of the lines (suggesting they contain a modern message) appears on pp72-74.

Wimpy A chain of fast food restaurants, one of which can be found in ST GILES'.

Wine It has been alleged, of the academic community, that many '… of them drank red wine all the time in Oxford – even with Dover sole' (NICQ: p19). See the section *Alcohol* under Morse.

Wise, Philip A neighbour of Morse (and living in the same block of flats), he attended EXETER College before the Second World War and then moved into Intelligence work. He is aged 71 years at the time of the DODO case. Both he and Dodo WHITAKER were members of the (Oxford) Record Library.

Witham Woods See WYTHAM WOODS.

Wolsey College Wolsey is sometimes known as 'The House' from its Latin name of *Aedes Archiepiscopi*, the House of the Bishop (CAIN: p81). Although CHRIST CHURCH is also known by this soubriquet, this derives from its name of *Aedes Christi* ('the House of Christ'). The college claims to have the largest quad ('Great Quad') in Oxford (p86). FELLOWS are known as Students (as they are at CHRIST CHURCH). The college has a House Matron (p119) and a Dean (p354). Both McCLURE and Matthew RODWAY had rooms on Staircase G in Drinkwater Quad, the former in G4 and the latter in G8. **Map D6**

Wolsey Road A street in NORTH OXFORD (NEIG: p142). **Map C2**

Wolvercote A small village some 2 or 3 miles to the north of Oxford. It is known to Morse because its pubs serve REAL ALE. From the south of the village, there is a good view across PORT MEADOW to the spires (dreaming, stately, or otherwise) and the RADCLIFFE CAMERA of Oxford. See The KING CHARLES and The PLOUGH. **Map B2**

Wolvercote Tongue, The (also the Wolvercote Jewel) An ancient bejewelled artefact (late 8th Century AD), discovered in 1873 in the waters below the bridge at Wolvercote, and now belonging to Laura STRATTON. She intends to present it to the ASHMOLEAN MUSEUM. The importance of the tongue is that the matching Wolvercote Buckle (found in the 1930s) was already in the Museum, and had been since 1947. The Tongue is triangular, made of gold, about two inches by three, and still carries one of its original three rubies. Dr KEMP is an authority on it and Sheila WILLIAMS has sketched it. A full description of it may be found in JWEL: pp58-59 (wherein a link to Alfred the Great is established).

Woodstock A town some 8 miles to the northwest of Oxford. BLENHEIM PALACE is a local attraction and the town is often crowded with visitors for the Palace, antique shops, and the general air of civilised charm; 'Church Street' (LBUS: p 222) is known to both Peter

NEWLOVE and Gaye McFEE. The town is bedevilled with parking restrictions ('double yellow lines'); these add to the attraction of the BLACK PRINCE with its own car park (though that car park is rather less attractive for Sylvia KAYE).

Woodstock Arms Morse drinks (at least) three pints of Morrell's Best BITTER here (REMO: p103) and, on a later occasion, a definite three pints (p148). The pub may be found at 272, WOODSTOCK ROAD (Honey 1998).

Woodstock Crescent The location of a fatal knifing which has absolutely no bearing on the case that is about to absorb Morse (JERI: p14). The crescent is in KIDLINGTON, not far from the HQ of the THAMES VALLEY POLICE.

Woodstock Road One of the main roads leading into (or out of) Oxford to the north of the city. It joins the A34 trunk road at the 'Woodstock roundabout'. At its northern end may be found the church of St Michael and All Angels – where Margaret DALEY is an occasional worshipper (WOOD: p242). (The 29th of September is St Michael and All Angels day, according to a diary in LBUS: p27.) At the southern end may be found the Oratory (the Catholic parish church for the centre of Oxford) and it is here that Morse follows a semi-irrational impulse and lights two candles (REMO: p207). **Map B2-C2-C3-C4-D4-D5**

Woolworths A chain of large general stores, very occasionally visited by Morse (and the suppliers of a cheap tie to George TAYLOR; WEAR: p44). The shop is referred to, in error, as 'Woolworth' in SERV (p102) but correctly in JERI (p125).

Worcester College The only mentions in the WORKS are JERI (p20) – and that only in connection with its gardens – and JWEL (p105). **Plate 89**, **Map D4-D5**

Workers' Educational Association Probably the largest United Kingdom provider of adult education. Margaret CROWTHER attends classes thus provided (on Classical Civilisation) at the Further Education Centre on Headington Hill.

Works, The Only the published and factual cases (as recorded by Colin DEXTER) can be found in this Companion. Details of fictional cases in other media are recorded in, for example, Bird (1998) and Bishop (2006). These cases have a certain amount of interest (one can almost picture how Morse may have looked) but they remain fictional. The change from the written word to, for example, television creates a few problems for the pedant – bizarrely, the beloved LANCIA car appears to have become a more televisual (and equally beloved) JAGUAR and this has been reflected in some printed editions. See also the notes on pages 4-5 in the Introduction.

Wormwood Scrubs see SCRUBS.

Wright, WPC She is a constable at ST ALDATES and helps Lewis (a little) in a search of various papers and artefacts. She does not know Morse (but wishes she did) and comments that:

"Everybody says he drinks far too much" (WNCH: p127). She is very blonde and, most useful in the days before recorded interviews, she has a Pitman shorthand speed of 130 words per minute (JWEL: pp250/253). And what an erotically charged sentence (for some) is: '... WPC Wright transferred her shorthand-book to her black-stockinged knee ...' (p262). In a later case, an interview is recorded and she types up the notes (WOOD: p295) without the usual Tipp-Exed alterations typical of Lewis. She is also described as small and attractive (WOOD: p360).

Wytham A charming village to the west of Oxford and location of the WHITE HART pub. The village affords (limited) access to WYTHAM WOODS and the village hall provides the setting for a production of *The Mikado* (WOOD). Morse has been known to hum the chorus from *A more humane Mikado* from Act 2 (WOOD: p270) – though making the punishment fit the crime is, of course, a matter for the judiciary rather than the police.

Wytham Woods (various spellings are Whitham, Whytham, or Witham). The Woods feature prominently in the WOOD case (and the published record contains a useful map). John Chavasse (under MINOR) suggests in a letter that the correct name should be Wood rather than Woods (and the Ordnance Survey Landranger map 164 agrees with him in naming Wytham Great Wood). However, Wytham Wood is directly joined by a number of other wooded areas and the appellation Woods is, understandably, in common usage. The Woods are administered by a University Committee to whom David MICHAELS, as head forester, reports with a University Land Agent as an Executive Officer. There is also a Wytham Trust (WOOD: p139) and the University Agricultural Research Station is based here (WOOD: p56). The Woods have been the location of a charity walk to 'Save the Whales' (CAIN: p16) and a postcard bearing the legend 'Bluebells in Wytham Woods' features a little later in the case (p46). Named areas of the Woods include Bowling Alley; Cowleaze Copse; Duck Pond; The Follies; Froghole Cottage; Hatchett Lane; Marley Wood; Pasticks (a good place for a body: p139); Singing Way; and Sparrow Lane (p131).

Plate 73 (Left) The Radcliffe Infirmary (p167).
Plate 74 (Right) John Radcliffe (p167).

Plate 75 (Left) The Randolph Hotel (p168).
Plate 76 (Right) Red Kite in flight (p170).

Plate 77 (Left) The Royal Oxford Hotel (p174).
Plate 78 (Right) Washing up at Ruskin College (p174).

X

Ximenes The CROSSWORD pseudonym of Derrick Somerset Macnutt (1902-1971). He appears twice in the WORKS – LBUS (p74) has: 'Crosswords were a passion with Morse, although since the death of the great Ximenes he had found few composers to please his taste'. And the heading to Chapter 16 of WEAR gives a clue example (recorded under CROSSWORDS). Robins (1975) has this: 'Perfection was always his aim, and seldom did he fail to live up to his own exacting ideal. His diagrams were a model of symmetry, his clues artistic, concise and accurate, with never a word wasted' (p20). A certain N. C. Dexter sent a poem to *The Observer* shortly after Macnutt's death. **Plate 17**

Plate 79 (Left) The Morse plaque at St Aldates police station (p175).
Plate 80 (Right) The War Memorial (p176).

Plate 81 (Left) St John's College (the entrance to the Great lawn and Groves) (p177).
Plate 82 (Right) St Mary's Church (p177).

Plate 83 (Left) Rewley House (p180).
Plate 84 (Right) South Parade (looking east) (p183).

Y

Yale The most common proprietary brand of key for house doors in England. References to such a key occur with some regularity in the WORKS and, perhaps, just one reference is enough: '… (she) slid her latchkey into the Yale lock' (ANNX: p12).

Yarnton A village a few miles to the north west of Oxford. Certain buses terminate here rather than continue to WOODSTOCK (LBUS). The village has little of interest bar Yarnton Manor, a fine building, used since 1973 by the Oxford Centre for Hebrew and Jewish Studies. A witness in the WOOD case – on his way to see his invalid mother in Yarnton – believes he sees Karin ERIKSSON.

Plate 85 (Left) The Trout in Lower Wolvercote (p193).
Plate 86 (Right) The Turf Tavern (p193).

Plate 87 (Left) The University Arms Hotel (p195).
Plate 88 (Middle) The White Hart at Wytham (p203).
Plate 89 (Right) Worcester College (p206).

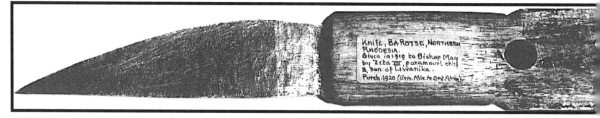

Plate 90 (Right) The murder weapon in *The Daughters of Cain* (p213).

Z

Zeta III A Paramount Barotse chief. The iron-bladed gut-cutter, – a possible murder weapon once stolen – was originally made for Zeta III (CAIN). The knife resides in the PITT RIVERS MUSEUM having been donated to the museum in 1919 by Bishop May (see APPENDIX D). **Plate 90**

Appendix A
Crosswords

Introduction

(1) *Listener* **Crossword 3715** *Coded Secret* **by Samson**

1	2	3	4	5	6	7	8	9	10	11
12					13					
14							15			
16			17				18		19	
20		21		22			23			
24						25			26	
27	28			29	30					
31			32			33		34		
35				36			37			
38						39				
40							41			

SECRET WORD: _____

From each across answer, only the odd or even letters should be entered. Each down answer should be entered with one letter removed, entries in the odd columns also being jumbled. A letter should be entered in the central square so that the diagonals form two different anagrams. You should now have enough clues to decode a secret word and write it below the grid.

ACROSS

1 Member of large family inhabiting street to one side (6)
4 Budget vice? It is twice cooked (16, two words)
12 Rent out in some measure after we change culture (10)
13 Ex-president trod in China and, disgraced, we find this man intended tapes to be destroyed (12, two words)
14 Producing two notes, order pint, good pub's ale lacking head (14)
15 Crown dropped in river - man's discharged (8)
16 Nights druids camp out for seasonal treat (16, two words)
18 Batting? Perform, or these nets will be required when it's wet (6)

20 With little space to move, packed theatre audience to crush bar! (14)
23 Fabulous winner to excite Tories (8)
24 Priest's gold taken by a friend for cure (10)
25 One coffin set off emotions (10)
27 Vessel's launch in which sailor must keep time (8)
29 A kinky sex shop to loan instruments (14, two words)
31 They think Blair's new – new but less Labour primarily (6)
32 Taking sexual activity outside is getting support in April mostly (16)
35 Make hard decisions in first year initially after starting school on Long Island (8)
36 One sort of tray made in factory – Head of Sales gets service awards (14, two words)
38 Improper, evil, base fool – priest sacked by archbishop (12)
39 Promote the surprisingly light measuring equipment (10)
40 Ed cut odds on Final to create a means of saving revenue (16, two words)
41 Inducement to run in RAC Rallies? (6)

DOWN

1   Signs of conflict around strike failing to close parts of hospital (9, two words)
2   Rashly pursued and overtook (7)
3   Advances Lothario's initial objectives (5)
4   Sloth condemned on mountain? Society's offences (4)
5   Immature crabs cross rough sea (5)
6   Fall requires epitaph put up outside (6, two words)
7   Very English artist had returned to front of National Gallery (8)
8   Trained Revolutionary Front inside London district (9)
9   Invalids' central heating on around end of October – one's cold inside (8)
10 The party where Henry's wife reveals jacket (6)
11 Some stones to make a home (4)
17 Crushed (nearly died from it?) (9)
19 Serenades – see bouquet recalled in records (9)
21 Old spire's crooked – one for quiet worshipper (8)
22 Temper aluminium instead of right metal (8)
26 One privileged and fashionable rides off (7)
28 Wrongly listed Spanish marks ... (6)
30 ... work the Spanish Academy returned and finally dropped like a stone (6)
33 Top us up from this ... (5)
34 ... a second tea or coffee (5)
35 Fish channel out of New Testament ... (4)
37 ... with these? You'll find nothing in Jordan when saint's not around on the Sabbath! (4)

Solution

¹S	²U	³N	⁴I	⁵E	⁶T	⁷V	⁸B	⁹S	¹⁰U	¹¹T
¹²W	S	E	N	Z	¹³I	H	R	N	X	N
¹⁴D	U	L	S	O	P	N	¹⁵E	C	E	E
¹⁶C	R	S	¹⁷M	S	U	D	N	¹⁸I	D	¹⁹O
²⁰U	P	²¹R	O	²²U	P	R	²³T	R	O	S
²⁴A	E	I	R	T	E	²⁵A	F	C	²⁶I	N
²⁷L	²⁸T	O	T	²⁹L	³⁰O	A	O	H	N	S
³¹R	I	S	³²I	A	P	³³O	R	³⁴A	I	G
³⁵S	L	D	F	³⁶M	L	T	³⁷R	M	D	L
³⁸L	E	I	I	A	E	³⁹P	O	O	E	E
⁴⁰O	S	L	D	T	D	U	D	⁴¹C	R	O

SECRET WORD: ENDEAVOUR

Answers were as follows:

ACROSS: 1 squint, 4 digestive biscuit, 12 westernize, 13 Richard Nixon, 14 double-stopping, 15 excreted, 16 Christmas pudding, 18 indoor, 20 bumper-to-bumper, 23 tortoise, 24 ameliorate, 25 affections, 27 flatboat, 29 alto saxophones, 31 brains, 32 misappropriating, 35 solidify, 36 military medals, 38 illegitimate, 39 photometer, 40 consolidated fund, 41 carrot.

DOWN: 1 war cl(o)uds, 2 usurpe(d), 3 len(d)s, 4 (s)ins, 5 zoe(a)s, 6 t(r)ip up, 7 v(e)randah, 8 Brentfor(d), 9 chr(o)nics, 10 (t)uxedo, 11 ne(s)t, 17 mortifi(e)d, 19 lo(v)e-songs, 21 idolis(e)r, 22 ta(n)talum, 26 in(s)ider, 28 til(d)es, 30 op(a)led, 33 (s)pout, 34 moc(h)a, 35 sol(e), 37 rod(s).

The diagonals are anagrams of 'Samuel Morse', inventor of the code, and 'Colin Dexter', author of the Morse detective stories. The letters removed from the down entries read 'Odds are dots, evens dashes': interpreting the across answers where odd letters were used in the grid as dots and those where even letters were used as dashes gave the Morse Code sequence for ENDEAVOUR (Morse's long-time secret first name).

(2) Crossword Dedicated to DI Morse and DS Lewis (Dexter 2006a)

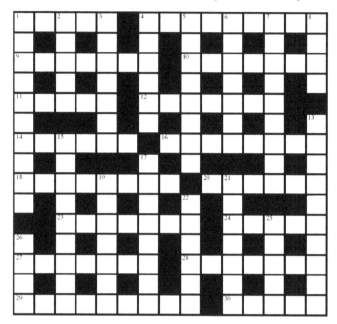

ACROSS

1 Detective Archer is a Sergeant (5)
4 'Hill almost a 100ft.? I start to relapse badly!' (Morse'll want *this*) (9)
9 Unproved proposition: that's the trouble with Morse – without a bit of savvy (7)
10 Where Morse (overweight?) could float around happily (4,3)
11 Enter two from Oxford CID and start of literary career for me (5,6)
12 Strange to argue, causing indignation (7)
14 Rum'd get drunk with *little* hesitation: this is right up Morse's street (6)
16 Troublesome lout? Let Morse loose! (8)
18 Almost the end for Morse – half the jury rated unfit. Change! (8)
20 I? Police chief in Spain and Portugal (6)
23 Of all the Dead, this took first place (7)
24 Morse was never this – unlike Venus de Milo (5)
27 Top car (top on ITV!) broken down – not the colour for Morse … (7)
28 … one monkeying around rarely in a tram (7)
29 Chips for Lewis? The usual _ _ _ _ _ _ _ _ _ with eggs (4,5)
30 Requirements to be born a Detective Sergeant (5)

DOWN

1 Those arriving after closing-time: the French 'tec and Morse unusually (10)
2 Sadly he, Lewis, is missing turn (5)
3 Extraordinary Chief Super (7)

4 Appearances for the writer came with odd parts in *Morse* (5)

5 Screen test for *German* car? No, it crashed (8)

6 Always turning up to catch gangster repeatedly is what Morse likes (4,3)

7 Person with crimes to unravel (9,5)

8 What could make a fine actor (4)

13 With no end of anger, Strange reads sourly: 'You dogs!' … (5,5)

15 … but relieved as criminal ruses are exposed in the end (9)

17 What Lewis did for Morse (8)

19 You'd find dead here – but not from the walls tumbling down (7)

21 Sir Don – a wicked fellow Inspector finally imprisoned (7)

22 See 11ac

25 See 7dn

26 Drink always cropping up in Morse's sabbaticals (4)

Solution

Answers were as follows:

ACROSS: 1. Lewis 4. Chairlift 9. Theorem 10. Dead Sea 11. Colin 12. Outrage 14. Murder 16. Molester 18. Readjust 20. Iberia 23. Service 24. Armed 27. Apricot 28. Tamarin 29. Side Order 30. Needs.

DOWN: 1. Latecomers 2. Wheel 3. Strange 4. Cameos 5. Audition 6. Real Ale 7. Inspector 8. Thaw 13. Great Danes 17. Assisted 19. Jericho 21. Bradman 22. Dexter 25. Morse 26. Bass.

Appendix B
The *Death is Now My Neighbour* Quiz

The following quiz appeared in the *Thames Valley Police Gazette* of, probably, December 1995 (but no later than January 1996) under the heading 'ARE YOU REALLY WISE AND CULTURED?' One needs to imagine that the world is to end in a week's time and this should inform one's answers.

Question One: Given the choice of only four CDs or cassettes, which one of the following would you be likely to play at least once?

- (a) A Beatles album
- (b) Fauré's *Requiem*
- (c) *An Evening with Victor Borge*
- (d) The complete overtures to Wagner's operas

Question Two: Which of these videos would you want to watch?

- (a) *Casablanca* (the film)
- (b) England's World Cup victory (1966)
- (c) *Copenhagen Red-Hot Sex* (2 hours)
- (d) *The Habitat of the Kingfisher* (RSPB)

Question Three: With which of the following women would you wish to spend some, if not all, of your surviving hours?

- (a) Lady Thatcher
- (b) Kim Basinger
- (c) Mother Teresa
- (d) Princess Diana

Question Four: If you could gladden your final days with one of the following, which would it be?

- (a) Two dozen bottles of vintage champagne
- (b) Five hundred cigarettes
- (c) A large bottle of tranquilizers
- (d) A barrel of real ale

Question Five: Which of the following would you read during this period?

- (a) Cervantes' *Don Quixote*
- (b) Dante's *The Divine Comedy*
- (c) A bound volume of *Private Eye* (1995)
- (d) Homer's *Iliad*

Answers given by Lewis:

1. Victor Borge
2. the football
3. Princess Diana
4. the champagne
5. *Private Eye*

Answers given by Morse:

1. Fauré
2. the sex film
3. Kim Basinger
4. the tranquilizers
5. none of them

Both officers give reasons for their choice of answers and any new insights gained into their characters are included under their entries or elsewhere in the text.

Appendix C
Literary Curiosities

This appendix is rather a catch-all for many of the felicities and amusements that DEXTER has recorded. It is clear that Morse loved the English language and such love has often led, indirectly or otherwise, to finding answers to many of the complexities in cases.

A bit clearer/a bit more clearly Lewis uses the former, Morse suggests the latter.

Air-Vice Marshal The correct spelling of the rank (for the then Deputy BURSAR of WOLSEY COLLEGE; CAIN: p86).

Alphabetical Items Three Bs: A phrase used by Morse to characterise public schools – 'bullying, beating, and buggery' (SERV: p136) – in contrast to the traditional three Rs of 'reading, writing, and arithmetic'. Morse refers to the 'alb, biretta and chasuble' as the ABC of ecclesiastical rig (SERV: p163). Beyond Morse, some guides at Lourdes refer to the 'ABC Tour' ('another bloody church'). "What does "P" stand for, sir?" asks Lewis (SERV: p222) and Morse gives him a number of examples based on his crossword experience (including, rather oddly, 'president').

Alternative/choice Morse corrects Strange when he talks of "… quite a few alternatives …" (NEIG: p189). The word should be 'choices' as 'alternatives' give only two options. Strange's Anglo-Saxon reply gives Morse little alternative.

Anagrams Some anagrams are straightforward – *carthorse* and *orchestra*, for example (WEAR: p100; MILE: p153), while others are somewhat more apt (*votes Lenin King* and *Ken Livingstone* or *a name is …* and *amnesia* (JWEL: p143 and NEIG: p106 respectively). Particularly fine is that eleven plus two is the same as twelve plus one (REMO: p263). Sheila POSTER may (or may not) use an anagram for her entry into a writing competition (STOR: p179), as might F.T. DONAVAN under other circumstances (WNCH); so also might Philip LAWSON (SERV: pp158-159). Not all anagrams necessarily work as one would wish – O.M.A. BROWNE-SMITH and Simon Rowbotham perhaps (MILE: p153), or *Truss Neatly To Be Safe* for *Fasten Your Seat-belt* (REMO: p328). Morse is, of course, reluctant to reveal what lies behind his initial of 'E'; this would lie happily (had his second name been Colin) with the coincidence that "EC once in CID" is an anagram of 'coincidence'. Unfortunately, it seems that Morse had no second Christian name. The young Morse was not particularly fast at solving anagrams at school (SERV: p158). An interesting anagram of 'courtesan' is given in CAIN (p55).

Apostrophes There are many places in Oxford that seem to invite the loss or addition of an apostrophe. As far as possible, correct punctuation is used herein: so ST GILES' (but see the entry thereunder) rather than the St Giles that occasionally appears (SERV: pp102-3 for example). Such errors are, of course, minor but in the spirit of Morse's pedantry some mention should be made – and one believes that he would support this. Morse has, for example, a particular bugbear about the parking sign at his block of flats ('Resident's Only') and has already mentioned the error to the Chairman of the Residents' Welfare Committee (REMO: p28). Truss (2003) devotes many pages addressed, in effect, to those who doubt how seriously such matters are taken; her book is subtitled 'The Zero Tolerance Approach to Punctuation'. One guesses that Morse would agree with her and with Fowler's (1968) advice on the difficulties surrounding the possessive case (ANNX: p16).

Boustrophedon The WORKS exhibit a rich vocabulary and it is not the intention of this Companion to act as a dictionary. However, this word (WOOD: p228) is *so* apt in describing the movements of a particular person that a little elucidation is given here. It means, simply, turning alternately from right to left and left to right and is applied to both writing and the movement of an ox when ploughing (from which latter use the word derives). Morse knows (of course) the word (SERV: p249).

Breakthroughs/breaksthrough The latter is suggested, anonymously, as the accurate plural (NEIG: p217). Also, Morse corrects Lewis's *moduses operandi* to *modi* (NEIG: p312). See also GIN AND TONIC.

Burnt Siena/sienna Morse prefers the former; Lewis has checked in Chambers (which gives only the latter: NEIG: p401). Siena is, of course, the correct spelling of the Tuscan city and province. A rare slip by Morse.

Coincidences Morse refers (WEAR: p303; MILE: p143) to the 46th Psalm in the Authorised Version (King James) of the Bible – where the 46th word from the start and the 46th word from the end should, when taken together, spell 'Shakespear'. This 'odd coincidence' has been used, by a few, to claim that Shakespeare may have been an author of that version. The coincidence disappears in the Revised Version. Anyone who spends more than a few hours in counting the 46th words of The WORKS (forwards and backwards) is likely to suffer a mild sense of disappointment if not acute embarrassment. It is, of course, mere coincidence that one learns (on p47 of SERV) that Morse is then 47 years old; a similar coincidence occurs in ANNX on p38 when one discovers that the number of guests at the HAWORTH HOTEL is reduced to 38. And two final examples here – in NEIG (pp88-89) one is introduced to Gerrard, Morse's barber. Gerrard quotes from HARDY's *The Photograph* and this prompts Morse to recall a photograph he had kept in his copy of the *Collected Poems of A.E. Housman* – between pp88-89. And a newspaper report of a murder at 17 BLOXHAM DRIVE (which takes place during a local election) has 'local' as the 17th word from the start and 'election' as the 17th from the end (NEIG: p115). As Morse says: "Coincidence. Life's full of coincidences" (JERI: p154). More precisely, Morse '... always looked upon any coincidence in life as the norm rather than the exception ...' (NEIG: p66). Or, "For me, Lewis, coincidence in life is wholly unexceptional; the readily predictable norm in life ..." (CAIN: p20); Morse is talking here of the number of items in an umbrella stand and the date. He glories in coincidences – that a woman born with name Bonnetti married a man of the same surname would have delighted him (JWEL: pp90-

91). Sarah JONSTONE thinks about the odd coincidence of seeing a word for the very first time only to see it again, in a different context, shortly thereafter (ANNX: p31) and Claire OSBORNE uses the word 'yard-arm' which has been seen by Morse in that morning's crossword (WOOD: p109). It may also be coincidence (or the relative dearth of Swedish surnames) that people named *Engström* and *Fastén* reside in the same block of flats in Stockholm as Irma ERIKSSON and similarly surnamed people work for the Swedish Embassy in London (see the MINOR named entries). And, finally, two cars bear '188J' as part of their number plate (NEIG: p267). Koestler (1972) has some relevant comments.

Dietitian/dietician A dietitian agrees with Morse that the former spelling is preferable (WOOD: pp78-79). Chambers (2003) gives both though suggests a slight preference for dietitian (in putting it before dietician, and out of alphabetical order, in a short list of noun definitions). The New Shorter Oxford (1993) also puts dietitian before dietician.

Farmer Giles (SERV: p113) Rhyming slang for 'piles' (as in haemorrhoids rather than 'lots of'). Also see *Slang* later.

Flouts/flaunts The former means to jeer or to mock and is incorrectly used of Shelly CORNFORD (who is flaunting her breasts one evening) (NEIG: p152).

Forlorn hope Morse is very much aware that the origins of the phrase have a little to do with 'forlorn' but less to do with 'hope'. The derivation is from the Dutch 'verloren hoop' and the translation is 'lost troop' (NEIG: p200) – a body of soldiers selected for a dangerous mission.

'... gone for a Burton' (CAIN: p295). Both Morse and Strange believe the phrase to have something to do with beer, in the sense of going for a (pint of) Burton beer. The phrase, during the Second World War, was RAF slang for a pilot who died in action. Some commentators have cleverly (or deviously) linked this to a series of pre-war advertisements that showed, inter alia, a football team with a member missing (who had gone for a beer) or from the practice of going to Montague Burton, the tailors, to get a suit (in which one may be buried). Of the complicated pulley arrangement (known as the Spanish burton), one must remain silent here (though others have given it as a source of the phrase).

Goodly The word chosen by LAWSON (SERV: p9) to describe his congregation. The word ('fine, excellent, ample' (Chambers 2003) is used in SERV to blur the distinction between 'good' and 'godly'.

Grammar As Bragg (2003: p234) has it: 'Correcting English is one of our great indoor sports.' Morse looks upon the written 'What's you're trouble' as a grammatical monstrosity (JWEL: p170) and corrects Lewis's "... as far as solving murders are concerned ..." to 'is' (NEIG: p182). Morse is, however, by no means perfect – he needs to turn to Fowler to clarify a use of 'should' or 'would' (LBUS: p155) and, "Well, that's them!" says an unwontedly ungrammatical Morse (NEIG: p81).

Harássment/hárassment Morse prefers the second pronunciation (REMO: p53), stating that the former is 'American'. Morse also places the stress on the first syllable of *subsidence* (STOR: p201).

Hidden meanings Two examples here (and both from letters reproduced in the WORKS). In LBUS (pp56-57) a phrase is cleverly buried; another is disguised in NICQ (p84).

Hyphenation There are many excellent examples, ranging from a 'hyper-handkerchief' (JWEL: p58) through 'William-Morris-patterned' (STOR: p171) to 'wraith-like' and 'gin-ridden' (JWEL: p77). Perhaps the finest example of hyphenation occurs in the description of DOWNES as a 'not-quite-top-echelon-public-school-man' (JWEL: pp78-79). The more artificial "you've-gone-and-done-it-once-again" appears in STOR (p202). Max produces a perfect example of tmesis when complaining of the frequency of his lumbago: 'Mid-*every*-bloody-season.' (MILE: p68) though another example of tmesis ('misapprefuckinhension' from CAIN: p190) is rightfully without hyphens as is "QE bloody D, Lewis – as we used to say in the Lower Fourth!" (ANNX: pp234-235). The Assistant Chief Constable uses the phrase "where-bloody-ever" (WOOD: p236) and Morse seeks an 'open-all-day' pub later in the same case (p323).

"I don't give a dam …" Strange uses this phrase and spelling (REMO: p11) when disturbing Morse. Both he and Morse attribute the origin of 'dam' to the name of a small Indian coin. They may well be correct but it is hard to find convincing support. The more usual (and with some backing evidence) is "I don't give a damn" and this is echoed in (choose your own expletive) phrases such as "I couldn't give a flying ....." or "I don't care a ....". Chambers (2003) has 'damn' rather than 'dam' when used in the phrase.

Kingfisher days (REMO: p49) Another name for halcyon days. And halcyon is derived from the Greek for kingfisher (which was once wrongly thought to build its nest on calm seas).

Miss/Mrs/Ms Morse finds the last "… ugly, pretentious, fuzzy …" (CAIN: p254).

Misspelling There are many examples in the WORKS of misspelling – often when Lewis is the perpetrator and Morse the corrector (with the odd lapses by Strange – REMO: p27 – thrown in). Morse is both pedantic and understanding (in the knowledgeable rather than sympathetic sense of the word). He recognises that not all have his educational background and gives examples of what some 'illiterate johnnies' sink to: *egog* for 'hedgehog' and *metantatopi* for 'meat and potato pie' (JERI: p 223). He also mentally corrects a PORTER's note (to 'until' and 'address') while putting in a major stop (MILE: p101). An anonymous love letter to Morse contains the misspelling 'embarassed' (ANNX: p243). The authorship of a note (MILE: p54) is called into question by Morse pointing out the misspelling of the word 'irresistible'. Morse mocks the spelling of 'afficionado' (as opposed to 'aficionado'; NICQ: p128). But Chambers (1993 and 2003) recognises the former though the Shorter OED (1993) only has the latter. Recognised spellings do, of course, change over time and (perhaps) Morse was nearer the mark in 1975.

'nairm' This word appears in a description of Laura HOBSON. Morse is interested in both her and in her accent: '… the broad north-country vowels in 'luv' and 'blunt'; the pleasing nairm she had …' (WOOD: p185). 'Nairm' does not appear in the major dictionaries. There seem to be three options – the word is a typographical error (but for what?), it indicates a flat pronunciation of 'name' in mimicry of a northern accent (but is Laura such a pleasing name?), or the word exists in a dialect form (but means what?).

Name and I/me and name Both may be used but the latter is more common in colloquial English (WOOD: p361). In REMO (p189) Strange uses both 'me and the missus' and 'the missus and me'; Morse prefers 'the missus and I'. In CAIN, Morse corrects '… me and Ashley' to 'Ashley and I' (p283).

Non-questions Morse recalls a number of these (all NICQ: p194):

'When was George Washington assassinated?'
'Who was Kansas-Nebraska Bill?'
'In what year did R.A. Butler become prime minister?'
'Who composed the Trout Quartet?'
'By what name was the Black Prince known when he became king?'

All of these are, of course, effectively nonsense questions (to which there can be no correct answer beyond 'never' or 'nobody' or some such other negative). Perhaps more correctly, as Morse points out, these are questions that cannot be properly asked. It may be worth noting that there is a similarity with the traditional 'Which came first – the chicken or the egg?' as a question that properly has no answer (beyond 'neither'). However, a potentially irrefutable answer used to be supplied to the question 'Which was first, the hen or the egg?' as 'The hen, when God made her.' (Worde 1511).

Overtaken by events An alternative to the normal meaning of the abbreviated medal (ANNX: p163; CAIN: p36).

Post-mortems/post-mortes Morse uses the former plural although he has suggested in the past that the latter is correct (REMO: p187). The plural is later confirmed as the former (p223). Max asks Morse if he thinks of death (*mors* in the Latin). Morse replies "… just add an "e" to the end …" (ANNX: p80).

Prepositions Morse has no blanket objection to a sentence that ends with a preposition and is quite happy with Lewis's: "But where are you going to get a photo from?" (STOR: p199).

Provision Morse mentally corrects a nurse for her use of 'providing' when she should have used 'provided'. A small example, perhaps, but it is followed by this telling text: 'Perhaps he should have told her that she'd meant 'provided', not 'providing'? No! Such things, Morse knew, were no great worry to the majority of his fellow men and women. But they were to him.' (WNCH: p168).

Put back/brought forward In a particular instance – relating to a change in a timetable – the latter is preferred (JWEL: p86).

Quantify/how much Morse, in trying to convince Strange that *how much* time he (Morse) spends in pubs is calculable, inadvertently prompts him (Strange) to use the word *quantify*.

> "A useful word, Morse. It means – well, it means to say how much …"
> "That's just what I said, isn't it?" (WOOD: p5).

Rang/rung Morse receives a letter from Ellie SMITH containing the phrase 'My mum rung me up …'. While the letter contains some fairly devastating news for him, he deals with it thus: "If I ever see her again, Lewis, I shall have to tell her that "rang" is the more correct form of the past tense of the verb "to ring", when used transitively." (CAIN: pp372-373). There is a further reference in CAIN (p53).

Reculer pour mieux sauter Morse casually demonstrates his knowledge of this phrase (NEIG: p362): 'step (or run) back to jump better'.

Registry Office A common mistake for a Register Office (where certain details of births, marriages, and deaths are recorded). A Register Office may also host marriage ceremonies (WOOD: p360). Ashley DAVIES visits the office in NEW ROAD to enquire about such a purpose (CAIN: p276) and Morse corrects SMITH's use of the word 'registry' (p283) and DIXON's (REMO: p320).

Riveting/rivetting During the WNCH case, Morse has occasion to consider the correct spelling (pp29/33). Chambers (2003) allows riveted and riveting and rivetted and rivetting (though the latter two are noted as being in 'former' use): Doyle (1981: p882) records Holmes saying: "One house, and only one, riveted my attention." (*The Adventure of Wisteria Lodge*)[1].

Sergeant/Serjeant These spellings are briefly discussed in JWEL (p287). The former is proper in such as a police sergeant, the latter in Coroner's Serjeant. The latter spelling is usually reserved for various officers in the legal profession – there is a Serjeant at Arms working in the House of Commons and, also, Serjeant's Inn in London; both spellings have exactly the same root – from the Latin *servire* (to serve).

Slang Only two examples are highlighted here. "She may have the decorators in." (CAIN: p46) means she may be having her menstrual period. And "Not as fit as a Stradivarius" is 'not as fit as a fiddle' (CAIN: p60).

Split infinitive Some reference is made (REMO: p14) to this much-debated area of grammar. Both Morse and Strange query the use, in a newspaper report, of the phrase '… to substantially further our enquiries …'

---

[1] Also see wistaria/wisteria later in this section.

Stet Difficilior Lectio Let the more difficult of the readings stand (heading to Chapter 33 of WNCH). The principle commonly applied by editors when faced with variant readings in ancient manuscripts. The principle is useful to Morse in deciphering a report.

"That's me! That is I, if you prefer it." Morse speaking (WNCH: p178).

Trade names DEXTER has been quite precise in his records in giving appropriate brands a capital letter (and examples include Biro, Hoover, Tubigrip, and Xerox).

V m t f y l An abbreviation for 'Very many thanks for your letter' (WOOD: p150). Max uses WASP (for White Anglo-Saxon Protestant) in ANNX (p74).

Who/Whom JWEL: p201. Morse's view of the distinction is crystal clear:

Lewis: "Who are you thinking of, sir?"
Morse: "Of whom am I thinking?" (WOOD: p148).

And in REMO (p390), Morse corrects Lewis's "Who are you thinking of?" to "Of whom am I thinking?" In a later case, Morse speaks to Lewis: "A she of easy virtue who old Felix spent a few happy hours with. Or, as you'd prefer it, with whom old Felix regularly ..." (CAIN: p23). STOR: p197 has:

"According to who, sir?"
"To *whom*, Lewis."

Lewis is corrected again in ANNX (p269). And, further – with Morse speaking: "To find out who knows who – *whom* if you prefer." (NEIG: p138).

Wistaria/wisteria The master's lodge at LONSDALE is 'wisteria-clad' (NEIG: p18). Chambers (2003) gives 'wistaria or more commonly wisteria' and notes that it is named after the American anatomist Caspar Wistar.

You and me/you and I Morse corrects Lewis when he uses the former phrase (REMO: p74).

Plate 91 (Left) Death is eleventh from the top (p238).
Plate 92 (Right) T. E. Lawrence (p248).

Plate 93 (Left) Advertisement in Walton Street (2007) (p249).
Plate 94 (Right) Samuel Pepys (p254).

Plate 95 (Left) Shepherd & Woodward (p258).
Plate 96 (Right) John Thaw as DI Jack Regan in *The Sweeney* (p261).

Appendix D

Minor (Individuals, Firms, and Organisations)

This entry records all those characters appearing in The WORKS (and from *Murder on the Oxford Canal* DENISTON 1978) who seem to have no immediate or future impact on any detective work. The word 'all' needs some qualification – a few, no doubt, have slipped the net and may never be caught here. Further, because this entry may otherwise appear too lengthy (and still might), some candidates for inclusion have been strewn carelessly in the main body of the text.

They are listed alphabetically by either forename or surname (with a reference to the case together with a page number now and again); a few are not included here but appear under other headings (such as, for example, the politicians Benn, Joseph, and Powell who appear under the entry for Morse). Unnamed individuals – such as the 'Maltese dwarf' at the PENTHOUSE CLUB – are not referenced. The occasional firm, organisation, or brand name also appears.

A

Abbott, Mr J From The Royal Grammar School, Chelmsford; attends a conference at LONSDALE COLLEGE (WEAR).

Achilles Ancient Greek hero referred to by BROWNE-SMITH (MILE: p166).

Ackroyd, Miss P From High Wycombe Technical College; attends a conference at LONSDALE COLLEGE (WEAR).

Adams, Arabella An 80-year old living at 19 BLOXHAM DRIVE (NEIG).

Addison Dr He is on the medical staff of the Littlemore Hospital (NICQ); perhaps he has treated both Richard BARTLETT (NICQ) and Dawn CHARLES' mother (NEIG: p16).

Adkinsons A firm of Surveyors, Valuers, and Estate Agents (CAIN).

Aga Khan, The Allegedly (and flippantly) a taxi passenger of Morse's father (JERI).

Aeneas Trojan leader (STOR).

Aguecheek, Sir Andrew A role in *Twelfth Night* (CAIN).

Alaric Leader of the Visigoths in their sack of Rome in 410AD (JERI).

Alexander the Great Macedonian hero (MILE). He is also quoted, by Strange, as an example of a short person (JWEL: p341).

Alf A customer of the JERICHO ARMS; his wife is a source of gossip (JERI).

Allsworth, Wendy A pseudonym (STOR).

Anderson, Gerald A guest, with his wife and two children, at the HAWORTH HOTEL (ANNX).

Anderson, Mr A pruner of the trees belonging to the CROWTHERS (LBUS). His Christian name is not revealed but it could, of course, be Gerald.

Andreasson A flat dweller in Stockholm (WOOD).

Andrews, Fred A guest at the HAWORTH HOTEL (ANNX); he might be a skipper ...

Andrews, Fred ...and visit hotels. The skipper of the *Iffley Princess* (CAIN: p305).

Annabel The wife of the bearded Chairman of the OXFORD BOOK ASSOCIATION (JERI).

Annie, Orphan Morse claims a relative by reference to this cartoon character (WNCH) and Della CECIL thus refers to herself (NEIG).

Ansafone A brand of answering machine; one may be found in Morse's flat (REMO: p148; CALL: p271 calls it an Ansaphone).

Anthony The fiancé of LONSDALE's (unnamed but attractive) college secretary. He is a Research Fellow at that College (MILE).

Archie A dog (NEIG).

Armitage, Rev Neil A curate at ST FRIDESWIDE'S living at 19 Port Meadow Lane (SERV).

Armitage, Peter A former Assistant Commissioner, New Scotland Yard (WOOD).

Armitage, Ronald A drinker of Bulmer's Cider, thief, and inhabitant of the streets of Oxford (ANNX). A fuller description of him appears under HOMELESSNESS. Whether or not he is related to the Rev Neil Armitage is, probably, neither here nor there.

Armstrong-Jones Morse's (deliberate?) mistake for the name 'Llewellyn-Jones' (CAIN).

Armstrong, Louis Jazz musician (REMO).

Artemis A naval sloop (DODO).

Ash Either the name, or the initials, of the author of a ballistics report (NEIG: p133).

Ashton, Jean Chair of Billingdon Rural District Council (CAIN).

Atkinson A police sergeant, removed from active duties because of his hearing problems (REMO).

Attila Leader of the Huns, Scourge of God, and (according to Strange), a short person (JWEL: p341).

Augustus Roman emperor (later deified), victor at the battle of Actium, and, according to Strange, a short person (JWEL: p341).

Austin One of Morse's examiners in GREATS (MILE).

Austin, A (1853-87) Allegedly the author of the SWEDISH MAIDEN poem (WOOD).

Austin, Alfred (1835-1913) Largely unadmired Poet Laureate (WOOD). According to Drabble (1985) '... he was much derided and parodied as a poet.' Harvey (1967) is equally scathing: '... he published twenty volumes of verse, of little merit.'

Austin Reed A shop (REMO).

A-Z A publisher of maps (NEIG).

B

B The sender of a postcard (STOR).

Babington Press A publisher of the Fine Arts and based in South Kensington, London (JWEL).

Baden-Powell, Robert Founder of the Scout movement; a camp-bed of his era, along with clothes fitting a young boy, are found in a loft (SERV: p161).

Bagshaw, Bert A drinker (REMO).

Baines, Mr and Mrs They run a newsagent and tobacconist shop in the BOTLEY ROAD (LBUS). It is unclear whether or not they are related to Mr BAINES, the teacher (WEAR).

Bakelite Originally a brand name but now used generically for phenolic resin products (NEIG: p271). The fascinating Bakelite Museum (at Williton in Somerset) is not, for some reason, mentioned in The WORKS.

Balaguer-Morris, J A dentist in SUMMERTOWN (CAIN).

Baldwin, Jn Esq. An eighteenth century benefactor of ST FRIDESWIDE'S (SERV).

Baldwin, Mary Ann A school contemporary of Valerie TAYLOR (WEAR).

Ballantyre, Jane A mistress (CALL).

Bamsey, Jonas A wharfinger (WNCH).

Banks, Friday A female's pseudonym; Friday is probably a diminutive of Frideswide (CAIN).

Bannister, Mrs A woman working at the LOCALS; she is known (rather unfortunately) for her weak bladder (ANNX).

Bannister, Roger An athlete (NEIG).

Barbara Bray The name of a narrow-boat travelled in by Joanna FRANKS (WNCH).

Bardot, Brigitte An actress and the object of a constable's fantasy (WOOD).

Barnardo, Dr Thomas Founder of a charity for children; John Westerby was a Barnardo boy (JERI).

Barenboim, Daniel Noted pianist and conductor, particularly of the works of MOZART (MILE).

Barker-Barker, the Hon. Amelia A character in a melodrama and played by Ruth RAWLINSON (SERV).

Barnes, Wilfred A private killed at the second battle of EL ALAMEIN (MILE).

Barnett, Augustus A chain of wine merchants (founded by Brian Barnett) with an outlet close to Morse's flat (MILE: p129).

Barron, Alice A troubled 6 year-old (REMO).

Bartlett, Mrs The tallish wife of Thomas BARTLETT (NICQ).

Bayley, Patricia An elderly lady, living at Collingwood in Sheep Street BURFORD. She used to work at the Oxford Eye Hospital (REMO).

Beaulah, Anthony He sends a letter (from Felsted School, Essex) on the SWEDISH MAIDEN verses (WOOD).

Beavers, Mrs A worker at the JERICHO Post Office (JERI).

Beeching, Dr Richard The author of a report that led to massive (and almost certainly irreversible) cuts in rural rail services in the 1960s (REMO: p89).

Belch, Sir Toby A role in *Twelfth Night* (CAIN).

Benedicta, Sister A nun (REMO).

Benham, Augustus Presiding judge at the second trial examining the murder of Joanna FRANKS (WNCH).

Bennett, Jennifer A Geography undergraduate at LONSDALE (MILE).

Benson, John A mechanic (NEIG).

Bergson, Sandra The leader of a sexy, savage, insatiable all-girl gang in *On the Game* (SERV).

Berridge, Sid A police constable on a search detail (WOOD).

Bert Possibly the landlord (or a mere barman) at a WHITE HORSE pub (WEAR).

Bertolese, Luigi The proprietor of the PRINCE WILLIAM HOTEL and a follower of the horses through Ladbrokes Turf Accountants (WOOD).

Bertolese, Maria The obese wife of Luigi (WOOD).

Beryl A sister of Brenda BROOKS (CAIN).

Betty A sister of Celia RICHARDS (JERI).

Bill A grey-haired receptionist at HQ (CAIN).

Bill and Ben Puppets and sometime television stars (REMO).

Birmingham Six A group of 'guilty' prisoners later found innocent (WOOD).

Bishop of Brighton, The A potential attendee at ST FRIDESWIDE'S Annual Parish meeting (SERV).

BiSoDoL A brand of indigestion tablets (NEIG).

Blair, David A Chief Superintendent from the Oxford City Force. He takes over a murder investigation, temporarily, while Morse is in hospital. Morse rates him highly (NEIG).

Blewitt, Alf A drinker (REMO).

Bloom, Molly A character (the main one, some would argue) in *Ulysses* by James Joyce (MILE*)*.

Bloxham, George A captain of a canal boat (WNCH).

Bob A worker at the TOWN AND GOWN ASSURANCE COMPANY (LBUS).

Bobbie A dog (WOOD).

BOMAC A misspelt brand of tractor (REMO: p134).

BOMAG A brand of tractor (REMO: p130). Abbreviated from the Bopparder Machinenbau Gesellscaft, apparently.

Bond, Robert A crew-hand on the boat *Isis* (WNCH).

Bonnetti, Angelo Husband of Georgie (JWEL).

Bonnetti, Georgie Sister of Ginger (JWEL).

Bonnetti, Ginger Member of the HISTORIC CITIES tour; her letter to her sister contains a number of misspellings (JWEL).

Boots A chain of chemists and cosmeticians with a number of branches – including one in Lower SUMMERTOWN (CAIN) and one in BURFORD selling Home Pregnancy Kits (REMO: p100).

Botanical Gardens Properly, the University of Oxford Botanic Garden (REMO).

Botham, Ian Terence A cricketer whose picture hangs in the BOWMAN's house (ANNX). Also, see the second of the footnotes to the entry for George DALEY.

Bott, DC A police officer with the Avon CID (NEIG).

Bowden, John Terence A passenger in a stolen car (WOOD). There is no obvious reason to assume that he is related to Jimmy BOWDEN.

Boycott, Geoffrey A notable Yorkshire cricketer, somewhat better with the bat than the ball (ANNX: p91).

Bridehead, Sue Cousin of Jude Fawley in *Jude The Obscure* (WNCH).

Bridewell, Marion An eight-year-old West Indian girl killed in a car accident on the BROADMOOR LEA estate (WOOD).

Briggs, DI A police officer with the Avon CID (NEIG).

Briggs, Gwendola A gay and somewhat gaudy 65-year old bridge player. She is chairman, secretary, treasurer, hostess, and general organiser of the Summertown Bridge Club (JERI). There is probably an end to her talents.

British Airways An airline (operating a Euro-Class service) and with a Lounge at Heathrow Airport (REMO).

British Diabetic Association An association for British diabetics and a beneficiary under Morse's Will (REMO).

British Legion An organisation whose primary purpose is the welfare of ex-soldiers (MILE: p169) and fund-raising (particularly before Remembrance Day, the second Sunday in November each year) by selling poppies. Such a poppy is thrown into the grave of an unknown (or, at least, unnamed) soldier who had fought from Normandy right through to VE Day (ANNX: p11). The Legion has a club in Lambourn (WNCH: p209), a branch in Swindon (MILE: p169) as well as, of course, most towns.

British Telecom A provider of telephone and other services, including '1471' whereby, on dialling this, one may discover the number of the last call made to that handset (REMO: p193).

Brogan A police constable (NEIG).

Brotherton, Alfred An alias of Alfred Musson (WNCH).

Brown, Mr and Mrs A fictional couple from Hill Top, Eaglesfield, Bristol (LBUS).

Brymer, Jack A classical clarinettist (CAIN); he made a number of recordings of MOZART's Clarinet Concerto.

Buckby, Martin Manager of Property Lettings Services at Finders Keepers (WOOD).

Bull, Jonathan A political candidate (NEIG).

BUPA Originally, the British United Provident Association; a private company in the field of medical care (CAIN).

Burford Garage A purveyor of Unleaded Premium petrol on the A40 (NEIG).

Burgess, Terry A dead councillor (NEIG).

Burke, William A criminal, associated with William Hare. They murdered to provide bodies for medical dissection in early 19th century Edinburgh. Burke's name became a verb meaning 'to murder' (WNCH), especially by smothering.

Burkitt, J The manager of the Summertown Curtaining Company (JERI).

C

Caesar, Julius Roman leader. Morse disdains the kind of finicky brigadier who would sit in Caesar's tent (WOOD: p132); a council of war is called in the same tent by Strange (CAIN: p353); Lewis is summoned under canvas (REMO: p249) and so is Morse, a little later (p273).

Calypso Quartet A group playing at the FRIAR BACON (ANNX). One (at least) of its members (Winston Grant) has beaded dreadlocks; Morse mentally compares them to the snakes that wreathed the head of the stone-eyed Gorgon (p279).

Camcorder A brand of video camera (GOLD).

Carolina Cutie A horse (REMO).

Caroline An assistant-receptionist at the HAWORTH HOTEL (ANNX).

Carrick, Daniel Father of Joanna FRANKS (WNCH).

Carter, DC An officer in the WOOD case.

Carter, PC An officer in the CAIN case.

Carter, Samuel Author of *Travels and Talks in the Antipodes* (Nottingham: Farthinghill Press 1886). His book contains an interview with Walter Towns – and several errors (WNCH).

Cash and Carry Stores A shop in Oxford (WATC).

Ceefax A news and information service (REMO).

Cewanika Barotse chief (CAIN).

Cézanne, Paul A painter (SERV).

Champs Elysées A road in Paris (REMO).

Chantry, Revd Robert Vicar of SUMMERTOWN parish in 1859 (WNCH).

Charisse, Cyd Actress and dancer (NEIG).

Charles, Prince Heir to the throne in 1986 (and later). It is suggested that he would stand a good chance of winning a Prince Charles look-alike contest (ANNX).

Charlie A removal man or, rather, boy (MILE).

Charlie The forename of (probably) a recovery truck driver (WOOD: p388).

Charlie A burglar (WATC). Perhaps a removal boy or truck driver who has gone off the rails.

Chartered Society of Physiotherapy One hopes the name is self-explanatory (NEIG).

Chavasse, John C. A letter writer on the SWEDISH MAIDEN verses; he lives at 21 Hayward Road, Bishop Auckland (WOOD).

Cicero, Marcus Tullius Roman orator, statesman, and writer. BROWNE-SMITH has a bust of him in his college rooms (MILE).

Clarke, Mr Husband of Mrs Clarke; Morse, having looked at the legs of the latter, envies the former (SERV).

Clarke, Mrs A young secretary at the ROGER BACON School (SERV).

Claude and Mathilde A unisex hairdressers in Lower Regent Street (tel: 01-417-8086) (MILE).

Cleopatra Queen of Egypt impersonated by Helen Smith (ANNX).

CND The Campaign for Nuclear Disarmament. Their march from CARFAX to Greenham Common was badly hit by the weather in 1986 (ANNX: p50).

Coleridge, Revd J Master of the Grammar School and vicar of St Mary's (Ottery St Mary); also the father of Samuel Taylor Coleridge (WOOD).

Collins, Jackie An author (NEIG).

Collins, Joan An actress and the object of a constable's fantasy (WOOD).

Comprehensive Assurance Company A firm in Shaftesbury Avenue (tel: 01-417-8081/2/3) (MILE).

Condon, Paul A Metropolitan police officer of high rank and an old friend of Morse (NEIG: p205).

Confucius A Chinese philosopher. Morse recalls the (probably apocryphal) Confucian gibe about the 'impossibility' of rape ('girl with skirts up runs faster than man with trousers down' as being hollow (WNCH: p67). The gibe is also told as a poor joke in LBUS (p95).

Cook, Cyndi A singer (REMO).

Cookson, Catherine A romantic novelist, read by Mrs Purvis (JERI).

Coole, Dr J.P.F. Author of *Carcinoma in the Brain* - a work that has some bearing on a particular case (MILE).

Coombs, Jennifer A resident of PARK TOWN (WOOD).

Cooper, Dr Assistant Curator (Documentation) at the PITT RIVERS (CAIN).

Cooper, Jilly An author (NEIG).

Cooper, Mrs A next door neighbour of the Phillipsons (WEAR).

Corby trouser-press Probably the best known brand of trouser-press in England (REMO; CALL).

Corner Shop A newsagents in Marine parade, Lyme Regis. Here Morse breaks his twin vows – to stop smoking and to avoid newspapers on holiday – and only just avoids (from embarrassment) buying a pornographic magazine (WOOD).

Coronation Street A soap opera (REMO).

Cox An aptly named officer in the Obscene Publications Squad (GOLD).

Cox, Stan(ley) A worker in waste (REMO).

Cram, Steve An athlete; his picture is in the BOWMANS' house (ANNX).

Crawford, Deborah A hostess at 53 Morris Villas, COWLEY (NEIG).

Cremosin A brand of paint (REMO).

Crufts Organisers of dog shows (WOOD).

Curtis, Paul The driver of a stolen car (WOOD).

Cust, Alexander Bonaparte A character in Christie's *The ABC Murders* (NEIG).

D

Daniel, Mr A bank employee (REMO).

David The fiancé of Sue WIDDOWSON; he is a postgraduate metallurgist at Warwick University (LBUS).

Davies, M. A doctor at the SUMMERTOWN Health Centre (JWEL) who has assisted Marion KEMP in the past.

Davies, Sergeant A police officer based at the City Police in ST ALDATES (SERV).

Davis, Steve A successful snooker player (ANNX). Morse attempts to emulate his expertise (WOOD).

Day of the Jackal, (The) A film (from a book) (LBUS).

Death, W.J. The name of a private on the Uganda Monument in BONN SQUARE (SERV: p141). **Plate 91**

Deniston, Margery The wife (soon to be widow) of Wilfred DENISTON (WNCH).

Denniston, Nigel A marker of O LEVEL English scripts (including that of Muhammad Dubal) (NICQ).

Devon Loch A racehorse remembered for failing with the winning-post in sight (REMO).

Dido Queen of Carthage and common crossword answer (STOR).

Disneyland An amusement park in California. Strange thinks Morse is 'in Disneyland again' when a particular theory (propounded by Morse) is seen as rather strange (by Strange) (CAIN: p296).

Disney, Walt A cartoonist (REMO).

Dixon Little is known of this person – presumably a detective – beyond the fact that he (or she) is sent to see if Morse is all right (WNCH: p15). If it is a 'he', then see DIXON.

Dods, Mr A guest at the HAWORTH HOTEL (ANNX).

Dooley, Father A well-read priest from Sligo (NEIG).

Dorothy A worker in the porn industry (WOOD).

DPP The Director of Public Prosecutions – the titular head of the body that reviews and initiates proceedings in criminal cases brought by the police (REMO: p71).

Dring, Eloise A pupil at the PROCTOR MEMORIAL School (CAIN).

Dubal, Sheik Ahmed Ruler of AL-JAMARA (NICQ: p36).

Dubal, Muhammad Son of Sheik Ahmed and a candidate in an overseas SYNDICATE examination in English Language O LEVEL (NICQ).

Duck, Donald Cartoon character (STOR).

Duckham An unsuccessful candidate for a position at the SYNDICATE (NICQ).

Dulux Manufacturers of a brand of paint called Super-White (ANNX: p48).

E

Eagleston, Tom On a conference list (WNCH).

Edberg, Stefan A Swedish tennis-player WOOD).

Eden, Anthony A British Conservative politician active in the 1940's and 1950's. He was, allegedly, the first to speak, in an interview, of a "property-owning democracy" (ANNX: p256) in 1949 (though that interview has not been fully traced here despite an idle hour or two).

Edgeley, Miss Catherine She lives in a flat in Summertown House, is an undergraduate at BRASENOSE (where she reads Jane Austen), and plays bridge (JERI).

Edgeley, Mrs The seriously ill (and then deceased) mother of Catherine Edgeley; she lived in Nottingham (JERI).

Edna A flat-bottomed barge (DODO).

Edwards, Barry A SOCO officer. A number of personal details about him may be found in REMO (pp176-177).

Edward the First Promoter of the Eleanor Crosses (one of which provided the inspiration for the design of the MARTYRS' MEMORIAL (JWEL).

Edward the Third King and father of the Black Prince (the soldier rather than *The BLACK PRINCE*) (LBUS).

Edwina The signatory on a postcard ('Greetings from Paradise Regained – I wish you were here') to Margaret BOWMAN and sent from the Lake District (ANNX: pp223/234). Morse is interested in the reference to *Paradise Regained* and suspects that Edwina may be a pseudonym.

Elaine She works in the porn industry (WOOD).

El Greco A painter with a most distinctive style (CAIN: xviii).

Elite Booking Services A provider of pornographic services (WOOD).

Elizabeth the First Queen of England whose relevance to an Arabian history O LEVEL is questioned (NICQ: p33).

Elizabeth the Second Queen (STOR).

Ellis On a conference list (WNCH).

Elton, DC A large police officer (NEIG).

Emmett On a conference list (WNCH).

Engström A flat dweller in Stockholm (WOOD: p212); do they also work at the Swedish Embassy in London? Also see *Fastén*.

Engström, Ingmar An official at the Swedish Embassy. It may be Ingmar that provides Morse with information about Swedish Civic Registration Numbers (WOOD: pp266/365).

Erotica Press The publishers of *Topless in Torremolinos* (NEIG).

Erskine On a conference list (WNCH).

Essex Young Conservative Association An association of young(ish) Conservatives in Essex (NEIG).

Euro-Ferry A cross Channel operator (JWEL).

Evans, Dick A Sergeant with the British Transport Police and an old friend of Lewis (REMO).

Evans, Mr The sometime bronchitic husband of Mrs A. Evans (NICQ).

Evans, Mrs A. Cleaner to Nicholas QUINN and his predecessors; she cycles to her work (NICQ).

Eve The two-year old daughter of the couple who follow Paul MORRIS into Home Close (SERV).

Ewers, Mr Husband of Susan EWERS; he is unemployed having been made redundant from the RAC in SUMMERTOWN (CAIN).

Eyres, Dr A houseman at the RADCLIFFE INFIRMARY (LBUS).

Ezekiel An Old Testament prophet and book of the Bible (MILE: p250).

F

Fab-Foam The makers, presumably, of the bath preparation in which Sarah JONSTONE relaxes (ANNX).

Farmer, Jack On a conference list (WNCH).

Fastén A resident of Stockholm in a flat (WOOD: p212); do they also work at the London Swedish Embassy? Also see *Engström*.

Fastén, Anders A very junior official at the Swedish Embassy (WOOD; p274).

Favant On a conference list (WNCH).

Favant, Donald (Don) A somewhat suspiciously named character (WNCH).

Fawley, Jude A character in HARDY's *Jude the Obscure* (JERI; ANNX).

Fawley, Sue Unmarried partner of Jude Fawley (ANNX).

Fiddler, The A racehorse (SERV).

Fielding An unsuccessful candidate for a position at the SYNDICATE (despite having achieved a First in History from BALLIOL) (NICQ).

Fielding On the list of a conference to be held at Hendon (WNCH). Perhaps, of course, he is the Fielding mentioned above (who, thwarted in his Oxford ambitions, took a career change from the academic world and joined the police).

Finders Keepers A letting agency (WOOD).

Fiona, (The Fabulous) A stripper in the CORN DOLLY (JERI).

Fiona, (The Fabulous) A stripper in the PENTHOUSE CLUB (WEAR). Perhaps she gets around a lot.

Fisher, Miss A guest at the HAWORTH HOTEL (ANNX).

Fisher, Mrs Winifred She experiences a freak October storm (LBUS).

Fitzgerald, Ella A popular singer (NEIG).

Flikscouten According to Morse, the Swedish Girl Guides (WOOD: p321). Modern foreign languages may not necessarily be his strong point.

Florestan The imprisoned hero of Beethoven's Fidelio, freed in Act Two. Morse feels like him on release from the confines of a hospital bed (WNCH).

Flowers, Bill A senior SOCO officer (REMO).

Foaming Bubbly A brand of bubble bath (JWEL).

Forbes-Smithson, Fiona The name of a honourable lady (one hopes) appearing in *Country Life* (JERI).

Forbuoys A newsagent (REMO).

Formula-One A standard of motorcar racing (REMO).

Fortuna A Roman deity (along with Jupiter and Venus) – the goddess of good luck (recalled by Morse in REMO).

Fowler, Betty An old flame of Howard BROWN (JWEL).

Francis, J A jockey who rides *Thetford Queen* to a win (JWEL).

Franks, Charles An ostler from Liverpool and the second husband of Joanna FRANKS (WNCH). His love for Joanna leads him to turn his back on the accused at the trial for her murder (p97).

Franks, Daniel Younger brother of Joanna FRANKS (WNCH).

Franks, Donald An astrophysicist and a member of LONSDALE (NEIG).

Freeman, Charlie 'Fingers' A member of the Oxford Blues jazz band who lives in KIDLINGTON (ANNX).

Freud, Sigmund Famed (though unappreciated by Morse) Austrian psychoanalyst (CAIN).

Friar's Balsam An aromatic inhalation of benzoic tincture which may ease some respiratory problems (CAIN).

Friends of the Earth An environmental group (WOOD).

Frusemide A synthetic diuretic drug (WOOD).

G

G The signatory to a letter (LBUS).

Gandhi Indian political leader assassinated in 1948 but impersonated by Mr Dods in 1985 (ANNX: p44).

Gardner, Margery A murder victim (heading to Chapter 16: WNCH).

Gascoigne, Douglas Manager of the RANDOLPH HOTEL with an office on the first floor (JWEL).

Gates, Bill Computer industry mogul and billionaire (REMO).

George A claret drinker from TRINITY who inadvertently leads the police to the discovery of a knife (CAIN: p207).

Georges Father of Georgette (JWEL).

Georgette An accident victim who was studying English as a Foreign Language (JWEL).

Gerrard Owner of a hairdressing salon and admirer of Thomas HARDY (NEIG).

Gibbs, Mrs The landlady of John MAGUIRE in London. Morse impresses her with his own style of search warrant (LBUS: p75).

Gibson, Miss The Secretary of the LOCALS; she is (rather marvellously) grey-haired, tight-lipped, and pale-faced (ANNX: p182). She is not impressed by the design of The Locals (which she thinks hardly deserves the Queen's medal for architecture).

Gielgud, Sir John An actor (REMO).

Gilbert, John The son of Alfred GILBERT (and his ex-wife, now living in Salisbury). He read Music at Oxford and obtained a very good 'second' (MILE).

Gill, Eunice 'A lovely girl' at the OUP (STOR).

Gloria Once a stripper at Le Club Sexy. She may well have changed her name and her luck (NEIG).

Godwin, Herbert An attendant at the PITT RIVERS (CAIN).

Golden Surprise A losing racehorse (JWEL).

Gordon A partner of Eileen Stanton (WNCH).

Grable, Betty Dancer and actress (NEIG).

Grace, Dr W.G. Noted early cricketer, impersonated in 1984 by John BINYON (ANNX: p41).

Graham, PC A police officer (NEIG).

Grainger, Robert A well-qualified geologist from Oxford (STOR).

Grainger, Sylvia Wife of Robert (STOR).

Grant, Winston An unemployed musician of 29 Rose Hill Gardens, Oxford where he lives with his wife and four children (ANNX).

Gray, René A professor who lives at 137 Victoria Park Road, Leicester. His attempt to interpret the SWEDISH MAIDEN verses is read in *The TIMES* by Morse while on holiday (WOOD).

Graymalkin A Persian cat (JERI).

Green, Dr Works at the SUMMERTOWN Health Centre (LBUS).

Green, Mr Possibly the occupant of 8 CANAL REACH (JERI: p92). It is likely that he became a mature student at London University (JERI: p301).

Greenaway, Nicholas John The newly named son of Frank and Joyce GREENAWAY (NICQ: p294).

Greenaway, Walter Algernon Known as 'Waggie', he is a patient in the John RADCLIFFE HOSPITAL at the same time as Morse. He is the father of Christine GREENAWAY (WNCH). He reads a book called *The Age of Steam* (possibly irrelevant) and it is unclear whether or not he is related to Frank and Joyce GREENAWAY (also possibly irrelevant). He is keen on CROSSWORDS.

Greenways Waste Management A waste management company (REMO).

Gregson, Dr Philip A practitioner at the COWLEY Health Centre (CAIN).

Grimes, A The owner of a locksmith's shop in JERICHO (JERI).

Grimshaw, (John) Atkinson A Victorian painter; reproductions of two of his dockside paintings adorn the office of QUINN (NICQ). Also see *His Flat in Oxford* under the main entry for Morse.

Gruby, Mrs A woman as miserable as her surname suggests (WOOD).

Gryce A senior schoolteacher from Bradford (NICQ: p83).

Guildford Four A group of 'guilty' prisoners later found innocent (WOOD).

GWR Preservation Society A society keen to keep alive the memories and rolling stock of the Great Western Railway (JWEL).

H

Halford Cycles A shop on the COWLEY ROAD (CAIN).

Halford, Roy Concierge at the RANDOLPH HOTEL and recipient of the British Empire Medal from the Queen; he joined the staff as a page-boy in 1945 and has worked there for the last 45 years (JWEL).

Harden, Roy The Senior Concierge at the RANDOLPH in 1994. Obviously, there is a tradition of hotel staff being called Roy (CALL).

Hardiman, Lady A peeress with an interest in polo (NEIG).

Hardiman, Lord A peer with an interest in the salacious (NEIG).

Harding, Louisa Thomas HARDY had an infatuation for her in his early life (ANNX: heading to Chapter 35) and often visited her unmarked grave (JWEL: heading to Chapter 50) in Stinsford (WOOD: p50).

Hardinge, Sarah The young daughter of Alan HARDINGE, killed by an articulated lorry while on her bicycle (WOOD).

Harrison A Constable in 1859 (WNCH).

Harrison, Joseph Allen Father of Frank HARRISON (REMO).

Hartwell's Motors A garage (NEIG).

Hawkins, Joseph A short-lived child (JERI).

Hawkins, Mr and Mrs A couple in North London; they adopted Joseph Hawkins (JERI).

Hawtrey, Eliza M The author of a monograph on JERICHO (JERI: p89).

Heath, Neville George Clevely A possible murderer (heading to Chapter 16: WNCH).

Height, Sally The daughter of Monica HEIGHT who takes (and re-takes) exams at Oxford High School (NICQ).

Heisenberg, Werner Karl A German physicist; Morse has a rudimentary grasp of Heisenberg's 1927 uncertainty principle (WOOD).

Helpston, DC An officer in the WOOD case.

Hertz Rent-A-Car A car hire firm in the WOODSTOCK ROAD (JWEL).

Heyer, Georgette A romantic novelist, read by Mrs Purvis (JERI) and Marion KEMP (JWEL).

Hickman, Sara A tall, slim, and attractive Deputy Manager (originally from Leicestershire). Perhaps she looks a little like Georgette Heyer.

Hill, William A firm of bookmakers (REMO).

Hillier, Monty Sometime President of an athletics association (REMO).

Hills, Jennifer A mistress of Charles RICHARDS (JERI).

Hills, Keith Husband of Jennifer Hills (JERI).

Hitler, Adolf A Fascist dictator of Germany. Lewis feels like a deaf man watching a film of Hitler addressing a Nuremburg rally while Morse rants (JERI: p236).

Ho, Susan A Chinese researcher at Oxford's Criminological Department (REMO).

Hodges, DC A police officer instructed to interview some guests; he is astute enough to recognise that Morse occasionally has the odd erotic fancy (JWEL: p128). A uniformed Sergeant Hodges appears in BAGG, some two years after the JWEL case and they may be one and the same.

Holmes, Kenneth A late husband (REMO).

Holmes, Mr Warden of the Riverside Club (or Centre) (CAIN).

Hornsby, Dr Clive He is Senior Reader in Social Sciences at LONSDALE COLLEGE and worried about the pressures put upon students (CAIN).

Hoskins The name by which a porter of a block of flats wishes to be known (MILE).

Hoskins, Arnold An Oxford coroner (CAIN).

Hovis A brand of bread (REMO).

Hudson, Marilyn A chamber-cum-kitchenmaid (NEIG).

Hughes, Anthony A passenger on the Iffley Princess (CAIN).

Hughes, James The young son of Anthony (CAIN).

Hurley, Ailish An Irish barmaid at the RANDOLPH (and Morse's favourite) (REMO).

Hurricane Georges A 1998 meteorological phenomenon (REMO).

I

Iffley Princess A pleasure-steamer on the Thames (CAIN).

Imbert, (Sir) Peter One time Chief constable of the THAMES VALLEY POLICE (1979-1985); at the time of the WNCH case, he is the Commissioner of the METROPOLITAN POLICE (p81). He backs a report suggesting that records of missing persons are so inaccurate that they should be scratched and started over again (WOOD: p289). He is keen on Verdi (particularly the Karajan recording of *Don Carlos*) and invites Morse to visit him in America (NEIG: p344).

Imperial War Museum A museum in South London but with 'branches' elsewhere (DODO).

International Information Computer A source (apparently available to car hire firms) that can verify such things as credit cards, driving licences, and home addresses (JWEL: p286). Its very existence is, however, a little hard to verify.

IRA (Irish Republican Army) Morse's cod Irish accent – to a hotel receptionist - arouses suspicion that he may be a member (ANNX).

Ireson, Julie Careers mistress at the Cherwell School (WOOD).

J

Jack The first of a list of male names (continuing with *James, Jason, Jasper, Jeremy, John, Joseph,* and *Julian*) that may be seen as tedious to repeat here (NEIG: p111).

Jack the Ripper Nineteenth century murderer (WNCH and REMO; in the latter case, Morse recognises the reference to the 1870s as inaccurate). A book (*Who was Jack the Ripper?*) is mentioned in passing in LBUS.

Jacobs, Mrs She lives, with her family, in BLOXHAM DRIVE (NEIG).

Jaeger A clothing manufacturer (WOOD). McCLURE wears one of their products (CAIN) as does JAMES (NEIG).

Jardine, Mrs The owner or rentier of a number of properties in KIDLINGTON (NICQ).

Jarnell, Joseph Witness in the second Joanna FRANKS murder trial (WNCH).

Jarnold, 'Jammie' A waste operative (REMO).

Jayne A worker in porn (WOOD).

Jeacock, Mr A co-operative and neatly competent postmaster in CHIPPING NORTON (ANNX).

Jenny Her partner is 'Keith'; her lover is Charles RICHARDS (JERI).

Jenny A friend living in NORTH OXFORD of Sarah JONSTONE (ANNX).

Jezebel A potential name to complete 'J' appearing in a torn letter (MILE).

Joanna A potential name to complete 'J' appearing in a torn letter (MILE).

Johns, Anthony QC Appears for the defence in the trial of Ruth RAWLINSON (SERV).

Johnson A cat (STOR).

Johnson, Dr Samuel Extracts from his works have a number of references in the WORKS; he is mentioned textually as 'an interesting man' (WOOD: p103).

Jones, Carole A pupil at the ROGER BACON school (SERV) who enjoys a glass or three of Babycham.

Jones, Karen A young lover (JWEL).

Jones, Mrs A resident of Cardigan Street in JERICHO (JERI).

Josephine A secretary at RICHARDS BROTHERS (JERI).

Judith The prim confidential secretary to PALMER (LBUS).

Judith A potential name to complete 'J' appearing in a torn letter (MILE).

Judith A slimly attractive personal assistant to Miss Gibson at the LOCALS (ANNX: p196).

Julie Morse's secretary (LBUS).

K

Karen A girl's name (CAIN).

Kate, Kinky A stripper at the PENTHOUSE CLUB (WEAR).

Kathy Another girl's name (CAIN).

Katie She is on the books of the Elite Booking Services agency (WOOD).

Keith Partner of 'Jenny', his absence in South Africa facilitates her potential liaison with Charles RICHARDS (JERI).

Kelly She is involved in the porn industry and appears to be on the books of the Elite Booking Services agency (WOOD).

Kennedy, Helena QC A leading barrister who champions civil liberties and promotes human rights. It is clear that Morse has a great deal of respect for her abilities (CAIN: p333). She has written on a wide range of subjects and is a regular broadcaster.

Kennedy, John Fitzgerald Former American President (REMO).

Kennedy, May A shopkeeper in LOWER SWINSTEAD (REMO).

Kenya Police The BEAR pub has one of their ties (NEIG).

Kimberley She is on the books of the Elite Booking Services agency (WOOD).

Kimmons Typewriters An Oxford firm who, not surprisingly, repair TYPEWRITERS (LBUS).

Kinder, John A blind amateur actor (SERV).

Kinder, Mrs Widow and mother of John Kinder (SERV).

King, Bob A courteous car park attendant (ANNX).

Kinsey, Dr Alfred A sex researcher, compared unfavourably by Morse to KIPLING (WEAR: p165).

Kirsty A girl's name (CAIN).

Klee, Paul An abstract painter (CAIN).

Klimt, Gustav A non-abstract painter (NEIG).

Krafft-Ebing, Richard A nineteenth century psychiatrist, famous for his studies of sexual perversion (REMO).

Kraft A Stockholm flat-dweller (WOOD).

Krebs, Hans A biochemist who discovered the urea cycle of metabolism (CALL).

Kronquist, Sam A member of the HISTORIC CITIES tour with incipient prostate trouble. This is probably unconnected to his reading of 1991 *The Good Beer Guide* (JWEL).

Kronquist, Vera Married to Sam and known to him as 'Birdy'. She is a reader of *Lark Rise to Candleford* and the magazine *Country Life* (JWEL).

Krooklok A brand of car immobiliser (WATC).

Kylie One of the many 'K' girls on the books of the Elite Booking Services agency (WOOD). An otherwise unidentified Kylie is mentioned in CAIN; Morse has (just about) heard of the Australian pop singer Kylie Minogue.

L

Lancaster A brand of pistol. The .577 heavy-calibre revolver was also known as a 'howdah pistol' from its occasional use while travelling on the back of an elephant (NEIG).

Lauren A mistress (REMO).

Laurenson, Agnes Wife of Matthew (WNCH) who travelled a short distance on the canals with Joanna FRANKS.

Laurenson, Matthew A wharfinger at TOOLEY'S YARD (WNCH).

Lawrence of Arabia Soldier and author (and a potential subject for a new sort of O LEVEL; NICQ: p33). T.E. Lawrence had some solid links to Oxford – an undergraduate at JESUS, a graduate at MAGDALEN, and a FELLOW of ALL SOULS. Also see POLSTEAD ROAD. He is also impersonated by a guest at the HAWORTH HOTEL (ANNX: p47). Morse visits his grave at Moreton, Dorset while on holiday (WOOD: p86). **Plate 92**

Lawson, Mr and Mrs Parents of Lionel and Philip LAWSON. They were killed in an air crash in Zagreb (SERV).

League of Friends, The A charity working in hospitals (REMO).

Learoyd, DC A police officer (NEIG).

Lee, Albert A lock keeper (WNCH).

Lee, Joanna The wife of Albert Lee (WNCH).

Len A customer of the JERICHO ARMS (JERI).

Levi and Goldstein Antiquarian booksellers in the Tottenham Court Road (tel: 01-417-8087) (MILE).

Levi, Dr S. A resident of PARK TOWN (WOOD).

Levin, Bernard Journalist (particularly for *The TIMES*) who was overly (if not excessively) fond (according to BROWNE-SMITH) of using brackets (MILE: p167).

Lewis, C.S. An Oxbridge man (with a little more of the ox than the bridge), academic, and author. He regularly drank, with others, in the EAGLE AND CHILD (ANNX).

Lewis, W.H. Brother of C.S. Lewis and co-drinker (ANNX).

Liebermann, Professor M An academic at LONSDALE College who holidays in Zurich (MILE).

Lilo A brand name of an inflatable mattress (WOOD).

Lindy-Lu One of the many workers involved in the porn industry (WOOD).

Lit and Phil Society Sheila WILLIAMS is a member (JWEL). It is unclear whether the Society promotes Literary and Philosophical endeavours or those of Literature and Philosophy.

Littlewoods A company running a football pools scheme (ANNX).

Llewellyn-Jones, Gareth A tutor at LONSDALE (CAIN).

Lloyd, G.W. A Welsh optician, originally from Mountain Ash, with a business in the High Street, Reading (ANNX).

Lloyds A bank with many branches and an Inspection Department near Bristol (NEIG).

Lone Ranger, The Morse forgetfully refers (twice) to David MICHAELS as this fictional cowboy character (WOOD).

Longford, Lord A peer, much interested in prison reform and the rights of prisoners (ANNX).

Lord High Executioner A character from Gilbert and Sullivan's *The Mikado* (and impersonated by John BINYON) (ANNX: p43).

Loren, Sophia An Italian actress (REMO).

Lotus House Margaret BOWMAN and Gladys Taylor enjoy a meal at this Chinese restaurant in the BANBURY ROAD (ANNX).

Louisa or Louise (both spellings appear) A worker in the porn industry (WOOD) who bears an uncanny resemblance to Claire OSBORNE.

Lowe, Angela A school contemporary of Valerie TAYLOR (WEAR).

Lucan, Lord A peer of the realm who absconded in 1974 (REMO) rather than the 3rd Earl who fought in the Crimean War.

Lucy A child with a doll called Amanda (WOOD).

Lumley, George A purveyor of tea in earlier days. His products were advertised at 1s 2d in Derby (WNCH: p222). Quite bizarrely, a similar faded sign can be found today, high up on a wall in WALTON STREET (though the price had risen to 2s 6d). **Plate 93**

Luxicars A firm of taxi operators in Oxford (JWEL: p170).

M

MAC A driving school (LBUS).

Mackenzie Construction A firm employing, inter alia, Edward WILKINS (ANNX).

Mackenzie, David A fat and mathematical member of LONSDALE (NEIG). He is also (probably) a patient at the Diabetes Centre (REMO: p37).

Madame Tussaud's A famous waxworks exhibition, favourably compared to the figures in the OXFORD STORY (JWEL).

Maddison, Katharine An assistant to Hannah McNeil when removing Joanna FRANK's clothing (WNCH).

Madigan, Elvira The eponymous heroine of a 1967 film. Its redolent theme is the second movement of MOZART's Piano Concerto in C major (K 467) (MILE).

Madonna An actress and pop singer and the object of a constable's fantasy (WOOD).

Maharaj Ji A possibly fake guru who appears on a poster (WEAR).

Mainwearing, Olive A brain tumour causes her to behave in an extraordinary manner – perhaps upsetting the citizens of Manchester (MILE: p122).

Mandy A cleaner at the HAWORTH HOTEL responsible for replenishing the sachets of Nescafé and the tubs of Eden Vale milk (ANNX: p82). She also works as a stand-in barmaid.

Mandy She works in the porn industry (WOOD); while 'Mandy' may well be a pseudonym, she may (of course) also work as a cleaner and a stand-in barmaid.

Mann, Thomas A writer tediously cited at a party (ANNX).

Marcinkus, Archbishop Paul Allegedly, a link between the Mafia and the Vatican City (ANNX).

Marlow, Norman His critical commentary, *A.E. Housman*, is cited by Potter (MINOR) (WOOD).

Marrinan, Tony Manager at the RANDOLPH in, at least, 1998 (REMO).

Marsden, Sylvia (née Prentice) A mother (REMO).

Marshall, Gilbert QC Appears for the Crown in the trial of Ruth RAWLINSON (SERV).

Martha Presumably, the partner of Brian Richardson (NICQ: p83).

Marx, Karl Philosopher buried in Highgate Cemetery; a postcard of his tomb is sent by BOWDEN to ASHENDEN (JWEL: p12).

Mary The flatmate of Jennifer COLEBY and Sue WIDDOWSON. She is freckled and dumpy and works for RADIO Oxon (LBUS).

Mary A person mentioned in a letter written by Matthew (WNCH).

Mary She works in the porn industry (WOOD). There is nothing to stop someone who is freckled and dumpy working in such an enterprise (tastes in pornography being what they are) but no link is apparent between this Mary and the flatmate of Jennifer COLEBY.

Matthew The author of a letter in which Mary is mentioned (WNCH).

Matthews, Dr David A Senior Consultant at the Diabetes Centre in the RADCLIFFE INFIRMARY (NEIG).

Maxim, Dr O.V. A cancer specialist (NEIG).

Maxim Removals A firm of hauliers (REMO).

May, Bishop A member of the University Mission to central Africa (CAIN).

Mayo, Mrs Philippa Janet From California, she is in Oxford researching the novels of Anthony Trollope. Unfortunately, she is also killed in a car crash; her death has much relevance to certain members of the HISTORIC CITIES tour (JWEL).

McBryde, Dr Alasdair An Australian resident of PARK TOWN. He is known to have drunk in the EAGLE AND CHILD and does not remain a resident in Oxford for too long (WOOD).

McCartney, Paul A famous pop singer and musician, he appears in a list of 'p m's' that Morse runs through his mind (SERV: p120).

McNeil, Hannah A serving woman at the PLOUGH in 1859 (WNCH).

McSevich, Manuel A talented photographer, well known to Morse. He has a studio in the High Street, ABINGDON (GOLD).

Measor, Jeff A company secretary (REMO).

Medusa A Gorgon (various references including JWEL: p238).

Melhuish A young and bearded Junior Fellow at LONSDALE COLLEGE (LBUS).

MENSA An organisation; its membership is restricted to those with a high IQ (CAIN).

Menzies A firm providing bookstalls at many railway stations (including Oxford and PADDINGTON) (WOOD).

Mercator, Gerardus Flemish geographer; WESTERBY has a bust of him in his college room which ends up in a recess to the east of High Table at LONSDALE (MILE).

Meyer, Dr The aged headmaster of a public school, possibly Uppingham, attended by the LAWSON brothers (SERV).

Michelle A bouncy brunette barmaid from the RANDOLPH (JWEL).

Midland A bank (NEIG).

MI5 and MI6 Intelligence departments of the British Government (WNCH).

Millie A burglar (WATC).

Mingella, Steve A character in the book *The Blue Ticket* (into which Morse dips while in hospital) (WNCH).

Mitchell, Bob A slightly out-of-condition officer with the British Transport police (REMO).

Mitty, Walter A character (created by James Thurber) who lives in a world of his own fantasies (CAIN).

M.L.O. A set of initials appearing on an envelope (REMO). The last two are probably 'letter office' and the first may be 'main'. There comes a point when such matters are possibly best left unexplored.

Mobiloil A brand name of a motor oil (WOOD).

Mona Lisa A work of art so valuable and famous that, effectively, it cannot be stolen and then sold (JWEL).

Monet, Claude Impressionist painter; OWENS has a reproduction of one of his miserable-looking haystacks (NEIG).

Monopolies Commission A UK Government organisation, existing to ensure free competition. Laura HOBSON refers to it while contemplating how much Morse has monopolised her thoughts (WOOD: p256).

Monroe, Marilyn A blonde actress of whom Morse has heard. The BOWMANS own two illustrated books about her (ANNX) and Ellie SMITH has a life-sized photograph of her (CAIN).

Monroe, Sally A young letter-writer on the SWEDISH MAIDEN verses (WOOD) from 22 Kingfisher Road (sic), BICESTER. Also see St Giles (MINOR).

Morecambe (Eric) and Wise (Ernie) A popular comedy duo (NEIG).

Morley, Joe A customer of the JERICHO ARMS, 'vast-bellied' and partial to GUINNESS (JERI).

Morris, Audrey A worker at a YWCA hostel and sister to Michelle Thompson (WOOD).

Morris, Peter A 17-year old, unrelated to Paul MORRIS, who buys a book from the OXFAM shop (SERV).

Morrison, Inspector A police officer (CAIN).

Morrow, Lieutenant Al An American police officer (somewhat overweight) and a reader of *The Finer Arts of Fly-Fishing* (JWEL).

MOT Ministry of Transport and now shorthand for the regular test that all motor vehicles must pass to remain on the road (CAIN).

Mother Teresa See Teresa, Mother.

Mouse, Mickey A cartoon character (REMO).

Murdoch, Mrs Mother of Michael and Edward MURDOCH (JERI) and hostess of the party where Morse meets Anne SCOTT.

Music Club Library Morse joins this club simply to get 2 free CDs (NEIG).

Musson, Alfred Crew member of the *Barbara Bray (WNCH)*.

Mustard, Colonel A character in Cluedo (ANNX: p34).

N

Napoleon French emperor, renowned military tactician and strategist, and (according to Strange), a short person (JWEL: p341). There is a further reference to the Emperor and Austerlitz in STOR.

NASA The National Aeronautics and Space Administration (STOR).

National Lottery Begun in 1994 to raise funds for good works and profits for its organisers. Morse is aware (in 1996 at least) of its existence and Lewis imitates its crossed-fingers logo as a sign of luck (NEIG).

National Trust, The An organisation dedicated to the preservation of buildings and the landscape (MILE).

NATO (North Atlantic Treaty Organisation) An international military body that exercises (at least) in Belgium (NEIG: p285).

Natwest Properly, NatWest. A bank (National Westminster) (NEIG).

Neighbourhood Watch A voluntary scheme that encourages neighbours to look out for any suspicion of criminal activity (WNCH: p169; NEIG: p121).

Nelson, Horatio Famed English naval commander, victor at Trafalgar, and (according to Strange), a short person (JWEL: p341).

Nescafé A brand of coffee (usually instant) and known to Morse (NEIG).

Newton, Josie (Josephine) Estranged wife of Paddy FLYNN and mother of two daughters (REMO).

Nielsson, Inga The incomparable star of *The Nymphomaniac* shown at STUDIO 2 (NICQ).

Nightingale, Florence A nurse of the Crimean War era. It is thought that she would find few faults with the nursing skills of Brenda JOSEPHS (SERV: p219).

Noakes, Charles The young caretaker at the SYNDICATE who works until 7.30pm each evening of his duty (NICQ).

Norris, Frederick A sorter of Her Majesty's mail in CHIPPING NORTON (ANNX).

Norris, Queenie Resident at 11 BLOXHAM DRIVE with her Cavalier King Charles dog (NEIG).

Nottinghamshire and Midlands Friendly Society Employers of Daniel Carrick (WNCH).

Novelty Emporium Its ranks of fruit machines (in Lyme Regis) fail to tempt Morse (WOOD).

NSPCC A charity concerned with the welfare of children (CAIN and REMO).

O

Oldfield, Jack 'Rory' Captain of the *Barbara Bray* (WNCH).

Old Wykehamists' Classical Association The possessors, perhaps though unlikely, of a particularly distinctive tie (NEIG: p82).

Olsson A dweller in a flat in Stockholm (WOOD).

Olympia An exhibition hall in London where a Beer Festival is held (REMO).

Olympic Games, The Included here purely to record the image of a large plane poised and ready for take-off being like a long-jump finalist in the said Games (ANNX: p285).

Open University Created in 1969 to provide home-based and distance learning (NEIG: p273).

Orphan Annie See Annie, Orphan (though it is one of the least exciting entries).

Orpheus A mythical character; Morse feels like him when emerging from the depths of Piccadilly Circus underground station (NEIG: p205).

Osborne, Cassandra Samantha Perhaps the mother of Claire OSBORNE (WOOD).

Oxfordshire, Buckinghamshire, Berkshire Athletics Association An athletics association, once running races at Cutteslowe Park (REMO).

Oxfordshire Building Society An organisation with a branch, at least, in CHIPPING NORTON from which Margaret BOWMAN makes a withdrawal (ANNX).

P

Palmer A police officer (STOR).

Palmer The name of a family living in Gloucestershire (REMO).

Palmer (Junior), Cyrus C. A citizen of Pasadena and sometime owner of the WOLVERCOTE TONGUE (JWEL).

Palmer, Philip The pseudonym used by Morse when booking into the GREAT WESTERN HOTEL (ANNX).

Pan Am An airline (JWEL).

Paolo A hairdresser (or his salon) visited by Monica HEIGHT (NICQ).

Paper Lemon A group providing live music at the HAWORTH HOTEL (ANNX: p22).

Parker, Dr A doctor at the SUMMERTOWN Health Clinic (NICQ: p211-13).

Parkes, Mr An old former headmaster now living in the WOODSTOCK ROAD; he plays bridge, is keen on codes and puzzles, and receives help from the Ferry Centre social workers. His wreath, from the Bridge Club, has twenty-two signatures (JERI).

Paula A lady of dubious virtue (MILE).

Pembroke A statue of the third Earl stands in the QUADRANGLE OF THE SCHOOLS (WNCH). He was Chancellor of the University 1617-1630.

Pepys, Samuel Famed diarist (SERV: p221) and graduate of MAGDALENE. **Plate 94**

Pete A boyfriend of Valerie TAYLOR (WEAR).

Pettiford, J A tobacconist in Piccadilly (tel: 01-417-8080) (MILE).

Philip II of Macedon Father of Alexander the Great. BROWNE-SMITH is preparing a book on his life and WESTERBY appears to send a postcard (postmarked Hellas) to LONSDALE College showing the remains of his palace (MILE).

Philips, Dr He is involved in the treatment of Michael MURDOCH (JERI).

Phillips A private in action at the second battle of EL ALAMEIN (MILE).

Phillipson, Howard The Literary correspondent of *The TIMES* (and possibly related to Philip Howard of that same journal). He plays an active part in reviewing the letters received in the WOOD case.

Phillotson, Richard A schoolteacher who marries Sue Bridehead in *Jude The Obscure* (WNCH). No relationship can be traced between this fictional character and DCI PHILLOTSON.

Pickford and Co. A firm that organised 'fly boats' (travelling round the clock, with a double crew working shifts) on the canal system (WNCH).

Ping Hong Restaurant To be found in BREWER STREET (telephone: 01-417-8085) (MILE); there is no further information on what type of cuisine is available.

Pippa A child of a wartime liaison (JWEL).

Plumeridge Simply a name in a telephone directory (JERI).

Plummer, Anthony An organ scholar at LONSDALE (NEIG).

Police Protection Order An order designed to improve behaviour (REMO).

Pollard Simply a name appearing (twice) in a telephone directory (JERI).

Polyfilla A brand of plaster and wood filler (LBUS).

Popper Simply a name appearing in a telephone directory (JERI).

Porridge A popular situation comedy, the situation being a prison (NEIG and REMO).

Portakabin A brand of temporary building (REMO).

Postill, Lt. Colonel Reginald Residing at 6 Baker Lane, Shanklin (on the Isle of Wight), he writes to *The TIMES* on the SWEDISH MAIDEN case and criticises the public investigation (WOOD).

Potter, J. Gordon A letter-writer on the SWEDISH MAIDEN verses; he lives at Arlington, Leckhampton Road in Cheltenham (WOOD).

Prentice, Mrs (née Jones) A mother and grandmother (REMO).

Presley, Elvis A legend of popular music; a collection of his records could be purchased via a card in a newsagent's window in Reading (ANNX).

Price, Agnes Elderly and widowed resident of 11 CHAUCER CRESCENT (BURG).

Price, Angela A resident in COLEBOURNE ROAD (MILE).

Price, Marcus A Fellow of ALL SOULS (WATC).

Price, Mr The husband of Angela Price (MILE).

Prince Consort Albert, husband of Queen Victoria (CAIN).

Prior, Mr James A security officer at the LOCALS (ANNX).

Pritchard, Tom A car hire firm manager (JWEL).

Protagoras A Greek philosopher (REMO).

Proust, Marcel French author (REMO).

Prudential An insurance company used by Morse (WNCH).

Purvis, Mrs Elsie The occupant of 7 CANAL REACH (and owner of a cat called Graymalkin) who, crucially, allows Morse to visit her back garden (JERI).

Pythagoras Greek mathematician (REMO).

Q

QE2 A very large ship (REMO).

Queen's Medal Properly, the Queen's Police Medal – an award for gallantry (REMO).

Quick Snack A rail station buffet (NEIG).

Quinn, Mr and Mrs The parents of Nicholas QUINN from Huddersfield.

R

Racquel Name of hostess in the FLAMENCO TOPLESS BAR (MILE).

Raffles A gentleman-burglar (WATC).

Randy, Ray, and Rick The members of the popular 3 R's entertainment trio (REMO). How the band got its name is not revealed.

Ratcliffe Infirmary One hopes a simple typographical error (REMO: p305).

Raven, Mr and Mrs A couple living in SQUITCHEY LANE. Mrs Raven plays bridge (JERI).

Rawlinson, Sergeant Joseph An officer at ST ALDATES, he is married with a 15-year-old son (WOOD).

Rayner, Polly A letter-writer on the SWEDISH MAIDEN verses; she is president of the WOODSTOCK Local History Society (WOOD).

Rayson, Nina Wife of Richard (CAIN).

Rayson, Dr Richard A Chaucerian scholar and fellow of TRINITY COLLEGE (Oxford) who lives in DAVENTRY AVENUE (CAIN).

Reading Motors A garage in Reading where John Smith sells a BMW car cheaply (ANNX).

Redford, Robert A blond actor (of whom Morse has not heard). The BOWMANS have a book in the *Hollywood Greats* series about him (ANNX).

Reeves, Beryl A cleaner, from Manchester, working at the RANDOLPH HOTEL (JWEL).

Rembrandt An artist (LBUS).

Removals Anywhere The name of a company owned by Albert GILBERT (MILE).

Rice, Colin A site manager at a waste centre (REMO).

Richard, Gillian A letter-writer on the SWEDISH MAIDEN verses; her address is 26 Hayward Road, Oxford (WOOD).

Richards, Father An old priest at St Michael and All Angels (WOOD: p245) and confessor to both Margaret DALEY and Karin ERIKSSON (though definitely not at the same time).

Richards, Viv A skilled cricketer, particularly with the bat (ANNX).

Richardson, Brian A schoolteacher from Bradford; married, one guesses, to Martha (NICQ: p83; 99).

Richardson, Mr and Mrs Their letter to *The SUNDAY TIMES* prompts Morse to seek a back issue (WEAR).

Ridgeway, Dr A micro-biologist from BALLIOL. Ill health means he is not considered for the Mastership of LONSDALE (NEIG).

Ridgway, Maxine A mistress (42 years old) *and* a law professor from Yale (REMO). And there are not too many of those.

Ringer, The A pseudonym (REMO).

RNLI The Royal National Lifeboat Institution; a charity that provides 24-hour assistance to those in peril on the sea (WOOD).

Roberts, PC A police officer (CAIN).

Robinson, Ann (sic) Morse's flippant alternative (as 'Ann Robinson') for 'before you can say Jack Robinson' (CAIN). The TV presenter is properly named Anne.

Roblin, Paul An Oxford (medical) doctor (CAIN). Morse consults him over his suspicion that he has diabetes (NEIG) and he is kept informed of Morse's progress (REMO).

Robson, Anna Wife of James (WNCH).

Robson, James A keeper of a lock (WNCH).

Rodney A short-lived Rottweiler dog (REMO).

Ronay, Egon A food critic (NEIG).

Rosemary An undergraduate at LONSDALE COLLEGE (MILE).

Rowena A party guest (JERI).

RSPB The Royal Society for the Protection of Birds (WOOD). Morse purchases one of their videos (REMO).

RSPCA The Royal Society for the Prevention of Cruelty to Animals; a sticker supporting this organisation may have been seen on Mrs BALLARD's coat (ANNX).

Russell, Mrs An employer of Joanna FRANKS and living at 34 Runcorn Terrace, Liverpool (WNCH).

Russian Embassy A place where vodka is drunk (REMO: p13).

Ruth A worker at the TOWN AND GOWN ASSURANCE COMPANY (LBUS).

S

Sacramento Temperance Hall of Christian Scientists A Californian place of worship attended by both ALDRICH and ROSCOE (JWEL).

Sainsbury's A supermarket chain (with one branch, at least) in Oxford (ANNX: p186). Morse has been known to use the branch at the KIDLINGTON roundabout; a small but no doubt typical shopping list of two small tins of baked beans, a small brown loaf, and a bottle of GLENFIDDICH appears in CAIN (p329).

St Christopher Morse originally believes his purchase of a pendant is of this saint (CAIN: p328).

St Giles A cat in Oxford (CAIN). He is re-housed at 22 Kingfisher Way (sic), BICESTER. See also Sally Monroe (MINOR).

St Jude His feast day is October 28th (CAIN).

St Richard of Chichester (1197-1253) His feast day is celebrated on the 3rd of April at ST FRIDESWIDE'S (SERV).

St Simon His feast day is October 28th (CAIN).

Salisbury's A shop in Oxford (JWEL).

Salter's Boat Yard A boat yard (CAIN).

Samson A Cavalier King Charles dog owned by Queenie Norris (NEIG).

Samuels, Bartholomew An Oxford surgeon (WNCH).

Sandra A nurse who works with Sue WIDDOWSON (LBUS).

Sandra A worker at the TOWN AND GOWN (LBUS).
Sandra, Sensational A stripper at the PENTHOUSE CLUB (WEAR).

Santa Claus Santa Claus (CALL).

Schwarz, Douglas A firm in Old Compton Street (tel: 01-417-8084) (MILE).

Schwenck, Mr An entrepreneur in SOHO (MILE).

Scott, Mrs Grace Emily The mother of Anne SCOTT, living in Burnley (JERI: pp54-55, 124).

Scott, The Rev Thomas Enoch A Baptist minister and the deceased father of Anne SCOTT (JERI: p55).

Self Hire A van rental company (WATC).

Selfridges A shop in London (ANNX).

Selina A worker for the Elite Booking Services agency (WOOD).

Shakin' Stevens A pop singer whose performance in St Paul's Cathedral may (or may not be) incongruous (MILE).

Sharif, Omar An actor (LBUS).

Sharon A police typist (REMO).

Sharpe, Mr The organist (in 1978) at ST FRIDESWIDE'S (SERV).

Sheehy, Sir Patrick His report (in 1993) made a number of recommendations (largely opposed by the police) on such matters as the ranking structure, pensions, and performance (or appraisal) related pay (CAIN: p4).

Sheila A friend of Wendy SPENCER (MILE).

Shelick, Nurse A young but old-fashioned nurse; she attends to Max shortly before his death in the John RADCLIFFE HOSPITAL (WOOD). She is also with Morse shortly before his death (REMO).

Shepherd and Woodward A firm with a number of establishments in Oxford. Morse has been known to get his hair cut (NEIG: p83) at one of their branches – where Gerrard's hairdressing salon may be found in the basement (p88). The firm is, perhaps, better known for supplying University gowns, schoolwear, and academic regalia. **Plate 95**

Shepstone, Basil A consultant and Senior Neurologist at the CHURCHILL HOSPITAL (CAIN).

Shergar A racehorse (REMO).

Sherwin-White One of Morse's examiners in GREATS (MILE).

Shylock A character in The Merchant of Venice. Morse confuses him with Sherlock HOLMES either in the heat of the moment or as a tease to Lewis (to whom he is speaking) (MILE).

Sid The first husband of Brenda BROOKS (CAIN).

Siddons, Sarah An eighteenth century actress (and still performing in the nineteenth) with a suite of hotel rooms named after her. Morse needs to caution Lewis about the number of d's in her name (NEIG).

Silken Dalliance A brand of condom (CAIN).

Sky A television company (REMO).

Smith, Mr A pseudonym of a hotel guest (MILE: p232). There are not as many Smiths (the most common English surname) in the whole of the WORKS as one may at first expect. A few others appear below and Eleanor SMITH appears in the main body of the text.

Smith, Mr John and Mrs Helen The true names, perhaps, of guests in Annexe 2 of the HAWORTH HOTEL. They give their address as Aldbrickham (HARDY's name for Reading), 22 Spring Street, Gloucester (ANNX) but seem to live at 45 Eddleston Road, Reading; Helen is a Yugoslav and Titoists killed her paternal grandfather; these facts are barely relevant but are included here from a perverse sense of completeness.

Smith, Trooper A fictional soldier (LBUS).

Smith, Wesley A TV worker (NEIG).

Smith, W.H. A stationery and book supplier (CAIN).

Snotty Joe A car driver (REMO: p182).

Snow, C.P. Author mistakenly called P.C. by Lewis (NEIG: p104).

Sodium Fluoroacetate A potent metabolic poison (CALL).

Soho Enterprises Limited The registered owners (under the name of Sullivan) of the FLAMENCO TOPLESS BAR (MILE).

Solomon A biblical king whose impartiality is emulated by Sarah JONSTONE (ANNX: p35).

Soros, George Financier (REMO).

Sotheby's An auctioneers (SERV).

Spastics Society A charity (since renamed) (WOOD).

Stanley A brand of knife, commonly used in DIY and thuggish attacks (REMO).

Stanton, Eileen A charge nurse (creamy-skinned, according to the ever-lustful Morse) at the John RADCLIFFE HOSPITAL. Married young and promptly divorced, she lives with an older man in Wantage. To Morse, 'She looked so good, so wholesome, in her white uniform with its dark-blue trimmings.' (WNCH: p36).

Steele, Danielle An author (NEIG).

Steinway A firm of piano makers; one of their Grand models may be found in the Lancaster Room at the RANDOLPH (JWEL).

Stephens, Geoffrey A judge at Oxford Crown Court (WOOD).

Stevens, William A clerk giving evidence in the second trial of the murder of Joanna FRANKS (WNCH).

Stewart, Mrs A music teacher at the ROGER BACON School (SERV).

Stewart, Winifred An attractive resident of COLEBOURNE ROAD and hostess at the Sauna Select in SOHO. Morse spends some four hours with her after initially refusing an offer of a drink and sex (MILE).

'Still a Mystery' A television programme (and still a mystery as to where in the WORKS the reference may be found).

Stockman, Denis An Oxford don and authority on the Grand Duchy of Lithuania in the fifteenth century (WATC).

Stockton One of Morse's examiners in GREATS (MILE).

Stokes, Mrs Mother of Linda BARRON (REMO).

Stride, Liz Victim of Jack the Ripper (WNCH).

Sturdy, The Rev David M. The vicar of St Andrew's in Norwich and a correspondent in the matter of the SWEDISH MAIDEN verses (WOOD).

Styler Another of Morse's examiners in GREATS (MILE).

Sullivan, Mr A gentleman found in SOHO who appears to be instrumental in introducing those seeking sex to those who, at a cost, provide it (MILE).

Summers, Jane A first class undergraduate (in Classics) at LONSDALE College (MILE); she was orphaned in 1974.

Summertown Travel A travel agency offering trips to both the hill-forts of Western England and the Himalayas (ANNX).

Susan The sender of a postcard of *Convent Thoughts* (STOR).

Susan, Sexy A stripper at the PENTHOUSE CLUB (WEAR).

Susie A daughter (possibly surnamed Marsden) (REMO).

Swain, Dr M.C. He is called to the RANDOLPH HOTEL and appears to be suitably qualified (bearing MA, MB, BCh, MRCP, MRCGP after his name). He is keen to leave the scene of death to attend a British Medical Association at which Max is to speak (JWEL).

Swift, PC A police officer (NEIG).

T

T The author of a postcard (LBUS).

TA The Territorial Army (NEIG).

Tampax A brand name of tampon (WOOD).

Tannoy A brand of loudspeaker (REMO).

Tao The name of a chain of clinics, one of which is likely attended by Mrs LEWIS (JERI: p162).

Taunt, Henry A photographer (1880s) of, at least, brewery drays (JWEL).

Taylor, Cecil Paul The former Head of the East Oxford Senior School and now living in the ABINGDON ROAD. He provides Morse with some welcome Scotch and with some useful information concerning Ellie SMITH (CAIN).

Taylor, Gladys A friend of Margaret BOWMAN; she is aged sixty years, a widow, and works at the LOCALS (ANNX).

Taylor, Liz An actress and an object of a constable's fantasy (WOOD).

Teresa, Mother An Albanian nun and worker for the poor of Calcutta (CAIN).

Thames Trains A company providing a rail service between PADDINGTON and a number of other places including, of course, Oxford (NEIG).

Thatcher, Margaret Conservative Prime Minister (1979-1990) (JERI: p138).

Thomas An undergraduate at HERTFORD College who assists at ST FRIDESWIDE'S (SERV).

Thomas, Alan or Allen (Alfred) A fruit-machine addict (REMO).

Thomas, Harold Alfred Father of Elizabeth HOLMES (REMO).

Thomas, Ivan A successful political candidate for the Gosforth Ward in KIDLINGTON (NEIG).

Thomas, Mr A drinker and father (REMO).

Thomas, Mr and Mrs Mr Thomas gives evidence about someone on the top of the tower of ST FRIDESWIDE'S (SERV).

Thomas, Mrs She is interviewed by DICKSON and then, more successfully, by Morse (largely by talking about her cat) concerning Mr BAINES (WEAR).

Thompson, Michelle A worker for the Elite Booking Services agency and sister to Audrey Morris (WOOD).

Thorogood, Mr He lives opposite to Jennifer COLEBY (LBUS).

Thorold, Walter An alias of Walter Towns (WNCH).

Todd, Sweeney The so-called 'Demon Barber of Fleet Street' who murdered his clients to provide meat for pies (MILE: p78). The name gave a rhyme for the police's Flying Squad, which became shortened to 'The Sweeney' (and a successful television series was made starring the late John Thaw). **Plate 96**

Tokyo Stock Exchange Margaret BOWMAN learns that the pound has perked up a little on this Exchange while listening to the news (ANNX).

Tolkien, J.R.R. Academic and author and regular in the EAGLE AND CHILD (ANNX).

Tom A letter-writer from Maidstone (WOOD).

Tomes, Philip A boatman and discoverer of the body of Joanna FRANKS (WNCH).

Tourist Buses The buses for tourists in Oxford (GOLD).

Towle, Kate A police officer (REMO).

Towns, Walter A crew member of the *Barbara Bray*. He serves time in the Longbay Penitentiary in Australia (WNCH).

Townsend, Sue An author (NEIG).

Traherene, Mr Justice Presiding judge at the first trial in the Joanna FRANKS murder case (WNCH).

Tutankhamun An Egyptian Pharaoh (STOR).

TWA The usual abbreviation for Trans World Airlines, makers of the Tristar airplane (JWEL).

Typhoo A brand of tea (REMO).

U

Ulysses Ancient Greek hero referred to by BROWNE-SMITH (MILE: p163). Also the title of a book by Joyce - from the reference to Bloom - being read by a brunette on the Piccadilly line (MILE: pp202-3).

V

Vera, Voluptuous A stripper at the PENTHOUSE CLUB (WEAR).

Velasquez A postcard of his *Rokeby Venus* was one of the few possessions of Karin ERIKSSON (WOOD).

Vermeer His *View of Delft* is reproduced in room 310 of the RANDOLPH HOTEL; the original is in the Mauritshuis in The Hague and was, allegedly, the favourite painting of Marcel Proust (JWEL). Morse has a reproduction of *The Milkmaid* in his flat (REMO).

Versace A fashion designer (CAIN).

Viagra A drug that may assist those with chronic erectile dysfunction (REMO: p276).

Villiers, Lt. Col. Basil (MC) A concerned citizen (WOOD).

Violet A provider of tea, Bran Flakes, soup and BOVRIL in the John RADCLIFFE HOSPITAL (WNCH).

Voss, Cedric Chairman of the History Committee, and a member, of the SYNDICS (NICQ).

W

Walkers A brand of potato crisp (CAIN).

Wallhead, Stephen RA He is a letter-writer from Wymondham Cottage, Helpston, Lincolnshire. His knowledge of the painting *The Woodman's Daughter* by John Everett Millais (and comments made by Arthur Hughes and Joanna Matthews RA thereon) leads him to speculate about the SWEDISH MAIDEN verses (WOOD).

Ward, Henry A wealthy coal-merchant who provided in 1838 a floating chapel for boatmen at the end of the OXFORD CANAL (WNCH).

Ward, John A fisherman (WNCH).

Warner, DCI Peter A policeman (NEIG).

War Office, The Part of the Ministry of Defence and responsible for army matters (DODO).

Warrener, Nurse She is involved in the treatment of Michael MURDOCH (JERI).

Wars of the Roses A series of conflicts in the fifteenth century. The English Examination Boards (apparently) encourage Rwandan refugees to study them (NEIG: p286).

Watson, DC A police officer instructed to interview some guests (JWEL); he is also present when David MICHAELS is interviewed (WOOD: p342) and has been known to comment on bicycle thefts (CAIN: p276). See also PC Barry WATSON.

Watt, Jimmy A police constable on a search detail (WOOD).

Webb, Mrs Secretary to PHILLIPSON (WEAR).

Webley The makers of a type of pistol issued to officers of the Royal Wiltshire Regiment in 1942 (MILE).

Webster, Mary The senior administrator at the LOCALS (ANNX).

Welch, Fiona A student nurse at the John RADCLIFFE HOSPITAL. Morse refers to her as the Fair Fiona (WNCH).

Wells Chairman of the GREATS examiners who faced Morse (MILE).

Welsh Schoolboys' Hockey Association One of their ties may be found in the BEAR pub (NEIG).

Westerby, John A Barnardo boy who failed in both his degree course and his marriage to Anne SCOTT (JERI). It is not clear if he is related to the WESTERBY who plays a prominent part in MILE.

Whiskas The brand name of a cat food (CAIN).

Whitaker, Agnes An elderly sister who attends a funeral (DODO).

Whitaker, Mrs A widow (DODO).

Wilkins, John He is mentioned in the OXFORD STORY recorded narrative and in a letter sent by Ginger Bonnetti (JWEL). He was Warden of WADHAM College and instrumental in founding the Royal Society.

Wilks, Roy A police constable who discovers a bullet (WOOD).

William, Mr A bearded entrepreneur in SOHO (MILE).

Williams, Charles Author and poet and a regular in the EAGLE AND CHILD (ANNX). He also worked for the OXFORD UNIVERSITY PRESS.

Williams, Jack An Oxford taxi-driver (JWEL).

Williams, Mr A keeper at BLENHEIM PALACE based at Combe Lodge (WOOD).

Williams, Sergeant Prosecutor in the trial of the Joanna FRANKS murder (WNCH).

Williamson, Mike The name of a modelling and photography business in Reading (CAIN).

Willis, Dr The author of a pre-post-mortem report (WNCH).

Wilson, Joyce A downstairs neighbour of Yvonne BAKER (WEAR).

Wimsey, Lord Peter A fictional detective (WOOD). A plaque celebrating his creator (Dorothy L. Sayers) may be found at 1 Brewer Street, Oxford.

Windolene The brand name of a window cleaner (CAIN).

Wiseman, Nancy A member of the HISTORIC CITIES tour; she is a librarian who hails from Oklahoma City (JWEL).

Woden Norse god and origin of the word Wednesday (NEIG).

Women's Institute (WI) An organisation for women with a branch in MIDDLE WAY (WNCH: 199). Margaret DALEY attends the WI weekly but it is not clear which branch (WOOD).

Women's Land Army The BEAR pub holds one of their ties (NEIG).

Woods, Michael A young lover (JWEL).

Wootton, Harold Samuel Carter's mistake for Thomas Wootton (WNCH).

Wootton, Thomas The youngest crew member of the *Barbara Bray* (WNCH).

Wright, Mr A builder (WEAR).

Wynne-Wilson, Laura An 82-year old; she is potentially an unreliable witness (CAIN).

Wytham Amateur Operatic Society Their performance of *The Mikado* in the late summer of 1992 features Cathy MICHAELS (WOOD).

X

Xerox A company known for its photocopying machines (ANNX).

Y

Yale University Fencing Club One of their ties may be found in the BEAR pub (NEIG).

Yellow Pages A telephone directory of businesses used by Lewis (ANNX: p164).

Yvonne A lady of dubious virtue with an appalling mock French accent (MILE). If Yvonne is her real name, why does her handbag carry the initials W.S.?

YWCA The Young Women's Christian Association (WOOD); since 2002 they wish to be simply known as 'YWCA'.

Z

Zeta III A Paramount Barotse chief (CAIN).

Appendix E
Place Names

The WORKS include a *very* large number of place names – towns, cities, villages, countries, and other – which are recorded here for the sake of completeness. Many place names appear alphabetically in **bold** in the text (and are not necessarily included here); many more appear within entries and are similarly excluded (or included at random). A few more place names are excluded (see the comments on page 7 – Entries in the Companion) but there are still plenty to list. Better, perhaps, duplication rather than omission.

Where potentially helpful, other references are given (rarely) and tend to illustrate Morse's travels, to underline annotations, for some matter of clarification, or for any other reason one may care to mention or invent.

It is worth adding that Morse admits to a poor knowledge of the world around him: "I never did any Geography at school" (CAIN: p224 is but one example). Further, at his '… local grammar school, the young Morse had been presented with a choice of the 3 Gs: Greek, Geography, or German. And since Morse had joined the Greek option, his knowledge of geography had ever been fatally flawed' (NEIG: p122). There is a very good chance that the reorganisation of English Counties in the 1970s may well have passed him by; he believes in Rutland rather than Leicestershire (SERV: p300). This is not to suggest that Morse is somehow automatically averse to change – it is just that some things have a certain historical resonance. Rather bizarrely, Morse can recall all the American states and (almost) their capitals (LBUS: p74; WNCH: p51).

ENGLAND (by traditional county where appropriate)

Bedfordshire Bedford; Luton (Airport).

Berkshire Goring;[1] Maidenhead; Newbury (for horse racing); Reading; Slough (see ANNX: pp88/89 for the mistaken belief that Slough is not in Berkshire and NEIG (p188) for Morse's recollection of Slough Borough Council); West Ilsley.

Buckinghamshire Beaconsfield; Buckingham; Gerrards Cross (erroneously called 'Gerrard's Cross' in REMO: p108); High Wycombe; M40 for the death of AINLEY (WEAR: p19); Stokenchurch – formerly in Oxfordshire (REMO).

Cambridgeshire Ely; Peterborough; St Neots; Cambridge (of course).

Cheshire Preston Brook.

Cornwall Bodmin.

Cumbria Derwentwater; Grasmere; Keswick; Ullswater; Windermere.

---

[1] 'Goring and Streatley' station is mentioned in NEIG (p85); the station itself is in Berkshire.

Derbyshire Derby.

Devon Honiton; Ottery St Mary; Plymouth; Torquay.

Dorset Bournemouth (where Morse enjoys the changing moods of Homer's deep-sounding sea (REMO: p29); Charmouth.

Durham Durham; Washington (NEIG: p345).

East Sussex Brighton.

Essex Chelmsford; East Essex; Saffron Waldon (sic) (MILE: p75; correct is Walden); Stansted (for the airport).

Gloucestershire Bourton-on-the-Hill; Bourton on the Water (hydrated rather than hyphenated); Charlton Kings; Cheltenham; Cirencester; Gloucester; Moreton-in-Marsh.

Hampshire Farnborough (and Longmead Road therein – WEAR: p149); Southampton.

Herefordshire Leominster; Ross-on-Wye.

Hertfordshire St Albans.

Kent Dover; Gravesend; Sidcup (though officially in the London Borough of Bexley).

Lancashire Blackpool; Bootle; Manchester.

Leicestershire Leicester; Lutterworth.

Lincolnshire Grimsby; Lincoln; Stamford.

Middlesex Kempton Park (horse racing).

Norfolk Thetford.

Northamptonshire (also referred to as Northants) Brackley; Daventry; Eason Hill (properly Easton-on-the-Hill); Kettering; Northampton; Peterborough (but only historically); Silverstone; Towcester (and the A5 - WEAR: p191); Weedon and Weedon Bec.

Northumberland Alnwick; Berwick-on-Tweed.

Nottinghamshire Nottingham.

Oxfordshire Appleford; Beckley; BICESTER (particularly as it is recalled by Morse when thinking about death in SERV: p263); Billingdon;[1] Burford; Carterton (for the postal sorting office in REMO); Charlbury; Chipping Norton; Cholsey; Culham; Didcot, Didcot power-station and Didcot Parkway; Eynsham; Faringdon; Headington Hill; Hook Norton; Long Hanborough; Nuneham Courtenay; Otmoor;[2] Radley; Streatley; Sutton Courtenay; Thame; Uffington (for the White Horse; formerly in *Berkshire*).

Rutland Rutland; Uppingham.

---

[1] This appears in CAIN: p275 as 'Billingdon Rural District Council'. Fairly hard to find on a map (though there is a pub, the Billingdon Arms, in EAST OXFORD).

[2] There is an area called Ot Moor (east of Oxford) but no village of exactly the same name, the 'nearest' being Charlton-on-Otmoor. Apparently, there is a shooting range (NEIG: p397). Williams (1935) suggests that Otmoor comes from the '… moor of Ota, an unknown individual who also gave his name to Oddington, one of the villages on the moor …' (p179).

Shropshire Bridgnorth; Church Stretton; Long Mynd (hills); Nesscliffe; Shrewsbury; Wellington.

Somerset Nether Stowey; the Quantocks (hills); Weston-super-Mare.

Staffordshire Burton; Fradley Junction; North Staffordshire; The Potteries; Stoke-on-Trent.

Suffolk Aldeburgh; Felixstowe; Newmarket.

Surrey Epsom (for the Derby).

Tyne and Wear Newcastle.

Warwickshire Leamington Spa; Rugby.

West Midlands Birmingham (and as Brum CAIN: p155); Coventry; 'Midlands'; Solihull.

West Sussex Fontwell Park (horse racing); Gatwick; Worthing.

Wiltshire Chalke Valley; Coombe Bissett; Devizes; Stonehenge; Swindon.

Worcestershire Broadway; Evesham; Kidderminster; M5 and M6; Pershore; Vale of Evesham; Worcester (and the Bromyard Road); 'Worcester Road' (to Evesham).

Yorkshire Doncaster; Leeds, Rotherham; York.

Greater London American Consulate; Arsenal (underground station); Bakerloo (underground line); Bethune Road; Bloomsbury; Bond Street; Brentford; Buckingham Palace; Canary Wharf; Chiswick; (inner) Circle line; Covent Garden; Croydon; Earls Court (which, referring to an underground station, should be Earl's Court - MILE: p39); East Croydon; East Putney; EC4 (as a postal district); Edgware Road; Euston; Finsbury Park (underground station); Great Windmill Street; Great Windsor Park; Greenwich (for the time-signal - REMO: p43); Hammersmith; Hanger Lane; Heathrow; Hendon; Holborn; Holloway (for the prison - CAIN: p384); King's Cross; Liverpool Street; Manor House; Mansion House (underground); Marble Arch; Marylebone; Mayfair; Mortlake (in connection with the Boat Race); New Scotland Yard (in connection with, but of course, the police NEIG: p204); North Circular Road; Oval (for the cricket ANNX: p277); Oxford Street; Park Lane; Piccadilly and Piccadilly Circus; Praed Street; Putney Bridge (separately and also in connection with the Boat Race); Richmond Road; Russell Square; St Paul's Cathedral; Seven Sisters (as a Road and an underground station); Shaftesbury Avenue; Shepherds Bush; Sloane Square; Soho; Spring Street; Stamford Hill; Stoke Newington; Strand; Sussex Gardens; The Thames; Trafalgar Square (and the National Portrait Gallery NICQ: p148); Upper Richmond Road; Uxbridge; Victoria; Waterloo; White City; Whitehall (in connection with Civil Service Selection CAIN: p147); Wimbledon.

IRELAND (*including* NORTHERN IRELAND)

Belfast; Connemara; Cork; County Meath; Dun Laoghaire; Galway Bay; Kerry; Killarney; Newry; Tralee.

SCOTLAND

Aberdeen; Inverness; Loch Ness; Loch of Kinnordy.

WALES

Bala; Bangor; Betws-y-coed; Bontnewydd or Bont-Newydd (WEAR: p223); Brecon; Builth Wells; Caernarfon (and Bay); Cambrian Mountains; Capel Curig; Dyfed (incorrectly as Dyffed WOOD: p320); Fishguard; Four Crosses; Llandovery; Llandudno; Llangollen; Llanwrtyd Wells; Llanystumdwy (and the Lloyd George Museum); Lleyn Peninsula; Llyn Tegid; Monmouth; North Wales; Pwllheli; Porthmadog; the Rivals (peaks); Snowdon; South Wales; Swansea; Tenby. A journey through Wales is central to the WEAR case (and less so to WOOD).

EUROPE

Aegean; Aegean Isles; The Alps; Amsterdam; Arlanda (Airport); Athens; Barcelona; Basel; Bayreuth; Belgium; Bergisch Gladbach; Bordeaux; Bosnia (NEIG: p383); Britain; Buchenwald; Carcassone (in a photograph in an office JERI: p213); Corinth; Costa del Sol; Crete; Cyprus; Denmark; the Dolomites; Dunkirk; Eiger (mountain); Etna; France; Gibraltar; Greece; Hamburg (and the Reeperbahn); Italy; Jutland; Lake Lucerne; Lugano; Macedonia; Malta; Münster; Normandy; Norway; Nuremburg; Paris (by implication from a reference to La Place de la Concorde in CAIN: p325); Pompeii (in a picture JERI: p213); Salzburg; Stockholm; Sweden; Switzerland; Thebes; Torremolinos; Triebschen (where WAGNER spent part of his life CAIN: p26); Trieste; Uppsála (WOOD: p38); Uppsála University (WNCH: p73); Venice (as 'the old harlot of the Mediterranean' ANNX: p17); Vienna; Yugoslavia; Zagreb.

NORTH AMERICA

Bahamas; Bermuda; British Columbia; Cambridge (Massachusetts); Canada; Chicago; Florida Keys; Harlem (New York); Kennedy Airport (New York); Los Angeles; Manhattan (for the cocktail in LBUS); Mississippi; New York; North Carolina; Oklahoma; Ottawa; Philadelphia; Sacramento; San Jose; South Carolina; South Dakota (as a reference to the USS *South Dakota* JWEL: p328 and its unmemorable State Capital WNCH: p51); Washington; Watergate Hotel (Washington DC; WEAR: p301) – it would be stretching a point a little too far to include this last entry under PUBLIC HOUSES.

REST OF THE WORLD

Africa; Antarctic; Argentina; Asia; Australia – also referred to as Oz (REMO: p78); Beirut; Bolivia; Bombay; Cairo; Cambodia; Canary Islands; Carthage; Cayman Islands; Chile; Erzincan in Turkey (STOR: p171); Ethiopia; The (Persian) Gulf; India; Isfahan; Israel; Jerusalem; Kathmandu; Kirgyzstan; Morocco; New Zealand; North Africa; Northern Rhodesia; Palestine; Perth (Australia); Rwanda; Sahara Desert; Samarkand; Sandwich Islands; Spain; Susamyr Valley; Tashkent; Timbuktu; Tokyo; Tonga; Turkestan; Vietnam; Zambia.

ELSEWHERE & OTHER

Atlantic Ocean; Australasia; Balkan States and Baltic States (NEIG: p122); Caribbean; Channel Islands (and Guernsey NEIG: p53); Black Country (largely in Staffordshire and the West Midlands); Chilterns; Cotswolds; East Anglia; Hell (CAIN: p94); Hibernia (WNCH: p180); the Home Counties; the Midlands; Peak District; the Pole Star (JWEL: p269); the Ridgeway; Trent and Mersey Canal (and the Barton Tunnel – which is surprisingly hard to trace); Watling Street.

Appendix F
Public Houses

A generic term for licensed establishments that serve alcohol (and, of less interest to Morse, occasionally food); their trading hours are governed by law (OPENING HOURS) and they are commonly known as 'pubs'. Oxford contains many notable examples, distinguished by their architecture, ambience, history, and clientèle; there are also many that are drab, seedy, and uninviting. All the pubs mentioned in The WORKS are listed here – Morse has drunk in most of them.

A number of pubs are mentioned though not named – for example, in WEAR (p54), Morse comments "If I remember rightly, Lewis, there's a pub just around the corner" (and, of course, there is). It may be safe to assume that he is aware of even those pubs where he is not explicitly known to have visited though he does (once) ask Lewis, while they are both in KIDLINGTON, where the nearest pub is (NEIG: p65).

A number of hotels (and even motels) and restaurants have been referred to, or visited by, Morse and the distinction between these and a public house is not always crystal clear; these are listed separately under their name if appropriate (such as the ELIZABETH, the SHERIDAN, and La SORBONNE). Some establishments are not so listed – for example, the Café Royal in London (WEAR: p94; MILE: p192), the Dorchester (JWEL: p198), Les Quat' Saisons (WNCH: p53), the Savoy (REMO: p135) or the Paris Ritz (REMO: p385) – but are referred to here merely for the pleasure of putting such a restaurant or hotel under the heading of 'public houses'.

Dunkling and Wright (1987) and Honey (1998) have been most useful in compiling this section. While the list below seeks to be comprehensive certainly no claim is made that Morse has been to *all* (a good number of other people in the WORKS seem to enjoy a drink as well). References are given but occasionally (to clarify any possible confusion or out of sheer bloody-mindedness); many pubs appear in more than one case. Every place listed below has an entry in the main text.

A
The Anchor (NEIG: p356); The Angel (WEAR: p139); Angel Inn (WNCH: p139).

B
Bay Hotel; Bay Tree Hotel; Bear Hotel (WOOD); The Bear (NEIG); Bell Inn; Black Dog; Black Horse; The Black Prince (LBUS); Boat Inn; Bonnington Hotel; Bookbinder's Arms; Brown's; Brunel Bar (see GREAT WESTERN HOTEL); Bull and Stirrup (LBUS); Bull and Swan (NEIG); Bulldog.

C

The Cape of Good Hope; Casa Villa; Cherwell Arms (JWEL: p224); Cherwell Motel (NICQ: p17); Chesterton Hotel; Corn Dolly; Cotswold Gateway Hotel; Cotswold Hotel; Cotswold House; Crown and Castle; Crown Inn.

D

Dew Drop Inn; Duke of Cambridge; Durrants.

E

Eagle and Child (various cases); East Oxford Conservative Club; Executive Hotel.

F

Fawlty Towers (WNCH: p81); The Flamenco Topless Bar (MILE: p177); The Fletcher's Arms; The Friar Bacon.

G

Gardener's Arms; The George; George and Dragon Inn; Golden Cross; The Golden Rose; The Grapes; Great Western Hotel.

H

Haworth Hotel; Horse and Jockey (JERI: p134); Horse and Trumpet (NICQ: p28).

J

Jericho Arms.

K

The King's Arms (various cases); The King's Arms, Dorchester (WOOD: p85); The King's Arms, Summertown (CAIN: p14); King Charles.

L

Lamb and Flag.

M

Maidens Arms; Manor Hotel; The Marsh Harrier; The Minster; The Mitre (JERI: p125); Moat Hotel; The Morris Bar.

N

Nag's Head.

O

Old Bull (SERV: p41); Old Orleans (CAIN: p104); Old Parsonage Hotel (CAIN: p96); Old Tom (CAIN: p84); The Ox.

P

Paddington Station Hotel (MILE: p228); Pear Tree Inn; Peep of Dawn; The Plough; The Prince of Wales; Prince William Hotel; Printer's Devil.

R

The Randolph (various cases); Red Lion (NEIG: p109); Richmond Arms; Rock of Gibraltar (see OXFORD CANAL); Rose and Crown; Rosie O'Grady; Royal Crescent Hotel (NEIG); Royal Oak (ANNX: p220); Royal Oxford Hotel (WEAR: p182); Royal Sun (WOOD: p61; also known as The Sun WOOD: p243); The Running Horses Inn.

S

Springs Hotel; Station Buffet (see OXFORD STATION JWEL: p162); Station Hotel (WEAR: p139); The Sun – see Royal Sun; Swan Hotel (JWEL: p215); Swan Inn (WNCH: p139); Swiss Lodore.

T

Three Pigeons; Three Tuns Inn; Trout; Turf Tavern (CAIN: p78); Turl Bar (NICQ: p199).

U

University Arms Hotel.

W

The Westminster; various White Hart(s); The White Horse – and more than one of them; White Swan, Abingdon; Woodstock Arms.

Plate 97 (Left) The Bastille (1789) (p274).
Plate 98 (Right) Hercules capturing Cerberus Sebald Beham (p275).

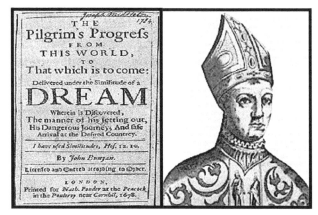

Plate 99 (Left) Title page of the first edition of The Pilgrim's Progress (p277).
Plate 100 (Right) Pope John XXIII (p279).

Plate 101 (Left) Achilles carries the body of Hector (p282).
Plate 102 (Right) A little unkind to strange – Gargantua (p283).

Appendix G
Quotations

The WORKS are somewhat studded with either direct quotations[1] or references to any number of poems, plays, books, or other artistic expressions; WEAR, for example, has quotes as headings to every one of the forty-two chapters (and a forty-third for the epilogue) though one is a CROSSWORD clue and another an examination question; other cases, NICQ and SERV for example, have no such headings though this does not mean that they are poor in quotations. Quotations heading Chapters have by and large been ignored here (though many are dotted around in other places). Rather, the emphasis in this entry is on those that appear *within* the chapters.

To save the reader a little time in tracking down sources – and to direct them to a higher quality of literature than they will find here – some (and only some) examples are included below. They are largely in the order of their chronological appearance with the definite exceptions of the first and last; all quotations taken from Diogenes SMALL are found under that entry. Biblical references are to the Revised Standard or the original (1611) King James versions.

'... tears shed for things ...'
DEXTER recalls both his own sixth form at school (and that of Morse) when they both first learned this from Virgil (in Bird 1998: p7). A fuller quotation reads: '*Sunt lacrimae rerum et mentum mortalia tangunt*'. 'There are tears shed for things, and mortality touches the heart'; the line is repeated as the heading to Chapter 34 of REMO with a slightly different translation.

'It's those abhorrèd shears.' (LBUS: p68)
Spoken by Bernard CROWTHER and a clear reference to the lines in Milton's *Lycidas*: 'Comes the blind Fury with th'abhorrèd shears, And slits the thin-spun life ...'

'Though your sins be as scarlet, scarlet, scarlet, They shall be whiter, yea whiter than the snow.' (LBUS: p70)
Isaiah 1, 19 has: '... though your sins be as scarlet, they shall be as white as snow ...'
These lines were turned into a (popular) hymn in 1887 with words by Fanny Crosby and music by W. Howard Doane. The hymn also features in SERV (p317).

'Like Hephaestus, thrown o'er the crystal battlements' (LBUS: p115)
This is an allusion to lines 739-743 from Milton's *Paradise Lost* (wherein Hephaestus is referred to as Mulciber).

---

[1] Fry (1997: pp375-376) cautions against taking quotations at face value. The mere fact that a quote comes from Shakespeare should, in the normal course of events, be seen as coming from the character who speaks the line – the evil Macbeth or the absurd Polonius – rather than representing Shakespeare's own view. This could (or even should) be borne in mind when perusing any of the Quotations here.

'Im Anfang war die Hypothese.' (LBUS: p119)

Morse translates this as: 'In the beginning was the hypothesis'. As such, it seems to have a direct link to *John 1,1* (starting with 'In the beginning was the Word …'). It is not exactly clear why Morse remembers the phrase in German and less clear (to the present writer at least) why he attributes the phrase to Goethe (p122).

'Bliss was it in that dawn to be alive, But to be young was very heaven!' (LBUS: p176)

Wordsworth wrote these lines in the poem *French Revolution – as it appeared to Enthusiasts at its Commencement*. The phrase later appears in *The Prelude* (Book XI). **Plate 97**

'Open weather, as Jane Austen would have called it.' (LBUS: p177)

The phrase open weather (high and white clouds with sunshine in LBUS) appears, at least, in *Lady Susan* (letter 8) and in Part Two of *The Watsons* ('Fine open weather, Miss Emma, charming season for hunting'). Morse recalls Jane Austen as wishing to swap the *expectation* of happiness for happiness itself (REMO: p98) but the source of this has not been traced here.

'The bride hath paced into the hall, Red as a rose is she.' (LBUS: p184)

Morse recalls (perfectly) these lines from *The Rime of the Ancient Mariner* by Coleridge.

'Not a line of her writing have I, Not a thread of her hair …' (LBUS: p189)

These are the opening lines of Hardy's poem *Thoughts of Phena At News of Her Death*. Morse regards these as 'the saddest lines of poetry he had ever read'. The lines also appear as a heading to Chapter 10 in WEAR.

'Babble no more o' green fields' (LBUS: p263)

Hostess Quickly recalls the death of Falstaff: 'For his nose was as sharp as a pen and a babbled of green fields' *Henry the Fifth* Act 2 Scene 3. Keats, writing to John Rice, uses the phrase 'like poor Falstaff, though I do not babble, I think of green fields'. According to Lee, the line was, until 1726, read as: '… as sharp as a pen and a table of green fields …' (1907: p176). The phrase '… babbled of green peas …' appears in the record of *The Adventure of the Three Students* as investigated by HOLMES.

'As far as I could see there was no connection between them beyond the tenuous nexus of succession.'

This appears as the heading to chapter 4 in WEAR and is attributed to the poet Peter Champkin. Despite a little effort, the source of the quotation has not been identified (though *The Waking Life of Aspern Williams* by Champkin is listed in the acknowledgements to ANNX, and quotes therefrom appear as the headings to Chapter 17 of that case and to 41 and 52 of CAIN).

'Tis a strange thing, Sam, that among us people can't agree the whole week because they go different ways upon Sundays' (WEAR: p133)

A quote identified as, and from, George Farquhar (1678-1707). It seems to be from a letter written in 1700. The quotation heads a chapter that describes how various people spend their Sundays; the quote refers to differences in religion but the Chapter does not.

'An editor of no judgement, perpetually confronted with a couple of MSS to choose from, cannot but feel in every fibre of his being that he is a donkey between two bundles of hay.' (WEAR: p165)
The quote comes from the first book of HOUSMAN's translation of *Astronomica* by Manilius (part IV). He drily continues by adding that the confused editor may imagine that if one bundle of hay is removed, he will cease to be a donkey.

'One morn I miss'd him on the custom'd hill ...'
A quote from Gray's *Elegy Written in a Country Churchyard*. This appears as a chapter heading (19) in WEAR. The poem subsequently explains the reason for the absence on the hill as being the death of the particular character.

'... he cursed the conscience that invariably thus doth make such spineless cowards of us all.' (WEAR: p226)
This is an obvious paraphrase of the line in *Hamlet* (Act 3 Scene 1) towards the end of the famous soliloquy: 'Thus conscience does make cowards of us all ...' Some editions give 'doth' for 'does'.

'All happy families are alike, but each unhappy family is unhappy in its own way.'
This Leo Tolstoy quotation appears in the heading to Chapter 27 of WEAR. It is the first line of *Anna Karenina*.

'Things are not always what they seem; the first appearance deceives many.'
This Phaedrus quotation appears in the heading to Chapter 34 of WEAR. It continues (most aptly): 'The intelligence of a few perceives what has been carefully hidden.'; it could almost apply directly to Morse.

'A sop to Cerberus ...' (WEAR: p299)
A saying that simply means a gift or a bribe to pacify a troublesome person (or, literally, a fearsome mythological dog). Ancient Romans and Greeks used to put a cake in the mouth of a dead person as a sop to the three-headed dog guarding the gates of the infernal regions. **Plate 98**

'The remorseful day'
The phrase exists as the title of the final case. It appears in two quotations: 'The gaudy, blabbing and remorseful day Is crept into the bosom of the sea'. Shakespeare *Henry IV Part II* (Chapter heading 37 in WEAR). And in the lines by HOUSMAN (for which, see the notes to the REMO case).

'... the Rock Improbable and the Rock Impossible ...' (WEAR: p310)
Morse feels that his reasoning has run aground upon these rocks. Exactly where these Rocks are has not been discovered here.

"You look for a leaf in the forest, and you look for a corpse on the battlefield." (WEAR: p319)
This is Morse speaking. There is a clear allusion to the G.K. Chesterton short story *The Sign of the Broken Sword* from *The Innocence of Father Brown* where Father Brown asks, 'Where does a wise man hide a leaf? In the forest. But what does he do if there is no forest?' (p219) and '... if a man had to hide a dead body, he would make a field of dead bodies to hide it in' (p226).

Coincidentally, perhaps, the quote to the next chapter heading (WEAR: p322) is by Chesterton. Lewis remembers, from Morse, the 'hiding a leaf' example when trying to solve the REMO case (p168). *The Innocence of Father Brown* is one of the few books found in the household of the BROOKS family (CAIN: p356); Morse is pleased to re-read a few lines that he remembers so vividly from his youth (p367).

"Remember what old Sam Johnson used to say? 'The fellow who doesn't mind his belly can't be trusted to mind anything.' Well, something like that." (NICQ: p22)
Well, something very much like that – the 'correct' quote is 'He who does not mind his belly will hardly mind anything else' Boswell's *Life of Johnson* (vol ii chap ix).

'... some of whom, as in Gibbon's day, well remembered that they had a salary to receive, and only forgot that they had a duty to perform ...' (NICQ: p24)
The reference is to Gibbon's *Memoirs of My Life and Writings* when he is recalling his time at Oxford (and a particular tutor).

'Oysters is amorous, Lobsters is lecherous, But Shrimps – Christ!' (NICQ: p37)
A slightly alternative reading – from the ribald (if not outright vulgar) *The Shearer's Lament* – is: 'Oysters is amorous, Lobsters is lecherous, But Shrimps, Shrimps is the most lascivious of all fish!'

'Morse recalled the passage from Gibbon about one of the tests designed for the young novitiate: stick him in a sack with a naked nun and see if ...' (NICQ: p74)
DEXTER (2008) is adamant that he had not invented this and Morse was unavailable for interview (being dead for some years). As to a possible location in Gibbons, Dexter is unsure and believes he may have 'overheard' the anecdote 'in the HIGH'. Gibbon was not enamoured of Oxford: 'To the University of Oxford I acknowledge no obligation ... I spent fourteen months at Magdalen College: they proved the fourteen months the most idle and unprofitable of my whole life'. Taken from his *Autobiography* in *The Oxford Dictionary of Quotations* (1953). It should be borne in mind that Gibbon was entered at MAGDALEN shortly before his fifteenth birthday; perhaps *too* young to appreciate the opportunity? Quennell has an apt phrase of Gibbon at this time: '... the sunny emptiness of his life at Oxford ...' (1945: p83).

'... the sin against the Holy Ghost ...'
This is the unpardonable sin of blasphemy against the Holy Ghost and to deny the Divine character of works that are manifestly Divine. Morse thinks, perhaps a little unkindly, that such a sin is, for BARTLETT, 'leaving filing cabinets unlocked whilst nipping out to pee.' (NICQ: p77). There is a further reference (p243) to the same sin as committed by those in charge of public examinations – to divulge the contents of exam papers before the exam. Morse recalls BROWNE-SMITH (one of his tutors) as barking away at a trivial '... spelling mistake as if it were the sin against the Holy Ghost' (MILE: p53).

'The grave's a fine and private place, But none do there, I think, embrace ...' (NICQ: p80)
This quotation is from Andrew Marvell's *To His Coy Mistress*. These lines have formed part of Morse's mental baggage for rather more years than he wishes to remember. The poem as a whole is, when devotedly recited to a reluctant lover, a supposedly excellent means of seduction (though it is unclear whether Morse has ever used this method – or indeed needed to).

'O tempora! O mores!' (NICQ: p83)
Usually translated as 'O what times! O what morals!' (though *The Oxford Dictionary of Quotations* gives 'O what times! O what habits!' and Chambers (2003) gives 'O what times! O what manners!'); the line is from Cicero. (Attempts to construct either an English or a Latin anagram containing the word 'Morse' appear to be fruitless.)

"The majority of men lead lives of quiet desperation." (Morse speaking; NICQ: p115)
The original is from Thoreau in *Walden* and reads: 'The mass of men lead lives of quiet desperation' (and it appears as such as the heading to Chapter 5 of JERI).

'... and the silhouettes on the furthest walls of the darkened cave were now assuming a firmer delineation' and *'... for a brief second one of the silhouettes on the cavern wall focused in full profile.'* (NICQ: pp126/147)
There is a further reference on p152. Morse is considering what he knows (or supposes) so far in a murder case; the reference is clearly to the 'Shadow in the Cave' from Plato's *Republic*.[1] Ignorant humanity is like those trapped in a cave who mistake the shadows on the wall for reality; only the rare individual will escape the cave through a long and rigorous intellectual journey to the world of ideas. Morse appears to be such an individual.

'No human action happens by pure chance unconnected with other happenings. None is incapable of explanation.' (NICQ: p186)
Morse recalls this quote of Dr Hans Gross (by heart) and it is a belief he has always cherished. Gross (1847-1915) was an Austrian criminal jurist and professor of Criminology at the University of Prague.

'Like Pilgrim he seemed to be making but sluggish progress – up the hill of difficulty and down into the slough of despond.' (NICQ: p197), *'... he felt like Pilgrim after depositing his sackful of sin.'* (WNCH: p131), *'Do you recall Pilgrim, when at last he confessed his sins to God?'* (WOOD: p2) and *'... like Pilgrim finally ridding himself of his burden of sin.'* (CAIN: p286).
These references are, of course, to John Bunyan's *The Pilgrim's Progress*. **Plate 99**

"Like somebody said, fish and visitors began to smell after three days ..." (Frank GREENAWAY speaking; NICQ: p209)
The somebody was Benjamin Franklin in *Poor Richard's Almanack* (1736) though it is the sort of quote that may well have an earlier source.

'But if Lewis had not been kept in the dark, neither had he exactly been thrown up on to the shores of light ...' (NICQ: p266).
There seems to be an echo here of Keats' poem *To Homer* with the lines: 'Aye on the shores of darkness there is light, And precipices show untrodden green ...' Horace's *Ode 4.5*, addressed to Augustus, is more specific: 'O father, O sire, O offspring born of the gods, You brought us forth into the shores of light'. There is a further reference (MILE: p197): '... the present case

---

[1] Plato is referred to as 'that old fascist' by an unknown writer (WOOD: p41). This seems a little harsh. In a vague attempt to salvage his academic career, Morse brushed up on a few chapters of the *Republic* while at university.

might never have been beached upon the shores of light'. And in REMO, one finds Morse thinking about death and '… being cast up on to the shores of light …' (p361).

'… his mind, like Yeats' long-legged fly, floating on silence.' (BARTLETT speaking; NICQ: p278)

The refrain is repeated throughout the poem (*Long-legged Fly*), which ends with: 'There on that scaffolding reclines Michael Angelo. With no more sound than the mice make His hand moves to and fro. (Like a long-legged fly upon the stream His mind moves upon silence)'.

'And ghastly thro' the drizzling rain On the bald street breaks the blank day.' (SERV: p15)

The lines come from section seven of Tennyson's *In Memoriam* and had been learned at school by Harry JOSEPHS.

'… wine-dark waves of the Aegean.' (SERV: p47)

'Wine-dark' is one of the more common adjectives from Homer.

'Riche, mais impuissant, jeune et pourtant très-vieux …' (SERV: p82)

The quotation is taken from Baudelaire *La Fleurs du Mal*. Morse recalls this line while trying to either enjoy or improve his listless feeling. The line can be translated as 'rich but impotent, young yet very old …'

'He worked like a Trojan.' (SERV: p132)

Dr Meyer (APPENDIX D) queries this phrase – why should Trojans be accredited with industriousness? Brewer's (1996) is not too helpful on the matter under the entry 'Regular Trojan': 'A fine fellow, with courage and spirit, who works very hard …'

'… to give the hooked atoms a shake.' (SERV: p164)

Possibly (or even probably) a reference to Lucretius who writes of hooked atoms affecting one's senses more harshly than smooth atoms (*De Rerum Natura*) but the phrase 'hooked atoms' can also be found in Epicurus and Democritus. Roberts (2005) has, of Epicurus, 'The swerve of atoms somehow accounts for the possibility of actions performed by choice, by humans and some other animals: without the swerve, apparently, all actions would be as fully determined as the fall of a stone dropped from a height'. At the back of one's mind there is a link with Coleridge who (somewhere) wrote of words as 'hooked atoms'. Morse also refers to the hooked atoms '… engaging and re-engaging themselves' when his mind is racing (MILE: p120) and says: "I take no delight in death, Lewis, and if one thing worries me above all else it is accidents – the random concourse of atoms in the void, as Epicurus used to say" (JWEL: p267). Morse also tries to shake the atoms while forging links between disparate issues in the WOOD case (p248). See also the entry under MARSTON FERRY ROAD for Lucretius.

''We're in, Meredith,' shouted Lewis from the depths.' (SERV: p193)

The phrase (according to Brewer 1996), is usually given as 'Meredith, we're in' and comes from a Fred Karno sketch called *The Bailiff*, first seen in 1907.[2] Each time the bailiff thought he was on the verge of entering a house for the purposes of distraint, he would call out the phrase to Meredith, his assistant. Rees (2005: p142-43) gives an alternative name for the sketch as *Moses and Son* and suggests it was performed by Fred Kitchen (who had the phrase, and Rees

---

[2] The character of Fred Karno was played by John Thaw in the 1992 film *Chaplin*.

has checked, placed upon his gravestone). Partridge (1977) notes the Kitchen connection but also refers to an unnamed music-hall song. It is a little unclear why Lewis should recall it.

'... a co-labourer in such an extensive vineyard.' (SERV: p212)
The reference is, presumably, to the parable found in *Matthew 20, 1-16* but without the details of equal pay for unequal labour.

"He's a better man than I am," (Morse speaking; SERV: p214)
The closing lines of *Gunga Din* by KIPLING read: 'By the livin' Gawd that made you, You're a better man than I am, Gunga Din'. Morse is, of course, familiar with most, if not all, of KIPLING's poetry and prose.

'He also was a man under authority.' (Lewis speaking; SERV: p224; REMO: p178, Morse speaking; REMO: p75, and KERSHAW speaking; REMO: p386)
Matthew 8,9 has 'For I am a man under authority, having soldiers under me ...'

'... sounding brass and tinkling cymbals.' (SERV: p229)
A clear reference to *1 Corinthians 1,1*: 'Though I speak with the tongues of men and of angels, and have not charity, I am become (as) sounding brass or a tinkling cymbal'.

'Ist dies etwa der Tod?' (SERV: p264)
These are the words recalled by Morse when facing a murderous death. They are the final words of *Im Abendrot* by Richard Strauss; a loose translation is 'can this perhaps be death?'

'The most scandalous charges were suppressed; the vicar of Christ was only accused of piracy, murder, rape, sodomy, and incest.' (SERV: p316)
Morse's favourite Gibbon quotation and one that he had committed to memory from boyhood. It concerns the fifteenth century Pope John XXIII and may be found in *The Decline and Fall of the Roman Empire* (Chapter 70, part VI). **Plate 100**

'Wash me, and I shall be whiter than the snow.' (SERV: p317)
The line comes from *Psalms 51.7*; as a hymn, it was set to music by William Fischer (with additional words by James Nicholson).

'There is a manifestation and there is a mystery.' (SERV: p318)
Morse recalls these words of St Paul to the Corinthians. The phrase as quoted does not seem to appear in any of the chapters or verses though the individual words 'manifestation' and 'mystery' do.

'Solitudinem faciunt: architecturam appellant.' (Morse speaking; JERI: p20).
According to Morse this phrase aptly describes the WESTGATE SHOPPING CENTRE. A loose translation is 'They make a desert (or wilderness) and call it architecture'. There is a clear resonance with 'solitudinem faciunt, pacem appellant' (... and call it peace) from Tacitus (*Agricola*, Chapter 30).

'Tarry ye at Jericho until your beards be grown ...' (JERI: p21).
Said to be the legend on a local inn – and therefore a possible source of the name of the area of JERICHO – the quote is found in *2 Samuel 10, 5*. It continues '... and then return.'

'We saw a knotted pendulum, a noose: and a strangled woman swinging there.'
This is given as the heading to Chapter 3 in JERI and identified there as lines from *Oedipus Rex* by Sophocles; the Second Messenger is replying to Chorus who has enquired how Jocasta died. Bishop (2006) uses the phrase 'Sophocles Did Do It' throughout his review of the WORKS to indicate where Morse's frequent flights of fancy lead him, temporarily of course, up and down a number of false trails and blind alleys.

'I lay me down and slumber And every morn revive. Whose is the night-long breathing That keeps a man alive?'
This quotation is taken from A.E.Housman *More Poems*. They are the opening lines of poem XIII and appear as the heading to Chapter 4 in JERI. See also the entry under HOUSMAN.

'The fatal key, Sad instrument of all our woe.'
This quotation is from Milton (*Paradise Lost; Book 2*) and appears as the heading to Chapter 6 of JERI. The 'fatal key' is the one that opens the Gate of Hell and lets out all manner of unpleasant people and things.

'... the qualms of his embering conscience.' (JERI: pp75-76)
This sounds rather like a quotation from another source; if so, the original has not been tracked down. One guesses that DEXTER, here, is simply being typically clever (but guesses are often mistaken).

'He can't write, nor read writing from his cradle, please your honour; but he can make his mark equal to another, sir.'
This quotation is by Maria Edgeworth (*Love and Law*) and is given as the heading to Chapter 11 of JERI. *Love and Law* appears to have been a play (performed in 1817) as the first part of *Comic Dramas in Three Acts*. The other parts were *The Two Guardians* and the intriguingly titled *The Rose, The Thistle, and the Shamrock*; surely this last play is overdue a revival?

'... (Morse) recalled that in Germany the situation might have been regarded as serious but not hopeless, in Austria, hopeless but not serious. Or was it the other way round?' (JERI: p106)
The latter is more common in English. According to a number of sources, the traditional Austrian saying is normally given as 'the situation is desperate but not serious'.

'The lads for the girls and the lads for the liquor are there ...'
A line from Housman's *A Shropshire Lad* (XXIII) and given as the heading to Chapter 16 of JERI. The line is particularly relevant because of the CLUE given on p129 (see under CROSSWORDS).

'... twin imposters ...' (JERI: p137)
Such is the reference to a speech invoking Kipling (much to Morse's delight). Although Chambers (2003) recognises 'imposter' the usual spelling is 'impostor' and it appears as such in the original of the poem *If* (Kipling 1940) where a fuller version of the quotation is: 'If you can meet with Triumph and Disaster And treat those two impostors just the same ...'

'Certum est quia impossibile est'
Tertullian *De Carne Christi* (heading to Chapter 20 of JERI). This may be translated as 'It is certain because it is impossible'. There has been, apparently, much academic debate concerning

this seeming paradox (and some of it attempts to link it back to passages in ARISTOTLE'S *Rhetoric*). From a sensitivity to relevance and from a feeling of ignorance, this debate is not rehearsed here.

'*The life of man without letters is death.*'

This is from Cicero, according to the heading for Chapter 25 of JERI. The source of this quotation has not been identified. The phrase 'vita sine libris mors est' ('life without books is death') seems to be proverbial.

'*Some clues are of the 'hidden' variety, where the letters of the word are in front of the solver in the right order.*'

From *Ximenes on the Art of the Crossword* (D.S. Macnutt; see XIMENES) and given as the heading to Chapter 26 of JERI. Some editions of *Ximenes on the Art …* carry a foreword by DEXTER. Such a clue, invented here (and but a poor example), could be 'ConstabLE WIShes police sergeant could be found within.' (5). A published clue from *The LISTENER* Crossword 3904 (18th November 2006) reads: 'PM down under delivered in cleAR VOice (4)'. One would need to know that Australian slang for the afternoon (pm) is 'arvo'. Also see the entry under XIMENES.

"*Cut out the weasel words, Lewis!*" (Morse speaking; JERI: p234)

Weasel words are those that suck the life out of those next to them, as a weasel sucks an egg (Brewer's 1996). Morse identifies 'actually' as a weasel word and is brought to task by Mrs Wynne-Wilson (MINOR) when he actually uses it (CAIN: p30). Only two other examples of Morse using the word have been identified – when he corrects Della CECIL's mistake of calling him 'Sergeant' with: "Chief Inspector, actually" (NEIG: p138) and when he points out that it is "Fifty minutes, actually" to opening time (REMO: p274). Ellie SMITH accuses Morse of using weasel words (with some justification; CAIN: p241).[3]

'*Facilis descensus Averno*' (MILE: p19)

The line is from Virgil's *Aeneid* (Book 6). A prosaic translation is 'easy is the descent to Hell'; more poetically, Dryden has 'smooth the descent, and easy is the way' (to Hell). Morse recalls the line in GOLD: p18.

'*But time cures hearts of tenderness – and now I can let her go.*' (MILE: p62)

This line, recalled by Morse, is from HARDY's *Wessex Heights*, is usually given as 'Well time cures hearts of tenderness, and now I can let her go'.

'*The boast of heraldry, the pomp of power …*' (MILE: p134)

Morse recalls this when considering the certainty of death. The line is from stanza 9 of Gray's *Elegy Written in a Country Churchyard* (which closes with 'the paths of glory lead but to the grave.').

'*Necesse erat digitos extrahere.*' (MILE: p135)

Morse is thinking that it was time he now did something. The phrase may be loosely translated: 'it was necessary to pull one's finger out'.

---

[3] Fleming's *Live and Let Die* has the following: 'The English word to be avoided at all costs, added Leiter, was (actually). Bond had said that this word was not part of his vocabulary' (2006: p28).

'... lente currite noctis equi ...' (MILE: p150)
Ovid has this phrase in *Amore* (Book 1.13); a loose translation is 'run slowly, horses of the night' and the reference is to the horses that pull Time's chariot (which Ovid wants to slow down so he can spend more time with his lover). Morse recalls the lines (in English) while he is impatient for the morning to arrive, and they also appear as the heading to Chapter 30 of WNCH. Morse also recalls the phrase during a most disturbed night – the night when he decides to abandon alcohol (NEIG: p304); and on a night when he is suffering any number of discomforts, he recalls the phrase again (REMO: p222).

'... as sharp as the sword of Achilles ...' (MILE: p166)
BROWNE-SMITH uses this phrase in a letter to Morse. There are, of course, a number of references in *The Iliad* to Achilles but one guesses that this refers to Book 21. **Plate 101**

'... a tide in the affairs of men that must be taken at the flood ...' (MILE: p203)
Morse recognises (and seizes) an opportunity while recalling these lines from *Julius Caesar* (Act 4 Scene 2).

'... a presence, and a bosom and a rose.' (MILE: p207)
Morse is recalling Molly Bloom in *Ulysses* by Joyce. The line in the original reads: '... preening for him her richer hair, a bosom and a rose.'

'... the veil of the temple had been rent in twain.' (MILE: p218)
Morse feels a sense of elation as things become clearer and recalls this biblical phrase. He recalls the same phrase (WOOD: p205) but on this occasion it is his heart that has been so rent. The reference is to either *Mark 15, 38* or *Matthew 27, 51* – or both.

'... the proposition that the wider the circle of knowledge the greater the circumference of ignorance.' (MILE: p252)
Morse becomes acutely aware of what he regards as the truth of this phrase. A source has not been tracked down though Albert Einstein is sometimes credited with something very similar (substituting 'darkness' for 'ignorance').[4]

'Abyssus humanae conscientiae!' (MILE: p262)
From St Augustine's *The Confessions* (Book 10.2.2). Morse is thinking about the actions of BROWNE-SMITH when he remembers this phrase, which loosely translates (in the italicised text) as 'And from thee, O Lord, unto whose eyes *the depths of man's conscience* are naked.'

'Nobody ever notices postmen, somehow ...'
A line from a Father Brown story, *The Invisible Man* (Chesterton; 1962: p111). It appears as part of the heading to Chapter 2 of ANNX and refers to a common deception in detection – one may see (but not remember) a sight so common that it does not register. The reference, in this case, is to the vans of postmen rather than postmen themselves.

'... in the Vale of the Great Dairies.' (ANNX: p26)
A reference to HARDY and *Tess of the d'Urbervilles*; this Vale is lush and fertile in contrast to the home vale of Tess.

---

[4] Einstein is referred to in GOLD (p36). Morse says of PC WATSON: "Not exactly an Einstein, is he?"

'… their shadows had passed gigantic round the walls of their childhood …' (ANNX: p42)
This has a tinkling echo of Platonic shadows and caves. It also has a clear echo of lines by Charles Heavysege (a nineteenth century Canadian poet) who wrote, in *Beyond the Veil*: 'E'en as gigantic shadows on the wall The spirit of the daunted child amaze.'

'… the last few hours of the death-struck year …' (ANNX: p48)
HOUSMAN has: 'Trod beside me, close and dear, The beautiful and death-struck year …' in *A Shropshire Lad* XLI.

'On Linden, when the sun was low, All bloodless lay the untrodden snow …' (ANNX: p48)
Sarah JONSTONE recalls the second line of this couplet. The lines begin Thomas Campbell's *Hohenlinden*.

'He was once a doctor but is now an undertaker; and what he does as an undertaker he used to do as a doctor.'
This is from Martial (and so identified) and is the heading to Chapter 10 of ANNX. The quote is from *Epigrams* 1.47 and the name of the undertaker is Diaulus.

'When I drink, I think; and when I think, I drink.'
From Rabelais and appearing as the heading to Chapter 11 of ANNX. Morse, of course, exemplifies this belief *par excellence*; it is quite hard to think of a character, from real life or fiction, who combines thinking and drinking to such a consistent degree or with such consummate dedication. The source of the quote is rather hard to track down. It does not seem to appear directly in *Gargantua and Pantagruel* (though Book III has '… drinking thus, I meditate, discourse, resolve, and conclude' Rabelais 1929: p255). And Strange says, of Morse: "… once he starts thinking, he'll start thinking about drinking …" (CAIN: p205). Watson (1933) has many pertinent comments on Rabelaisian drinking; Strange has a girth that is described as 'Gargantuan' (REMO: p16). **Plate 102**

'… and something that sent the four guardians scurrying from the portals of her sanity …' (ANNX: p145)
A little unclear on sources here but there may be a link to the four guardians of the divine throne (*Ezekiel 1,10 and Revelations 4,6-8*).

'… as some great Master of the Tides drew in the foam-fringed curtains of the waters …' (ANNX: p154)
Morse is musing (in the PEEP OF DAWN pub) about 'thinking and drinking'. There is a clear allusion to *The Wreck of the Deutschland* by Gerard Manley Hopkins, which has the phrases 'I admire thee, master of the tides' and 'the cobbled foam-fleece'. In the poem, the Master of the Tides is God.

'… sans warning, sans farewell, sans payment, sans everything.' (ANNX: p159)
This has a very clear echo of Jacques in *As You Like It* (Act 2 Scene 7). His speech opens with: 'All the world's a stage …' and closes with the description of second childhood as '… sans teeth, sans eyes, sans taste, sans everything'.

'... the affair was engendering the sort of bloom on the cheek which ... Aristotle himself had once used to define his notion of pure happiness.' (ANNX: p178)

Aristotle suggests in the *Nicomachean Ethics* (Book 10) that happiness, among other things, can be found in an activity, which may (or may not) create the bloom on the cheek (the blush of exertion or the flush of romance).

'It is a bad plan that admits of no modification.'

Heading to Chapter 27 of ANNX and referenced to Publius Syrus. This appears as maxim 469 in his *Sententiae*; Morse would no doubt agree with maxim 571: 'It is only the ignorant who despise education'.

'... with his bottom on the top sheet, as they say.' (ANNX: p192), *'... get his bottom on the top sheet ...'* (JWEL: p240), and *'... he's probably got his bottom on the top sheet ...'* (REMO: p94)

This seems to be indicative of sexual activity (confirmed by the later reference to 'the old charpoy ... creaking' (p200) where charpoy may be rendered as 'bed'). The phrase reappears (WOOD p201) but does not appear in common parlance. Perhaps it should.

'Dominus custodiat introitum tuum et exitum tuum' (ANNX: p209)

An inscription on the face of the top step of those leading from the rear of ST MARY'S to the RADCLIFFE CAMERA. It is noticed but not understood by Margaret BOWMAN. A loose translation is 'May the Lord preserve thy coming in and going out'. The original can be found in the Douay Bible at *Psalms 120, 8*. **Plate 103**

'A certain document of the last importance has been purloined.'

This is the heading to Chapter 34 of ANNX and referenced to Edgar Allan Poe. It is, of course, from *The Purloined Letter* and in the quote above it is the Prefect speaking to Dupin. Just as one may hide a leaf in a forest (or a body in a battlefield), one may hide a letter in the most obvious place.

'Felix qui potuit rerum cognoscere causas.'

From Virgil (*Georgics*) and appearing as the heading to Chapter 44 of ANNX. A rough translation is 'Happy is he who knows the causes of things.'

'Which orders having been obeyed ...' (WNCH: p23)

Morse recalls this phrase from his study of the Classics. It is likely to have come from Caesar's *The Gallic Wars* though an exact source has not (here) been identified.

'And though drink (as the Porter once claimed) might take away the performance, who could gainsay that it frequently provoked the desire.' (WNCH: p67)

The reference is to *Macbeth* (Act 2 Scene 3). The Porter, in replying to Macduff, states that drink, inter alia, '... provokes the desire, but it takes away the performance'.

'... the boatmen's robes of honour (in Fitzgeraldian phrase) ...' (WNCH: p68)

Quatrain 71 of Fitzgerald's translation of *The Rubaiyat of Omar Khayyam* reads: 'And much as wine has played the Infidel And robb'd me of my robe of honour – well, I often wonder what the Vintners buy One half so precious as the Goods they sell'. Quatrain 37 appears at the heading to Chapter 13 (p77); perhaps Morse was re-reading an old favourite when discussing the case with DEXTER.

'The wages of sin was death ...' (WNCH: p79)
The line is from *Romans 6,23*.

'... treading that narrow way by Tophet flare to Judgement Day ...' (WNCH: pp79-80)
KIPLING's *Buddha at Kamakura* has: 'Oh ye who tread the narrow way By Tophet-flare to Judgement Day, Be gentle when 'the heathen' pray To Buddha at Kamakura!' **Plate 104**

'... nescit vox missa reverti.' (WNCH: p82)
The original can be found in Horace (*Ars Poetica 390*) and means, in effect, that the word once spoken cannot be recalled.

'... like Tennyson's lily sliding slowly into the bosom of the lake ...' (WNCH: p89)
The lines can be found in the poem *The Princess* as: 'Now folds the lily all her sweetness up, And slips into the bosom of the lake.'

'... Doctor Johnson's advice to all authors that once they had written something particularly fine they should strike it out.' (WNCH: 116)
The passage, from Boswell's *Life* is usually given as 'Read over your compositions, and wherever you meet with a passage which you think is particularly fine, strike it out'. Johnson is recalling advice from an old tutor to one of his pupils.

"Better to have fought and lost than ... something ... something ..." (WNCH: p168)
Morse is trying to recall some lines of poetry. It is likely that he was grasping for Tennyson's lines from *In Memoriam*: 'I hold it true, whate'er befall; I feel it, when I sorrow most; 'Tis better to have loved and lost Than never to have loved at all'.

'Morse sat back with the self-satisfied, authoritative air of a man who believes that what he has called 'nonsense' three times must, by the laws of the universe, be necessarily untrue.' (WNCH: p189)
An echo – and perhaps a small one at that – of Lewis Carroll's *The Hunting of the Snark*: 'Just the place for a Snark! I have said it thrice: What I tell you three times is true.'

'... their present mission was a lost cause. But then Oxford was not unfamiliar with such things.' (WNCH: p218)
Matthew Arnold is the original source. His *Essays in Criticism* has, of Oxford: 'Home of lost causes, and forsaken beliefs, and unpopular names, and impossible loyalties'.

'Lead on Macduff!' (JWEL: p31)
Does Morse deliberately misquote this line – only to be corrected by Lewis with 'Lay on Macduff!' (though his exclamation mark is, perhaps, optional)? The line is from *Macbeth* Act 5 Scene 8.

'Never apologise, never explain.' (ASHENDEN speaking JWEL: p65)
This phrase is attributed primarily to Disraeli. The quote has also been attributed to Benjamin Jowett, Admiral John Fisher, the Duke of Wellington, and others. There is a rumour – no more – that it is firmly given as being by Disraeli in Morley's *The Life of William Ewart Gladstone* (London: Macmillan vol 1 1903). As a mere aside here, Nicolson (1967: p307) records Stanley Baldwin's words of advice: 'never complain, never explain'.

'... the source, in Milton's words, of all our woe.' (JWEL: p70)

Morse is recalling a past love affair and it is likely that he is not recalling 'the fatal key' but rather the first lines of *Paradise Lost*: 'Of Man's first disobedience and the fruit Of that forbidden tree whose mortal taste Brought death into the world and all our woe ...' (Capitalisation and punctuation varies.)

'Solvitur ambulando'

This appears as the heading to Chapter 13 of JWEL and is translated there as: 'The problem is solved by walking around'. The original appears to come from (or at least refers to) Diogenes the Cynic and his proof of motion. Slightly confusingly, the reference appears in *Lives and Opinions of Eminent Philosophers* by Diogenes Laertius (in the section on Diogenes the Cynic) where '... he replied to one who had been asserting there was no such thing as motion, by getting up and walking away'. Morse believes that the delights of walking are often ludicrously exaggerated and determines that the *ambulando* may be taken figuratively (CAIN: p120).

'... something pale and long and white ...' (JWEL: p114)

Attributed by Max to 'as the young lady said'. The reference is to a body; the quotation seems to be to a punchline of an easily-constructed rude joke.

'... much blood, methinks ...' (JWEL: p114)

Spoken by Max. No clear reference has been discovered here but the Shakespearian echoes are there – 'much blood' appears in *Richard II* (Act 3 Scene 2) and 'the lady doth protest too much, methinks' in *Hamlet* Act 3 Scene 2).

'Tomorrow and tomorrow and tomorrow ...' (JWEL: p116)

Quoted by Max in reply to Morse. The line is sometimes punctuated differently and comes from *Macbeth* Act 5 Scene 5.

'... Rumour had probably lost little of her sprinting speed since Virgil's time ...' (JWEL: p145)

The reference is probably to *The Aeneid* Book IV wherein rumour is defined as: 'The report of evil things than which nothing is swifter'. There is also a reference to 'many-tongued rumour' in LBUS (p110) – which is likely to be from the same source. In *Bleak House*, Morse read (no doubt) of 'Rumour, always flying, batlike ...' (p128).

'Ignorance, Madam, sheer ignorance.' (JWEL: p146)

Sheila WILLIAMS says to Morse: 'Like Dr Johnson, I must plead ignorance, Inspector, sheer ignorance'. Johnson's reply to a question about why he wrongly defined 'pastern' in his *Dictionary* as the knee of a horse was recorded, as above, by Boswell. **Plate 105**

'Till that her garments, heavy with their drink, Pull'd the poor wretch from her melodious lay, To muddy doom.' (JWEL: p56)

Max slightly misquotes these lines from *Hamlet* (Act 4 Scene 7) describing the death of Ophelia. As Morse points out, the last word is not 'doom' but 'death'.

'Thou shalt not covet thy neighbour's house, Lewis. Just ring the bell!' (JWEL: p174)

This is Morse speaking and quoting, of course, the traditional rendition of the Tenth Commandment from both *Exodus* and *Deuteronomy*. A little later (p178), Morse recalls (also) that: 'Thou shalt not covet thy neighbour's wife' – without fully recalling its location in *Exodus 20,17*.

'Hell hath no fury ...' (JWEL: p182)
Lewis (unfortunately in the presence of Morse) gives the common misquote and then, horror of horrors, attributes it to Shakespeare. Morse corrects him: 'Heaven has no rage, like love to hatred turned, Nor Hell a fury, like a woman scorned'. (Congreve *The Mourning Bride* Act 3 Scene 2).

'Just a song at twilight When the lights are low And the flick'ring shadows Softly come and go ...'
This appears as the heading to Chapter 35 of JWEL and attributed to The English Song Book. A fuller attribution would give the song (from which the above chorus is taken) as *Loves Old Sweet Song* (1894) with music by James Molloy and lyrics by Charles Bingham; *Loves Old Sweet Song* is heard one afternoon on the piano (and possibly on many, many afternoons) at the RANDOLPH (JWEL: p201).

'... a damn close-run thing.' (JWEL: p215)
The Duke of Wellington's remark about the battle of Waterloo is more correctly (though less memorably) given as: 'It has been a damned serious business ... It has been a damned nice thing – the nearest run thing you ever saw in your life.' (*Oxford Dictionary of Quotations* 1953).

'Tried to cross the nighted ferry ...' (JWEL: p219)
This is a reference to crossing the River Styx to Hades in Greek mythology. Housman has, from *More Poems XXIII*: 'Crossing alone the nighted ferry With the one coin for the fee ...'

'... amo amas amat ...' (JWEL: p231)
Traditionally the words of the first Latin lesson taught to schoolchildren. 'I love, you love, he (she or it) loves'.

'Vanity, all is vanity, saith the preacher.' (JWEL: p276)
Taken straight from *Ecclesiastes 1,2*.

'It provokes the desire, but it takes away the performance.' (JWEL: p292)
The phrase refers to drink and is quoted (correctly) by Morse. The original is found in *Macbeth* Act 2 Scene 3.

'Unusual as a fat postman.' (JWEL: p293)
Said by Morse but also believed to have been used by Raymond Chandler in *The Long Goodbye* (Chapter 12) as '... rare as a fat postman'.

'... would have to vie with Caesar's wife in immunity from any suspicion.' (JWEL: p325)
Julius Caesar is reported to have said, of Pompeia (his wife), that: 'I thought my wife ought not to be even under suspicion'. There are a number of sources for this, not least Plutarch in his *Parallel Lives*. 'Caesar's wife must be above suspicion.' appears in GOLD (p6) and is quoted by Strange in a rather convoluted discussion on police corruption. Also see the entry for CRAWFORD.

'... Accipe fraterno multum manantia fletu, Atque in perpetuam, frater, ave atque vale.'
This is the heading to Chapter 60 of JWEL and given there as from Catullus. A rough translation is: 'Accept (them), with many flowing brotherly tears, and for eternity my brother, hail and farewell'.

'Like a stricken deer ...' (JWEL: p345)
The phrase has a common history but was most poetically (a matter of debate, perhaps) used in William Cowper's *The Task*: 'Like a stricken deer that left the herd, Long since; with many an arrow deep infixt ...' There seems to be little doubt that Cowper took the line from *Hamlet* (Act 3 Scene 2): 'Why, let the stricken deer go weep ...'

'All in a hot and copper sky, The bloody sun at noon, Right up above the mast did stand, No bigger than the bloody moon.' (WOOD: p8; punctuation added)
Strange's recollection of these lines – taught to him many decades before – from *The Rime of the Ancient Mariner* by Coleridge are nearly word-perfect. Just one less bloody and he would have been spot on. Morse, who obviously knows the poem well, is unsure whether or not the 'monstrous misquotation' is deliberate. **Plate 106**

'But now I only hear its melancholy, long withdrawing roar.' (WOOD: p22)
Morse recalls this line from Matthew Arnold's *Dover Beach* while on holiday in Lyme Regis; he regards Arnold as 'much-underrated'. A number of commentators have seen *Dover Beach* as a recognition that the faith of the past has now been lost to an uncertain present (and as such it is quite apposite for a man of Morse's current atheism).

'Titvre tu patulae recubans sub tegmine fagi ...' (WOOD: p31)
Titvre is usually rendered *tityre*. These are the opening words of Virgil's first *Eclogue*. A rough translation is: 'Tityre, you, reclining beneath (the shade) of a broad beech tree ...'

'Water's all right ... in moderation.' (WOOD: pp44-45)
Morse, in pursuit of Louisa HARDINGE, admits that this line is not his but Mark Twain's. The original – which has not, despite several hours enjoyable enquiry, been definitely sourced here – appears to be: 'Water, taken in moderation, cannot hurt anybody.'

'Work without Hope draws nectar in a sieve, And Hope without an object cannot live.' (WOOD: p46)
Morse knows and quotes these lines from Coleridge from heart. They also have relevance to a CROSSWORD clue. The lines are the final two from *Work without Hope* (written 1825; published 1828).

'I seem but dead man held on end To sink down soon ... O you could not know That such swift fleeing No soul foreseeing – Not even I – would undo me so.' (WOOD: p91)
A diarist tracks down these lines from HARDY. They are the closing lines of *The Going* (and the first line is usually rendered as: 'I seem but a dead man ...').

'... the bawdy hand of the dial is now upon the prick of noon.' (WOOD: pp109/394)
Claire OSBORNE recalls this from *Romeo and Juliet* (she had played Nurse in a university production) and thus impresses Morse. It is from Act 2 Scene 4 and spoken by Mercutio. The same prick occupies Ted BROOKS as he clock-watches in bed (CAIN: p158).

'I do arrest thee, Antonio ...' (WOOD: p110)
Morse explains that he was never much on the boards – just the once really – and his only line was as above. If this refers to the part of Second Officer in *Twelfth Night* then not only did Morse wrongly recall the line – it should be 'Antonio, I do arrest thee ...' – but he also forgot that the Second Officer has several lines (in Act 3 Scene 4). The fact that his recital of the line 'made the audience laugh' suggests that this was a mature performance and that his audience were well aware of his professional status. Although Antonio in *The Merchant of Venice* is also arrested, there is no comparable line.

'... for there was something sadly amiss when a man couldn't get drunk ...' (WOOD: p171)
The reference is to *Love-o'-Women* (KIPLING) and indicates a rotten soul. Morse is very aware of the quote; Alan HARDINGE vaguely recalls it (WOOD: p277).

'Nothing matters very much ... and in the end nothing really matters at all.' (WOOD: p180)
Max says this, after his heart attack, to Morse and the latter assigns the quote to Lord Balfour. The quote is also rendered as: 'Nothing matters very much, and very few things matter at all'. It does not appear in *The Oxford Dictionary of Quotations* (1953) and Bloomsbury (1991) gives it as 'attributed' without a source.

'The cart is shaken all to pieces, and the rugged road is at its end.' (WOOD: p186)
Morse recalls this line from *BLEAK HOUSE* (Chapter 47) after the death of Max. The end of the line is usually given as '... road is very near its end'. And is so when used as the heading to Chapter 75 of REMO.

'The day thou gavest ...' (WOOD: p208)
Morse is contemplating his own funeral and thinks that the above hymn – a good tune – might be suitable. The line also appears to have a slight reference in the SWEDISH MAIDEN verses (WOOD: p238). The hymn is fairly common at funerals and the first lines read: 'The day Thou gavest, Lord, is ended, The darkness falls at Thy behest; To Thee our morning hymns ascended, Thy praise shall sanctify our rest' (words John Ellerton; music Clement Scholefield).

'... the waters to be drained from the poisoned cistern.' (WOOD: p246)
This sounds remarkably like a part of a quotation (and it may well be) but, if so, its source has not been traced here. The phrase is used in the WOOD context to refer to 'confession'.

'Jenny kissed me when we met ...' (WOOD: p265)
Sally Monroe (MINOR) cites this line in correspondence on the SWEDISH MAIDEN verses. She knows the origin – it is from the poem *Jenny Kissed Me* by Leigh Hunt. She may not know that the Jenny has been alleged to be Mrs Carlyle, wife of Thomas.

"Prayer and fasting, Lewis. Prayer and fasting." (WOOD: p323)
Morse explains, ironically, his method for inspiration. There are, of course, many references in both Old and New Testaments to these twin attributes – but, perhaps, most notably in *Matthew 6,5-18.*

'The west yet glimmers with some streaks of day: Now spurs the lated traveller apace To gain the timely inn.'

This is the heading to Chapter 56 of WOOD and is from *Macbeth* Act 3 Scene 3. It is only repeated and included here because of the immediate and complete resonance between 'timely inn' and Morse ...

'Caeli, Lesbia nostra, Lesbia illa, Illa Lesbia, quam Catullus unam Plus quam se atque suos amavit omnes, Nunc in quadriviis et angiportis Glubit magnanimi Remi nepotes.'

Catullus Poem LVIII (heading to Chapter 8 of CAIN). A rough translation: 'Caelius, our Lesbia, that Lesbia, That same Lesbia, whom Catullus loved More than himself and more than all his own kin, Now loiters at the crossroads and in the backstreets Ready to toss off the grandsons of the brave Remus'. In McCLURE's translation (p42), quadriviis is given as CARFAX (which Morse appreciates).

'If you love her set her free. If she loves you, she will gladly return to you. If she doesn't she never really loved you anyway.' (CAIN: p42)

Morse recalls these embroidered words from a Maidstone bed and breakfast establishment when contemplating an early love. It has not been possible here to track down the original author but the phrases (or paraphrases of them) appear to have passed into the common realm. Variations include: 'If you love her, set her free. If she won't come back, she's here with me' and a very much ruder one.

'And like a skylit water stood The bluebells in the azured wood.'

These lines are the heading to Chapter 9 of CAIN and cited there as from HOUSMAN's *A Shropshire Lad* XLI. The line 'dry the azured skylit water' appears in the SWEDISH MAIDEN verses.

'Somebody once said that was his favourite music – the sound of bagpipes slowly fading away into the distance.' (CAIN: pp164-165)

Morse is speaking to Lewis; the 'somebody' has not been traced here but the quotation has the traditional structure of a statement-and-answer joke (where the first part deliberately misleads).

'O Love That Wilt Not Let Me Go' (CAIN: p194)

This hymn is played at the cremation of Mrs PHILLOTSON. Had he been there, Morse would no doubt have joined in. The words are by George Matheson and the music by Albert Peace.

'He had not been born great, Lewis was aware of that ...' (CAIN: p204)

The reference is to *Twelfth Night* Act 2 Scene 5: 'Some are born great, some achieve greatness, and some have greatness thrust upon 'em'.

'Greatness is but many small littles.' (CAIN: p204)

The original Latin proverb may well be *'maximus in minimis'*; perhaps *'multum in parvo'* (much in little), the motto of Rutland is a little wide of the mark; perhaps there is another proverb altogether.

'... she beheld an image of the Pale Horse; and knew that the name of the one who rode thereon was Death ...' (CAIN: p246)

Julia STEVENS is not having a particularly good night's sleep (and with some cause). The reference is to *Revelations 6,8*. **Plate 107**

'And – there – was – a – great – calm …' (CAIN: p247)
Mary RODWAY uses this phrase after counting while trying to get to sleep. It may well have come from the title of HARDY's poem (of the same name but without the dashes) and written on the occasion of the 1918 Armistice.

'I've got a truly marvellous demonstration of this proposition which the margin is too narrow to contain.' (CAIN: p263)
This is what Morse recollects Fermat writing (after checking up in his flat). The marginal note has led, of course, to much activity trying to prove Fermat's Last Theorem (which suggests something about cubes and the impossibility of a fourth power to be the sum of two fourth powers). The original marginal note ends with: *'Hanc marginis exiguitas non caperet'*. Morse notes, later, that not every case may be solved: it took '… over three hundred years to solve Fermat's Last Theorem' (REMO: p20).

'… had clearly taken some of the cream from Lewis's éclair.' (CAIN: p273)
This is only included here to draw attention to the joke in Chambers (2003) under 'éclair'.

'Paradise enow.' (CAIN: p273)
Morse is listening to WAGNER, smoking, and drinking whisky. The line is from *The Rubaiyat of Omar Khayyam*: 'And Wilderness is Paradise enow' at the end of the loaf of bread and flask of wine quatrain.

'Dis aliter visum.' (CAIN: p289)
'The gods thought otherwise' is from Virgil's *Aeneid* Book 2 line 428.

'… kneeling on the Golden Floor …' (CAIN: p299)
The 'Golden Floor' is usually taken to mean Paradise. HOUSMAN's last words (recounted by Laurence Housman in *The Unexpected Years*), on hearing an off-colour joke, were: 'That is indeed very good. I shall have to repeat that on the Golden Floor.'

'… Tithonian immortality.' (CAIN: p351)
The phrase is used in connection with '… the hessian lining …' (properly, Hessian) for cabinets by the PITT RIVERS. Tithonus was the lover of Eos, the dawn, in Greek mythology. Eos asked Zeus to make him immortal (but forgot to also request eternal youth, with the predictable outcome).

'… like Abraham, (Morse) had made his way forth from the tent in the desert …' (CAIN: p352)
It is quite difficult to establish more of a reference than *Genesis*. Abraham does seem to go forth from his tent a good few times and the direction is not always clear.

'Unmanned with anguish, Morse turned away …' (CAIN: p373)
The poem *Carnot* by Swinburne has the following lines: 'The staff of state is broken: hope, unmanned With anguish, doubts if freedom's self be free …'

'Dreaming when Dawn's left hand was in the sky …' (NEIG: p12)
The opening line to the second quatrain of *The Rubaiyat of Omar Khayyam*; it is skilfully used by an undergraduate to impress Dawn CHARLES.

'*Kept tears like dirty postcards in a drawer.*' (NEIG: p141)

Morse recalls Auden's 'immortal line' on A. E. HOUSMAN while thinking of Rachel JAMES. It comes from the sonnet *A. E. Housman*.

'*Lewis seldom expected (seldom received) any thanks.*' (NEIG: p143)

An imagined link, no doubt, but perhaps the phrase echoes that used by Oscar Wilde (in *De Profundis* and of Lord Alfred Douglas): 'You demanded without grace and received without thanks'.[5] Pretty apt description of Morse for much of the time.

'*Tempora mutantur: nos et mutamur illi.*' (NEIG: p153)

Literally, the times are changing and we are changing with them. The phrase is often attributed to Ovid (*Metamorphoses 15, 165*) but there it begins *omnia mutantur* and continues somewhat differently.

'*No wise man ever wished to be younger.*' (NEIG: p186)

Attributed by Morse to Jonathan Swift; it may be found in his *Thoughts on Various Subjects* (along with the somewhat contradictory: 'Every man desires to live long; but no man would be old').

'*... something about never climbing in vain when you're going up the Mountain of Truth.*' (NEIG: p205)

Morse's breadth of reading rarely fails to astonish; the quotation, which he almost recalls perfectly, is from Nietzsche (*Human, All Too Human*) and is usually translated as: 'In the mountains of truth, you will never climb in vain ...'

'*... rough as a bear's arse ...*' (NEIG: p225)

Morse's description of how he feels after a long night. The phrase often has 'badger' instead of 'bear', may (or may not be) Irish in origin, and usually has connotations of a hangover. Morse also feels as rough as 'a bear's backside' in STOR (p199). The phrase also has a specific engineering definition but that is of no concern here.

'*But there's so much to do!*' (NEIG: p236)

This is Morse speaking – or remonstrating, rather – with Dr Matthews (who has told Morse that he must stay in hospital). The doctor suggests that those were the last words of Cecil Rhodes (and Morse agrees). The last words are usually recorded as: 'So little done, so much to do'.

'*I trace the rainbow through the rain And feel the promise not in vain That Morn shall tearless be.*' (NEIG: p250)

Lines from one of Morse's favourite hymns, heard on the radio and accompanied by his bleating, baritone voice. They are from *O Love That Will Not Let Me Go* by George Matheson and Albert Peace.

'*Sans teeth, sans hair, sans ears, sans eyes – and very soon, alas, sans everything.*' (NEIG: p262).

A slight adaptation of the 'seven ages of man' speech from *As You Like It* (Act 2 Scene 7): 'Sans teeth, sans eyes, sans taste, sans everything'.

---

[5] The text of Wilde's letter is reproduced in Hyde (1982).

'Let us walk honestly, as in the day; not in rioting and drunkenness, not in chambering and wantonness, not in strife and envying.' (NEIG: p277)
The text for the Second lesson in Chapel at LONSDALE – to be read by Denis CORNFORD. It is from the King James Bible – the *Epistle to the Romans 13,13*.

'Benedictus benedicatur' (NEIG: p287)
The grace after the meal in LONSDALE. The more usual is *benedicto benedicatur* – let the blessed be blessed.

'In thought, word, and deed.' (NEIG: p290)
A major source (although not the only one) is St Augustine when categorising sin (though he may have taken his analysis from St Jerome). The Roman catholic Mass has the prayer *Confiteor* (often known as the *mea culpa*) with the line *'quia peccavi, nimis cogitatione, verbo et opere'* ('that I have sinned exceedingly in thought, word, and deed'). Apart from anything, the English phrase does confirm a sensible, appropriate, and significant (or whatever) use of the OXFORD COMMA. **Plate 108**

'Nothing? Was it nothing to you?' (NEIG: p300)
Correctly identified as (almost verbatim) from *Lamentations 1, 12* (on p298) but mistakenly attributed to either *Proverbs* or *Ecclesiastes* by Clixby BREAM.

"'In our beginning is our end,' somebody said – Eliot, wasn't it? Or is it 'In our end is our beginning?'" (Morse speaking; NEIG: p313)
This is Morse speaking (to Lewis). Eliot's *East Coker* (the second of the *Four Quartets*) starts: 'In my beginning is my end.' Suitably confusingly, the last line is: 'In my end is my beginning'.

'Der Garten trauert Kühl sinkt in die Blumen der Regen …' (NEIG: p381)
These words, from 'September' in *Four Last Songs* by Richard Strauss, are amateurishly translated here as: 'The Garden mourns (and) the Rain sinks coolly into the Flowers …'

'Waiting for breakfast while she brushed her hair' (NEIG: p409)
Morse recalls this line of Philip Larkin while in the ROYAL CRESCENT HOTEL (the line also being the poem's title). Aptly, it continues: 'I looked down at the empty hotel yard Once meant for coaches'.

'… that little tent of blue that prisoners call the sky.' (REMO: p8)
Morse remembers the line from Wilde's *The Ballad of Reading Gaol* when looking, from his flat, at (presumably) his small 'tent' of garden (or the sky above). The original has '… which prisoners call …' Wilde's line about taking a comma from a poem in the morning (and putting it back in during the afternoon) may be found in the ROSIE O'GRADY pub.

'… fast-fading violets, globèd peonies, the fields of asphodel …' (REMO: p8)
Morse, in a horticultural frame of mind, recalls his interest in flowers. The violets are probably from Keats' *Ode to a Nightingale*: 'White hawthorn, and the pastoral eglantine; Fast-fading violets cover'd up in leaves;' And the peonies from the same poet (*Ode on Melancholy*): 'Or on the rainbow of the salt sand-wave, Or on the wealth of globèd peonies …' The 'fields of asphodel' is a little more enigmatic. Morse will, no doubt, remember the reference in the *Odyssey (XI)* to such fields as being a certain particular region of Hades. He may also have remembered the lines of Wilde (from *Phedre*): 'The heavy fields of scentless asphodel, The

loveless lips with which men kiss in Hell.' Or, even, those of Tennyson: '... and the shadowy warrior glide Along the silent field of asphodel' (*Demeter and Persephone*).

'You holy Art, when all my hope is shaken ...' (REMO: p10)
A translation from Schubert's *An die Musik* (To Music). Morse follows what appears to be Basil Swift's English version of the text while listening to Elisabeth Schwarzkopf singing in the original.

"... as the poet said, we have not got." (REMO: p18)
This is Morse speaking (about new evidence). It seems likely that he is merely being facetious, referring to the two basic rhymes of 'not' and 'got'. But (and this is one of the larger buts) there may be an echo of Christina Rossetti's line in *No, Thank You, John*: 'That I don't give you what I have not got'.

'... the soothing secret of counting up to however-many.' (REMO: p34)
Morse has clearly read *Little Dorrit*. In Chapter 16, Mr Meagles advises Tattycoram to: 'Take a little time – count five-and twenty ...' (not once, but twice).

"Oh Lady in Pink – Oh Lovely Lady in Pink!" (REMO: p41)
Said of the pro-hunting Sarah HARRISON by a work colleague. One guesses that this is simply a paraphrase of the song *Lady in Red*, adapted for the (correct) name of the red coat worn by many foxhunters.

'... the words, in Homeric phrase, had escaped the barrier of her teeth.' (REMO: p114)
The 'barrier' appears in *The Odyssey* (books 5 and 23 at least). This allusion links with the idea of words being winged – like a bird escaping from a cage or a feathered arrow being let loose. Once beyond the barrier, they cannot be recalled.

'From May to September.' (REMO: p116)
Mentioned as a song title, there may be a confusion here with *September Song* (Kurt Weill and Maxwell Anderson) and its haunting lyric: 'It's a long, long while ... From May to December For the days grow short When you reach September'. Or there may well be an old song simply called *From May to September* reflecting a like-named romance between a younger and an older person.

"Only two things we can be sure of Morse – death and taxes." (Strange speaking; REMO: p186)
Strange is unsure of the provenance of the quote. Lewis (surprisingly) knows that it is Benjamin Franklin. The original appears in a letter (13th November 1789) as 'But in this world nothing can be said to be certain, except death and taxes'.

'When I play on my fiddle in Dooney, Folk dance like a wave of the sea ...' (REMO: p189)
Morse recites these lines and Strange remembers them. They are the opening lines to *The Fiddler of Dooney* by Yeats.

'Far from the madding crowd' (REMO: p211)
Part of a line from Gray's *Elegy Written in a Country Churchyard*. The full couplet reads: 'Far from the madding crowd's ignoble strife, Their sober wishes never learn'd to stray ...' The line as given in REMO is, of course, the title of a HARDY novel.

'… rosy-fingered Dawn …' (MILE: p56; REMO: p223)
A common Homeric phrase.

'lash-wide stare' (REMO: p227)
Morse refers to this phrase of Larkin. It is from the poem *Love Again* and the full line reads: 'Someone else drowned in that lash-wide stare …' The poem is not for those of a faint-hearted or prudish disposition.

'Nunquam ubi sub ubi!' (REMO: p252)
Used as a heading to Chapter 45, a literal translation would be 'never wear underwear'. The contents of that Chapter do have a certain sense of the erotic as Morse 'interviews' Debbie RICHARDSON.

'I wonder how we would have been together?' (REMO: p254)
Morse notes that this line is an almost verbatim quote from Eliot. The actual line, from *La Figlia Che Piange*, is: 'And I wonder how they should have been together!'

'Tomorrow and tomorrow and tomorrow …' (REMO: p362)
In *Macbeth* (Act 5 Scene 5) one finds: 'Tomorrow, and tomorrow, and tomorrow Creeps in this petty pace from day to day To the last syllable of recorded time, And all our yesterdays have lighted fools The way to dusty death'.

'Yet he wanted to go (as Flecker had said) 'always that little further' …' (REMO: p371)
In *The Golden Journey to Samarkand* one finds: 'We are the Pilgrims, master; we shall go Always a little further …'

"Do you know that lovely line of Thomson's about villages 'embosomed soft in trees'?" (Morse speaking; REMO: p399)
So asks Morse of Lewis – who has the grace to admit that he doesn't even know Thomson. The line is from *The Seasons* (Spring): 'And snatch'd o'er Hill and Dale, and Wood, and Lawn, And verdant Field, and darkening Heath between, And Villages embosom'd soft in Trees …'

'The long day's task was almost done …' (REMO: p415)
Morse is thinking, shortly before his death. *Antony and Cleopatra* (Act 4 Scene 15) has: 'Unarm Eros. The long day's task is done, And we must sleep.'

'Honour rooted in Dishonour stood, And Faith, unfaithful, kept him falsely true.' (GOLD: p32)
Morse remembers the lines but not the author. They are from Tennyson's *Idylls of the King: Lancelot and Elaine*. The opening is usually 'His honour rooted …' and punctuation also varies.

Plate 103 (Left) The inscription (the Radcliffe Camera beyond) (p284).
Plate 104 (Right) Buddha at Kamakura (p285).

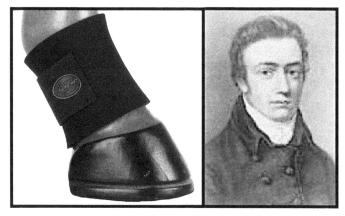

Plate 105 (Left) A wrapped pastern (p286).
Plate 106 (Right) Samuel Taylor Coleridge (p288).

Plate 107 (Left) Death on a Pale Horse (William Blake) (p290).
Plate 108 (Right) St Augustine (de Champaigne) (p293).

References

Works consulted or quoted. One's attention is drawn to the warnings given in both Bird (1998) and Bishop (2006).

AA Illustrated Guide to Britain, Drive Publications, (1982).

Alden, Henry (ed), *Alden's Guide of Oxford*, Alden and Co, (1948).

Allen, Paul & Allen,Jay, *Endeavouring to Crack the Morse Code*, Meadow Books, (2006). A guide to a number of Oxford locations.

Andrews, P. W. S. & Brunner, E., *The Eagle Ironworks Oxford*, Mills and Boon, (1965).

Armstrong, M., *Laughing*, Jarrolds, (1928).

Ashley, Mike (ed), *The Mammoth Book of New Sherlock Holmes Adventures*, Robinson, (1997).

Baring-Gould, W. S., *Sherlock Holmes*, Panther, (1975).

Batsford, Harry & Fry, Charles, *The Cathedrals of England*, Batsford, (1934).

Beerbohm, Max, *Zuleika Dobson*, Penguin Modern Classics, (1952).

Beresford, Ross (ed), *The Listener Crossword*, Times Books, (2002).

Bintliff, Russell, *Police Procedural: A Writer's Guide to the Police and How They Work*, Writer's Digest Books, (1993). Although based on American crime, a worthy attempt to assist those who would write on detective matters.

Bird, Christopher, *The World of Inspector Morse*, Boxtree, (1998). Well illustrated (and containing photographs of well-known and illustrious actors), the book does give rather more away – not necessarily the full plots – than one would wish. There is also a concentration on 'cases' outside and beyond the WORKS (which is, nonetheless, enjoyable).

Bishop, David, *The Complete Inspector Morse*, Reynolds and Hearn, (2008). A detailed and interesting book (updated from the 2002 edition); however, it pretty much reveals the full plots – and hence the murderers and most of the twists – of the WORKS (which, one suggests, if not urges, should be read first).

Bleak House, *Charles Dickens and his Bleak House*, Canterbury Printers. Undated leaflet – available at the house circa 1980.

Bloomsbury Dictionary of Quotations, Bloomsbury, (1991).

Booth, James, *Personal communication*, Hull University, (2007). James Booth is the Literary Adviser to the Philip Larkin Society.

Boswell, James, *Everybody's Boswell*, Bell and Sons, (1930). An abridged edition of *The Life of Johnson* (1791), and the *Tour to the Hebrides* (1785). There are, of course, many editions of the *Life*.

Boswell, James, *London Journal 1762-1763*, William Heinemann/Yale University, (1950).

Bradbury, Malcolm (General editor), *The Atlas of Literature*, de Agostini, (1996).

Bragg, Melvyn, *The Adventure of English*, Hodder and Stoughton, (2003).

Brewer's Britain and Ireland, Ayto, John & Crofton, Ian (eds), Weidenfeld and Nicolson, (2005).

Brewer's Dictionary of Phrase and Fable, Revised by Adrian Room, Cassell, (1996).

Brindley, Giles *Oxford – Crime, Death & Debauchery*, Sutton Publishing, (2006).

British Waterways, *The Oxford Canal: an Explorers Guide*. Undated pamphlet – though obtained in 2006 – available from lockkeepers and various information centres.

Broadbent, D. E., *Perception and Communication*, Pergamon Press, (1958).

Browne, Richard, *Personal communication*, (2006). Richard Browne writing as Crossword Editor of *The Times*.

Bryson, Bill, *Mother Tongue*, Penguin, (1991). Chapter 15 has some helpful comments on anagrams and crosswords, the whole book a pleasure.

Bunson, Matthew E., *Encyclopaedia Sherlockiana*, Macmillan, (1994).

Catholic Encyclopaedia, The, Robert Appleton, (1907).

Chambers, *The Chambers Dictionary*, Chambers Harrap, (1993, 2003, and 2008). The Preface to the 1993 edition has the following: 'At a lunch in Oxford in 1991 to celebrate the publication of the *Observer's* AZED 1000 crossword, Richard Morse toasted *Chambers* as: '… the immensely readable book. Just as one can frequently take a short shopping list into a supermarket only to emerge with several additional purchases, so more pleasantly the checking of a single word in Chambers may lead to a more extensive acquisition of lexical items than had originally been intended'. Oxford, crosswords, Chambers, and Morse – how serendipitous … Morse refers to '… that most faithful of all his literary companions, Chambers English Dictionary …' (WNCH: p51).

Chambers, *Crossword Dictionary*, Chambers Harrap, (2000).

Chambers, *Dictionary of Literary Characters*, Chambers Harrap, (2004).

Chesterton, G. K., *Autobiography*, Hutchinson & Co., (1936).

Chesterton, G. K., *The Innocence of Father Brown*, Penguin Crime, (1962 edition).

Colvin, H. M., *Ackermann's Oxford*, Penguin, (1954).

Crowther, Jonathan, *The A-Z of Crosswords*, Collins, (2006).

Crystal, David, *The Cambridge Encyclopedia of the English Language*, Cambridge University Press, (1995).

Deniston, Wilfred M., *Murder on the Oxford Canal*, The Oxford and County Local History Society, (1978).

Dexter, Colin, *As Good as Gold*, Pan Books/Kodak, (1994). A compendium containing, inter alia, seven cases.

Dexter, Colin, *Oxford and Me* (in *Oxford – One City, Many Voices*), Gatehouse. (2004).

References

Dexter, Colin, *Chambers Morse Crosswords*, Chambers, (2006a).

Dexter, Colin, *Personal communication*, (2006b).

Dexter, Colin, Article in *The Times* 10th June 2006, (2006c).

Dexter, Colin, *Personal communication*, (2008).

Dickens, Charles, *Bleak House*, Collins Clear-Type Press, (Undated but from circa 1920s).

Douglas, Mary (editor), *Rules and Meanings: the Anthropology of Everyday Knowledge*, Penguin (1973).

Doyle, Arthur Conan, *The Penguin Complete Sherlock Holmes*, Penguin, (1981).

Drabble, Margaret (editor), *'Lady Susan, The Watsons, Sanditon' by Jane Austen*, Penguin, (1974).

Drabble, Margaret (editor), *The Oxford Companion to English Literature*, OUP, (1985).

Dunkling, Leslie & Wright, Gordon, *Pub Names of Britain*, J. M. Dent, (1987).

Ekwall, Eilert, *The Concise Oxford Dictionary of English Place-names*, OUP, (1960).

Festinger, Leon, *A Theory of Cognitive Dissonance*, Stanford University Press, (1957).

Fleming, Ian, *Live and Let Die*, Penguin, (1954).

Fowler, H. W., *Modern English Usage*, OUP, (1968). Revised by Sir Ernest Gowers.

Fowler, H. W. & Fowler, F. G., *The King's English*, OUP, (1931).

Fry, Stephen, *Paperweight*, Arrow Books, (1997).

Fry, Stephen, *The Ode Less Travelled*, Hutchinson, (2005).

Gerasimov, M. M., *The Face Finder*, Hutchinson, (1971).

Goodwin, Cliff, *Inspector Morse Country*, Headline, (2002).

Gowers, Sir Ernest, *The Complete Plain Words*, Penguin, (1977). Revised by Sir Bruce Fraser

Greer, Brian (editor), *The Times Crossword 2001*, Times Books/HarperCollins, (2000).

Haining, Peter (editor), *The Orion Book of Murder*, Orion Books, (1996). The case of *The Burglar* is on pp288-293.

Harvey, Sir Paul (editor), *The Oxford Companion to English Literature*, OUP, (1967).

Herbert, Rosemary, *Whodunit?*, OUP, (2003).

Hibbert, C. (editor) & Hibbert, E. (associate editor), *The Encyclopaedia of Oxford*, Macmillan, (1988).

Hobhouse, Christopher, *Oxford*, Batsford, (1939).

Honey, Derek, *An Encyclopaedia of Oxford Pubs, Inns and Taverns*, Oakwood Press, (1998). This fine (and regrettably brief) volume has an Introduction by DEXTER who writes: 'I can see (Morse) in his bachelor flat in North Oxford, turning the pages as he listens to his beloved Wagner with a glass of his beloved beer beside him.' (p3). The book has been extremely helpful – not just in compiling this companion but also as a practical guide which has made location visits somewhat more targeted.

Housman, A. E., *Collected Poems*, Penguin, (1956).

Howarth, T. E. B., *Cambridge Between Two Wars*, Collins, (1978).

Howells, W. D., *Certain Delightful English Towns*, Harper and Brothers, (1906).

Hyde, H. Montgomery, *Oscar Wilde*, Orbis, (1982).

James, P. D., *Cover Her Face*, Sphere, (1962).

Jenkins, Simon, *England's Thousand Best Churches*, Penguin, (2002).

Keating, H. R. F., *The Bedside Companion to Crime*, Michael O'Mara Books, (1989). Keating also appears in STOR (p174).

Kennedy, Ludovic, *10 Rillington Place*, Pan, (1963).

Koestler, Arthur, *The Roots of Coincidence*, Hutchinson, (1972).

Kipling, Rudyard, *Love-o'-Women* (in *Many Inventions*), Macmillan and Co., (1893).

Kipling, Rudyard, *The Definitive Edition of Rudyard Kipling's Verse*, Hodder and Stoughton, (1940).

Lang, Andrew, *Oxford*, Seeley and Co., (1909).

Lee, Sidney, *Shakespeare's Life and Work*, Smith Elder &Co., (1907).

Leonard, Bill, *The Oxford of Inspector Morse*, Location Guides, (2004).

Lovelock, William, *A Concise History of Music*, G. Bell and Sons, (1959). The opening words ('… this is a book for the beginner, not for the specialist …') have a certain attraction for the present writer.

Mackenzie, Donald A., *Teutonic Myth and Legend*, William H. Wise and Company, (1934).

Marchand, L., *Byron's Letters and Journals*, Harvard University Press, volume 3, (1974).

McSpadden, J. Walker, *Stories from Wagner*, George Harrap, (1905). Written for children, this book has the merit of being easy enough to swim through if one has been struggling through Teutonic treacle.

Morris, Jan, *Oxford*, OUP, (1978).

Morton, H. V., *I Saw Two Englands*, Methuen and Co., (1942).

New Shorter Oxford English Dictionary, The, Clarendon Press, (1993).

Nicholson, Robert, *Guide to the Waterways 1: London, Grand Union, Oxford and Lee*, Harper Collins, (2000).

Nicholson, Robert, *Guide to the Waterways 4: Four Counties and the Welsh Canals*, Harper Collins, (2003).

Nicholson, Robert, *Guide to the Waterway 7: River Thames and the Southern Waterways*, Harper Collins, (2006).

References

Nicholson, Robert, *Nicholson's Guide to the Waterways: South east*, (undated).

Nicolson, Harold, *Diaries and Letters 1939-1945*, Collins, (1967).

Onions, C. T., *A Shakespeare Glossary*, Clarendon Press, (1911).

Oxford Dictionary of Quotations, The, OUP, (1953).

Page, Adrian, *Cracking Morse Code: Semiotics and Television Drama*, University of Luton Press, (2000).

Partridge, Eric, *Usage and Abusage*, Penguin, (1963).

Partridge, Eric, *A Dictionary of Catchphrases*, Routledge & Kegan Paul, (1977).

Pevsner, N. & Metcalf, P., *The Cathedrals of England: The South-East*, The Folio Society, (2005).

Picard, Barbara Leonie, *Tales of the Norse Gods and Heroes*, OUP, (1953).

Putnam, Don, *Crosswords for the Devotee*, Paperfront, (1974).

Puxley, Ray, *Britslang*, Robson Books, (2004).

Quennell, Peter, *Four Portrait*, Collins, (1945).

Rabelais, Francois, *The Heroic Deeds of Gargantua and Pantagruel*, Dent and Sons, (1929).

Rees, Nigel, *I Told You I Was Sick*, Weidenfeld and Nicholson, (2005).

Richards, Antony J., *Inspector Morse on Location*, Irregular Special Press, (2008).

Richards, Antony J. & Attwell, Philip, *The Oxford of Inspector Morse*, Irregular Special Press, (2015).

Ritter, R. M., *The Oxford Manual of Style*, OUP, (2002).

Roberts, John (editor), *The Oxford Dictionary of the Classical World*, OUP, (2005).

Robins, Alec, *Crosswords*, Teach Yourself Books/Hodder and Stoughton, (1975).

Roud, Steve, *The English Year*, Penguin, (2008).

Shepherd, Walter, *On the Scent with Sherlock Holmes*, Arthur Barker, (1978).

Sutherland, John, *Inside Bleak House: A Guide for the Modern Dickensian*, Duckworth, (2005).

Symons, Julian, *Bloody Murder*, Penguin Books, (1985). Symons also appears in STOR (p174).

The Times: 75 Years of The Times Crossword, HarperCollins, (2005). Contains an interesting foreword by Colin Dexter.

Tracy, Jack, *The Ultimate Sherlock Holmes Encyclopedia*, Gramercy Books, (1977).

Trask, R. L., *Mind the Gaffe: The Penguin Guide to Common Errors in English*, Penguin, (2001).

Truss, Lynne, *Eats, Shoots & Leaves*, Profile Books, (2003).

Tyack, Geoffrey, *Modern Architecture in an Oxford College*, OUP, (2005).

Venables, D. R. & Clifford, R. E., *Academic Dress of the University of Oxford*, (1973), pp 209-211 in Douglas (1973).

Wain, J. & Wain, E., *The New Wessex Selection of Thomas Hardy's Poetry*, Macmillan, (1978).

Watson, F., *Laughter for Pluto*, Lovat Dickinson, (1933). A generous book on the life of Rabelais.

Wells, Stanley & Taylor, Gary (editors), *The Complete Oxford Shakespeare*, OUP, (1987).

Williams, Ethel Carleton, *Companion into Oxfordshire*, Methuen, (1935).

Worde, Wynkyn de, *The Demaundes Joyous*, Wynkyn de Worde (reprinted London by Gordon Fraser), (1971). The 1971 reprint was made with the permission of the Syndics of the Cambridge University Library (obviously unrelated to the SYNDICS appearing in this companion).

Young, Wayland, *Eros Denied*, Corgi, (1969).

Yurdan, Marilyn, *Oxford in the 1950s and '60s*, The History Press, (2009).

Information to be found on the Internet

Many entries have been cross-checked by visits to sites on the World Wide Web (but always with the caveat that some of such sites may contain errors). Because of the very nature of the web (with its rapid changes and updates) it has not been thought wise to include a list of sites. Rather, the interested reader may wish to use an appropriate search engine to explore any matters of further enquiry (for example, Oxford colleges maintain their own sites and a simple 'name of college oxford' in an engine will produce a list of any number of results – usually containing one that is patently the college's own site).

A number of websites dedicated to Inspector Morse exist and others may well be in the process of creation; their contents, for the most part, have been very helpful but their quality and accuracy varies. The suggestion above is repeated: use a search engine to find what you are looking for and use your own powers of induction and deduction (just imagine Morse looking over your shoulder while you sit at the keyboard) to find and verify what you wish. At the time of writing, the phrase 'Inspector Morse' produced about a million entries in a well-known search engine; one may need to be rather selective.

Acknowledgments

There are many people to thank for assistance and, as is traditional, some mention is made here. Firstly, Colin Dexter for his patience, help, wisdom, and humour (and allowing me to quote so extensively). Secondly, James Booth and Jim Page for advice on Larkin and Housman; Ian Wilkes for the same on Holmes; Cathryn Scott of the Welsh National Opera and Liz Feeney of the *Oxford Story*; Mike Davis and Jimmy Brett for turning blind eyes when I should have been working; Ged and Marian Taylor for many pictures and Derek Arthur for *Listener* crosswords; Rebecca Webber and Claire Brand (Press Officer and Photographer respectively of the Thames Valley Police) – their kind assistance provided the photograph of HQ (which I had been denied from taking one Sunday by a zealous security guard); Hazel Norris and Ian Brookes at Chambers and Jane Cramb at Pan Macmillan; Francis Hamel for permission to reproduce *Aristotle Lane Allotments* and Al Partington for a rather attractive pub photo; Richard Browne of *The Times* for information on crosswords; and Antony Richards, my editor, for much guidance, many helpful suggestions, and midwifery skills.

Colin Dexter has the copyright on the crossword, dedicated to Morse and Lewis, in Appendix A. It is from *Chambers Morse Crosswords*, published by Chambers Harrap Publishers Ltd 2006 and is reproduced with permission. Daily Information Ltd. have the copyright on the map of Greater Oxford and it is reproduced with their permission.

Finally, there are well-meant thanks to my wife and children for much patience and help (particularly Jessica for her scientific eye), a little encouragement, and less interruption than I deserved (or, indeed, usually get).

Lightning Source UK Ltd.
Milton Keynes UK
UKHW030630311221
396440UK00007B/499